NO NEWS
IS BAD NEWS

by

Maureen Milliken

S & H Publishing, Inc.
Purcellville, Virginia

Maureen Milliken/S & H Publishing, Inc.
P. O. Box 456
Purcellville, VA 20134
www.SandHpublishing.com

Hunter cover photo by Scott Monroe

LIFE DURING WARTIME
Words and Music by DAVID BYRNE, CHRIS FRANTZ, JERRY HARRISON
and TINA WEYMOUTH
Copyright © 1979 WB MUSIC CORP and INDEX MUSIC, INC.
All Rights Administered by WB MUSIC CORP.
All Rights Reserved

No News is Bad News/ Maureen Milliken. -- 1st ed.
ISBN 978-1-63320-038-8 – print edition
ISBN 978-1-63320-039-5 – ebook edition
    Fiction: Mystery: Amateur Sleuth: Woman Sleuth: Maine

COLD HARD NEWS

The snowbanks in a small Maine town start to melt, and the town's secrets begin to emerge.

Bernie O'Dea, the editor of the *Peaks Weekly Watcher*, is jazzed to finally have a big story to cover when a body is found in a melting snowbank. But as spring turns into a long, hot, explosive summer in Redimere, Maine, the story gets bigger — maybe too big for Bernie to handle.

As secrets are revealed, the town is ripped in half and the body count rises, Bernie is forced to question her part in the town's tragic tale, a part that may cost her and others their lives.

Note: While *No News is Bad News* is set in Franklin County, Maine, Redimere is not a real place and any resemblance of the town or its people to any real places or people, living or dead, is a coincidence. While most of the geography is real, some liberties have been taken, so if things aren't where they're supposed to be, or there are rivers or highways in the book that don't exist, it's simply because it's a work of fiction.

TO MY TRIBE:
Liz, Jimmy, Becky, Billy, and
Nicki

CHAPTER 1
2009
Redimere, Maine
November 7

Guy Gagne was ready to give up and head home when he saw the blood.

There was just a little on some leaves. It looked fresh, though it was drying in the crisp morning air. Guy was deer hunting and his first thought was deer, wounded, maybe now dead. But he'd seen enough in the Maine woods in his seventy years to know it could be something else entirely, something less innocent than a wounded deer during hunting season. Later, r police asked, he couldn't put his finger on it, but when he saw the blood, he had to find out what it was.

The silver-dollar size drops were close together, then got farther apart, smaller, the way they do when something that's bleeding is fleeing. The deer—had to be what it was—had stayed on the tote road Guy had been crossing all morning. His heart pounded as he followed the trail. He was excited, tingly, weak in the knees—the way he felt when he jumped a deer. It wasn't really the same. Either he'd find one dead or worse, wounded, and he'd have to put it down. *Or he'd find something else.*

The drops had gotten smaller, hard to see on the dried leaves in the dim light of the woods. *Dim light of my old eyes,* he admitted. He thought he'd lost it, was almost ready to give up, when he saw a drop where the weedy brush at the trailside was crushed, a copper spot on a green frond, then more beyond, in the woods. That one was dark and thick. Not a dollop, really, more like it was poured from a gravy boat.

A crow beyond the brush gave a sharp warning caw, circled around. There were three or four crows, circling, diving. He pushed broken branches aside, sidestepping the tacky puddle of blood. A woodpecker's rattle echoed somewhere.

A few feet off the trail the crows dive-bombed and hopped around a couple mounds, bright red, some with traces of brown or gray. He let out his breath, let go, for just a second, of that fear this was something else. The crows were attacking a fresh deer gut pile picked over and scattered by critters, but new enough to still be mostly intact.

Guy had been out since six-thirty, just after sunrise, and hadn't heard shots out this way, or triumphant shouts. Hadn't seen a group of happy hunters loading their trophy into a truck. But, like his eyes, his ears weren't what they used to be. The leaves were disturbed, he could see that now, two parallel lines in the spongy ground that could be drag marks. The feeling was back. Yeah, drag marks, but not like what you left when you dragged a deer.

There was more blood, broken branches. Now that he looked closely, it seemed to be everywhere.

Someone had field-dressed the deer and dragged it out. That's what Guy kept telling himself, even though the mounds of gut, the blood, the drag marks, weren't right.

Guy had seen plenty of gut piles from deer of all sizes in the decades he'd been hunting. There was a sameness to them. This one was different, smaller. There was something else different, small and

2

shriveled, centered on top, like it had been placed there on purpose. More gray than pink.

Guy hadn't only been hunting for most of his life, but he was a Maine guide. He wrote about hunting in his newspaper column. He was probably more of an expert on hunting and everything that came with it than anyone else in town. Still, it took a minute of staring, more than a minute, to figure out what he was looking at. It finally registered. It didn't belong to a deer. It was pathetically, obviously human.

Guy fumbled for his cellphone—stupid, he thought, even as he did, it won't work back here—the full force of what he was looking at connecting with his brain, then his stomach.

He plunged back to the trail, only slowing to vomit, the coffee and eggs he'd had hours earlier soaking his camouflage pants. He barely noticed. All he wanted was to get to fresh air and to unsee what he had just seen.

. . . . .

A few hours earlier, around the time Guy Gagne was drinking the coffee and eggs he'd later lose all over his camouflage pants, Bernadette O'Dea awoke with a start. She'd been sleeping in fits and pieces, uncomfortable in someone else's bed, not quite drunk enough to not care where she was. Pretty sure she'd made a huge mistake.

Pete was breathing heavily beside her. He'd been like that for hours as she watched the red numbers of the digital clock tick away, willing sleep, but more urgently willing morning to come so she could leave. Neither seemed like it was going to happen. She watched Pete, on his side, facing her. His brow furrowed, even in sleep. Bernie wished she could turn back the clock several hours, erase what had happened. They'd been drunk. The entire event was over before she'd even started, too fast for her to really enjoy it or fully partake. She'd known from the start it was a bad idea. Bad bad idea.

Afterwards, as he'd pulled her close and wrapped himself around her, he'd murmured, "This isn't finished, just give me a

3

couple minutes." Then he fell asleep.

Now, a couple hours later, he still slept, uneasily, as she watched, waiting for morning. Would it be rude to leave? She wasn't sure, but it seemed like it would. She had to get up early, had a lot of work to do. "Pete," she whispered.

The skin of his shoulders and chest was deathly pale in the moonlight coming through the window, contrasting with the tan on his lower arms, even the one that had been in a sling and cast for the past few months. Farmer's tan, they used to call it when she was a kid. The dark jagged scar on his triceps was angrier looking now than when she'd first seen it earlier that night. She touched the scar, running her finger along it, feeling a surge of compassion despite her regret. The scar felt just like she'd thought it would, crusty and thick against the surprisingly soft skin of his inner arm, his triceps rock hard underneath.

He said something.

"What?" Bernie jerked her hand away.

His breathing was more rapid. He said something again, with more urgency.

"Wake up," she said, but not loudly, not sure if she should wake him. The boyfriend she'd lived with before she moved back to Maine used to fall asleep with the assurance of a grizzly lumbering off for hibernation. He never talked in his sleep or seemed bothered by dreams, just snored steadily until it was time to get up. This was new to her.

Pete shouted now. "No, no, oh no." An urgent plea.

"Pete, wake up," she said, putting her hand on his chest and shaking him.

He sat up, gasping for breath, fully awake and covered with sweat that hadn't been there a few minutes earlier.

"Are you okay?" she asked.

He looked bewildered, terrified, but it faded to a grimace in seconds. "Sorry." He untangled his legs from the sheet and hurried into the bathroom, where the sound of running water seconds later didn't mask the sound of him throwing up.

4

"Guess we're done with the romantic portion of our program," she said, though not loud enough for him to hear. She looked around the floor for her clothes. Definitely time to go.

She was balancing on one leg, trying to put a sock on, as he came back into the room after several long minutes punctuated by flushing and running water.

"Are you leaving?" he asked.

She swayed on one foot, then hopped to regain her balance as she looked up. "I have a long day coming up and should get some sleep. I'd just as soon go home now. Under the cover of darkness." She tried a smile. "No sense in everyone in Redimere seeing me." She was over-explaining, she knew, to cover up the awkwardness. It was only making it worse, as usual.

While she talked, he'd pulled the edge of the sheet over his lap. She sat down next to him to put her shoes on.

"I could drive you home later," he said.

"I could use the walk. You left your car at the bar, anyway."

She took his hand, and he turned it over and intertwined his fingers with hers. His hair stuck to his temples in wet tendrils, like he'd splashed water on his face.

"Are you okay?" she asked.

"Yeah."

"You had a bad dream."

"I had a lot to drink."

"It seemed like more than that."

He shrugged. She kissed him. A chaste kiss on the lips that tasted like peppermint toothpaste. His grip on her hand tightened, but other than that he didn't move.

She waited for him to say more, but when it became clear he wasn't going to, she pulled her hand out of his and got up.

"Sorry, I gotta go." She left him sitting on the bed.

She hoped the walk home would clear her head of the embarrassment, confusion, and regret.

There was a dim glow in the east, but it was still dark. So quiet. Too early for the hunters. She was glad. She wasn't wearing orange

5

and everyone in Maine knows what that can mean, even in town. Your fault if you get shot. There were a dozen court cases over the years to prove it. The air was crisp, a light sheen of frost covered leaves and browning November grass. She loved this time of morning. It reminded her of when she used to deliver papers in Augusta as a kid. The only person in the world. Early morning in fall smelled like wood smoke, the paper mill, a hint of skunk. There was no paper mill in Redimere anymore, but she swore she could smell the sulphury wet cardboard.

She knew in a couple hours, when the sun came up and the second it was legally possible, gunfire would punctuate the morning. Like being in a war zone. *The sound of gunfire, off in the distance, I'm getting used to it now...* She sang the Talking Heads song as she made her way up the hill. "Life During Wartime." The song had been going through her head long before hunting season started the week before. Emotional wartime had been declared months ago. Add the encounter with Pete to the list. Bad idea. Bad bad bad. The song taunted her: *No time for dancing, or lovey-dovey, I ain't got time for that now...*

She'd only had a few one-night stands in her life. They were always awkward. The sex was never great because of the drunkenness. Anyway, she liked to like a guy before she slept with him. At least Pete had that going for him. She liked him too much maybe. Redimere was too small a town. As the owner and editor of the local newspaper, the *Peaks Weekly Watcher,* Bernie wondered, wouldn't a relationship with the police chief compromise her as a journalist? She didn't do complicated well. Especially not now. Too much going on to deal with someone else's feelings, the uncertainty and complexity of being with someone. *I ain't got time for that now...*

He'd been so intense. That's what was really bugging her. He'd whispered something and she hoped she'd heard it wrong, or that he'd forget he'd said it. They'd been through a lot together, but that would wear off and he'd realize she was who she was, not whoever was causing all that intensity. She'd be worried about how he really felt, and sooner or later it would become painfully clear and

6

ultimately they wouldn't even be friends anymore. She could see the rise and fall of the relationship in one depressing trajectory. Things were better the way they had been, avoiding the whole exhausting, heartbreaking dance.

She'd spelled that out to her friend Carol several times over the past months. Carol had said Bernie was overthinking it, especially since she and Pete weren't in a relationship. Well, now they'd had sex, and even though it lasted about two minutes, Bernie figured that gave her the right.

She turned into her driveway, so lost in thought that at first it didn't register that her usually placid dog was barking inside and there was a figure on her front stoop. Hadn't she left the porch light on when she'd come home to eat lunch and walk the dog in the late afternoon, when darkness was already creeping into the day? She couldn't remember. In the dark, all she saw was a silhouette, hunkered. She had an irrational thought it was Pete, and her heart soared and sank at the same time.

"Good morning, Bernie."

It was one of the last people she would expect to see on her porch in Redimere, Maine, at four-thirty in the morning.

"Salvatore, what the hell are you doing here?" She was happy, but confused.

"Is that any way to greet your baby brother?"

She gave him a hug.

"Taking the walk of shame? How eighties of you."

"It's not what it looks like," Bernie said as she unlocked the door, even though it was exactly what it looked like. At least her bra wasn't hanging out of her pocket, college style.

"Sure."

"You want coffee?" He smelled like cigarettes, pot, and alcohol.

"I'm beat. Can I just crash in your guest room?"

"Don't we need to talk about why you're here? My guest room is full of boxes and has no furniture. It'll be the couch."

"That works. Can we talk in the morning? Or afternoon?"

7

"I have to spend the day at the office. I have a mountain of work to catch up on."

"Night then?"

She let out Dubya, whose joy at meeting a new person made his "I have to go out" dance a jerky spin, becoming more frantic and happy as Bernie and Sal laughed at him.

"When did you get a dog?"

"Recently." She got a pillow and blanket from the closet, in no more mood to talk than he was.

"You never mentioned it."

"We haven't talked much, remember? You're busy. I'm busy. Cellphone, voicemail, blah blah blah."

Sal settled on the couch, and she let Dubya back in. The dog did a more subdued happy dance, then launched onto the couch with his too-short legs, snuggling against her brother. "Just like a Jack London story," he said. She could see in the glow of the pellet stove his eyes were closed, his hand on Dubya's head.

"Goodnight, little brother and dog."

"Night, big sister. Thanks."

Bernie thought she'd fall asleep right away, her usual insomnia beaten by the long day and alcohol, if not the brief, unsatisfactory sex. But the night with Pete had become a monster in her head, regret gripping her and not letting go. Another monster kept it company. Why was her little brother, a professor of art history at an upstate New York university, and presumably well into the school year, asleep on her couch?

. . . . .

There was no sense going back to bed after Bernie left. Pete didn't blame her for going. What a disaster. He stood under the shower until the water ran cold, watching dawn break through the bathroom window. He wished he could enjoy the luxury of his first shower with his cast off, no fiddling with plastic bags that leaked, trying to wash with one hand, the cast always in his way. His arm and shoulder ached, his ribs still hurt from where they'd been broken. He'd been told they'd take months to heal. What hurt the most, though, was that look of unhappiness, maybe even pity, in Bernie's eyes as she dressed to go.

Pete put on his uniform and went into the kitchen. He was wide awake and sober, enough at least to see the note on the table, next to a dirty plate and empty bottle of beer.

"Hi Loser. I see you still are one. I was on the couch when you got home. Didn't want to interrupt, so I left. Got news for you. 'JP' ☺"

Damn Benji Reeves. In his apartment, no less. Somehow he wasn't surprised but it still shook him. He knew he'd locked the door when he left for work the previous morning. He always did. He'd lived in the city all his life until he moved here the year before and he still couldn't get over the naïve Maine practice of not locking up. He tried to remember if it was still locked when he got home with Bernie. He'd been in a hurry to get in, but he must've unlocked the door. He hadn't turned on the lights, too anxious to get to the bedroom. There could have been an elephant in the living room as he led Bernie through and he wouldn't have noticed.

He thought he'd seen Benji Reeves a week or so ago, walking down Ridge Road with that familiar slouch, in a too-big hoody, but Pete was riding shotgun and Dawna was driving the cruiser and he'd let it go. Wouldn't have been able to explain why he'd wanted her to stop or turn around. How could he not sense he was here, in his apartment, last night? He knew why. All he could see was Bernie, her big brown eyes, the way she shivered when he touched her, melted against him.

Reeves had been there, watching. He'd like to find him and kick the shit out of him. He wondered how long Reeves had sat in the living room while Pete was there with Bernie. Pete would have heard the door close. Well, maybe not.

He glanced at the boxes stacked in the living room, half full of his belongings. He'd been slowly trying to move. He was going to pick up the pace now that his arm was available. He knew deep down Reeves could just as easily show up at his new place, and his other demons were as tightly packed in his psyche as his dishes and

9

books were in their boxes, but he felt the need all the same.

His nightmares had started up again since summer, a terrifying mix of dumpsters, ducks, bodies, fire that he'd thought he'd put behind him. The Donovan family and Reeves were there, too, part of a web that left him disgusted and exhausted. When he saw Reeves last week, he'd hoped it was his imagination fueled by one last blast of that old familiar terror. It'd almost gone away since he moved here, came back strong in July, but had been ebbing. It usually shot through him, then went away just as quick.

He knew, deep down in his soul, that this time it wouldn't.

CHAPTER 2
2003
Philadelphia
August 12

The kid's body hadn't been in the dumpster for long, but the hot day had done its work and it was already bloating, already stunk, mixing with the summer smell of full dumpster as Pete dropped into the soft pile of garbage next to it, one of his shoes sinking into something, wetness seeping over the top into his sock.

"Isn't it your turn for the dumpster?" he'd asked Sid.

"Nope, never my turn," Sid said. "Bad back. Funny how I have to keep reminding you."

As Pete had pulled himself up and swung over the top, a flash of terror and a yellow and white blur tinged pink played through his head, there for a second and gone, pushed away as he dropped into the cooking stew of garbage and got to work on the latest body.

. . . . .

Back at the station, Pete and Sid started the process of trying to figure out who the kid was. No ID—what kid that age carried ID? One shoe missing, the other a sad, impossibly large size 13 basketball sneaker. Blue and white basketball shorts, a sleeveless 76ers T-shirt.

Pete booted up the computer and started checking missing kids while Sid called downstairs to find out if anyone's child had disappeared in the last few days. Kid looked to Pete like he'd been dead several hours, maybe a day. Hard to tell in this heat, especially when the body was surrounded by the metal walls of a dumpster.

"About thirteen or fourteen, maybe one-hundred-twenty pounds, five-foot-four, skinny kid," Sid was saying to someone on the phone. "Caucasian, dark blond, light brown. Eye color, can't really say, wait for forensics. No, they were full of blood. Looked like the kid's neck was broke and someone beat him around the head."

When Sid got off the phone, Pete said, "Look at this." He slid over so Sid could see his computer screen.

MISSING: JP Donovan. Height 5' 5", weight 125. Hair light brown, eyes hazel. Last seen, Philadelphia, August 7, 2003. Identifying jewelry or tattoos: a cross on a gold chain worn around the neck. Two photos of the kid, one close-up of the cross.

"Weird cross," Sid said. "Ours today didn't have one."

"It's a Celtic cross. Irish," Pete said. "That's a pretty elaborate one. Wonder if those are real stones?"

"Maybe a robbery."

"Yep."

The Donovans lived in a worn-down townhouse split into apartments in an equally worn-down neighborhood. A woman answered their knock, her look of annoyance changing to a smile as she took in Pete.

"We're the ones who called about JP Donovan," Pete said. "Are you his mother?"

"I'm JP's sister, Cheryl. His older sister."

No shit, Pete thought. She was probably around thirty, but the kind of thirty he saw a lot on this job. Smoker's wrinkles around the mouth, circles under the eyes. Hair too teased and makeup too thick in a sad effort to distract from the damage of poverty, stress, and substance abuse.

She led them into the apartment. "Sit down, sit down. Ma!" The last she yelled toward a door down the hall as Sid took the lone chair, so Pete sat on the couch next to Cheryl, who moved closer as she leaned to pick up a bottle of soda on the coffee table, their thighs almost touching. He could smell cigarettes, sweat, a cloying fruity smell, too thick to be shampoo or the gum she chomped with ferocity, even as she drank the soda.

"Ma's in the kitchen making you guys some coffee. She got all nervous when you called, so I figured she could keep busy and take her mind off it." Cheryl giggled and picked one of those subscription cards that are always falling out of magazines, folded, refolded it. "Just gave up smoking. Shitty time to give up smoking."

Sid nodded. "I know what you mean. Gave it up eighteen years ago when I had my first kid. Went to smell her head one night and smelled cigarette smoke. Stopped right then. I still reach for a cigarette when I'm stressed out, only there's not one there."

"I don't smoke around my kids." Cheryl gave a shaky smile, but there was defensiveness behind it. She was skinny, twitchy. If she wasn't a drug user, she'd recently quit that, too. Pete caught himself. They were here to talk to her about a body that could be her murdered brother, and he was looking at her like a suspect.

"When can we ID JP?" she asked as the mother came in, a heavier, older Cheryl. She was carrying a tray, four mugs on it, with spoons sticking out. It clattered as she set it down on the coffee table. "That picture they showed us, it was hard to tell, so they said we need to see the body."

"I didn't know what everybody wanted, so I just put cream and sugar in all of them," the mother—Linda—said, her voice quavering.

She sat down on the couch on the other side of Pete, forcing him closer to Cheryl. He wished there was another chair in the room. He didn't like to interview people when he couldn't look at them full-on. He'd have to turn to watch Cheryl speak, turn the other way to watch Linda. He looked at Sid, and Sid shrugged his eyebrows. *Whatcha gonna do?*

"So they're going to check JP's dentals, we're just having trouble tracking them down," Linda said. "The dentist shut down, and we don't know what he did with the records. So we can't tell if it's him. Someone stole his chain." She started crying.

13

"Ma, it's okay. Maybe it wasn't him. We can hope," Cheryl said. "He always wore that chain with a Celtic cross." She said it like the basketball team. "Ma's dad brought it from Ireland. A family heirloom. Worth some money."

"Celtic," Pete said, the correct pronunciation, the C sounding like K.

"What?" Cheryl said.

Sid shot Pete a look, then asked Cheryl. "He always wore it?"

"Yeah," she said. "Even swimming and to bed and in the shower. He loved it. Called it his good luck charm. He didn't have it on in the picture they showed us. Maybe someone killed him to steal it."

"That picture was awful," Linda said softly.

Cheryl reached around Pete to squeeze her mother's arm, brushing it across his shoulder as she did. "We took care of JP. He went to the dentist," Cheryl added, defensive again, though no one had asked. "That dentist just moved and we can't find him."

"It's okay," Pete said. "Why don't you tell us about him?" He took a sip of coffee. Instant. Way too much sugar.

"He's my baby," Linda said. "I thought I was done having kids, years before, then he came along. Seventeen years after I had this one, my first." She smiled sadly at Cheryl. "He was my little miracle baby. My miracle boy."

Pete and Sid exchanged glances—Pete knew Sid well enough to know he was thinking something like *yeah, a miracle performed by Saint Vodka.* Pete fought a smile, hoping the noise he made into his coffee cup sounded like a sympathetic murmur.

"I can't say no to him," Linda added. "He just gives me that look, and I can't say no. He's a devil, but in a good way. A good boy. Just has a lot of energy. That devilish little smile." Her voice trailed off.

Cheryl rubbed Linda's back, her forearm again brushing Pete's shoulders. He squirmed forward. He could feel her looking at him out of the corner of her eye. He kept his eyes on his coffee.

"That's right, Ma. He's a good boy."

Cheryl's face, turned toward her mother, toward Pete, was inches away. He could feel her breath, smell it. The hand that had been patting her mother moved to his shoulder. "He got in trouble, ran away a lot. That's why no one was looking for him. We called it in, they said they'd look, but nothing. We was gonna make some posters, have a visual. Some people were going to come over this afternoon to help, when we got that call."

Pete got up and moved across the room to the fireplace and picked up a photo. "This is JP?" he asked, hoping that would seem like why he left the couch. It was the same photo as on the missing poster, but clear, not the bad fax reproduction.

Sid wiggled his eyebrows at him again. He'd seen where Cheryl's hand had been. Pete pretended he didn't notice, stared at the photo. A school picture, typical, with the kid's shirt buttoned all the way up to the collar, bad home haircut slicked down for the photographer. The devilish grin his mother had referred to made him look older, knowing. There was another photo next to it, JP sitting in a lawn chair, gesturing in a white-kid gang sign, shirtless, the Celtic cross shining on his skinny collarbone, the same knowing smirk.

Sid was talking. "Sometimes the police are doing their job, but it doesn't seem like it from your perspective. People were looking for your boy, no doubt."

Pete had doubt, but there was no point in saying anything. "What's JP stand for?" He looked up from the photo at Cheryl and Linda. Cheryl, her hands folded in her lap, looked at Pete, annoyed, then away. The room was hot, the windows closed despite the summer swelter. He heard an air conditioner running somewhere in the apartment, but the cold air wasn't circulating into the room. His mind slipped to the dumpster. Dumpsters. He felt lightheaded, nauseated. The family seemed weird, off. Or was it just him? The heat?

"It didn't stand for anything," Linda said. It took him a second to remember what he'd asked. It hadn't been important, just a question to get them talking.

15

"I just liked the way it sounded," she continued. "It's JP, no periods. Like that actor? A Martinez from *Santa Barbara*? The soap opera? I always liked the way he had that initial with no period. It was classy. He was very handsome."

Cheryl rolled her eyes. "They don't care about that."

"Tell us about the day JP disappeared," Pete said. "Five days ago, right?"

"I was working. I clean offices," Linda said. "I got home around six in the morning, had breakfast. JP was still asleep."

"You see him? Are you sure he was in bed?" Sid asked.

"Where would my boy be at six a.m.?" Linda asked. "They already asked us that." Same defensiveness as her daughter.

"Just trying to establish a timeline," Sid said. "We want to help."

"You guys keep asking the same questions. Days after, now that he's dead. This would have been a lot more help the day he went missing," Cheryl said, again shooting daggers at Pete.

"What happened then?" Pete asked, ignoring Cheryl, trying to concentrate on the nuance, on what was being said, but also what wasn't.

"He was playing basketball with his friends down on Diamond. The end near Temple?"

"Not a great neighborhood," Sid said. "That's what? Couple miles away?"

"JP walked all the time," Cheryl said, still defensive. "He liked to."

Linda continued as though Cheryl hadn't broken in. "He called for a ride in the afternoon, too hot to walk home. Brandon answered the phone."

"Brandon?" Pete and Sid both said at the same time.

"We told this all to the cop we made the missing report to," Cheryl said.

"We like to hear it ourselves," Sid said, smooth, conciliatory. "Different ears. We're homicide detectives. We may hear something they didn't."

16

Good old Sid. One or two smooth sentences and Linda and Cheryl were smiling again, purring like kittens.

"Brandon's my brother. JP's half-brother. He's a year younger than me," Cheryl said. "Brandon didn't want to wake Ma, so he told JP to walk. That's the last anyone talked to him."

Linda put her coffee down with a shaky bang on the table and let out a sob.

"Where's Brandon?" Pete asked.

"Oh, he don't live here," Cheryl said. "Well, he does, but only when he's on the outs with Cassidy, his girlfriend. He was here for a couple weeks, but he went back the other day."

"He felt bad," Linda said, wiping at her eyes. "Brandon feels so bad. When JP never came home, he felt bad. But Brandon gets worried about my health, with the diabetes and all, and he knows I need my sleep. He never even said that day JP called for a ride because he didn't want to upset me. It's only when JP never came home he told me."

"It's okay, Ma," Cheryl said. "No one is saying this happened because you were asleep."

Linda began to sob again. "But my baby, my baby. My baby's gone."

Pete's stomach clutched. He looked at his hands, afraid it showed on his face. His mother had sobbed the same thing when Joey died. The heat in the room had become suffocating. He smelled the rotting stench from the dumpster, a physical assault that wouldn't go away. Just like that other dumpster a few months ago. Why was he thinking about that? He could feel his shirt stuck to his body under his suit jacket. He had a desperate need to get out of the house. He took a deep breath, pushed it all way, way back.

"Pete," Sid said. He looked over. Sid glared, a subtle shake of his head, then turned back to the women. "When did you know JP was missing?"

"When he didn't come home for supper, Ma called me to see if he was at my place. Sometimes he came over to hang out," Cheryl said. "But he wasn't. We weren't really worried, though, were we,

17

Ma?" Linda, still sobbing, didn't answer. "Sometimes he took off. Especially in the summer, when it's this hot out. Hung out with his friends. We thought maybe he was mad about the ride. Brandon went to look for him, driving around, but didn't see him."

"I had to go to work and he still wasn't home," Linda said.

Cheryl murmured, "Ma, it's okay, I can tell them."

Linda brushed her away. She gathered herself and looked at Pete, then Sid. "I went to work. I didn't know he was missing. I was mad at him, thought he was fooling around, just being himself, not coming home. So I went to work. I didn't know he'd called for the ride."

"It's okay," Sid said. "Understandable. Lots of people would do the same thing. What time did you go to work?"

"Around eight at night. When I got home in the morning, though—" She started sobbing again.

"We called the police when Ma got home and it was clear he hadn't been in his room all night," Cheryl said. "But they said he hadn't been missing long enough, and because he'd run away before, he wasn't a high risk or whatever they said. So we waited until later, twenty-four hours from when he called, then we called again."

"Can we talk to Brandon?" Sid asked.

"He won't tell you anything different than what we said," Cheryl said.

"True, but we'd like to talk to him anyway."

"I'll write down his cell." She went to the kitchen.

．．．．．

When they were outside, Sid turned on Pete. "Where'd you go in there, man? You left me all alone with those women."

"I was right there."

"In body."

"You were doing such a good job, I figured I'd let you keep going." Now that they were outside, despite the heat simmering off the pavement, it felt like fresh mountain air. "What's with Cheryl? She's coming on to me while we're talking about her brother's

18

murder?"

Sid laughed. "Pete Novotny charm. It's like a lethal weapon."

Pete didn't laugh at the old joke, Sid making fun of his lack of charm. "Notice how she slipped into past tense about JP, but Linda didn't?"

"Don't read too much into it. We found a body, so maybe Cheryl's come to terms."

"Maybe. But none of that felt right. Weird."

"You were weird, man," Sid said. "Just try to keep your head in the game."

Keep my head in the game, Pete said to himself. Maybe that was the problem, and none of that was weird at all. He was having trouble telling.

. . . . .

They found Brandon at his apartment with his girlfriend the next morning. A bigger, more muscled version of Cheryl, without the bleached blond hair and makeup.

"Look at this, Salt 'n Peppa. Do you have a warrant, Salt 'n Peppa?" First thing he asked when they asked if they could come in.

"We've never heard that before," Sid said. "It's because I'm black and you're white," he added to Pete.

"I get it now," Pete said. "Good one."

"We done?" Brandon asked, making to shut the door.

"We just want to talk to you about your brother," Sid said.

"Half-brother," Brandon said. "You can do that from the hallway. I told the other cops everything, anyway."

"That all may have changed," Pete said. "Now that he may be dead."

Brandon looked at him with contempt. "That kid isn't JP."

"How do you know?" Pete asked.

"Because my mother just called. Different kid."

"Is that so?" Sid asked, just as his cellphone rang. He stepped away to answer as Pete and Brandon had a stare-down. Pete knew Brandon's type, all tough-guy show with his black skull earing and Lenny Dykstra Phillies jersey with the sleeves torn off, tattoos

19

covering his muscled arms. He'd love for this guy to be guilty of something. Anything.

"He's right," Sid said, closing up his phone. "Someone else's kid. Parents reported him missing today and ID'd him."

"Case closed," Brandon said.

"Where's your brother?" Pete asked, grabbing the door and blocking it with his body as Brandon started to shut it.

"Half-brother," Brandon said. "He was a spoiled brat, and he ran away because he was a giant pain in the ass. Now get the fuck out of my house."

Pete stepped back and Brandon slammed the door.

"Was," Pete said, as he and Sid turned to go down the stairs.

"Uh huh," Sid said.

They solved the murder of the kid in the dumpster within days. JP Donovan remained a missing person, not a homicide. At least that's what Sid said every time Pete brought it up.

CHAPTER 3
2009
Redimere, Maine
November 7

Bernie fully intended to get a lot of work done. A quiet Saturday in the newspaper office, no one around. She even turned off her cellphone. But as she sat at her desk staring out the window at Main Street while her computer hummed, untouched, in front of her, all she could do was think about the night before. She tried to remember how, exactly, she'd landed in Pete's bed.

She'd planned an early night. A quick beer and chili at the Pour House, then home to TV and bed.

When she got to the Pour House, she was surprised to see Pete's car in the parking lot. He told her once that alcohol, being police chief, and hanging out with townspeople, was a recipe for disaster. He was at the end of the bar, eyes on the Celtics game.

"Hey, sailor," she said.

Pete had an empty shot glass and a half empty pint of beer in front of him. "Hi, yourself."

He signaled the bartender and pointed to Bernie.

"Chili, too," she said to the bartender. "What's up?" She nodded at the shot glass in front of him.

"Friday, I guess. My out-of-the-sling celebration."

"I'll drink to that," Bernie said, as the bartender put a pint of beer and a shot glass full of something amber in front of her. *Uh oh.* Pete held his glass in salute, waiting. *What the hell.* She raised the shot glass and got her Irish on. "Here's to the end of one season and the beginning of the next, to the coming darkness, but the warmth inside. Here's to fall back tomorrow night, which is an hour better than spring forward."

"Here's to having two arms again," Pete said.

"Two arms," Bernie agreed. The whiskey burned her throat, then warmed her stomach.

"When are we going to go shooting again?" he asked her.

"Never," Bernie said.

Pete laughed. "Come on, you're not that bad."

"It's not a matter of good or bad, it's a matter of me not liking it."

"You need a means to protect yourself."

"My mouth and personality continue to be my greatest weapons."

"Seriously." He *was* serious. The crinkly smile was gone, and he fixed her with that laser look from his green eyes that always unnerved her. "I'd feel more comfortable."

She was already buzzed, never diplomatic anyway, and she wasn't about to be now. "So many answers to that. First of all, I can't believe you're one of those guys who thinks everyone having a gun makes them safer. Second of all, I think you know me well enough to know if anyone shouldn't have a gun—"

"Bernie." He was laughing again.

"Let me finish. Third of all, why is it up to you to feel any level of comfort at all about me?"

"I think you know the answer to all three of those," he said.

"Can I see your arm?" A change of subject would do them good.

"Why?"

"I want to see what it looks like after being in a cast all those months."

He took off his flannel shirt, which he wore open, a T-shirt underneath. His arm was pale, but still had the hint of a tan, still firmly muscled, just a little thinner than the other. A scar snuck out from under the short sleeve of the T-shirt and ran down his triceps.

"Does it hurt?"

"No." He stared into her eyes and she felt the heat of the alcohol and maybe some other things burn her face. She remembered how a few months ago, he'd kissed her and how it felt, and how she'd found herself thinking about it a lot. Like now. Maybe that's when the night had started to go off the rails.

She broke the gaze. "I didn't realize you'd have a scar like that."

"They had to put a plate in. Four screws to put the bone back together."

"So it must hurt."

"Nope."

She knew he could have a white hot poker going through his eye and he wouldn't admit it hurt. "Right."

"You want to touch it?"

Bernie was about to say yes when she realized he was teasing. "Of course not," she said, but her fingers itched. Despite the fact the arm had been immobilized for months, his triceps still looked rock-hard. Damn right she wanted to touch it.

So that could have been the moment.

. . . . .

Walking back into town with Pete, many hours and glasses later, Bernie shivered, her jacket open in an attempt to hasten sobriety. She shuffled through the clumps of leaves that littered the roadside, their tangy smell mixed with the wood smoke. The tip of her nose was cold. Their breath came out in bright puffs. It all made her a little giddy. That and the alcohol, of course. At least the anxiety, her constant companion for months now, had waned.

One or two lights shone in homes. Bernie almost felt like they should tiptoe, to avoid waking the slumbering town. The scarecrows left from Harvest Fest slumped against utility poles, some still standing, some sunk down, sitting or lying in lumps by the gutter.

"Don't the scarecrows look like bodies?" she asked, mostly to break the silence. Pete had become quiet as the night wore on. He

23

didn't answer, so she tried again. "Harvest Fest was over two weeks ago. Halloween was last week. Somebody should pick them up."

They were at the corner of Church and Main, where she'd turn to go up the hill to her house, he'd go the other way, to his apartment.

He spoke, his first words in several minutes. "Ever since that time I kissed you, I've wanted to do it again."

Bernie too. That didn't stop the alarm bells, their clang clear through the haze of alcohol. She wanted to say something, like it wasn't a good idea, but couldn't get the words out.

He gently took her upper arm and turned her to face him. "No one's around to see us." His smile was warm, his eyes caught hers and held. He put his arms inside her open jacket, pulling her against him. He kissed her, a long warm kiss. She hadn't realized how cold her lips were until his warm ones touched them. What else could she do? She kissed him back.

"I'll take that mouth and personality any day," he said, soft and low. "I like them just fine. Everything else about you, too."

He held her tight against him. He wasn't a big, muscle-bound guy, but his arms were like steel bands, even the bad one. "It's great to have two arms again," he said. He kissed her again. He pulled back and looked in her eyes. "I don't want to go home alone." A husky whisper. The way he looked at her, the way he sounded, it was more a plea than a line, and sent her heart rocketing up to her throat. He pulled her close again, and she could feel his heart pounding against her chest.

"I don't want to go home alone," he repeated into her ear, his warm breath brushing her skin.

A voice in her head screamed *Bad idea! Bad idea!* "Okay," she whispered back.

In his apartment, she took off her jacket and threw it on a kitchen chair. She was about to say something, she wasn't sure what, suggest he turn on a light or something, when she was in his arms again. He kissed her again, even longer than the ones under the streetlight. He put his hands inside her shirt, pressing them, hot, against her stomach. The voice in her head was back, or maybe a different one, telling her she shouldn't have gone on that recent eating binge. Definitely a different voice, because it was almost drowned out by the first voice, still urgently telling her what a bad idea this was.

His hands moved up her rib cage, resting under her breasts, just slightly touching, barely brushing them.

A third voice, louder, chimed in. *Oh boy. Okay.*

He took her hand and led her through the dark living room into the bedroom. He pulled her close, kissing her again, then started unbuttoning her shirt.

Voice one was now hysterical. "Stop! Bad idea! Don't do it!"

Voice two said, "You DO NOT want him to see you naked."

The third voice, though, the loudest one, was saying something wordless and her body was agreeing.

Her head couldn't catch up with what was going on. She wanted to slow it down, slow him down, but her body wasn't letting her. Or Pete. He may have been drunk, but there was nothing sloppy about what he was doing. He pulled her close, his arms tight around her, his flannel shirt hot and soft against her bare skin. His mouth was against her ear. "I am so glad you're here," he whispered.

The third whooped in triumph. The other two shut up.

Now the scene played on a non-stop loop throughout the morning as she tried to get the newspaper's finances up to date, reconciling bills with revenue. The paper was a little bit in the black. Just a little. Despite the economy, the Great Recession, the worst year for newspapers in the history of newspapers, Redimere's few minutes in the spotlight a few months before, when the entire town had been pulled into a horrific double shooting and its aftermath, had boosted the paper's revenue and circulation. Despite the relatively good numbers, she hated dealing with them. They were like hieroglyphics to her and even simple addition and subtraction took forever, had to be checked and rechecked. It didn't help that they were dancing against the backdrop of her one-night stand with

Pete.

The paper was in the black, good enough that she could afford to hire a full-time reporter. Something she desperately needed since she handled most of the reporting duties herself, with Guy writing his column and helping with editing and layout. But the thought of hiring one made her nervous, considering what was going on with newspapers and how easy it would be to plunge into the red. It was a moot point, because she was having a lot of trouble finding someone who wanted to work for a remote Maine weekly despite the fact reporters all over New England were all losing their jobs. As she went over her budget again, or tried to, the moments that weren't taken up with vowing never to sleep with Pete again were filled with vowing to find a nice, eager intern who could work part-time.

The fact that she'd had a call a couple days before from an old colleague, Fergus X. Kelley, gave the vow new urgency. Feckless, she always called him, to herself and sometimes to others after a few beers. He'd taken a buyout at her former paper and was looking for something to tide him over until he found something "bigger."

"I pay a fraction of what you were making. It's a small-town weekly. In Franklin County, Maine. No lobsters or lighthouses here. I can't imagine this is what you want."

"It'll be fun," he said. "I got money from the buyout. I just want to stay sharp."

She told him she'd think about it. She didn't want to, though. He'd be a disaster. She'd never liked him and his lazy ways.

The police scanner, which had been quietly humming with the usual mundane things, popped to life. A possible 10-61, the dispatcher said. Bernie checked the yellowed police code list taped on the wall next to the scanner. Hunting accident. So much for the quiet morning. She grabbed her bag and her camera and ran out the door.

. . . . .

Pete was talking to the state police major crimes investigator when Dawna arrived, still in her hunting clothes.

He looked relieved to see her. "You know Sergeant Dawna Mitchell?" he asked the state investigator.

"I certainly do," the investigator said. Dawna knew him, too, and braced herself. George Libby was one of those state guys who thought the Redimere cops were backwoods clowns. She knew things were changing with Pete here, but she also knew the state guys would never admit it.

"We can't even really call this a hunting accident," Pete said to Libby.

"Without a body, it's hard to say what it is," Libby said. "But not an accident."

Guy Gagne was talking to an investigator. He was stooped, his usual ramrod posture wilted. He looked tired. The front of his pants was caked with what looked like vomit. She'd seen enough, both in Afghanistan and as an EMT, to recognize it, even if the faint whiff hadn't already carried to where she stood with Pete.

Dawna had also seen the gut pile, but not clearly, too many investigators surrounding it. The blood, though, was too scattered and messy to be from field-dressing a deer.

"What's going on?" she asked.

"Human gut pile," Libby said.

"Hunter mistakes a person for a deer, I get that, I guess," Pete said, his gaze riveted to the organs. Dawna could see them more clearly now, some in a pile, some scattered nearby. "They don't field dress him and drag him off. The rectum? The genitals? Not like a deer, right?"

Dawna processed it, the information neatly falling into place. Human gut pile, complete with genitals and rectum. "Some people do that with a buck. Keeps it cleaner. I do it, and so do a couple other hunters in town. More don't do it than do."

Pete gave her a long look and she felt that annoying blush burn across her face.

"The rectum," she said. "Some hunters start with that, remove it, to keep the meat from getting contaminated. I tie it off with a boot lace. I carry a bunch in my knapsack. Some people don't tie it

27

off." She couldn't tell if Pete, who didn't hunt and was from the city, thought she was a sicko, or if he understood.

"This one was not tied off," Libby said.

"The big thing is," Pete said. "This was a person. A man, obviously. So even if it was a hunting accident—"

"Right," said Libby. "Whoever shot him would have realized it wasn't a deer long before he field-dressed him." Dawna heard the implied condescension. *We get it.*

Pete shook his head. "What's the point? Where's the body?"

"If he was even shot," Dawna said.

The three watched the crime scene crew comb through the thick woods and brush.

"So far we've got two shell casings back in that clearing near that old hunting camp, down by the Ridge Road, and another one here," Libby said, pointing to an evidence marker a couple yards from the gut pile. "Other than that, and an extraordinary amount of blood, not much more."

"Lots of blood for a field dressing," Dawna said.

"Wouldn't a deer have a lot of blood?" Pete asked.

Libby rolled his eyes.

"It would," Dawna said. She didn't expect Pete to know. "But when you field dress, you usually try to get it on a rise or angled spot, then you cut it, gut it clean, and tip it, so the blood goes out in a nice stream. Some people are messier than others, but this, well, it just plain looks more like a messy crime scene. Those congealed puddles scattered around? It's not like you'd do with a deer. It's like someone was manhandling the body."

"Anyway, it wasn't a deer," Pete said.

"It wasn't," Dawna said. "I guess what you'd do with a deer doesn't matter."

"The killer was making a statement?"

"Maybe," she said at the same time Libby said, "That's pretty clear."

An officer handed Libby an evidence bag with what looked like a clump of bloody string inside.

"What's this?" Libby asked.

"Found with the guts," the officer said. Pete and Dawna leaned in to look. "Looks like a cord from a sweatshirt or something."

"Is it brown?" Pete asked.

"Covered with blood, hard to tell," Libby said. He managed to make it sound like an insult, but Pete didn't react.

"There's another thing," Dawna said. Pete hadn't taken his eyes off the blood-covered cord and she wondered if there was something she was missing. "I heard gunshots. Around five. They sounded like they were coming from this direction."

Libby cocked his head, looked at her like she was a sideshow curiosity.

She took her lead from Pete, ignored the insult. "I was hunting. Heard two shots and thought it was way too early. Heard another one about ten minutes later."

Libby wrote it down. "I'll fill you two in once we know more."

Pete nodded, expressionless, but his quick glance at Dawna looked rattled, and that rattled her.

. . . . .

When Bernie arrived on Ridge Road, two things struck her. The first was there were an awful lot of law enforcement agencies there for it to be a simple hunting accident. State police investigators, game wardens, Franklin County sheriff deputies, a variety of other cops and other responders milled around. Even the U.S. Border Patrol from the Rangeley station. The state police crime scene mobile van was there, too. She wondered if it was a local or one of those guys who'd been roaring through town all week in big SUVs with out-of-state plates.

The next thought was that they weren't going to let her in to the scene. She was right.

She leaned against her car, waiting to see a friendly face from the Redimere department. Hopefully Dawna. She wasn't sure she wanted to talk to Pete.

The day had started out sunny, but had gotten cold, winter on the wind. She occasionally snapped a few photos. Stomped around a little to keep warm, tried to see if she could overhear conversations whenever someone came out of the woods, but she got nothing.

Eventually Dawna did come out. She shook her head before Bernie even said anything.

"You might as well go home," she said. "No one will tell you anything today."

Bernie opened her mouth to ask a question.

"Seriously," Dawna said. "Sorry. I'll have the chief call you later."

Bernie went back to the office, forcing herself to do at least some of the work she'd been putting off. Hours later, exhausted, hungry, and dispirited, she walked into a house extraordinarily cleaner than she'd left it, and smelling of beef stew and homemade bread. Her mood lifted more than she thought capable. She had almost forgotten her brother was there. "Honey, I'm home," she sang.

Sal turned from the stove, nearly tripping over Dubya, who was planted at his feet, grinning adoringly up at his new hero. "I cooked supper. I also cleaned. You were verging on hoarder status. Some of those dirty dishes looked like, I don't even know. I thought maybe the vacuum was broken, but I tried it and it wasn't."

"Wow, Mom. You look so much like Sal." She didn't want to explain that she had too much on her mind to even think about cleaning. "Did you go to the store?"

"No," Sal said. "When did you become a hoarder? You have a zillion empty prescription bottles."

She lifted the top of the pot and sniffed the stew. "I had meat?" She tried to think how old it would be.

"In the freezer. Smelled okay. I threw them all out. The bottles."

"Don't throw out my stuff," she said, annoyed. "They come in handy." She opened the kitchen wastebasket and there was a clean garbage bag in it. "Where are they?"

"Then why are they all empty?"

"There are some non-empty ones holding tacks, nails, screws, stuff like that. Anyway, I don't want to bring them to the dump. I don't want the world to know my secrets."

"I put them in a garbage bag. I was going to do the same with the mountain of unopened mail on the table, but a lot of it looked like bills, so I put it on the desk in your bedroom."

"Did you get out anywhere today or just spend the whole day throwing out my stuff?"

"You're welcome. No, I didn't go out. A cop came by."

"When?" When she got back to the office, she'd turned her cellphone on in case Pete called about the accident. Still wasn't sure she wanted to talk about the other stuff. She'd noticed he'd called earlier in the morning, before the accident, but hadn't left a message. She'd been relieved.

"Couple hours ago."

"Did you talk to him?" she asked Sal. She'd been at the office, but she didn't have a lot of lights on and the door had been locked, so even if he'd driven by, he may have thought it was closed.

"Nobody was home."

"You could have at least answered the door. He's going to think I was hiding from him."

"No car in the driveway. It wouldn't take Sherlock Holmes to figure out you weren't here."

That was another thing. "Where's your car, anyway? How'd you get here?"

"Who is he, friend or foe?"

"We have bigger things to talk about. Like why you're not in New York and where your car is."

He stirred the stew, tasted it, nodded. "Not much to talk about."

She was about to argue when the sound of tires on the gravel driveway interrupted and headlights swept past the window.

"I'll just skedaddle into the other room." Sal, rucksack in hand, disappeared down the hall to her bedroom.

It was Pete. He gave her a peck on the lips as he came in. "I called you this morning."

"I was at work. Had the phone off. I turned it back on later, though." He looked strong and official in his uniform, a lot different from when she left him on the bed so many hours before. "Did Dawna tell you I was at the hunting accident scene?"

"She did." He took in the pot of stew on the stove, the homemade bread on the counter.

"I made those yesterday, just heating them up," Bernie said, wondering why she was lying. "So what was that hunting accident all about?"

"Guy Gagne found something today in the woods. I'm not sure it's a hunting accident."

"What did he find?"

"Human body parts."

Bernie's radar clanged. "What parts? Whose? How old?"

"Press release Monday, once we get it sorted out. State police is the primary."

"Thanks. Is that why there were so many law enforcement agencies there?"

"Yeah. That and it was a slow day." He gave her a big smile. She wondered if they were going to pretend last night hadn't happened. That would work for her. "I wanted to talk about last night."

Okay, guess not. She hoped, as embarrassing at it would be, it was going to be "let's just be friends, it can't happen again." She was afraid, though, it wouldn't.

"I was really drunk," he said.

"We both were."

"I'm usually not—" He blushed. "I usually take more time."

Bernie shrugged. She was embarrassed he was embarrassed. The last thing she wanted to talk about was the sex. *Just skip to it can't happen again.*

"I didn't want you to think it was a drunken thing, that I was taking advantage."

"I didn't think that. But we've both been around the block." She'd speed things up. End the conversation. Everything back to business as usual.

Pete looked into her eyes. "I would like a do-over."

Bernie laughed. It was the last thing she wanted to hear—at least she was pretty sure it was—but unexpected, cute even. "You bring the Jack Daniels and I'll bring the case of beer."

"That's not what I mean." Pete took a deep breath. His eyes wandered to the steaming pot on the stove, to Dubya panting happily on the kitchen floor, the cats curled and snoring on the couch, back to Bernie. Those green laser eyes boring into her soul. "Last night was about how I feel, not sex."

That's what she was afraid of.

"You must know," he said, taking her elbow looking into her eyes, ducking at the knees, to be sure he caught her gaze, because now hers was wandering.

"I have so much going on," she said. "I like you a lot. We definitely have a bond, after what happened in July, but—" She wanted him to let go of her elbow, stop looking into her eyes. "It's just, you know, we make such good friends." She felt as lame as it sounded. The stare unnerved her. His grip on her elbow, firm, but not painful, burned. She wished he'd let go but didn't want him to. She cast about for something else to say but couldn't come up with anything. She didn't want to hurt his feelings. Didn't want to lose their bond. What did she want? She didn't know. Wanted this to be over.

Pete, ever the hero, broke the silence. Dudley Do-Right, as Bernie sometimes called him. To herself, of course. "All right." He let go. Smiled even. His radio crackled, as if on cue. She followed him to the door. He leaned over and kissed her on the lips, gentle and warm

Bernie still didn't know what to say.

He took a deep breath. Way too deep. She braced herself.

"Drunk as I was, I want you to know that when I said I loved you, I meant it."

Bernie's heart sank. "I know." His smile, warm and sincere, made her feel worse.

33

"I just wanted you to know."

Bernie watched Pete's cruiser back out of the driveway.

Sal came out of the bedroom after the door shut. "You're screwing a cop?"

She'd forgotten Sal was there. "No."

"Looks like it to me. Sounds like it, too. 'Let's just be friends.' Sheesh."

"You were listening?"

"It's hard not to in this house."

"I'm not sleeping with him."

"I like the way he warmed you up by talking about body parts. What a charmer."

"Don't change the subject. I want to know why you're here. Where's your car? Have you talked to anyone else?" They both knew by anyone else, she meant their siblings.

"You're the only one who knows." Sal went over to the stove and ladled a bowl of stew. He cut a big piece of the bread and sat at the table, pouring himself a glass of wine, slipping a piece of meat to Dubya. "Sit down and eat. *Mangia.* I'll tell you everything."

She sighed, got her helping, and sat down. Sal grinned at her. Her Irish dad and Italian mom had tried the DNA mix seven times with varying degrees of success before finally getting it right with her youngest sibling. He looked like a skinny Roman warrior, a tangle of black curly hair, big brown eyes, perfect Roman nose over a thick beard and beautiful, perfect smile. Dimples even behind the beard. On top of it, he was easy-going in family of uptight, type-A overachievers.

"I got fired."

Bernie nearly spit out her stew. "What?"

"Fired. You of all people should understand."

"I didn't get fired," Bernie said. Nearly three years after her "you can't fire me, I quit" moment the fact, the circumstances still made her cringe. "Did you do something?"

"Plagiarized." She could tell he was trying to look matter-of-fact, but a blush crept up his neck, a growing ruddy patch visible even under his beard.

She was stunned. "It was an accident, right?"

He sighed again. "No. It was a purpose. I had a student who did this brilliant paper. Then she dropped out, left the paper behind. You don't know how much pressure I'm under. Tenure's coming up next year. I have to publish. My dean had already had a talk with me about it. I was up nights. I was panicked." He shook his head. "You know how that feels? So I thought what's the harm? She's not here anymore. She'll never know. So I did it. I won't bore you with the details. Then I got caught."

"Geez, Sal."

"You have to help me tell the others. Mom and Dad. What am I going to say?"

"I don't know. What *are* you going to say? I don't get that you'd do something like that. You're so smart. So talented. You don't need to steal someone's work."

Sal took a gulp of wine. "Maybe I'm not that smart. I like to teach. I really like to create art. If I didn't have to make a buck, I'd just do that. I liked the job, the people, but the competition, the ambition, all the politics? I hate it. What's with our family that I'm expected to take part in all that? Why can't I just be me?"

"Don't blame the family. You could have done whatever you wanted."

"Come on. You're the only one in this family without an advanced degree. The only one who's not a medical doctor or lawyer. Hell, some of them even have two degrees. Look at all the shit you get. Look at the shit I got when I dropped out of med school."

"I don't get shit," Bernie said. "They just tease. I'm perfectly happy with my life."

"When you were a big-shot reporter, winning awards and kicking ass, it was okay. But here?" He looked around her little house, the living room and kitchen one room, barely enough space for the furniture. "Come on."

"We're not talking about me. What are you going to do?"

35

"Crash here until I figure it out." He smiled, raised his eyebrows.

She laughed, couldn't help it. "Sure."

"They gave me severance. Smoothed it over so there wouldn't be a fuss. Can't embarrass the university."

"You have to tell the family."

Sal smiled again. She could see why he'd left a string of broken female hearts in his wake over his nearly forty years.

"I'll think of something," she said.

"Let's talk more about the body parts," he said. "What's that about?"

"I don't know, but I'm looking forward to finding out."

"Weird job you have."

"I know! Isn't it great?"

CHAPTER 4
2007
Redimere, Maine
June 17

There was no one there, then there was. In the beam of Sgt. Ray Morin's cruiser headlights, through the driving early summer rain, it was more an impression than a shape.

Not a person at first. Ray thought it was a deer. Then maybe a ghost, but in the two seconds it took him to skid the cruiser to the shoulder and realize that was crazy, the shape was gone.

The back of Ray's mind had caught a split-second shadow darting into the woods. It wasn't a ghost. Or a deer. Wasn't his imagination.

Obviously not. Because now, an hour later, after a slogging sprint through the woods, a slip, a fall, a half-assed tackle, there the kid was, soaking wet and streaked with mud in the plastic chair crammed into the corner of the office, under the bulletin board and next to the filing cabinet, in what little free space the Redimere Police Department's basement headquarters had.

Ray didn't have time to think much about it until it was all over—splashing through the mud, tripping over roots, the tackle, the struggle. But back at the office as he sat there feeling the aches and pains begin to pop all over his forty-five-year-old body, he knew what made him stop the cruiser. It was two in the morning in the driving rain and there was someone on the shoulder of Route 27, a road to nowhere Maine and even more nowhere Canada past that.

Every cop knows that the first thing to look for is something that shouldn't be there. When that something runs, you run, too, right after it. Ray had to admit, that was the limit of his brilliance on this one. In the dank police station, he was at a loss.

"C'mon, tell me your name and I can get you somewhere and we can both get some sleep." Ray said it like a recitation, the cajoling, ordering, begging of the past forty-five minutes or so.

The kid didn't respond. Sat there, unmoving, except to occasionally wipe his nose. The peanut butter crackers and Mountain Dew Ray got him out of the vending machine still sat untouched on the edge of the desk.

Now it was after three a.m. and, Jesus Christ, Ray wanted nothing more than to go home.

The kid—Ray had started thinking of him like that, though he could be anywhere from fifteen to twenty, hard to tell under that soaked, sagging hoodie—didn't seem to hear. Ray didn't know whether to be concerned or pissed off, but pissed off was winning.

"Just a name, okay?" Ray asked for the sixth, seventh, twentieth, whatever time.

The ticking clock was the only answer. Three-sixteen. Ray wanted to go home to his warm bed, his warm wife, look in on his daughters, anything but sit here in the damp police station with this kid. The rain pounded on the ground outside the windows of the basement office. He could feel the damp seeping in, smell it.

"If you tell me who you are, I can help you," Ray said.

The kid sat slumped in his chair, staring at his shoes.

Ray had to do something. Nothing he was going to say was going to move this along. "Okay, I have to find someplace to put you tonight." Ray knew he couldn't call the chief. Cal Littlefield liked his sleep and he'd have Ray's hide for waking him up for something like this. Ray clicked through the computer resources file, no idea who to call at this time of night. It was the deepest, darkest hour of the morning in Redimere, Maine, one of the deepest, darkest reaches in the state. Not a lot of resources handy.

Ray settled on the Department of Health and Human Services hotline for child abuse. Not quite right, but better than nothing.

"Okay," he said, more to himself than the kid. "This'll have to do." He picked up the phone, reciting the number to himself, only half registering that the kid was moving.

"Wait." The kid's first words since the soft "fuck" when Ray had tackled him. He stood, turned to the bulletin board plastered with missing kid photos from the past decade. So many pictures, Ray always thought, so many missing kids. The kid scanned the fliers, some tacked over others, some yellow with age. He rifled through them as Ray watched his back with one eye, the other eye on the phone number, his finger suspended above the buttons.

The kid, purposeful, impatient, seemed to know what he was looking for. The dial tone kicked back in as he tore a flier from its tack, one that had been buried underneath a bunch of others, yellowed and smudged. He put it on Ray's desk.

MISSING: JP Donovan. Height 5' 5", weight 125. Hair light brown, eyes hazel. Last seen, Philadelphia, August 7, 2003.

He poked the smudgy fax picture with a dirty, nail-bitten finger.

"That's me."

. . . . .

The party was in one of those Philadelphia social club halls—the Ancient Order of Hiberians or something. Smoking ordinance? Not in our freakin' hall. Pete hadn't wanted to attend JP Donovan's celebrated return, four years after that August day in 2003 when he'd first met the Donovans. But he knew he had to if he was ever going to get answers. He tried not to breathe the smoke in the hot summer closeness of the hall, a bubble of bile working its way up his throat. He also wanted to see for himself. He'd been so sure JP was dead. So sure Brandon had something to do with it, that Cheryl and maybe even Linda were complicit. He'd spent the last four years trying to figure it out, spending way more time with the Donovans than he wanted, waiting for that break. So JP's back, picked up hitch-hiking by a cop in some remote Maine town, and he was wrong all along? He had to see for himself.

"There you are, stranger," Cheryl Donovan, looking much like she had when he last saw her months before, grabbed him by the elbow and gave him a quick dry kiss on the cheek. He tried not to pull back as she leaned in, too close as always. "Come over and see the boy of the hour," she said, dragging him through the crowded room.

Pete had felt dizzy since he got there. The room was packed, hot. TVs in the corners and over the bar blared the Phillies game, although none of the shouting, already drunk, crowd seemed to notice. The air was heavy with cigarette smoke, sweat, other smells he didn't want to try to figure out. He was overdressed. Why had he put a suit on? He wasn't sure. Hadn't worn one since he'd been put on leave the month before. Now the necktie was strangling him. His T-shirt, damp with sweat under his suit, stuck to him, the backs of his knees wet against his trousers. He tried to tamp down the panic, tried to breathe, as he followed Cheryl.

"Brandon here?" he asked her.

"Who? Oh, no. He had to work," she said over her shoulder. "Here he is." She pulled Pete in front of a young man. Oversized Yankees baseball cap, a hoodie, loose jeans. The kid looked away, down at the floor, then behind Pete's shoulder as Cheryl spoke. "JP, this is the cop that helped us. He was looking for you all this time, all these years, all the four years since you went away," she said, her voice loud over the crowd. "He's like a member of the family."

The kid's eyes met Pete's, then darted away. Kid's as shaky as I am, Pete thought. He held his hand out. "Pete Novotny."

The kid, not looking at him, briefly shook it, then shoved his hands in his pockets. A small smirk flashed, then was gone in a split second. That knowing smirk from the photos.

"JP got shy since he was gone," Cheryl yelled in Pete's ear. "JP! Pete's a homicide cop, but he helped us look for you anyway. Even though you weren't dead!" She laughed as though it was the funniest thing on earth. She was the only one laughing. The kid stared at the ground, shuffled his feet.

"Glad you came home safe," Pete said, holding his hand out again.

The kid again took his hand. Smirked. Looked at Pete, his eyes not darting away this time, meeting Pete's. They were half-closed slits in a smooth, unlined face. Pete felt a shift. The one that had eased up just a fraction since his breakdown. The back of his neck locked and his vision blurred. The bile bubble in that hollow between his stomach and chest get bigger, his stomach clutched. He couldn't breathe.

"Gotta go," he managed to say to Cheryl and the kid, then turned and pushed through the crowd toward the exit sign, feeling Cheryl's hand on his arm, then slide off as he moved, pushing, desperate for fresh air.

Outside, he leaned back against the brick wall of the building, taking deep gulps of the warm June night. Trying to get his breath, willing his heartbeat to return to normal. What triggered the panic attack this time? Seeing the kid he'd been sure was dead? When he shook that hand, grudgingly offered from the sleeve of the hoodie, he'd felt something. He'd never known JP Donovan. Never seen anything but photos. Those sad snapshots from Christmas and barbeques that when they're taken no one ever imagines are going to find their way to a police desk or missing kid poster. All those photos had that smirk. Was it the same smirk? He couldn't say.

When he took that hand, clammy, reluctant, he'd tried to look past it and into those slitted eyes. He felt a hint when he took his hand, but when he looked into those eyes, he was sure. They weren't hazel. They were a deep brown, almost black. And as old and soulless as Methuselah. That's when he knew it wasn't JP Donovan.

. . . . .

JP Donovan's story was barely plausible. He'd been kidnapped off the city street while he was walking home that hot day in August 2003. Thrown in the back of a van and blindfolded. The van ride took hours—he didn't know how long. He was brought to a farm in the middle of nowhere. He was kept in a basement, fed just enough

41

to keep alive. Beaten and raped by a series of men. Sometimes there were other kids there, too, sometimes not. He didn't even know it was Maine until he escaped nearly four years later, he'd said. That's the night he was found hitchhiking on a desolate two-lane road in a tiny Maine town about fifty miles from the Canada border.

So far the FBI and Maine State Police couldn't find evidence any of that had happened. Not a shred.

"I've heard more believable stories on the Sci-Fi Channel," Sid said as he and Pete sat in lawn chairs in Sid's backyard, watching Sid's kids run through the sprinkler.

"If nothing else, you'd think he would have left out the barely eating part," Pete said. "He's a small guy, but definitely not underfed." It was the day after Pete had gone to the party. He'd told Sid about it, but not about the panic attack. It wasn't a big one, anyway. There were going to be aftershocks from his breakdown, he wasn't cured, but he sure as hell wasn't going to talk about it.

They drank their beer and watched Sid's kids run and shriek through the water. "Easy on your brother, Ashley," Sid yelled.

Sid's daughter shrieked again, louder, and his little son chortled. Ashley laughed, too, a fit of giggles that dissolved into happy squeaks.

Pete felt that old chill. "They sound like ducks."

"What?" Sid said, startled.

"The kids." Heat rushed up the back of his neck, prickled his hair. He could tell he'd put Sid on alert. He didn't know why he'd said it. "Remember those ducks in the dumpster in the summer of '03? A couple months before we found the kid we thought was JP?" Even as he said it, he wished he hadn't.

Sid reached over and rested his big catcher's mitt of a hand on Pete's head. His eyes filled and he looked like he was about to say something. Pete didn't want to hear it. His embarrassment burned, mixed with shame. He nodded his head from beneath Sid's hand and Sid looked away.

Pete pushed the demon down, way to the back where it belonged, changed the subject. "The weirdest thing is the Donovans insisting he's JP. I know he's not."

"You gotta let that go, man. Four years have gone by since the kid went missing and wherever he's been, no matter how made-up his story is, he's been through something. People change."

"Their eye color doesn't."

"How many times are we going to have this conversation? The family says it was wrong on the poster. It's impossible to tell from those old snapshots. You said yourself he had the same smirk. Or devilish smile, as Linda put it." He chuckled and looked at Pete to share the joke. "I know they're weird. I know you've put four years into this, but let it go. It's nothing to us."

Pete knew what was coming.

"I worry about you," Sid said quietly, even though the kids were too far away to hear.

"I'm fine."

"You still have a ways to go. We need you back. I need you back. Have you talked to Karen? She's worried, too."

"I'm fine." Pete wasn't going to argue, and he certainly wasn't going to call his ex-wife to whine about his mental health. He also wasn't going to let the Donovans go. "How does everyone buy in? He's obviously lying."

"Everyone lies. You know that."

Pete's friend in the FBI said they knew the kid was full of shit about what he said he'd been through, but he hadn't broken any laws. The FBI didn't seem much interested in Pete's insistence he wasn't JP Donovan. "The family says he is," his friend said. "He's gonna be 17 in a few months. Whatever he's been up to, it's not worth pursuing."

Pete tried again with Sid. "Did you read that newspaper story I sent you? The one from the paper up there that said people don't think he's JP Donovan, but he's 21 and had been in the town for a while? That's after JP said whatever happened to him was hours from that town and he was just passing through."

"We going to keep talking about this?" Sid asked, taking two more bottles out of the cooler by his chair. "I didn't read the story.

43

I'm not interested. The kid made up an identity. Lied about his age and where he was. Unless he tells the truth, we'll never know where he was those last four years, but it's not our problem."

Sid used to joke with Pete about his obsession with the Donovans and the fact he thought they knew what had happened to JP. So had Karen before their divorce two years ago. Pete was already shaky, spinning, before that, but losing Karen had made him focus on the Donovans with added intensity. Something to keep him busy. Sid had stopped joking about it around then, his comments becoming concerned and pointed. So Pete had stopped talking about it despite the amount of time he devoted to it. He'd talked to Brandon, or tried. More or less stalked him. Brandon had a lengthy criminal record and Pete waited for him to slip up. Cheryl had called a lot, long drunken rambles that Pete listened to, hoping for a clue, something to go on. He'd visit Linda once in a while, listen to her cry, tell the same stories. He never got much, but he could wait them out.

Now JP was supposedly back. Pete knew it could stir things up, make someone slip. Now he had a new angle, totally new information. He was on leave, at loose ends, and if he could finally solve this one, he'd be back on track. His old self. He couldn't let it go.

"What are you thinking, buddy?" Sid asked.

"I'm thinking I'm going to Maine," Pete said.

CHAPTER 5
2009
Redimere, Maine
November 7

The gunshot split the black night. It was close, really close.

Gunshots weren't rare in Redimere this time of year. Bernie'd been hearing them since hunting season had started a week before. *The sound of gunfire, off in the distance, I'm getting used to it now...* the Talking Heads song was constantly in her head. But on this dark, dead-quiet night, when the only noise was distant cars on routes 27 and 16, and not even the bugs and birds of summer, not even the wind in the trees in the cold November night air, it stopped her short.

She was half an hour into her nightly walk, a habit she'd developed over the past couple months driven by anxiety over money, owning a newspaper, feeling on the edge, the bad summer. Tonight was worse, with worries about Pete and her brother mixed in. She'd wandered to the outskirts of town where houses and mobile homes were nestled on lots snug inside the dark woods, many not visible from the road, their porch lights or lit windows blinking through the trees, revealed, now that the trees were bare of leaves.

The dooryard of the house she stood in front of was cut out of the woods, an expanse of shrubless, treeless still-green lawn that sloped down to the road, a small ranch that in the dark with light seeping out from the drawn curtains of every window, looked cozy and inviting. The drapes of the large picture window next to the front door were slightly parted, and Bernie could see movement.

She'd heard nothing since the gunshot, but it seemed to have come from inside. Her hand gripped her cellphone in her jacket pocket as she walked up on the lawn for a better look. Another line from that song dodged through her head as she tried to make sense of the situation. *You oughta know not to stand by the window, somebody see you up there...*

It'd be foolish to call the cops if it were someone in his backyard testing his gunsights or shooting at cans. Even though that would be idiotic in the dark, and possibly illegal—she should look it up when she got home—it happened all the time.

She didn't have to think about it at all, though. There was another shot, then a short, sharp scream. She couldn't tell if it was male or female, just terrified. She moved up farther on the lawn, not yet where the dim light from the window spilled out, and took the phone from her pocket, not wanting to tear her eyes from the house, but also not one of those people who could punch a number into a cellphone without looking. She'd just looked down at the phone when the door burst open, the storm door banging against the house like another shot. A woman ran out, followed by a man. Bernie backpedaled down the lawn and across the street. No streetlights out here in rural west-central Maine to reveal her. Their attention wasn't on her anyway.

The woman was wearing a cardigan thrown over a T-shirt, pajama bottoms. She sobbed and gasped for breath as she sprinted across the lawn in long, graceful strides that made her flight, the shot, the scene, even more surreal. Bernie stupidly thought of the deer that loped through her backyard at dawn.

"Get back here you bitch," the man said, firing the gun—a rifle—into the air. "Where is it?"

The woman screamed again at the sound as she hit the pavement and ran down the country road, disappearing almost immediately into the black night. A baby was crying somewhere in the house, a ragged raw, hiccupping wail.

46

The man stood on the lawn, breathing heavily. "Bitch," he said, not yelling, but loud enough for Bernie to hear. She still had her cellphone in her hand but hadn't hit the numbers, paralyzed, afraid he'd see her, hear her.

As he looked down the street, not making a move to go after the woman or to go back in the house, there was movement in the doorway, a tiny silhouette. "Colton's crying," a tremulous voice said.

The man turned toward the doorway, and as the light played on his face, Bernie recognized him. Tim Shaw, the supervisor at the town dump. She felt a moment of embarrassment, now that it was someone she knew. She knew his wife, too. Wendy from the deli counter at the store.

"Where's Mommy?"

Bernie, like Tim, looked down the street. A black expanse with no sign of life.

"She went for a walk," Tim said. "Let's get back in the house." Still, he stood, looking down the street.

"She forgot her shoes," the boy said, on the verge of tears.

"She's fine," Shaw said.

"She threw it in the garbage," the boy said, though it sounded like a question.

What? Her shoes?

"Let's get back inside." Shaw guided the boy into the house with one hand, gun in the other. He took one last look down the street before slamming the door.

Bernie dialed her phone, her fingers shaking. She didn't call 911. Didn't want to go through the questions and transfers from one dispatch center to another that was the reality in rural Maine this time of night, repeating herself and all the details over and over when she just wanted someone to get the hell out here.

"Hi," Pete said, in the middle of the first ring.

"I'm out walking on Ridge Road, and I just saw Tim Shaw chase his wife out of the house with a rifle. He went back in, but she ran down the street. He was shooting it. Not at her. That I know of, since I didn't see that part. But still shooting, a couple—"

"Did you call 911?"

"I called you."

He started to say something, then bit it off. "You're at their house?"

"Yeah, about a mile out of town, a little past the intersection of County." She tried to keep her voice a low stage whisper, but it kept rising and cracking.

"I know where it is. If your cell isn't on vibrate, do that now. And for god's sake, stay out of sight." He hung up.

Bernie had crossed the street back to the yard while she was talking, walking over to the driveway and up to the garage, hoping she was in a spot where she couldn't be seen from the house. The sound of the baby crying was faint but unrelenting. The night crisp, cold. The kind of night that was a reminder winter was on its way down the mountains. The smell of wood smoke hung in the air. Bernie wondered where shoeless, coatless Wendy was.

Her phone vibrated. "A state cruiser should be there in five minutes. Ten at the most. Me, too, maybe sooner. Stay out of sight and quiet. Don't knock on the door. Don't go looking for Wendy. Don't talk to anyone. Got it?"

Bernie murmured what she hoped sounded like agreement, but it was too late.

Tim Shaw, the rifle still in his hand, was crossing the dooryard toward her. "What the fuck are you doing here?" he asked.

She was trying to form an answer when the sound of sirens split the night. "Waiting for them," she answered, smiling, hoping he hadn't heard the tremor of fear in her voice.

. . . . .

Pete was surprised to find Vicki in the office Sunday morning. He was exhausted, the previous day had felt like a month, beginning with the gut pile, then the depressing visit to Bernie, the scene at the Shaws'. He wanted some quiet and to do his paperwork alone.

"You can go home," he said. "You don't have to work on Sunday."

"There's just so much to do," she said.

"Nothing that can't wait until tomorrow." He went into his office. One nice thing about the new public safety building, at least he had somewhere private to go instead of everyone sitting on top of each other like in old days in the dank basement department under Town Hall.

He took the bottle of aspirin out of his desk drawer and popped three, swallowing with no water so he wouldn't have to go back to the outer office. His arm was killing him, screaming in pain. Don't do too much too soon, everyone at the hospital had said when the cast had finally come off, two surgeries and several weeks later than originally predicted. What was too much? He had no idea.

The pain was no distraction from the gut pile, though, and that bloody brown string they'd found at the crime scene. He knew the minute he saw it in the evidence bag. When Pete had seen Benji Reeves last week on Ridge Road, skinny, hunched over in that brown hoodie, he shouldn't have questioned it. Should have made Dawna stop the cruiser, should have grabbed him with his one usable arm.

"You got a message yesterday. I mean Friday." Vicki was standing halfway in, halfway out of the door.

"Friday?"

"I forgot."

She came over to his desk holding a message slip and handed it to him. "Sorry," she said again, and scurried out of the room. Pete had a private line, but most of his calls went through the front desk. It'd worked fine when Dawna sat out there, before they had an actual receptionist. But now Dawna was a sergeant, out on patrol. You'd think hiring an office administrator would make things more organized, not less.

"What's this?" He went to the door, the slip in his hand.

"He said you'd know?"

"There's no name or number." Pete read the message out loud. "A man called. He wants to talk."

Vicki's eyes welled up.

"No number off the caller ID?" he asked.

49

"It said 'unknown.'"

He looked at the slip, wet with his sweat and wadded up. Took a deep breath. Shaky. "Okay, thanks."

"I told him you'd be back." She looked like she was going to cry.

"Did he say anything else? Anything?" He tried to soften his tone. It wasn't Vicki's fault.

"He didn't say anything else, but his voice was funny. Kind of high. He had this laugh. I'm sorry, there's just so much here to do."

"It's all right. See you tomorrow, okay?" He went back into his office, trying not to slam the door behind him as he heard her weak "okay" somewhere behind him.

Sid answered on the first ring. "Hey, buddy, how ya doing?"

Pete loved Sid but hated the question. Hated that it was more than just a greeting and hated the concern in Sid's voice. "Fine. Any reason Benji Reeves would be in Redimere?"

"Yeah, I don't like small talk either." Pete knew Sid wanted him to laugh, joke back. When he didn't, Sid continued, "Reeves? I thought you were done with all that."

"Me too. That's why I'm calling. Anything going on there?"

"What part?"

"Any of it."

"Haven't heard anything."

"Nothing? You sure? Think."

"I'm not the bad guy, no need to interrogate me. What's going on?"

Pete took a deep breath and reminded himself he was talking to his best friend. "He wanted to talk to me. He was in my apartment Friday night, but I wasn't there. He said in a note he had news. Earlier Friday he called the station looking for me."

"He hasn't caught up with you since?"

"We found a gut pile in the woods yesterday. Something tells me it may be him."

"Gut pile?"

"Just what it sounds like."

50

"What tells you it was him?"

"Cord from a brown hoodie."

"And from that you deduced the gut pile is Benji Reeves?"

"I think I saw him last week, and he was wearing a brown hoodie."

"Again, a gut pile is?"

"When someone kills a deer, they field dress it. Slit it open from its throat to its groin and take out its guts. Leave them for the elements."

"Maine is a weird and wonderful place."

"Hunters do it everywhere, even in Pennsylvania. Some of them also cut out the deer's rectum and castrate it. They did that to this guy, too."

"Reeves."

"I think so."

"I'll see what I can find out," Sid said.

"It's fucked up."

"That's right. Whatever it is, it's fucked up." Sid took a deep breath. Pete could feel him getting ready on the other end, 500 miles away. Knew what was coming. "Let it go. You're okay now. You need to stay that way."

Pete didn't respond.

"I worry about you, brother."

"I know." Pete felt his irritation wash away on the familiar wave of weariness.

After Pete hung up, he tried to sort through the nearly year and a half since he'd last talked to Reeves. He knew there was only one thing that Reeves would want to talk to him about. But he didn't want to feel humored, hear more warnings. He didn't need it. So he didn't tell Sid that part. Those crazy days were over. Now if he could just get rid of the needle of dread that was pricking at him. He balled up the phone message and threw it in the waste can.

51

CHAPTER 6
2009
Redimere, Maine
Sunday, November 8

Bernie and Sal both slept until noon Sunday, despite the extra hour from the end of daylight saving time.

"Where did you go last night?" he asked as they shared a pot of coffee.

"I take walks. Can't sleep." She didn't want to talk about it or what happened at the Shaws. "You need to call Theresa." Their oldest sister would take charge, disseminate the information, tell their parents. She would also give both of them a giant helping of her opinion, but that was the price to be paid.

"Later. Maybe tomorrow."

Bernie didn't argue. Once it was done, the phone calls, explaining, and agita would be at a fever pitch. She wasn't looking forward to it any more than he was. "I know. It's too much." She turned on the TV for the day's first football game. There were too many things that were too much.

"Too much," Sal agreed, not looking up from his newspaper.

They hung around the house, reading the Sunday papers, watching football, eating leftovers. Bernie set some of the clocks back, but that was too much, too, so she stopped.

She liked having Sal there. It was good to have someone from her own tribe around, who knew the language and the customs. Still, she wanted to be alone to think. About Pete, about Tim and

Wendy Shaw. She was glad she didn't know much yet about the body parts in the woods or she'd have to think about that, too. She'd been tempted to call Guy Gagne and ask, but it was all too much now.

Mid-afternoon, the phone rang. Bernie looked at the caller ID. Not Pete, thank God. It was her friend Carol, inviting her to dinner.

"Can I bring a guest?"

"Pete?"

"Why would you say that?" Bernie asked, annoyed.

"People are talking."

"That's not possible. It's my brother," she said, ignoring Sal's waving arms and mouthing "no no no."

"Your brother is in town? I'd love to meet him. Is this one of the lawyers? Skinny Pat or Tommy?"

"Little Pat. Pat Jr., actually. No. It's Sal. The youngest. You know, the professor."

"Great. He and Vince will have a lot to talk about. See you at six."

"Why did you tell her I was here?" Sal asked when Bernie hung up.

"Why are you so uptight? It's my friend Carol. She's great, and so is her husband. She feeds me and helps me out at the paper sometimes. They don't know any of the sibs. Your secret's safe with them."

. . . . .

Bernie handed Carol a bottle of wine from her dwindling collection. She'd told Sal as she pulled it out of the cupboard that if he was going to stick around, he was going to have to start contributing to the wine budget.

Carol gave her a hug, then hugged Sal. She opened the wine and poured everyone a glass.

Vince emerged from somewhere in the back of their rambling farmhouse and joined them at the scarred wooden kitchen table.

"Bernadette," he said with a big grin and shook his head after introductions were made. "Bernadette."

"You have something to tell us," Carol added.

Bernie heard Sal take in a breath.

"What?" Bernie asked, feigning ignorance.

"You and Pete."

"Nothing to tell."

"Come on," Carol said. "I know you spent the night together. It's about time. Let's hear all about it."

Carol and Vince, and even Sal, were looking at her with open interest.

"Where did you even hear that?"

"Walt Pecoe," Vince said. "He saw you two kissing under a streetlight. Then you walked down the street to Pete's holding hands." Vince beamed like a proud father.

"Walt? What was he doing out at that time of night? I didn't see anyone."

"He was doing inventory at his store. Stepped out to take a look at the Milky Way."

"Shit," Bernie said. She hadn't seen him, but then she hadn't been looking down Main Street. She'd been looking at Pete. "You know what I was wondering? You know Wendy Shaw, right?"

"Yeah," Carol said.

"Do you think she'd talk to me?"

"About?"

"Domestic violence. Being a victim." Bernie tried to look matter of fact.

"No," Carol said. "She's got to live in the house with that man."

"I don't know why women do that," Vince said.

"Oh my god," Bernie said.

Carol cut off her rant buildup. "Explain what you'd envisioned as far as writing a story, especially one involving exposing Wendy."

Bernie felt her face burn, maybe a little from the wine, but also from having to explain something she could tell others thought was ridiculous. It happened often enough she wondered why she wasn't more used to it. "I was hoping to get her to talk off the record, warm up to me. Then start talking on the record. I was actually hoping—I know this seems dumb—that by talking to me she'd smarten up and get her and her kids out of there. Once she was out safe, I'd do the article."

"They're never safe," Carol said.

"I agree with Carol," Sal said. "You know better, Bern."

Bernie didn't want to argue about it, she just wanted to do it. She knew she could make it work. "I'd be sure no one was in danger."

"You'd never be sure," Sal said. "You saw enough of Dad's cases. He was defending the husbands and boyfriends, but still said none of those women had a chance."

"Your dad defended murderers?" Vince asked, interested, not judgy.

Bernie opened her mouth to answer, but Sal beat her to it. "Couple times," he said. "A few. Only a couple were domestic violence murder, though. The others were the usual stuff—bar fight, drug deal gone bad—you know, Augusta stuff."

"He took a lot of heat," Bernie said. "But he was defending their constitutional rights, no matter how bad they were. They had the right to a defense."

Sal was nodding, jumped in. "Everyone gets worked up about certain parts of the Constitution, but the one that makes sure everyone gets a fair shake in the justice system is one of the most important parts of all."

"That and the First Amendment," Bernie said.

"I'm not sure everyone gets a fair shake," Vince said.

"No, they don't," Sal said. "People like my dad and our brothers and sister try to make it happen as well as they can."

"Tim Shaw is an interesting guy," said Vince.

"In what way, aside from the wife-beating?" Bernie asked.

"He was a big shot athlete in high school, got a football scholarship to Maine, hurt his knee, and now look at him, years later. I'm on the transfer station committee, so I get to see him up close and personal. He's a despot over there."

"Where?" Sal asked.

"Tim's the manager at the transfer station. You know, the dump," Bernie said. She hadn't told anyone about Saturday night's incident at the Shaw's house. It was still too fresh and she only wanted to talk to Pete about it. "How does that make him interesting? He must be in his mid-thirties. You'd think he'd be over the end of his big-shot sports career by now."

"Some people never get over it," Vince said. "I think it haunts him, the life he has now. Take yesterday for instance. He was in a rare mood. Snapping at everyone. No one can do anything right. Yelling at the guys. I thought he was going to haul off and sock Brian Plourde."

"Wendy was a sports star, too," Carol said. "Basketball scholarship to Maine. But she married Tim when he left college, came back here. You don't see her yelling at people and beating them up."

"Men are different," Vince said. "Dreams die harder."

"That is so much bullshit," Bernie said. "How—"

"Can't we talk about something fun?" Carol asked.

"This isn't fun?" Bernie asked.

"Vince, you and Sal are both college professors. Discuss," Carol said.

"Not fun either," Bernie said.

Sal said, "Not a professor anymore. Speaking of dreams dying hard."

"Why not?" Vince asked.

"Didn't work out."

"How did you become a professor instead of a doctor or lawyer like everyone else?" asked Carol. "Well, almost everyone." She smiled at Bernie.

"I went to med school for a couple years, but it didn't interest me," Sal said. "I'm also an artist, a sculptor, but you can't make a living at it. I needed a paying job. Art history interests me too. Teaching. Since I was the youngest, everyone left me alone, and I developed a lot of interests on my own. I'm a doctor. I have a

Ph.D."

"So what are you going to do now?" Vince asked.

"Don't know," he said. "I'll figure something out. I'd be happy to find something just to pay the bills so I don't burn through my severance and can get out of my sister's hair." He winked at Bernie, but it seemed more forced than cute.

"Staying in the area?" Vince asked.

"For now."

"Do you want to work at the transfer station?" Vince asked.

"Wow, harsh," Bernie said.

"I'm serious. We're really short-handed. Pays ten dollars an hour and it's thirty-two hours a week. Could help tide you over."

"Vince, I don't think—" Bernie started.

"I think I'd like that," Sal said. "Even under Danny the despot or whoever. I'd like a job where it's cut and dried, and I don't have to think. It'll help pay for groceries. And wine." He gave Bernie a gotcha look.

"Seriously, Sal?" Bernie asked.

"What do I have to do?" he asked Vince.

"I'll expedite it. We're open six to two tomorrow, so show up at five-thirty and I'll get Don Littlefield there with the paperwork. He's the public works director and your new boss. Tim is your direct boss, but Don's the big guy in charge."

"Excellent," Sal said, lifting a glass. He and Vince clinked.

"Whatever," said Bernie, annoyed, though she wasn't sure why. "I thought you were just saying what a jerk Tim is."

"Sal doesn't seem like the type Tim likes to push around."

"Okay, now that's taken care of, tell us about Friday night," Carol said.

The wine had done its work and Bernie was ready to talk. "Okay, but if you say anything to Pete about me talking about it, I'm never, ever telling either of you anything ever again."

"Our lips are sealed," Carol said, leaning forward. Vince topped off the wine glasses. Sal gave her a silent salute with his, then chugged it empty.

.....

After they got home, Bernie, a little tipsy, did something she knew was a bad idea even as she was doing it. When she got in her bedroom and closed the door, she called Pete.

He answered on the first ring.

"I wanted to talk about last night, the Shaws," she said.

"Okay."

"Are you guys charging him?"

"Is this for a story?"

"I just need to talk it out."

"No, we're not."

"I can't believe how Tim and Wendy lied to you guys."

"Happens all the time."

"I can tell you for a fact, his gun didn't go off by accident scaring the cat, and she wasn't running out of the house looking for Fluffy. That's ridiculous. I bet they don't even have a cat."

"I know, but there's not much we can do."

"What about the kid saying 'she threw it in the garbage'? What about Tim asking Wendy where 'it' was, and then her pretending he didn't say anything? Something was going on."

"Bernie." His voice had a warning in it.

"What?"

"I can hear those wheels turning all the way over here."

"I'm thinking of doing a domestic violence story. I was already thinking it, but after last night I can see an angle."

"What angle?"

"I'm thinking Wendy will talk to me."

"No. Absolutely not. You shouldn't have even talked to them before we got there last night."

"I told you, I couldn't help it. They spotted me. What was I supposed to do? Anyway, they acted like nothing was going on. She even went into the house and put her shoes and coat on and came back out with the baby, for chrissake." Bernie could still picture the tow-headed boy, his face red and snot stuck to his nose, clinging to his mother's neck as she smiled and pretended everything was okay.

58

"You didn't have to talk to them."

When Wendy came back up the lawn, shoeless and coatless, Tim had asked "Where is it?" Wendy had smiled at Bernie and ignored him. It had been bizarre. Surreal.

"You get involved, you can get someone killed," Pete said.

"It's Wendy and Tim who are going to get her killed," Bernie said. The fact their story sounded rehearsed was one of the things that scared the shit out of her. Like they'd done it so many times before. Another thing was the look, for a second, of appeal, mixed with terror, in Wendy's eyes.

"Situations like that are very dangerous for everyone involved," Pete said. "You shouldn't be one of the people involved. Dawna gave her the domestic violence hotline number. It's the best we can do when we don't see anything happen. Everyone lies and no one wants to press charges. We're doing our best."

Bernie had a feeling if she could get Wendy alone, talk to her, eventually she could do a story. Domestic violence, tied to the poverty, drug use, and frustration in this part of Maine was an epidemic. Maybe Wendy and Tim didn't have those issues, but they had something. It was a way to take a deep dive, as her boss at her last job would say. Bernie was tired of the smattering of domestic violence stories that covered the pages of her paper, arrests or court hearings, never a big one that tied it all together about the people and the causes. She wanted to do something that got to the heart of it. She just wanted to do it, not have to explain it to Pete.

"Please? I know you mean well. But please." He said it softly, affectionately.

Her heart did a Dubya-style happy dance, despite the fact she didn't want it to, but she still wasn't going to agree.

"Anything else?" he asked.

"Body parts?"

"Tomorrow. Actually today. Good night, Bernie."

CHAPTER 7
2009
Redimere, Maine
Monday, November 9

P lagiarizer! Plagiarizer!" a shrill voice cut through the crisp fall
air.

Bernie looked up to see the dirty gnome that was Wayne
Daggett waddling down Main Street as fast as his bowed legs could
take him, shopping bag in one hand, a handful of newspaper
clippings wadded up in the other, waving wildly above his head.

"What fresh hell could this be?" she muttered. The words may
have been Dorothy Parker's, but she knew they were written for
Bernadette Clare O'Dea. The last eight or so months were evidence
of that. The past weekend was just par for the course. This morning
had already been long and it wasn't even seven yet.

She bent her head back down to the lock on the front door of
the *Peaks Weekly Watcher*, juggling the keys in one hand, a cup of
coffee in the other, as her bag, heavy with laptop and notebooks,
and all the other crap she lugged around all day, slid down her
shoulder.

In her haste to get the key in the lock, herself in the door, and
the door shut behind her, she dropped the bag and the coffee on
top of it.

"Plagiarizer!" Wayne yelled, his shrunken apple face red with,
well, not rage, more like righteous satisfaction, spit coming out from
between the few tobacco-stained teeth he had left. "Plagiarizer!" He

waved the clippings in her face.

How could he know about Sal? Why would he care? "It's plagiarist," Bernie said as she kicked the coffee cup off her bag before it could do serious damage.

It was the last thing she needed this morning, which had already started out annoyingly with Sal giving her crap about her call to Pete, like it was any of his business.

"Why are you talking to that guy at midnight, especially with a buzz on?" he'd asked her as she drove him to the transfer station at five-thirty.

"We're friends, we do that," she said. "If Pete doesn't want to talk to me, he doesn't have to pick up. I don't have to explain it to you."

"I'm just saying, as a guy, he's picking up because he likes you and you're taking him for granted."

"I'm not discussing my love life with you."

"Ha, you said love life."

Now this. She set her dripping bag down on the nearest desk and looked for the ever-elusive roll of paper towels.

Wayne put his bag down on the desk, too. He leaned over Bernie as she wiped up the mess from her canvas bag, then from the filthy wood floor, a century of dirt, ink, and other spills coming up black. He thrust both his hands in front of her face, one holding a clipping of an article she had written months before, the other from *The New York Times*.

"They're the exact same story. You copied! You're a plagiarizer!"

Bernie sat back on her heels, taking the clipping from him. "The Associated Press picked up my story. It's the same story because it's the same story. See the byline? They're both me." She gave the clipping back and booted up her computer.

"Ah!" Wayne chortled, and rifled through his shopping bag. "Aha!" He pulled out two more articles. Bernie saw they were from the press conference the state police held in August to announce the resolution of the Stanley Weston murder case. "Look, same quotes

61

as Waterville *Sentinel,* but there's a different name on the story." He grinned in triumph.

"Look," she said to Wayne, hands on hips, in what she hoped mimicked the no-nonsense posture that got results for her mother, "We were at the same press conference. If it proves anything, it proves neither of us misquotes people. You have to go, because I have work to do."

Dawna appeared in the open door. The police to the rescue.

"Everything all right, Bernie?"

"I think Wayne wanted to talk to you about some things," Bernie said.

Wayne blinked, confused.

"Okay, Mr. Daggett," Dawna said. She took his arm, her linebacker's bulk towering over him. "I need to talk to you, too, about going through everyone's dumpsters. They don't like it. Let's go to Choppy's and get a cup of coffee. I'm buying." She turned to Bernie as she led Wayne out the door. "The chief said he tried to call you but kept getting voice mail. Could you give him a call?"

"You're very nice to him," said Annette, who had come in with Dawna.

"He's okay," Bernie said. "He's not well, and he's harmless."

"He's also a big pain in the butt," Annette said as she settled behind the front counter, put her purse in her top drawer and turned on her computer.

"True," said Bernie. *There but for fortune go I.* She punched Pete's office number in on her desk phone. "Hey, guess what? My voice mail is full again."

"Maybe you should check it once in a while," Pete said without a trace of humor.

Okay it's going to be one of those days. "Sorry, usually it's stuff I don't want to hear."

"We're not having a press conference about the body parts after all. Just a news release state police is emailing later, but I can give you the particulars since Guy was involved and I assume you'll see him today."

"He's not here yet."

"We've asked him not to talk." Pete let that sink in. "You get that, right?"

Geez, he was a bear this morning. "Of course I do."

"Pretty simple. I'll read it to you. Same thing they're emailing later. Ready?"

She cradled the phone against her shoulder and held her hands over the keyboard. "Shoot."

"Ten oh seven a.m., Saturday, November 7, Franklin County Dispatch received a 911 call regarding body parts in the woods in Redimere, off Ridge Road, north. Caller was Guy Gagne, seventy, of Redimere. He reported finding intestines and other internal organs."

"Whoa, intestines?"

"Yes, and other internal organs. Preliminary findings suggest they are from an unidentified male human—"

"How do you know it's male?"

"I'm only reading the release, okay? Not answering questions. I'm doing you a favor. Unidentified male, age undetermined. Organs appeared fresh. They were taken to the state medical examiner's office for further investigation and testing. State Police Major Crimes Unit is investigating other evidence found at the scene please don't ask me what it is. Maine State Police, Redimere police, the Maine Warden Service, Franklin County Sheriff's Department, U.S. Border Patrol, and Redimere Fire and Emergency Department all assisted at the scene."

"I knew there were way too many agencies there to be a hunting accident."

"Got all that?"

"Yeah."

"I have to go."

"Wait."

"What?"

She wasn't sure what she wanted, but she didn't want him to hang up yet. In the greenish warped reflection of her computer, she could see her hair was coming out of its scrunchy, going all Medusa on her. She tried cramming it back in with one hand, the other pressed the phone to her ear. "Do you guys have any missing person reports that would fit in with this? Someone gets gutted a couple days ago, seems like someone would miss him."

"I'm not answering questions about the gut pile."

"That question was about missing person reports."

He sighed. Loudly. "I haven't heard of any. You can come over and see what Vicki can dig up, but if there were any in Redimere I would have heard. Your best bet is the county sheriff."

"Thanks." She felt a little better. That had to be at least three sentences.

"That it? I gotta go."

She typed up what she had for a story, hoping she'd have more in a day or two, before she had to send the paper to be printed. Hoping in a way there wasn't a lot more for a day or two so the daily papers didn't beat her before the *Watcher* hit the streets Thursday.

She was about to run over to the police station to check on missing person reports when Eli Perry came in.

"I have to take out an ad," he said. "My truck is out of commission, so I can't pick up this week."

"Shirley's out of the office, but I can take the info," Bernie said. "I thought you had email contacts for your customers, a website updated daily." She tried to remember what she'd written in the feature she'd done a few months before on Eli's private garbage hauling business. Nice feel-good piece. Man gives up lucrative log-hauling career to start a business when he becomes a single father. Well, almost feel-good since he used to be a member of the Outlaws motorcycle gang and people in town were either scared shitless of him, thought he was a drug dealer, or both.

"I did," he said. "But apparently the world wants to know. When I brought my own rubbish to the transfer station Saturday and the guys found out I wasn't picking up this week, they freaked."

"Freaked?" Bernie wondered if there was a story there but

couldn't figure out what it would be. The town didn't have garbage service. Most people went to the dump themselves, but a handful of private haulers charged to pick it up for people. She didn't understand why anyone but Eli's customers would care. "Why?"

"Got me. You know Brian Plourde? Flipped out. Shaw gave me a ration of shit, but he always does. I don't mind helping you out with an ad, though. If people want to know, who am I to question it?" He scowled, but she knew he was laughing down deep.

"Works for me. How's single fatherhood?"

"Scarier than being in the Outlaws. I wasn't that involved before her mom died. Now I'm tying pigtails and making pancakes." He correctly read the look on Bernie's face. "Not worth a feature story. Former biker gang member is tying pigtails after life on the edge? No thanks. I appreciate the other story, but that was business-related, and I want to keep my private life as private as I can."

Bernie laughed. "Was worth a thought. Guess I'm that transparent."

"I know I owe you. The feature on my hauling business got me customers. I appreciate being treated like a contributing member of society. You know what you ought to do? Find out what's going on over at the transfer station. Those guys need to get over themselves."

. . . . .

Pete walked down Main Street back to the police station, coffee in hand. Vicki's coffee was awful—how can you wreck coffee-maker coffee?—and he felt guilty going out to get a cup, so he always told her he needed to get some exercise and fresh air. He wasn't sure she believed him.

Dawna came out of Choppy's and joined him. "See you needed exercise." She nodded at the coffee cup.

"Am I that obvious?"

"I'm a trained detective," Dawna said, falling into step with him. "Had to do a little community relations with Wayne Daggett. He was harassing Bernie again."

"She didn't mention that," Pete said. "Not like her to not tell me every single thing that's in her head."

"Nothing serious. I'm just trying to keep an eye on him. He seems wackier since he got out of jail. I know his yard had to get cleaned up, but when he got home and none of his junk was there, I think it put him over."

"Thanks." If they had a stretch of time where their biggest worry was baby-sitting the town's more challenged residents, he'd be thrilled. He'd been hoping things were going that way, but after the weekend it was obvious they weren't yet.

They passed the Redimere Crisis Center and Pete glanced in the window, catching the eye of Bill Chapman, who smiled and waved. Pete raised his coffee cup. Chapman pointed to Pete, then his own right arm and gave a thumbs up. Pete smiled, flexed the muscle of his wounded arm, then thumbs-upped back. *Everything great, thanks.* His doctor in Farmington had given him a referral to see Chapman, but Pete didn't need medication for his head any more than he needed it for his physical pain.

"How's that feel?" Dawna nodded toward his arm.

"Fine." Pete was grateful she didn't probe, just nodded as though she understood. "Let's talk about the gut pile," he said as they walked through the outer office. He tried to avoid Vicki's accusing glare at his Dunkin' Donuts cup.

"As a hunter, what do you make of it?" he asked Dawna as they sat down. "I don't get any of this. Why do that with the organs?"

"I think whoever did it hunts, but it doesn't have anything to do with hunting, if you get what I mean." She recited again the process of field-dressing, the reasons for cutting off certain organs, the fact that only a few hunters went to that extreme.

Pete closed his eyes as he listened, feeling that familiar weariness bear down. Dawna stopped talking and he opened his eyes.

"I'm one of them," she said, looking at him steadily.

He almost laughed. If anyone was not a suspect, it was Dawna.

"Who else?"

She reeled off a couple names, then added, "Eli Perry—I only know because when we were kids we went hunting together." She looked guilty. Pete knew his dislike for Perry was no secret. "His daughter's mother was a cousin of mine. She died last year. Cancer."

"Eli Perry." Pete considered. He'd make a good suspect. Pete never bought that he'd gone legit in the not-very-lucrative garbage hauling business.

"This doesn't seem his style, assuming he were to kill someone."

Pete closed his eyes again. "Maybe someone was trying to send a message, so that would go beyond style."

"Maybe," Dawna said. "You still sure it's Benji Reeves?"

"Now that I've had two nights to sleep on it? Yeah. I was over at the transfer station this morning to see if anyone had seen or talked to him, and they played the usual games, but it could be any one of those guys. He pissed off a lot of people."

"You think it's someone at the transfer station?"

He could tell her question was pointed. Knew the question behind it. "Seems logical. That was the group Reeves hung out with. It doesn't have anything to do with how I feel about them."

She played with nonexistent lint on her knee. He knew she was leading up to something.

"When we were at the scene Saturday, you seemed, I don't want to insult you, but a little rattled?" She looked up, her black, wise eyes with a question, a bigger one than what she had just asked.

"Maybe. I was tired." He caught a blink of disappointment, that she knew he wasn't being honest, before she looked down again.

"George Libby always treats us like idiots," Dawna said. Back at the station Saturday, when Pete had told Libby about Reeves' visit to his apartment, seeing him a week before in a brown hoodie, Libby had been his usual condescending self. Dawna had tried to smooth it over, explain the tangled connection, Pete working in Philly, coming to Redimere on the case, then coming a year later to work here, Reeves and JP Donovan. Libby had held his head in mock confusion, then told them to write up a report. "I don't think he paid much attention to what we were saying."

"Don't let Libby bother you," Pete said. Pete had also told Libby what he'd uncovered over the years about Reeves' extensive criminal history, his aliases, fraud charges, con jobs. Libby's only comment was that it seemed like there were a lot of people who'd like him dead. Pete agreed, but Reeves was dead in Redimere, after trying to contact Pete. That meant something. He said as much to Dawna. "And on top of it, he was wearing a brown hoodie and when he wasn't couch surfing, he used to camp up in the cellar holes past the crime scene. I think it's him. It possibly has to do with the case in Philadelphia."

"That upsets you."

"It brings up things I'd rather forget, and also makes me worry that if someone could do that to him, there's something ugly going on. I'm worried about what we don't know."

She picked at her knee again, not looking at him. "The transfer station guys, they know better than to do anything like what happened a couple years ago."

"I'm not worried about them." His face was burning, the old shame and embarrassment coming back up. "I haven't had trouble with them since I came to work here and don't expect to."

"Things are different now. People have your back."

"Thanks." He wished she'd drop the subject.

"I don't want to upset you more, but what do you think, knowing what you do about what happened in 2007, would bring him back and make this happen?"

She must be taking lessons from Bernie. "I'm not sure. It could be nothing to do with that and I have to sort it out in my head first. Does that make sense?" He didn't want to have to explain his nightmares, the growing panic, his fear everything could all go to hell.

"It does." She didn't look convinced.

CHAPTER 8
2007
Redimere, Maine
Wednesday, June 27

Pete's first stop when he got to Redimere, even before he found a place to stay, was the police station. It was a maze of tiny dank rooms underneath an ancient town hall. Exposed wires and ducts, the smell of mildew, the chief's office the size of a closet, which he'd been ushered into by a blushing female officer who, when she saw his badge, hadn't asked him what his visit was about or if he had an appointment. Must be nice working in such a remote little town that a an out-of-town detective is treated like royalty. He wanted to laugh. If they only knew.

"You'll want to talk to Ray," the chief, Cal Littlefield, told him. "We didn't have that kid long. Not much to tell. You got a place to stay yet? That's a long drive."

"It was fine. Six hours."

"Since the season is starting up, with Fourth of July next week, you might have trouble finding somewhere to stay."

"I'll find something," Pete said. He hadn't expected the town to be so small, so far from everything. He'd had a vague idea of staying in a nearby city—Augusta, maybe—but after he'd left the interstate in Augusta and kept driving for what seemed like forever, past farm fields, through woods, over rivers, without hardly a hotel or motel to be seen, he'd started to wonder. Even Farmington, where there was a collection of dreary motels on Route 2, seemed too far away.

A cop poked his head in the door. Balding, glasses, irritated. "Cal?"

"Ray," Cal said with delight, as though he hadn't seen the guy in weeks. "Here's your man, Sergeant Ray Morin. Ray, this is Pete Novotny, a detective out of Philly. He's up here to ask some questions about the missing kid"—Cal used air quotes around missing kid—"you picked up a couple weeks ago."

"I already told them what I knew, which wasn't much," Ray said.

Pete was about to say, "Tell me anyway," in the nicest way he could, but Cal stepped in.

"Pete is looking into it in relation to another case, so anything you can do to help him out." He winked at Pete.

Pete hadn't told Cal he was on leave, had fudged why he was here, yet Cal seemed in on the game. Disappointing to think he'd become that transparent.

Ray frowned. "Come on into the break room, I gotta get a soda."

Pete and Cal followed.

"What's your poison?" Ray asked as they edged into an alcove jammed tight with a fridge, microwave and two folding chairs. Ray opened the fridge. "Pepsi. Orange Crush. Mountain Dew. Water."

"Water," Pete said.

Ray handed a bottle to him and pulled out a Pepsi. He didn't sit down, so neither did Pete.

"What do you want to know?"

"What happened. Your impressions. What you think of his story."

"Not much then, right?" Ray grinned tightly.

Cal broke in. "I'm sure you know a lot of folks up here think that kid was a transient who'd been around town for some time, right? They don't think he's the missing kid."

Pete nodded. "Yeah, but the family's saying it's their kid. So—"

"So none of that makes sense," Cal said.

"I'm confused as hell," Pete agreed, laughing.

Cal laughed, too. Ray didn't.

"All I know is he told me he was that missing kid, showed me the flier," Ray said, irritation showing. "He could be sixteen. It was hard to tell."

"No need to get worked up, Ray," Cal said. "Let's go back in my office, where we can be more comfortable."

They walked the few feet back into Cal's office, and he shut the door. Cal sat behind his desk, and Pete and Ray took the two other chairs. Pete watched Ray's Adam's apple bob as the cop chugged his soda. Pete was hot, tired from the drive, and wondered, not for the first time, why he was here himself. He didn't want to think about it too deeply, though, so he pushed it away.

Ray drained the soda and put the bottle on Cal's desk. He sighed, the weight of the world on his shoulders. "The guy could have told people here he was twenty-one when he wasn't. It's hard to say. He could be either age. That type, you know?"

"Shape shifter," Cal said. Another wink.

"Anyway," Ray said, ignoring Cal. "I called the missing persons hotline number that was on the flier and they got in touch with the family. I took him home with me for the night. The sister drove up the next day."

"Cheryl?" Pete asked.

"Yeah," Ray said. "Nice lady. JP was nervous as a cat all day, so nervous I expected him to take off, but he stayed in the house. It was still pouring out, anyway. He played video games with the kids. Cheryl got here and he went in the guest room. He didn't want to come out at first. I put it down to being nervous about being away all that time without calling home. Cheryl had to coax him through the door. Finally, he comes out, with that damn hoodie on, hood up—my wife had washed it for him—and Cheryl starts screeching like a banshee." Ray shook his head. "I thought something was wrong at first, but I guess they were screeches of happiness. She hugged him. Didn't even take a good look, and said, 'JP, you're home,' or some bullshit."

"Bullshit?" Pete asked.

71

Ray frowned deeper, defensive at first, but then thought about it. "Didn't feel right. She seemed determined to greet her brother, so that's what she was going to do. That's how it felt. The kid, he didn't hug her at first, then did, but it kind of felt like he wanted nothing to do with it."

Cal broke in. "Teenage boy. Been gone four years. Probably felt guilty. Lots of reasons to react like that."

Ray shrugged. "Maybe." His defensiveness was gone. He was now a cop talking to other cops about a case. "It felt funny, like I was watching a play."

"That's how I felt at the welcome home party," Pete said.

"Listen to you two," Cal said. "Why would she pretend some stranger was her long-lost brother?"

"Beats me," Ray and Pete said at the same time. Pete fought the urge to say "jinx," drank his water instead.

"When you picked him up, if he'd been around town, wouldn't you have recognized him?" he asked Ray.

Ray's defensiveness was back. "Not necessarily."

Cal broke in. "It's a small town, but we're a landing area. Ski bums, people on their way to Canada, people looking to hide. Lots of hidey-holes in the woods. We're a small police force and got our hands full as it is. If someone isn't causing a problem, we're not always aware they're there. People keep to themselves."

Pete didn't get it, but then he'd never lived anywhere like this. "The story in the paper, it seemed like a lot of people in town seemed to know him."

Ray flushed. "Look, I picked up a guy who told me he was sixteen and missing. He said he was passing through. I handed him off to his family, who were absolutely delighted to have him back. He didn't break any laws, so whatever he was doing and whoever he may have been was none of my fucking business." He stood up. "Do you need anything else from me?"

"No," Pete said, with a mild smile, the one that drove his wife—ex-wife— nuts. The one that said "Sorry I pissed you off, but that's your problem."

Ray jerked the door open—it stuck—and went down the hall. Pete heard another door, sounded like the one to the street, open and close.

"Ray gets a little irritated," Cal said. He gave Pete a long look. "I bet you're tired after that drive. Why don't you come on to my house? My wife would get a kick out of having someone besides me to cook for. You can stay with us. Guest room has a nice view of the lake. No need to pay for a room, if there's even one to be had."

The last thing Pete wanted was to be someone's guest, to have to make conversation and pretend he was okay. To lie awake at night rather than take the chance they'd hear his nightmares. "Thanks, but—"

Cal picked up the phone. "Fourth of July coming up next week, the Four Seasons Lodge and the B&Bs are full up, I'm sure. Cecile would have my hide if I made you find a room, anyway. Fellow officer from out of town." He gave Pete a big grin. "Honey? We got room for a guest? Couple days?" he raised his eyebrows at Pete and Pete nodded, caught up in the tidal wave. "Take those steaks out of the freezer and we'll be there in a tick."

Cal grinned at Pete. "We can talk some more about your case. I get tired talking to the same old people about the same old things."

Pete figured there were worse things than having time to pick the chief's brain. Anyway, maybe what he needed was some home cooking.

"Sure," he said. "Great."

. . . . .

Pete was prepared to regret taking Cal up on his offer but found he enjoyed the company. It had been a while since he'd spent time with people who didn't know his history, his embarrassing breakdown, who weren't concerned about him, watching every word and move for evidence of instability, another one coming.

Cal's house—a log cabin at the end of a dirt road overlooking a lake—was cozy and homey, Cecile friendly and attentive. After a dinner of steaks, potato salad and sautéed greens they called fiddleheads, Pete and Cal sat on the screened deck with drinks,

73

watching the stars come out and listening to the loons.

"I could get used to this," Pete said.

"A lot different from Philadelphia, I'm sure," Cal said.

"Oh yeah."

"You a city or country boy?"

"Mostly city. I grew up in Milwaukee. I've been in Philadelphia since college. Spent some summers on my uncle's farm in northern Wisconsin as a kid, though."

"I spent some time in Wisconsin," Cal said. "I played minor league ball after I got back from Vietnam. 1968, '69. The Appleton Timber Rattlers. Used to go to Milwaukee to tie one on."

"They were with the White Sox then, right? I played in college."

"Where'd you say you went to school?" Cal asked.

"I didn't. Penn."

"Oh, Ivy. Smart fella," Cal said, but in a friendly way. "I went to Maine for a year, before 'Nam. Baseball scholarship. Then I joined the Marines. Thing was, I was still a good ballplayer after I got out, but it wasn't fun anymore."

Pete had the same experience after his brother died. He'd quit the team. Started working two jobs, concentrating on getting done with school and getting out. He almost said it out loud.

"I was one of the lucky ones," Cal said. "Two tours and not a scratch. I lost something, though. Still not sure what. I didn't have that fire. You need fire to be good at ball, and it just didn't matter anymore. I miss it though. Ball. Whatever it was I lost, too."

Pete nodded and took a sip of the whiskey Cal kept pouring into his glass, felt it burn down his throat into his stomach. Thought of his brother Joey, driving that motorcycle straight into the brick wall. Karen, who'd light up whenever she saw him when they started dating in college. She stopped lighting up at some point. Dumpsters and bodies. Cal was easy to talk to. Hell, he did most of the talking. Pete liked listening. He wasn't about to wreck it by spilling his guts.

"Look at me getting all morose," Cal said, a booming laugh

echoing across the lake. "You don't want to hear that. What position did you play?"

"Pitcher. Backed up the shortstop on off days. I could hit okay, not for power. Lefty." He held up his left hand, the one holding the drink.

"I could have guessed. You have that pitcher look. I played outfield. Big slugger." He held up his glass. "Here's to old baseball days."

They clinked glasses.

Cal put down his glass and leaned back, hands folded on his stomach. "Now why don't you tell me what you're really doing here?"

.....

The next morning, Pete walked the mile or so into town to talk to the newspaper editor. The paper had run a story the week before that several town residents questioned the identity of JP Donovan. Pete knew enough reporters to know for every word printed there were a lot that stayed in notebooks.

He'd told Cal a little the night before—that he was poking around while he was on vacation because he didn't like the threads left hanging from the Donovan case. Cal accepted the explanation. It was the truth, anyway, Pete told himself, just not the whole truth.

"Editor's name is Bernie O'Dea," Cal had said over breakfast.

"What's he like?"

"He's a she," Cal said, winking. "Nice little ice cream cone. Smart, straightforward, likes to talk. She's only been here a few months but seems like she knows what she's doing."

Pete turned from the dirt road onto the main road into town, trying to clear his mind, enjoy the surroundings. He hadn't been for a walk in the country in—well, he couldn't remember. Maine was a surprise. He'd expected it to be like northern Wisconsin, but it wasn't. It felt thick and old, crowded with trees, a spectacular view of mountains to the west opening up in the gaps, the smell of the earth, the sound of birds in the trees and squirrels clicking away. The road was quiet, a car only every few minutes, drivers raising their hand in greeting. At first he thought they mistook him for someone else, but after two or three, he accepted that it was what people do here. The woods were dense, dotted with weather-worn houses, or more often mobile homes, with dirt patches for yards. Aside from the waving drivers, he didn't see a soul in the ten or so minutes it took him to walk into town.

Downtown was three or four blocks of clapboard two- and three-story buildings, a few brick ones thrown in. A rocky river rushed along one side, a hill with small frame houses, church steeples poking out, narrow roads winding up it; on the other, thick woods with the mountains in the background. A shambling ancient brick mill hunkered next to the river, bright signs over the doors and a half-full parking lot shouting out with hopeful optimism that it wasn't a mill anymore.

When he'd asked Cal how to find the newspaper office, Cal had said just walk until you get there. And there it was, a storefront with a wooden sign hanging over the street: Peaks Weekly Watcher.

At first he thought the dim room was empty, but then he saw a young woman, intern maybe, with flyaway hair in a sleeveless blouse, pedal pushers and sandals, squinting at him, her fingers frozen over her keyboard.

"Can I help you?" As she came to the counter he realized she was a woman about his age.

"I'm looking for the editor."

"That's me. Bernie O'Dea," she said.

He introduced himself. "I wonder if I could talk to you about JP Donovan."

She grimaced and rolled her eyes. He couldn't tell if it was amusement or annoyance. "I don't know how much I can tell you. What's this about?"

"Is there somewhere we can talk?"

She looked around the empty room, then back at him, the message obvious: there's no one here.

"I don't want anyone walking into the conversation."

"Follow me. So what's this about, anyway?" She turned to look

76

at him over her shoulder as she walked through the cluttered newsroom to a back door. They were at the top of a wooden staircase that went down to a mostly empty dirt parking lot, backed by the rushing river.

"My summer office," she said, walking down the stairs. There was a picnic table on a strip of grass and trees between the parking lot and river. "At least we'll see them coming."

They sat down and she cocked her head, an obvious punctuation to her unanswered question.

"There are questions about JP Donovan's identity, and your story implied it's unlikely it was him."

"Wasn't a very good story. It raised more questions than it answered."

"That's why I'm here."

"Are you investigating my story?" She seemed like she was laughing at him.

"Your story points me in the right direction."

"As it said, there are some guys in town who think he was twenty-one, his real name is Benji Reeves. He's not originally from here, but also not a missing kid from Philadelphia."

"You agree?"

"I do. Though I don't know why he'd pretend to be the missing kid. I tried calling the Donovans to interview them and him, but no one picked up or returned my calls."

"How does he live in town, and the police don't know who he is? Particularly if he was into the things implied in the story?"

"What did the police say?"

"I'd like to hear what you think."

"It's hard to explain what it's like here." To people from away, he heard, though she didn't say. He'd already heard it from Cal, sensed it was a mantra in town. "Lots of places to stay out of sight. Small, not very inspired police force. Just because someone's committing a crime doesn't mean they get caught or arrested. You know that."

"I do. It just seems so…"

"I know. Reeves was a slippery character. 'Chameleon' came up a lot. Even in a small town like this there are parallel universes. People like you and me who go to work and the store, say hi on Main Street. Then there're these other people doing stuff we can't imagine." She gave him the big smile again. "I can't. You probably can."

Pete watched the bright river rush and jump over rocks, beyond it the dark, dense woods. He tried to think of another way to approach it, because in her friendly way, she wasn't telling him much.

"I wonder if there were things that weren't in the story that would help." He returned her big smile to show how harmless he was.

She wasn't biting. "What is it again you want? Because normally I'd want a subpoena before I'd release my notes."

"This isn't Watergate or the Pentagon Papers. I'm just looking for information that can help the family of a missing kid."

She stood up, her sunny smile gone, her fists on her hips. "First of all, don't patronize me. Second of all, I don't care how little the story is, it's the principle of protecting information and the people who give it to me. If I didn't put information in a story, I had a reason. Third, I'm under the impression the family is okay with the guy, so I'm not sure how you're helping them."

Pete started to say something, but she wasn't done.

"Fourth," she said. "Who are you again? What exactly are you doing?"

Pete was ashamed he'd underestimated her. Why did he think a journalist in Redimere, Maine, would be any more of a pushover than the ones in Philadelphia? He wanted her on his side, too, as she stood there, her curly black hair coming out of its pony tail, looking like a teenager ready for the beach but so pissed off that he had no doubt she'd shut him down.

"Sit down. Please? I'll tell you what's going on. You can decide what to tell me."

"Damn right I'll decide." She sat down. Then she smiled, the sun breaking through the clouds. "That was fun."

"I'm a homicide detective," he said. "If that's not the real JP Donovan, he's still missing. Too many things lead me to believe it's not him. The family's reaction is troubling. We're still investigating JP's disappearance as a possible homicide." He felt bad about lying, but it was necessary. If she knew the disappearance wasn't being investigated as a homicide by anyone but him, that JP was considered just another runaway and his "return" meant case closed, she wouldn't tell him anything.

She pulled a notebook from her back pocket, disengaging a stubby golf pencil from the binding coil.

"This is off the record," Pete said. "I can't give you anything for a story."

"I understand," Bernie said, flipping to a blank page. "I'll respect your request to keep it off the record, but I have to take notes to remember the conversation accurately."

"I'm not so sure—"

"Look." Her voice was sharp again. "You're asking me to help you out. You have to let me do it my way."

"Okay," Pete said. The fact that she was taking it so seriously, combined with big brown eyes that seemed like they could see straight into him, didn't make him feel good about stretching the truth. He knew he didn't have a right to make the rules. "I'm looking for any details that would point to him being someone else, names and contact info, so I can talk to people who knew him."

"The story quoted Tim Shaw, the manager at the transfer station—that's the town dump—"

"Yep."

"Saying he worked there as a casual, someone who comes in and works when they need help, but isn't full-time or regular part-time. Shaw's known him for a couple years, said there's no way he's sixteen. The story also quoted Eli Perry, who'd let Benji—let's call him that to make it easier—crash on his couch. Eli's a rough customer, used to be in the Outlaws motorcycle gang, probably deals drugs, drives a logging truck. But no criminal record to speak of, a few misdemeanors. He said Benji claimed to be from the Boston area and told a lot of stories, but nothing like the one he told when he came out as JP. Eli said all his stories seemed like bullshit. Sorry, language."

"It's okay," Pete said. "I've heard that word before." He smiled big, hoping they would stay on track. "So what happened when you checked out the stories?"

Bernie looked as embarrassed and uncomfortable as Pete had felt a few minutes before. "If I'd had the time and resources, there were things I could have pursued. Should have. But I just had to whack together the story. That's why it wasn't very good."

"So what wasn't in it?"

She took a deep breath. He could tell she was struggling with giving him the information. He tried to look benign, not too expectant.

"Shaw and Perry both said Benji's a con man, rips people off. People were after him and that's why he got out of town. Neither would give details. You can't print that about someone without checking it out, getting their side. Like I said, I tried to talk to Benji, but it was nothing doing. Both said he's a manipulator, messes with people's heads and pretty cocky about it."

"Sounds like him."

"You've talked to him?" she asked, pencil poised.

He looked at the notebook, then at her laughing eyes.

"Off the record," she said. "Don't worry."

"I went to his welcome home party."

"When and where?"

He told her, watched her write it down.

"I could write about the party, right? That wouldn't have to be off the record."

"I'd just as soon my whole visit to Maine is off the record."

Her head was bent to her notebook, but he could see her lips purse. "What were your impressions?" she asked him.

"He's not JP. When he was reported missing the posters and his family emphasized a cross he always wore, but when he was

80

found and the FBI asked what happened to it, he didn't know what they were talking about. When they reminded him, he said he lost it. His family said he never took it off, so you'd think he'd remember."

She was writing furiously, nodding in rhythm to the pencil.

"The missing posters said his eyes were hazel, but Benji's are as dark as yours."

The tips of her ears turned pink as she continued to write.

"The family never said, all those years I kept in touch, that the eye color on the posters was wrong. Then all of a sudden they did."

She looked up. "In touch how many years?"

"My partner and I found a body in a dumpster a few days after JP Donovan was reported missing in 2003. We thought it was him. Turned out it was some other kid."

"And?"

Pete laughed and shook his head. "I'm trying to figure out how the tables got turned here."

She smiled. "And?"

"I felt at the time there was something odd about the family and the disappearance, so I kept tabs on them, hoping something would come to light."

"And?"

"Nothing did."

"Until now." She was smiling wider.

"Can we get back to my stuff?" he asked.

"In a minute," she said.

"This is totally, totally off the record," he said. "I'm up here on my own time—"

"On your own time? So it's not an official investigation?"

He could kick himself. "I'm on vacation."

"It sounds like a good story."

"Back to my stuff?"

"Perry said I should check Benji's other names but wouldn't elaborate." She made air quotes around other names. "I checked police records here, Franklin County court records, the paper's archives, Google, even. Couldn't come up with anything under

81

Reeves whether it be Benjamin, Ben, BJ or any variation. Checked Donovan, too. Didn't have time to check other county court records in the state. I did a pretty sorry-ass job with that story."

"It's tough when no one gives you enough information to go on."

"It is. The people at the transfer station were skittish, probably because Shaw told them not to talk to me. I talked to some guys on the transfer station committee, kind of a longshot, but maybe they knew of Benji. They wouldn't talk about personnel. Speaking of Shaw, Benji's only friend was Shaw's wife, Wendy. She works at the deli counter at the Country Grocer. She wouldn't talk either."

"Can I have contact information for these people?"

Bernie's big brown eyes were steady on his, disconcerting him. "You can't tell them you got it from me. Tell them you got it from the cops, whatever, not from me."

"Okay," he said.

"I have their cell numbers. I don't normally do this." She found the numbers in her notebook, copied them onto a blank page. "Hunt them up in person and call them only if you have to. That would help me out."

He took the paper from her—a number for Shaw, a number and address for Perry. Next to Wendy Shaw she'd written "Country Grocer." The names of some of the transfer station committee members.

"Shaw and Perry know more than they're saying. You can find Wendy across the street at the store. I don't have a cell number for her. The transfer station committee and town officials wouldn't talk to me because it was about personnel, but since you're a cop it's different."

"Thanks. I truly appreciate it." He held out this hand. Hers was soft, warm and strong, accompanied by another big laughing smile.

As she walked with him across the dirt parking lot, she said, "I want you to promise me—" She stopped and opened the notebook, wrote on a page and tore it off. "Here's my name and cellphone number. If this ever can go on the record, give me a call? The years of trying to figure out what happened to JP Donovan, the real one, sounds like a good story."

"Sure." He folded the paper and put it in his wallet. Something in him would like to call her anyway, but he pushed it back.

"It's up to you, but I'd like an exclusive," she said as they started walking again. "I wouldn't normally give out that contact info. So, ya know, quid pro quo."

"Gotcha."

"I don't pull out the Latin for just anyone," she said, turning to go up the stairs to the office back door.

"An arrest or body will be the sine qua non for that to happen."

She grinned, another delighted happy smile that knocked Pete back a little. "Fortes fortuna iuvat."

He laughed, "You got me. I don't really know Latin, just phrases from law school."

"Fortune favors the brave. Go get 'em and I'll be waiting for that call."

As he walked down Main Street, he realized he was still smiling.

CHAPTER 9
2009
Redimere, Maine
Monday, November 9

Bernie's long Monday just kept getting longer. Mondays were always busy. Not as bad as Tuesday and Wednesday, when the paper was put together and sent to be printed, but long enough. Too long for her to be happy about taking the time out for her annoying monthly doctor visit. Her prescription wasn't refillable, so every month she went through the indignity of his indifferent inquisition that would get her the magic pill that helped her act "normal" for eight to twelve hours a day.

Bernie kind of liked Dr. Chapman, but part of it was for the superficial reason that with his height and the way his elbows and knees were all over the place, his lank blond hair and his glasses, he looked like the actor Ed Begley Jr. She called him, in her head of course, Dr. Ehrlich, Begley's character on "St. Elsewhere," which she'd watched obsessively in the eighties. Sometimes she pretended he actually was Dr. Ehrlich, and then his phony jolliness and pretending to be interested when he wasn't didn't bother her as much.

At least he pretended, unlike the doctor who'd diagnosed her several years before. When she first went (at the urging of her regular doctor), she said she was sure she didn't have ADHD, and if she did, it was a mild case. Almost imperceptible. After putting her through his hoops, he said with pomposity she found comical, "I treat thirty to forty cases of ADHD a week. I am the leading New England expert on ADHD. You have the most extreme case I've seen in years."

She figured he was just saying that to make sure she knew who the boss was and sell her the drugs. She was sure he got kickbacks from the drug company to push them on people. He'd also made a point of telling her that while he was a psychiatrist, "I'm not here to listen to your problems. Get a counselor for that." She'd get one sentence out, maybe one and a half, before he'd hold his hand up like a traffic cop. "Enough!"

Chapman let her ramble. She knew he wasn't listening. He'd talk a lot himself sometimes, but it was two separate conversations, each on its own track to nowhere.

He was the same as the other guy in one respect—they were pushers, plain and simple. She went to get her fix, and as far as they were concerned, she was just another pathetic junkie.

Chapman also chomped gum nonstop. She couldn't think of him without the sound of his mastication crashing in her head, drowning out her thoughts, especially on a day like today, when she was jumpy and tired. You'd think a psychiatrist would know how insane that could drive someone already on the edge.

"How we feeling today?" he asked. "We good?"

"A little stressed out." She wanted to say "*we're* a little stressed out but otherwise *we* are *well*." She knew it'd be jerky and he probably wouldn't even notice, so she didn't.

"What's going on?" he said as he looked at his computer screen, she hoped at her record and not fantasy football or something. Chomp chomp went the gum. He always asked, despite the fact he wasn't there to hear her problems. He told her it was a diagnostic tool so he could decide her medication and dosage. She had trouble figuring out the distinction. Sometimes she answered, "Nothing," or "the usual." He never pressed or asked for details.

Today she needed to talk, even if he wasn't paying attention. She tried to ignore the gum, the noise pulling at her thoughts, hammering at her concentration. "Work is really hectic. I still can't find a reporter, except maybe this jerk I worked with at my last paper, who I know would do an okay job, but I'd end up regretting it. I'm desperate, so maybe I'll hire him even though I know I'll hate myself. There's this girl from UMO who emailed me and seems like she wants to, but I'm not encouraged, because she just seems to have no energy. My brother showed up out of the blue and he lost his job for plagiarizing—can you believe it?—and there's something weird going on with him. Where's his car? I don't know. He won't answer when I ask. I'm worried about money. Both mine and the paper's. What happens if it goes under? Newspapers all over America are shutting down. I'd lose my house. I already have trouble making ends meet. I don't even open my bills, just let them pile up. That's not normal, right? I can't sleep, so I go for long walks at night. It comforts me, but that's weird, too, right? I like looking at people's lit windows. Is that weird? I'm not sure. It's comforting, but I don't know why. I'm not a peeping Tom. I don't look in, just at. I, um, kind of, had relations with a guy I really like but don't think I should be having relations with. I feel this darkness sometimes. Right in my soul. A rising anxiety. Like things are out of control. It's this spiral and I'm just going to go flying off the planet out into space. That can't be good, right?"

"Safe sex, k?" Chomp chomp. He didn't look up from the computer screen.

The chomp chomp chomp drilled into her brain. "I'm still pretty stressed from all that stuff over the summer."

"As you should be." Chomp. "How're the meds working?"

"Okay, I guess," she said, trying to focus on that rather than the booming chomp of the gum. "Depending on how much sleep I get, what I have to eat, how stressed I am. Sometimes they last a long time, sometimes it feels like I haven't even taken it. I haven't been sleeping well at all. You know, that's why I'm walking at night. I feel jumpy and irritable —"

"Mmm hmmm." Chomp chomp. He wrote the prescription. "I'm going to give you a stronger dose. Just for a week. See if it makes a difference. Come back in a week and we'll see if you need something else. Anxiety meds. Sleep meds. You want those now? I can do that, too."

Bernie didn't want more meds. She wanted to feel better. To sleep. There had to be a way to do it without medication, but she knew better than to say it out loud. Last time she suggested behavior modification, he stopped her in mid-sentence and said, "You know I'm not a therapist, right? I diagnose and prescribe." Right.

"Did you pee in the cup?" Chomp?

Instead of answering directly—how could he not know? The nurse always had her do it first thing when she came in—she asked, "Am I going to have to do that every time? Why don't I get to bring my bag in with me? Like I'm going to smuggle in pee from someone else who's taking methylphenidate? Seems like too much work." She was trying to force him to engage. Bad habit she had. Some would say attention-getting, but she didn't think it was attention-getting to want her doctor to pay attention during a visit that was costing her health insurance company a lot of money and a not-too-cheap co-pay on her part.

He stopped chomping. One time she had called him Dr. Ehrlich to see if he got the joke. The look he gave her was so withering, she never tried it again. Now he gave her that look again. "I know you're an honest girl, but those pills go for a lot of money on the street. Maine's got a big illegal prescription drug problem. We're required to make sure you're actually taking it."

"I wouldn't sell it on the street. First of all, I need it. Second of all, I'm not a drug dealer."

"You'd be surprised who's a drug dealer." No chomping, she noticed.

"I can't imagine anyone wanting to take it who doesn't have to," she said. "I know it makes me less stressed, but it also slows me down. I don't get high, just less irritable. I also forget words and can't answer people's questions. I'm under water. I'll be doing something and I'm under water. Then I resurface and feel like I've missed a dozen things."

87

Chomp. Chomp. "That's what's called focusing. You're just not used to it." He grinned. At the computer screen, not her. "People grind it up. Snort it. It's a stimulant. Gets them high, no question. I wouldn't recommend trying that though." He looked up and winked. Almost seemed delighted by that fact. Chomp chomp. He went back to the screen. "As for you leaving your purse in the exam room—"

"It's a courier bag. It has my life in it. Lots of stuff to leave lying around."

"As for you leaving your purse, it's regulation. People do smuggle urine in. I met your brother today."

"Really?" Bernie tried to adjust to the change of subject while fighting off her irritation at the gum, the conversation, the fact he said purse after she said courier bag.

"Working at the transfer station?" Chapman said. Chomp chomp. Type type.

"Really?"

"I'm chairman of the committee. Was in the office this morning when he filled out his paper work. Overqualified. Still, he seems to be a relaxed guy. No drama. You could take a lesson."

Friggin' Sal, she thought as she walked to the pharmacy to get the prescription filled. Why did it piss her off? Didn't matter, everything did these days. It was great having Sal around, but there was something going on. Something more than him being at loose ends and upset over losing his job. Why couldn't everything be simple? Including Pete? Every time she started thinking about Pete, she decided to put it on a back shelf in her head for another time, a time when she didn't have so many other things to think about. But it was there, always hovering, along with the feel and smell of his hot skin and his strong, warm hands…

She opened the door to Redimere Drug and walked down the narrow aisle filled with medication, cosmetics, candy, to the prescription counter in the back. What she really needed was supper. She hadn't eaten in hours. She eyed the overpriced bags of candy hanging from racks above the candy bars. Shook it off.

Leftover beef stew would do fine. Unless Sal had made something else. At least she was eating better since he'd moved in.

Someone was at the counter talking to Herb Varney, the pharmacist. Annoying. She was jittery to get home, to eat. As she neared, she saw it was Tim Shaw. Her instinct was to turn around and leave, but she had to get the prescription filled or she wouldn't have her pill the next day on a busy, busy Tuesday.

"Those back problems never go away," Herb was saying. "You can have surgery and it'll still bother you the rest of your life. Knee problems, too."

"Don't I know it," Tim said, shaking the pill bottle Varney gave him. Bernie pretended she was engrossed in the cold medicines. She could feel his glare as he turned around, feel it like a cold hand grabbing her neck, but she didn't look up.

"Help you, dear?"

Herb gave her a nice smile, his eyes wide and watery behind thick glasses as she handed him her script, and she felt the cold grip seep away.

"Let's see if we have this," he said. That's what he always said. They always did. You'd think the only pharmacist in town would know she'd be in for it every month and would stock it special. The ways of pharmaceuticals were a mystery to her. "I see Dr. Chapman upped your dosage."

"Yeah." She wondered if this conversation was okay or if he was crossing some ethical boundary.

"Just one week? That's good, see if you can handle the higher dose."

"Uh huh." She was embarrassed enough about taking the meds without discussing it with Herb Varney. She wondered if he went home and gossiped to his wife about who was taking what drug for what embarrassing condition or disorder. He looked like the type who would, with his big watery eyes and little bird nose and non-existent chin. Though maybe hunger was just making her impatient and judgy.

When he gave her the bottle she shoved it in her coat pocket, shrugging off his offer to answer any questions.

She stopped at the Country Grocer to get more wine. Wendy Shaw was behind the deli counter. Bernie decided she needed some deli meat, too.

"Hi," Bernie said. "You're working later than usual."

"Walt's been doing inventory, so he needs me for longer hours." She shot Bernie that "boy, you're nosy" look Bernie was so used to. Still, people answered. Their choice. Bernie knew a normal person would also say to Wendy, "I just saw your husband. Said hi. We had a nice conversation about the Patriots," or something. But the last time she saw Wendy, her husband was chasing her out of the house with a gun, so it didn't seem right.

"What can I get for you?" Wendy asked. Bernie guessed they were going to pretend nothing happened the other night, just like they had on the lawn waiting for the police.

"How are you?" Bernie asked.

"I'm fine. We're closing in a few minutes."

"Half a pound of that white American cheese that's on sale. Really thin. Seriously, how are you?"

Wendy sliced a piece and held it up for Bernie's inspection. "Like this?"

"That's great," Bernie said. "Do you want to talk sometime about what happened the other night?"

Wendy watched the cheese slicer with a focus Bernie envied.

"Wendy."

"Nothing to talk about." Her voice was a whisper.

Bernie whispered, too. "Off the record." She wanted to ask what it was about, why Tim would chase her out of the house, what he'd asked her for, maybe try to explain to Wendy what she hoped to accomplish with the article. Not exploit her or reveal her pain to the world, but make a difference by bringing the issue out into the open. She heard the owner, Walt, say to someone, "I'll go ask Wendy."

"Anything else?" Wendy asked in a normal tone, her face back to bland and helpful.

"Roast beef, same cut."

"Hey, Bernie," Walt said. "What's new?"

"Nothing," Bernie said, watching Wendy take the slab of beef out of the glass case and put it on the meat cutter.

"I'm really happy for you and Pete," he said.

"Did Pete say something?"

Walt smiled and Bernie swore she saw a blush under his ebony skin. "No, you know Pete. Doesn't kiss and tell. I saw you guys the other night."

"We're not an item."

He laughed. "Sure you're not. I can keep a secret. So can Wendy."

"I can," Wendy said, looking at Bernie with an emphasis that left no doubt about the message. She held up a slice of roast beef. "This okay?"

Bernie nodded.

"Are you getting anything else?" Walt asked Bernie as Wendy sliced, then wrapped the beef. "I need Wendy to help someone with a question about ordering an organic turkey."

Wendy took off her apron without looking at Bernie.

"I guess I'm all set," Bernie said. She tried to catch Wendy's eye, but Wendy walked up the narrow aisle without looking at her, her hiking boots rapping a firm goodbye on the wooden floor.

Walt lingered. "If you and Pete aren't together, I'll lose my faith in humanity."

Bernie half-listened, her thoughts on Wendy. The former high school and college basketball star, almost six feet tall, always seemed strong and in charge. Yet she was sometimes beaten and terrorized by her husband. Wendy didn't seem surprised Bernie knew, that Bernie didn't believe the charade from the other night, that cold five or so minutes the three of them stood there the other night as Tim awkwardly joked about his gun accidentally going off and Wendy jiggled the whimpering toddler on her hip, not looking Bernie in the eye.

"Right," she said to Walt, not remembering what she was

responding to. "We'll see what we can do." She walked back down the aisle, brushing by Wendy, who studiously ignored her.

Wendy was good at hiding it, but Bernie had felt her terror Saturday night, felt it like a hand reaching out to grip hers. She could feel it again tonight, not as powerful, but as clearly as she'd felt Tim's cold glare in the pharmacy. She knew it wasn't going to go away, but would keep simmering in her head, drawing her to Wendy's story.

.....

Bernie walked into the house to the smell of sauce simmering on the stove, making her feel more warm and cozy than she'd felt in ages.

"I got some deli stuff," she said, throwing the packets in the refrigerator. "Apparently free, at least for now, since I forgot to pay for it. Smells good in here." She picked a bottle of wine up from the counter. Expensive. Not one of hers. "Can you afford this?"

"I'm an employed man. We're celebrating."

"How'd that go at the transfer station? How the hell have you already met my doctor?" She made sure to say it so he'd see how annoyed it made her.

"The gateway of garbage. The receiver of rubbish. The Shangri-la of shit."

"So how'd it go?"

"Good, aside from losing my cellphone. Very elemental. Recycling, garbage hopper. Branches go here. Bulky plastics go there."

"You lost your cellphone? Where? Where's your car?"

"If I knew where, it wouldn't be lost. Anyway, I can live without one for a while."

"You were never great about calling."

"You know my motto: Let my admirers come to me."

Bernie rolled her eyes. "You met Dr. Chapman?"

"Bill? He was in the office when I did my paperwork. One thing led to another once he found out we're both doctors. So to speak. You know who else stopped in? Your cop boyfriend."

"At the transfer station?"

"When I was in the office. He was asking those guys, Bill and my new boss, the despotic Tim Shaw, who didn't really seem that bad, and my bigger boss, Don Littlefield, if they'd seen some guy recently. Got everyone all worked up."

"Who was Pete asking about? I don't want you and my doctor to be friends." That anger that was always right below the surface lately surged up.

Sal dipped a piece of bread in the sauce and handed it to her. "Don't be such a fussy-pants."

He knew she loved bread with sauce on it. She took a bite, despite herself. The thick, hot sauce tasted just like their mom's.

"Those guys don't like your friend Pete very much," he said.

"How do you know that?"

"Because they were bitching about him after he left. Sounds like there's a history. I talked to Bill for a while, turns out he's yet another guy come here from away to escape the hustle and bustle for the way life should be, you know, the Maine motto. He said he'd keep an ear out for anything I'm more qualified for. I told him I'm happy for now, but he seems as bothered by a Ph.D. working at the dump as you did."

She grunted with annoyed indifference through her sauced bread, then opened the refrigerator again. "He's been here forever. Long before I got here. From California to Maine. I asked him once what brought him here and he said 'an airplane.'"

"So you guys have the same sense of humor. The lure of Maine is what brought him here."

"Probably running from something." She gave Sal a significant look, hoping he'd get the hint.

"You know, Maine's motto, the way life—"

"I know what the motto is!" she said.

"I'm going hunting with some of the guys Saturday."

"I'll warn the deer. And the people. So, your car?"

"I'm a good hunter. You should give it a try. It'll calm you down."

She slammed the refrigerator door shut. "Why does everyone feel the need to tell me to calm down? I've told you a million times, I have no interest in shooting and killing something. None. Zero. Zilch. Nada. Do you really think me with a gun is a good idea?"

Sal shrugged. "Who's everyone? Anyway, we'll eat venison stew all winter. I've never seen you turn that down."

Bernie got another piece of bread and dipped it in the sauce, giving him the stinkeye as she chewed.

He seemed unaffected. "You know what else is cool about the dump? You can spy on everyone's life. What they had to eat, who the drinkers are. People put piles of mail in the recycling. Prescription bottles—I can see why you didn't want to bring yours—boxes that held stuff no one should know about."

"I bet."

"The guys are pretty cool. They think I'm funny as hell."

"No doubt." Bernie poured some wine.

"I even made a friend."

"Won't Bill be jealous?"

"Brian Plourde. You know him?"

"Wicked goofball. Kind of a pain."

"That's the guy. A little excitable. He's funny as hell too."

"Not on purpose."

"He's harmless. He's also my driver. His truck smells worse than your car does."

"Maybe you should be buying a car instead of wine," she said. "Where *is* your car anyway?"

He looked uncomfortable. "I'd been, for a week or so, staying at Leslie Lark's in Vassalboro before I came here. It's there. I need to get it. And my gun and some other stuff. Any way you can give me a ride to Vassalboro Wednesday? It's Veterans Day and the dump is closed. It's my only day off before Saturday."

"Are you kidding? Leslie Lumpkin?"

He turned red. "We'd kept in touch. You know, first love and all that."

"Aside from the fact that I can't get my head around that, I have a paper to put out. I don't have time to go to the bathroom between now and Thursday much less drive you to Vassalboro. I don't take holidays off. What's that, two hours or more? Why did you leave your car there? What the hell were you doing at Leslie Lumpkin's? Maybe your new friend Brian can drive you in his smelly truck."

"Lark. She made it legal. She was using it when I left and I wanted to get out without a lot of hassle. Left a note that I'd be back for it. Brian can't, I already asked."

"Using what? Her name?"

"My car. I wasn't sure where to go when I got canned, so I went there. Then I came here." He rushed the words out. "I'll find a ride. I want to get it as soon as I can."

"Maybe you can get good old Leslie to drive it up here. Since she's been using it anyway, she owes you."

Sal turned to the sauce and started stirring with a lot more vigor than it needed. "Her coming up isn't going to work."

"What's the problem?"

He didn't answer.

"Really, what's the problem?"

"I don't have time for her bullshit."

He gave Bernie his biggest most charming smile, but she wasn't biting. She glared at him, fuming.

"She has a lot of my stuff. I want to get it. End of story."

Bernie stomped off to her bedroom to change. "Find a way that doesn't involve me."

CHAPTER 10
2009
Redimere, Maine
Thursday, November 12

Bernie watched Sal snore on the couch Thursday morning as she filled the coffee maker, wondering if she should wake him up. She knew he had to be at work by ten. *Hell, I'm not his mother. He can get himself up.*

He'd managed to get himself to Vassalboro the day before, night actually, she'd been told by Jody Mercier, who picked up the *Watcher* in Waterville at the printer. Jody had dropped Sal off near the Carter Bridge in Waterville, where Sal had said he'd hitch the rest of the way. She'd heard him come in about two hours before. A second duffle bag was on the floor next to the one he'd arrived with the week before, a gun case next to it.

In the week since Sal had arrived, he'd vaguely talked about finding his own place. She wished he would. Him always being there, on the couch, clicking through the channels, was getting annoying. But she also wanted to keep him close. Something with him wasn't right. He was pretending he was okay when he wasn't, and it worried her. On top of it, he still hadn't told the family he'd lost his job or that he was in Maine. The more he put it off, the worse it was going to be for both of them. After all, she was the one harboring him.

He was dead to the world, her three cats, Billy, Becky and Poopoo, curled up on or next to him. Dubya alternated between lying on the floor gazing adoringly up at him and seeing if she was doing anything food-related in the kitchen. Sal's snores and the cats' loud purrs made a rhythmic chorus as they slept, undisturbed by the kitchen light and the gurgles from the coffee maker.

A knock on the door changed that. The cats shot down the hall to her bedroom. Sal sat up, startled. "Who's that?"

"I'll see," Bernie said, not sure if she was more annoyed by Sal looking at her accusingly or at whoever the hell was knocking at six-thirty in the morning. She looked out the window. Pete and a state trooper, both in uniform.

"What the hell?" Bernie said.

Sal wrapped a blanket around his waist and followed the cats down the hall as she opened the door.

"Bernadette O'Dea?" the trooper asked.

"Yes," Bernie said, looking at Pete. He was as expressionless as the trooper.

"I'm Sergeant Joe Frazer. You have a brother, Salvatore O'Dea?"

"You better come in," Bernie said. "Sal!"

Nothing.

"Sal, get out here." No nonsense.

He came down the hall. She was relieved to see he'd changed out of his underwear into sweatpants and T-shirt.

"You guys want some coffee?" Bernie asked, hoping to put off whatever was coming.

"We just have a few questions," Frazer said.

Sal jutted his chin at Pete. "What's he doing here?"

"Chief Novotny gave me the courtesy of coming along. He said he knew you."

"He doesn't know me," Sal spat.

"I know your sister," Pete said quietly.

"Right. In the biblical sense."

"Sal!" Bernie said, her face hot.

"I thought I could lend some support," Pete said.

"I don't need any support," Sal said.

97

"What's going on?" Bernie asked. Everyone ignored her.

"Do you know a Leslie Lark?" Frazer asked.

"Maybe."

They'd been taught at their lawyer father's knee that whether you were guilty or innocent, you don't have to answer police questions. More prosecutions were built on the stupid blurtings of people who didn't know their rights than on forensic evidence, despite what TV had people believe. "Jails are full of people who couldn't shut up," their dad always said.

But this was Pete. "Jesus, Sal. Answer the question," Bernie said.

"When did you last see her?"

Sal tore his glare from Bernie and looked back at Frazer. "Last week? Thursday maybe? Friday?"

"Are you asking me or telling me?" asked Frazer, sounding like Bernie and Sal's mom.

"Friday? Thursday, actually. A week ago," Sal said. "Why? What's she saying?"

"What time Thursday?" Frazer asked.

"I don't know. Midnight. Why?"

Bernie wanted to ask, "You didn't see her when you got your car?"

Pete's eyes hadn't left Sal. Watching him, Bernie thought. Studying him. It pissed her off. This was her brother, whatever the issue was, not some potential criminal to be studied.

"She's missing," Frazer said.

It was brief, but Bernie saw relief pass over Sal's face. That didn't make Bernie feel any better. Pete saw it too, she could tell. She was trying not to look it, but nervous apprehension was changing to dread, crawling up her spine, buzzing her brain.

"Missing?" Sal asked, more puzzled than worried.

"She'd missed important appointments. Turns out no one's seen her since Monday."

Sal shrugged. "Can't help you."

"I'm told you lived together."

"Sal?" Bernie asked. She wanted to say "Visited. For a week." Frazer sounded so sure.

Sal ran his hand through his black curls, something Bernie guessed made women's hearts melt but had no effect on the trooper. "Yeah. We were. Since, um…" he looked at Bernie and stopped.

"Tell the truth, Sal. It can only help you," Pete said, matter-of-fact, almost friendly. Bernie knew better. Pete was focused on every gesture, every nuance of Sal's face, body language, voice.

Sal shot him a dirty look. "I am. I showed up there in April. I needed a place to crash. We used to go out, and we're still friends."

"April?" Bernie said. The dread that had been creeping through her fuzzy morning brain took full grip.

"It was a relationship?" Frazer asked.

"No. Well, yes. Not really. Hell we were in the same house. Me man, she woman. You know how it is." He looked at Pete, gave a little leer, but without the bravado of before.

No reaction.

"So, sure, we shared a bed. Then she started thinking it was more than what it was, so I left. Came here."

"You came here when?" Frazer asked, his eyes going from Bernie to Sal.

Pete's were on Bernie. The same look he had while watching Sal. Two can play at that game, Bernie thought, trying to look only mildly curious, casual. But her heart was pounding so hard she felt like Pete could see it.

"Friday night. Saturday morning, actually. Got here around one-thirty in the morning and sat on the steps. My sister showed up a few hours later." He winked at Pete. "I have no idea where she could have been."

"Again, you last saw Ms. Lark when?"

"Thursday night. We had a, well, not a fight, a difference of opinion on where the relationship was going. I slept on the couch. She left before I got up. She'd been using my car because her pickup was in the shop, and she took it that morning. I hung out, did some of the farm chores just to show there were no hard feelings. Left her a note. Ya know, goodbye. Hit the road. Hitched. Walked some. Stopped in that coffee place in Waterville. Figured out what I was going to do. Then I hitched here."

"She left for where?" Frazer asked.

"Beats me. She had a lot of stuff do to, errands. She runs a farm. She's always doing something. We didn't report to each other."

"Okay, that's it for now," said Frazer.

"That's it?" Sal asked, obvious in his relief. Bernie was surprised, too. There had to be more.

"Don't go anywhere," Frazer said. "I'll talk to you again soon."

Bernie held open the door as he and Pete went out. Then Frazer pulled a Columbo.

"Mr. O'Dea, one more question."

Sal didn't look at him, didn't respond.

"Why didn't you wait for her to get back with your car? Seems like a lot of work, hitching, walking all the way here, when you had a car."

Sal shrugged. "Wanted to slip out without having to talk."

"Do you know where your car is now?"

"I thought it was one question. I assume she still has it."

"It's not at her farm."

Sal looked guilty. Bernie hoped she didn't look as confused as she felt. Isn't the car out front?

Sal said, "Neither is she, right? Like I said, Leslie had it. It was gone when I got up Friday. I figured I'd go back and get it when she cooled down."

Frazer nodded as though it made sense. Pete looked away. Bernie knew he heard Sal's obvious lie, even though he couldn't know Sal had gone to Vassalboro to get his car the day before. Could he? She hoped her panic didn't show. She felt Pete's eyes on her and tried to look calm.

The two cops walked out the door toward the state cruiser. The only other car in the driveway was Bernie's.

"I'll call you," Pete said to Bernie as he opened the cruiser door. She didn't answer. She couldn't imagine what they would say to each other.

. . . . .

Trooper Joe Frazer dropped Pete off at the police station. It was early, but Pete didn't feel like going to Choppy's or anywhere else he'd have to have small-talk conversations. Frazer had called him last night, told him about Leslie Lark missing and that they needed to talk to a Salvatore O'Dea, who was thought to be in Redimere. He wondered if Pete would like to assist. A courtesy call but also a fishing call—did Pete know Salvatore O'Dea? Well, no he didn't, Pete told Frazer.

"I know his sister," Pete said, biting back his irritation at Bernie, that with all the information that poured out of her, he somehow didn't know anything about her brother who'd recently arrived in town. A brother who'd caught the interest of the state police. Frazer had filled him in that morning over Dunkin' Donuts coffee as the two sat in the cruiser in the still-dark morning.

No one had seen Leslie around since Monday, and they were worried. It wasn't like her to miss appointments, not be in touch. A neighbor late Wednesday night had checked on her and found the door ajar, very unlike her. Her purse and cellphone weren't around, so that was a good sign, but she hadn't shown up Wednesday morning to pick up some goats she'd been firm about buying and had also missed a veterinarian visit for one of her horses Tuesday late afternoon, which everyone who knew her said was totally out of character. No one had been able to reach her on her cellphone. The neighbors had been tending to her animals, something she would have arranged if she was going somewhere. While it wasn't an unusually long amount of time for an adult to be missing, the Vassalboro police chief was also her cousin. He wondered if maybe that ne'er-do-well who'd been sponging off her for months had something to do with it. The chief had found a smear of blood on the kitchen floor, smudged like someone had tried to wipe it up quickly, in an otherwise immaculate kitchen. That was enough,

Frazer told Pete, to make a call on the ne'er-do-well, one Salvatore O'Dea, who Leslie had told her cousin the police chief several times she wished would go up to Redimere to stay with his sister and get out of her hair.

Frazer acknowledged to Pete it may not be enough to set off alarms, but it sure was enough to take a look.

"What do you know about Salvatore O'Dea?" Frazer had asked as they waited for six-thirty, which they'd determined was reasonable enough not to be too early, but early enough to catch O'Dea at home. Main Street was quiet in the dark, the occasional pickup truck or SUV loaded with hunters drove by, slowing at the sight of the cruiser.

"Not much," Pete said. "I know he started work at the transfer station, because I was there when he arrived. I know his sister pretty well. Editor of the newspaper. Owner."

He and Frazer both sipped their coffee, watching a loud group of hunters come out of Dunkin's and pile into a luxury SUV with Massachusetts plates.

"She's a good person," Pete said.

"I'm sure she is," Frazer had said, starting up the cruiser. "Let's go find out what kind of person her brother is."

.....

Now Pete sat in his office, staring out the window. Nice view of mostly woods, with a shining corner of the river visible. The trees that weren't pine had been a riot of red, orange, and yellow, even some purple, through October and even early into November. It seemed like the leaves had died overnight a few weeks ago. Then they were gone. Dead and shriveled on the ground, brown, ugly. The thought matched his mood.

He blamed Reeves and his damn eviscerated guts. The DNA from the guts would be tested, but they'd need DNA from Benji Reeves to make the connection. Even with his criminal record, Reeves didn't commit the type of crimes DNA samples were taken for. They'd need the rest of his body to determine if it was really Reeves.

Pete had gone to the transfer station Monday to see if anyone had seen him and got the usual crap, Brian Plourde skittering by him nervously, Tim Shaw smirking. It'd put him more on edge than he already was.

Now this thing with Bernie's brother. He didn't have a good feeling about Sal. What's a guy with a Ph.D. doing working at the dump? Pete had a law degree and he was a cop, but that wasn't really the same thing. Sal was definitely hiding something. Bernie seemed antsy herself. She wasn't good at duplicity. He hoped her brother had the sense to come clean. He really hoped Leslie Lark would turn up, but had a bad feeling she wouldn't. Alive at least.

No, the police certainly weren't done with Sal O'Dea. They were just starting. It wasn't Sal Pete was worried about, though; it was Bernie. Among all the bad feelings he had about this, the biggest one was that she was in for a world of hurt, and he wasn't going to be able to protect her.

. . . . .

The cruiser wasn't out of the driveway before Bernie was back in the house, slamming the door behind her.

"What the *hell?*"

"It was those pot guys," Sal said.

"Why didn't you tell them you went out there yesterday? Where the hell is your car? You've been in Maine since April?" There were so many things. So many. Bernie's anger and disbelief multiplied with each question, the rage that was always crouching, waiting, roaring up.

Sal looked stunned. "The car wasn't there yesterday. Leslie wasn't there. Telling them didn't feel right."

"Didn't feel right?" Her head was going to explode. Blow up and paint the walls and ceiling with blood and bone and tissue. She knew she was screaming at him, but she couldn't control it. "I don't even know which thing—oh my god. You've been up here since April? *April?*"

"Whoa, Nelly," Sal held up his hands. "Whoa."

"When the hell did you get fired?"

"April."

"Jesus, Sal."

"I didn't know what to tell people. I was trying to figure it out. Help Leslie on the farm."

She was already late for work. She had a newspaper to put out. "Dammit, Sal—"

"Calm down. It's not a big deal. Don't worry. Everything's okay," he said, hands still out, trying to ward off her anger.

"Everything's okay? I got woken up by two cops at my door wanting to know why my brother's secret girlfriend is missing."

"You were already up," he said with a hopeful grin, trying a joke.

"You're lying to them. Lying! You don't think they're going to find out—and soon!—that you went there to get your car yesterday? What pot guys?" Her brain had finally registered that he'd said that.

"She had this idea to grow pot for the medical marijuana clinics. She got involved with these guys. Way over her head. I didn't want them to know I was back at her place yesterday. Tell the cops I was there? I might as well broadcast it. Anyway, she'll show up." He didn't sound like he believed that last part.

"You have to tell them the truth; then you're off the hook," she said, wondering if she believed it herself.

"Like the cops would believe me."

She'd had it. "You're right. Why would they?"

. . . . .

Bernie couldn't concentrate once she got to work. Thursdays, the day the paper came out, were payroll and administrative day, not things she enjoyed doing. She still needed to find a reporter so she could cut her weeks back to, oh, maybe seventy hours or so. She'd heard back from a University of Maine student, Carrie, who'd sent her an email in response to feelers she'd put out looking for a reporter. But now, with the Sal development, she intended today to start pressing her friends and contacts in New England for an experienced reporter, needed ASAP. Sal was in serious trouble. It wasn't all fine. It wouldn't blow over. She was going to need help because her brother was the story and she couldn't cover it. One thing about the fall of 2009, there were a lot of out of unemployed journalists. She'd find someone.

Mid-morning, Pete showed up, just like she knew he would.

"Your office?" he said. Annette and Shirley exchanged glances. Bernie pretended she didn't notice. She didn't want to talk to Pete until she talked more to Sal, but she didn't see how she could avoid it. They crammed into the little room and Pete closed the door behind him. Bernie perched on the edge of the desk and he leaned back against the door. They were inches apart and she could smell his comforting soap smell, feel the warmth coming off his body. It didn't reassure her.

He got right to the point. "What's going on with your brother?"

"What do you mean?"

"Don't play games."

"I'm not playing games. I mean, do you mean what's he doing here? Or the thing with Leslie Lark? Because he had a situation with his job. Okay, he was fired, so I was trying to figure out if you were asking me —"

"The woman. Leslie Lark."

"Are you interrogating me?" Bernie knew she was stalling because she'd have to lie and she didn't want to. She was a shitty liar. He'd know. Maybe knew right now she was about to lie. Not maybe, probably She didn't like lying to Pete. It felt like shit. But Sal was her brother, and she felt stubborn and defensive, way more stubborn and defensive than bad about lying. She knew he hadn't done anything wrong no matter how many secrets he was keeping.

"I'm trying to help," Pete said.

"You seem like you're mad."

Pete bumped his head back against the door, looked up at the ceiling, and sighed. A huge exaggerated sigh. Bernie knew it—he was mad.

"It's not like you to not be honest with me," he said.

It isn't? "I don't know any more than you do. Sal showed up

105

and it turned out he got fired. That's all I know. That and what we both heard this morning. I thought he had been at Leslie's for a week, not since April." Bernie was pissed at Sal but more pissed at Pete. He didn't seem like he wanted to help. He seemed like he wanted to go after Sal.

She felt pinned down. She knew he could see it, read the lies and the guilt.

She reached behind him for the doorknob. He took a second to move. They were almost touching, her chin even with his shoulder. She felt like if she put her head on his shoulder, he would wrap those steel cable arms around her and squeeze all the fear out of her. Because she knew now she was scared shitless about her brother. Pete moved aside, and she opened the door, and the moment was gone almost as fast as it came, except for the scared part.

Annette, Shirley, Guy, and a customer at the counter acted overly busy. It was obvious they'd heard at least some of the conversation. Bernie didn't have an indoor voice. She tried to think how loud she'd been but couldn't; her focus had been on how she felt, how Pete felt. That probably meant loud. "I'll let you know if I find anything out," she said to Pete's retreating back as the door to the street closed behind him.

Bernie sat down at her computer. She'd wanted to ask him if there was anything new about the body parts. Gut pile. It had all gotten lost in the last painful five minutes. Too late now. She hoped by Monday Leslie Lark would be back home and the gut pile would be her biggest story. *Thank god those guts belong to a man.*

CHAPTER 11
2009
Redimere, Maine
Thursday, November 12

The door opened and Wayne Daggett waddled in. Bernie groaned, inwardly, of course. She'd wanted an interruption as she'd listlessly poked at her computer, trying to get the payroll done in the aftermath of that painful five minutes with Pete, but not this one.

"I need to talk to the editor," he said, walking by Annette's counter to Bernie's desk. Annette grimaced and shrugged.

He carried a paper grocery bag, as usual arriving with props. "Everyone's talking about the drugs," he announced to Bernie.

She always felt with Wayne like she was entering the conversation somewhere in the middle. "Everyone's *always* talking about drugs," she said. It was the root of most crime in this area of Maine. Theft, robbery, assault, domestic violence, you name it— addiction and drugs seemed to always be at the bottom.

Wayne showed his usual impatience with Bernie's inability to translate the words that came out of the tangled jungle of thoughts in his head. "The guts and the drugs." He clutched the grocery bag close to his chest, his wild eyes, whiskers, and wispy hair dancing as he trembled with excitement. His shirt and workpants looked like the same ones he'd had on last time Bernie had talked to him, right down to the food stains. But who was she to talk? She was probably wearing the same thing, too, with the same stains. Could he really know anything about the gut pile? She considered it as he quivered in front of her.

"What are you talking about?"

He put the grocery bag on her desk and opened it, close to his body so she couldn't look inside. She heard plastic clink, but he pulled out a newspaper, yellowed. She could tell by the font and design it was *The New York Times*. "This is the key," he said, looking around to make sure Annette and Shirley weren't listening. Bernie was sure they weren't.

"Let me take it and read it when I have the time." She reached out, but her heart had sunk. More Wayne and his nutty crap. The newspaper was obviously decades old.

"No. You read it right here then give it back."

"Wayne, I don't have time today."

He put the newspaper back in the bag, carefully sorting it with whatever junk was in there. "I'm just trying to help," he said. "But now I don't want to." He looked at her with deep regret, and she felt bad for a split second. He was just another lost soul looking for someone to understand him.

"Sorry, Wayne. Maybe when I have more time."

He shook his head and waddled out of the office.

"You should ban him," Annette said. "He was going through the dumpster again."

"It's all right," Bernie said, turning back to the payroll, wishing the tinge of guilt would go away. "He means well."

.....

Pete stayed in his office working, not wanting to run into Bernie, or anyone really. She'd called him briefly late morning with an out-of-left-field question about whether the gut pile had anything to do with drugs.

His reply, he knew, had been unnecessarily terse—he wasn't commenting, it was the state police's case. He'd wanted to say "it's a gut pile, how the hell do I know?" He'd also wanted to say, "Everything has to do with drugs." He figured better to be terse than impatient. He didn't have time to go down the rabbit hole of her thought process today. Still, he knew if she had a question she

108

had a reason. He couldn't always follow how her mind was working, but he knew it usually went places that made sense to her and got results. *One of the reasons I like her so much.* He amended that. Love her. Then did some more amending. *Don't think about it until the thing with her brother goes away.*

"That Ms. O'Dea can be really annoying," Vicki said, coming into Pete's office.

"What now?" he asked.

"She's asking for all sorts of reports again. She wants to know if she can come in tomorrow and go through all our drug arrests."

"They're public record."

"I just think she's a pest. That's a lot of work for me."

"She's doing her job," Pete said. "It's our obligation to help her. Dawna sorted arrests by category in the computer program, so it shouldn't be too hard to give her a printout."

"She's loud and always interrupts, or finishes my sentences before I can."

"It's because her brain is moving so fast. Speed of light." He gave Vicki a big smile.

Vicki rolled her eyes and turned to leave.

"Vicki, just to be clear," Pete said. "Anything she asks for, give it to her. You don't need to check with me. If she's asking for something, she has good reason. I trust her." He knew he was going overboard, but if he couldn't stick up for Bernie with her brother, maybe he could make up for it in this small way.

"Oookaaayy," Vicki said.

When he stepped out of the office to get a coffee, the sun was already going down. He still hadn't gotten used to the way the day faded so fast into night, the sudden, early darkness, the lack of twilight this time of year. A lumpy shape against a nearby utility pole made him jump, until he realized that it was one of the scarecrows. He'd have to talk to Don Littlefield about getting them off the streets. They'd given him the creeps to begin with and had become part of his nightmares, along with the chewed up pieces of Benji Reeves' organs. They were no closer to identifying them now, five days after Guy had come across them, but he knew without a doubt it was Reeves. He would have been back in touch. The sweatshirt cord was the same color as the hoodie he'd seen him in on Ridge Road. He wish he knew what the hell it meant. He wondered what Bernie's question about drugs meant, wondered if he should have quizzed her about it, gone down the rabbit hole instead of shutting her down.

As he turned the corner on School Street, the sound of kids laughing and a frantic voice yelling, "Give it back" broke the late afternoon silence.

Boys on bicycles, three of them, were playing keep-away with a knapsack, papers and books falling out and scattering on the playground pavement. A girl, younger, maybe ten or eleven, was jumping at it, her chubby face scrunched in frustration. "Give it back," she repeated.

"Fatalie. Hey, Fatalie, come get it," one of the boys said as he threw it to another.

"Pork-o-hontus," another one said, punctuating it with an Indian war whoop.

"What's going on?" Pete asked. The activity stopped, the knapsack dangling from one boy's hand. "Is that yours?" Pete asked the girl, who was angrily wiping away tears with the sleeve of a too-small jacket. She nodded, her braids bobbing, looking at the ground.

"Give it to her," Pete said to the boy, even and matter-of-fact, glad to have something this simple to distract him from the gut pile, the problem of Benji Reeves, Bernie and her brother.

The boy held the torn and gaping backpack at arm's length, letting go a second before the girl could snatch it. She knelt down and began picking up books and papers.

"Help her," Pete said, hearing in his voice how tenuous his control was, the last of his patience disappearing.

"I don't want them to touch my stuff," the girl said.

"She doesn't want us to touch her stuff," one boy said. "Guess we should go."

"You need to apologize," Pete said.

The lead kid rolled his eyes. Pete stared him down.

"Sorry," the kid mumbled.

Pete looked at the other two. "Sorry," they said, sounding anything but.

"What's your name?" Pete asked the girl.

"Natalie," she mumbled into the front of her coat, not looking up from the scattered papers.

"Sorry, Natalie," Pete prompted the boys.

"Sorry Natalie," they said, sing-song.

"Do you guys have any idea how stupid you look picking on someone half your size?"

"Hardly half," one said, rolling his eyes at the other two, who snickered.

Natalie flinched. His heart broke for her, a determined little barrel of a kid. His voice low and steady, but venomous, he said, "That's right, because it's a small person who picks on someone smaller. You ought to be ashamed. Go home. If I ever catch any of you pulling a stunt like this again, we'll talk about it at the station with your parents."

The boys took off, the ringleader popping a wheelie as they rounded the corner.

"Are you okay?" Pete asked, squatting down and gathering papers, trying to wipe the grit from the playground off and smooth out the wrinkles around the penciled scrawl and smeared eraser marks. He picked up a construction paper cat, its ears bent and dirty, cotton-ball nose half torn off. He tried to stick the nose back, but the glue was dry, the cotton dirty with sand.

She nodded, not looking at him, wiping her nose again with her sleeve. She reached for the cat and he handed it to her.

"What's your last name?"

"Perry."

"I'm Officer Pete. The police chief."

"I know who you are," she said as she smoothed out the cat, then tried to make it and the crumpled papers and books fit into the torn bag. Pete handed her more and she jammed them in with the

111

others.

"Where do you live?" he asked, though he already knew.

"Timberwoods."

"I was just going that way. Mind if I walk with you?"

She looked at him for the first time. Behind the tears, coal-black eyes burned. "I didn't need any help."

"I know," Pete said. "I thought I'd help anyway."

They began walking.

"I don't need you to walk me home," she said after a minute of silence.

"I'm going in that direction anyway."

She didn't answer.

"Are you related to Eli Perry?"

"He's my dad."

He could see it in her shape. A tiny version of his six-foot-five, three hundred pounds of muscle. But his long, braided hair was red, flecked with gray, his pale skin covered in freckles, the parts that didn't have tattoos. She was dark, Native American. "How old are you?"

"Ten."

"Do those boys bother you a lot?"

"I told you, I don't need any help," she said, angry, picking up her pace.

"I know you don't," Pete said. He looked at her out of the corner of his eye, marching beside him, the torn knapsack clutched to her chest with the wad of papers and sand-smeared books sticking out, the face of the damaged cat staring up at him. "Everyone can use it once in a while, though, right?"

She wiped her running nose on her shoulder.

"You live with your dad?" He knew it but wanted to keep the conversation going.

"My mom's dead." She said it like he should know, the biggest reality in her ten-year-old world.

"I'm sorry," he said, mentally kicking himself. "Has your dad been hunting yet?" An awkward question, but he knew Eli Perry hated Benji Reeves. The man topped Pete's list of possible suspects.

Natalie didn't bite, rolled her eyes. They walked down the dirt road of the trailer park and Natalie turned into the dooryard of an unadorned single-wide. Unlike some of the other trailers, there was no patch of grass or garden, no lawn ornaments. Construction-paper pumpkins and ghosts, what looked like it was supposed to be a witch on a broom, danced across the windows.

The tin door flew open.

"Hi, Nat."

"Hi, Dad. You didn't get your truck back yet?" she asked. Seeing them next to each other, despite the difference in coloring, the resemblance was striking. The same wide brow, furrowed, the same dimpled chin now that Perry no longer had a beard. He'd also cut off his braid, his hair looked barbered, short and respectable.

Perry gave his daughter a hug, glaring over the top of her head at Pete. "Nope. Don't worry though, we won't starve to death." He gave her a quick kiss on top of the head, not taking his eyes off Pete. "In fact, I thought we could get pizza. How was school?"

"Whatever," Natalie said, pushing past him.

"Hi, Eli," Pete said.

"What's going on? My kid okay?" He wasn't friendly. Pete didn't expect him to be.

"We were going in the same direction, so I walked her home," Pete said. "Some kids were giving her a hard time."

"It wasn't anything," Natalie said quickly from inside.

"Those ones from before?" Eli asked her.

"Just some kids." Her voice was more muffled, as though she'd moved farther into the trailer.

Perry leaned into the doorframe, his huge tattooed arms holding onto either side, his bulk filling it. Every single inch of him, from his scowl, to his bulging T-shirt, to his biker boots said just give me a reason to pound you into the dirt. As much as he filled the doorframe, Pete could still see the deer head on the wall behind him.

They regarded each other for several cold quiet seconds.

113

"Okay, officer. We done?" Perry finally said.

"Have you talked to Benji Reeves lately?"

Perry didn't say anything.

"He's back in town, and I'm wondering if you talked to him."

Perry, his eyes locked with Pete's, gave away nothing. "Get off my steps."

"Did you hunt off Ridge Road last weekend?"

"None of your business where I hunt or when."

"Now that you pick up rubbish, you probably see a lot of what's going on. Maybe you've just seen him around town lately?"

"Can't help you."

"If you've seen him around, know anything about Reeves, or about anything happening in the woods off Ridge Road this weekend, that'd help me out," Pete said.

"Can't help you officer."

"Where's your garbage truck?"

"None of your fucking business."

"Right," Pete said. "Take care, Natalie," he called into the house. He was surprised to hear a small "okay" from inside. "Take care," Pete said, turning to walk back down the road. He could feel Perry's eyes on his back until he turned the corner out of the trailer park.

.....

Bernie took one last look in the mirror. Her hair, out of its pony tail, wouldn't part the way she wanted it to and sprang up in an annoying way, Medusa-like, but it would have to do. Her dad called the tangle her Irish ringlets. She called it a mess and cursed once again that she'd gotten only the worst from the Italian-Irish DNA mix, including the round Italian shape and the "gift" of Irish gab. She was saved, maybe, by skin that tanned nicely, unlike the lobster burns some of her siblings endured. It was little comfort given the rest of the package. She had put on dress pants, a nicer than usual blouse and her for-special-occasions-only cardigan. Not exactly dressed for the Ritz, but good enough for Bobby Dolan.

Sal needed a lawyer, and Bobby was the first guy who came to mind. She didn't want to use one of Redimere's two attorneys, because things were too gossipy as it was. She sure as hell didn't want to call her lawyer sister or two lawyer brothers, though once Bobby knew, they would, too.

She didn't want to go to dinner with him, either. He'd seemed too eager when she called, but she didn't see any other way. Anyway, when was the last time she was out on a Friday night? She couldn't remember. It'd be a nice meal, if nothing else.

Despite the fact it wasn't a date—she'd have to make that clear—it'd be interesting to see Bobby. He'd been her older brother Pat's best friend in high school. They played football, basketball, and baseball together. Bobby was the ultimate sidekick—cheerful, friendly, easy-going to Pat's type-A best-at-everything, win-at-all-costs personality. Pat was president of the class, valedictorian, all-state and went to Harvard. Bobby cheerfully rode the bench, got good not great grades, was voted class friendliest, and went to Boston College, the college of his father, uncles, and older brothers.

Bernie had a huge crush on him in high school, and even went out for a couple beers when she was a freshman at Boston University and he was a junior a mile up the road at BC. Possibly classified as dates, they'd even involved a trip or two to second base. By then, though, she had a huge crush on another guy who wouldn't give her the time of day, and Bobby wasn't that interesting any more.

She met him at a restaurant in Farmington, a good halfway point between Redimere and Augusta. Bobby looked about the same as the last time she'd seen him, about thirty years before at Pat's graduation party. Heavier, but the same thick blond hair, rosy cheeks, and cheerful smile.

"You haven't changed," he said, giving her a too-tight hug. She knew she had—he didn't need to be squeezing her so tight to know she wasn't the skinny bundle of nerves she'd been at eighteen.

Bernie got down to business with what she knew about Leslie Lark and Sal's possible involvement. As she wrapped up, she told him how worried she was. "Sal doesn't have anything to do with this, but it looks bad, her gone as well as his car, and no one's heard from her, a smear of blood on the floor."

"Non-starter," he said, tucking into his steak. "Inconsequential," he added when Bernie didn't say anything.

"How can that be? People have been convicted on less."

"Convicted of what? A crime hasn't been committed as far as we know. Leslie's missing, no one knows where she is. That's it."

"Her purse, her cellphone aren't there."

Bob shrugged, concentrating on his steak. "That's good, it means they're with her. She's an airhead. Leslie Lumpkin. God help us."

"Smear of blood on the floor."

"Could be anything."

"Then there's Sal getting fired. That doesn't look good," Bernie said.

He laughed. "It's a big leap from plagiarist to murderer."

"They'll use anything to make a person look bad."

Bobby beamed as though they were talking about the Red Sox. The winning ones. "I'll see what I can find out. But if they had anything, he wouldn't be back at your place lounging on your couch, would he? He'd be in jail down the street here. No evidence, no case. You know that."

"I guess."

"Let's talk about you," Bob said. "Last I saw you, you were skipping down Commonwealth Avenue, a trail of fellows in your wake."

Bernie wanted to talk more about Sal. "Not quite."

"Pat probably told you I got divorced. We waited until the kids were out of the house. Then I moved back up here from Connecticut to be nearer my folks. The girls are all scattered across the country, anyway. No reason to stay down there."

"Yeah, he did. That must have been tough." He'd married a fellow lawyer, Bernie remembered, a woman as blond as him. Christmas cards with four blond daughters, everyone in matching sweaters with big overly cheerful smiles. It always made her glad she'd gotten over her crush.

"Tough, yeah." His eyes filled with tears. Pat and his other friends used to call him Blubby because he cried so easily.

"I hear your law practice in Augusta is doing great," Bernie said, trying to detour the flood.

"Yeah," he perked up. "Pat and Theresa have been great, helping me reconnect. Your family is the best."

"If you say so," Bernie said. *Best bunch of pains in the ass.*

"How're the rest of the tribe? Tommy? Amy? Angie? Mary Kate? How about you? How'd you end up back here? You broke up with Steve? Pat used to keep me up to date."

"Those guys are all fine. You know. Lawyer, doctor, doctor, doctor. Single, married with four kids, single, married for Mary Kate finally since Massachusetts legalized it." She let all that sink in, giving him the usual time people needed to mull over the magnificence of her siblings.

When she could tell he'd absorbed it, she continued. "I broke up with Steve. I got laid off. I bought the *Watcher*, and he didn't want to leave Massachusetts, so that was that."

"Now you're dating the police chief?"

Bernie felt a surge of annoyance. "We're just friends. Where did you hear that?"

Bobby looked relieved, unfortunately. "Kermit O'Neil. He mentioned it. I do a lot of Franklin County work, run into Kermit all the time."

In what world, Bernie wondered, was a Redimere lawyer discussing her love life with Bobby Dolan? "We've been through some things together," she said.

"Yeah, I saw that in the papers and on TV," he said. "Hell of a tragedy."

"It's over. We're back to normal."

"Be careful of that cop."

Bernie looked up from mashing sour cream into her baked potato, trying not to smear it all over her plate. His cheerful smile was gone, and she saw, for the first time, the steely resolve that made him the unbeatable criminal defense lawyer her brother and sister insisted he was.

"What?"

"He's not your friend right now, okay? If something's happened to Leslie, Sal's in trouble, no matter he didn't do anything. You know as well as anyone police aren't our friends. Can't trust 'em."

Bernie was unnerved. She knew that, but she also knew that Pete was one of the most trustworthy, solid people she'd ever known. No, not one of the, but *the*, period. Her concern actually was that he was so honest he wasn't going to protect Sal if he'd really done something wrong, but that was different from what Bobby was saying.

He stared, waiting.

"Don't worry," Bernie said. "Sal's my top priority."

"Good," Bobby's grin was back. "I guess that means we'll be seeing a lot of each other."

CHAPTER 12
2007
Redimere, Maine
Thursday, June 28

Pete drove to the transfer station, wondering why he'd worn a suit. No one had told him Maine was this hot in June, not as bad as Philly, but still hot. When he'd packed the suit, he thought it would give him credibility, but he seemed to be the only person in the state wearing one. It was one more thing to brand him as someone from away, a phrase now burned in his brain.

He turned onto Transfer Station Road, which wound into the woods outside of town. A quarter mile in, through an open gate, the woods cleared to reveal a buzzing village, dirt roads circling around outbuildings and assorted piles of debris, signs showing the way to bulk plastics, brush pile, compost, appliances. Cars were double-parked in front of the recycling shed, a long, low, wooden building with eight or nine large openings. A sign promised an office, swap shack, and a variety of other delights down around behind. The biggest sign, with two large arrows, declared "HOPPER" the featured attraction. Beyond the woods was a spectacular line of mountains, fronted by green foothills, capped by an achingly bright blue sky. No one involved in the serious business of dumping and sorting garbage seemed to notice.

Workers wore orange vests, but even without them it wasn't hard to pick out Tim Shaw. He was on a forklift, barking at two workers hovering below him, who nodded and shuffled their feet. No doubt who the boss was.

When Pete introduced himself and asked if they could talk, Shaw didn't bat an eye.

"Sure, why not?" He hopped off the forklift and began walking. Pete assumed he was supposed to follow. He led Pete down the dirt road that circled the recycling building to a trailer up on cinder blocks. "My swanky office," he said as he opened the door.

The room was hot and musty. Battered office furniture and filing cabinets were piled with papers. Yellowed safety pamphlets papered the walls. There were glasses in the sink, a couple beer bottles. File boxes and buckets lined the walls, as did folding chairs, a couple easy chairs. Half office, half big-boy clubhouse.

Shaw didn't sit down. Now that they were out of the sun's glare, Pete saw dark circles under bloodshot eyes. He looked tired and wary.

"It's about Benji Reeves," Pete said.

"You guys weren't that interested a couple weeks ago," Shaw said.

Pete smiled. "I am now."

"What do you want to know?"

"I'm trying to find anything definitive that says he's not JP Donovan, as well as anything that may tie him to the Donovan family, even if he's not their missing kid."

"He just isn't. That's definitive. He worked here on and off for a couple years. Petty criminal."

"Anything specific?"

"This and that. Break-ins. Drug stuff. We get a lot of that around here."

"But you hired him?"

Shaw laughed. "These guys sort garbage for minimum wage, a little more if they have a head on their shoulders and are reliable, but not much more. We take what we can get. Anyway, lots of guys around here, the kind of guys who would work here, have some kind of record. Goes with the territory."

"But the police didn't know him?"

Shaw laughed again, a harsh bark. "Keystone fucking cops. Reeves is slippery, good at what he does—and I'm not talking his career as a town employee—unlike our police force. He didn't get caught."

"Where he was from? Family? Anything else?"

"Don't know. I'll say this, he was always watching, never taking part. Then suddenly you'd realize he knew too much." He bit off the last word.

"Like what?"

"Nothing specific. Just that smirking way he has of letting you know he knows your shit. He didn't have nothing to do with that missing kid's family, just saw an opportunity and took advantage. That's his way. Always working an angle. If he could fuck you over while doing it, all the better."

"How did he fuck you over?"

"Nothing specific. I gotta get back to work." He opened the door, held it, squinting up into the sun, let it slam shut as Pete moved past him down the cinder block stairs, and went back to his forklift.

Pete walked over to the garbage hopper. He'd never thought much about what happened to garbage after it went in the garbage can—thought about dumpsters, dreamed about them, but his dreams didn't have anything to do with garbage. Metal steps led to the control booth, which had a window looking down at the works. The hopper itself had a cement wall about two feet high on two of the three sides not taken up by the control tower. The third side had no wall, and a pickup truck had backed up, tailgate open, the driver tossing bags in. They slid down stainless steel walls, shiny with garbage and from thousands of sliding bags. The walls angled down to a rectangular hole about fifteen feet below. The garbage slid into the hole, which was maybe five feet deep, as a metal wedge slowly pushed it through an opening into a dumpster trailer behind the control tower.

121

"Pretty impressive, huh? That's 1,800 cubic feet of pressure," a voice said above the grinding of the hopper's motor. A skinny guy in an orange transfer station vest stood next to Pete. "Packs everything right into the dumpster, tight as a nut. I'm like you, I like to watch it."

"How long have you worked here?" Pete asked.

"A few years. It's just until I find something better. I had to drop out of college because of the money. I was an English major. I think I'll be a writer or something, or go into web design, maybe video game design."

"Lots of people take a little time to find themselves," Pete said, thinking the guy looked older than college age. Hard to tell with the wispy mustache and almost nonexistent beard, wide child-like eyes. "I went to night school to be a lawyer. Took me years."

"Are you a lawyer? Here in Redimere? I don't think I know you. I usually know everyone. Everyone comes through the transfer station. Most everyone. Busiest place in town."

"Visiting. I'm a police detective."

"Wow. Really? That's cool. I could've been a lawyer. Thought about it. I think I would've been good at it. *Law and Order* is one of my favorite shows."

"It's a lot of school."

"I know, right? Not enough time or money. Hey, I'm Brian."

"Pete." He took the hand the kid had offered, damp but strong. "You didn't know Benji Reeves did you?" He'd heard the forklift start up, sounded like it was getting near.

"Oh yeah. We were really good friends."

"I'm investigating—"

"Brian," a big red-headed kid lumbered up, wheezing, looking at Pete with alarm. "Tim says he needs you right now. He don't want you talking to people."

"Doesn't want me talking to people? Moses, I always talk to people. It's what I do. I'm a people person." Brian rolled his eyes, letting Pete in.

"Brian." The redhead looked like he was going to cry.

"I don't want to get you in trouble with your boss." Pete said. "Sounds like he wants you back to work. Here's my card. That's my cellphone number. Give me a call, and we can talk about Benji. I'll be in town another day or two."

"Sure thing." Brian looked at the card. "Philadelphia, now that's a city I always wanted to go to. That museum they have, you know the Rocky one? I—"

"Plourde, get your ass over here!" It was Shaw.

Brian's grin faded. "Uh oh. The boss says jump and I say 'how high?' Ya know? I'll give you a call tonight."

"Thanks," Pete said as Brian hurried away toward the idling forklift.

"Don't make Tim mad," the big redhead said to Pete.

"No, wouldn't want to do that," Pete said.

He felt Shaw's glare follow him as he walked back to his car. Pete gave the friendly wave he'd seen around town. *See ya, buddy. See ya later.*

. . . . .

Pete had seen the Country Grocer across the street when he was at the newspaper office. It was a low-slung wooden building with a long porch stacked high with bundles of camp wood, car antifreeze, an ice cooler, angled parking spaces out front. He made it his lunch stop.

The store inside wasn't air-conditioned, just like every other building he'd been in so far. It smelled like coffee and something baking. There didn't seem to be any customers, and as he walked up to the counter, it occurred to him the guy behind it was the first black person he'd encountered in the town.

He introduced himself.

"I'm Walt Pecoe, the owner." He glanced at Pete's badge, wary.

Pete didn't blame him. He was sure it was the same in Redimere as it was in Philadelphia and everywhere else in the United States, for black men and cops.

"I'm trying to find out about Benji Reeves."

"Benji," the store owner said, relaxing. "Never Ben. Benji.

123

Kind of affected if you ask me. Not really a name for a grownup."

"You knew him?"

"Not well." Walt glanced toward the back of the store, lowered his voice. "My deli manager, Wendy, they were friends. He'd come in here and talk to her. I think he always pocketed a little present when he left, though I never saw him or could prove it. Never trusted him. Too ingratiating."

"Is Wendy here now?"

"She's out back."

As Pete approached, he could see a woman sorting meat through the glass front of the deli counter. She stood up, tall and rail thin. Had that look about her that women did who'd played basketball and been good at it. He didn't know her at all, yet couldn't picture her being friends with the Benji Reeves he was coming to know.

He told her he wanted to talk about Benji Reeves.

She stared at his badge, just like the owner had, only more wary, looked like she was trying to figure out how to answer. "Why?" she finally asked.

"It has to do with a murder investigation in Philadelphia." Not really a lie.

"I can't help you."

"I heard you were friends."

"He followed me around and bugged me. I had no interest. I'm a thirty-three-year-old mother of a toddler with another kid on the way, a mortgage, a husband to cook for, and a house to clean, when I'm not working here to pay the bills. He was twenty-one and lived like a gypsy. He was looking for something I couldn't give him."

"Looking for what?"

"What do you think?" she said, exasperated. "I barely knew him. I don't know why he latched onto me. I can't help you."

"You know he's twenty-one."

She leaned on the counter, closer to Pete, eye level. "I know he's twenty-one. Or that's what he said. He said he was from Boston. He said he was an orphan. He said his name was Benji

Reeves. I don't know how much I believed. I didn't care."

"Anything—"

"I have to get back to work. I'm sorry." She walked through a door behind the counter.

"I couldn't hear most of that," Walt said as he rang up Pete's pre-made sandwich and bottle of water. "But it's probably a good idea to leave Wendy alone. Her husband isn't a nice guy." He gave Pete his change. "Not a nice guy at all."

Pete had picked up a chamber of commerce map at the store, and checked it out as he ate his sandwich in the car. He'd called the public works department before he left that morning to see when he could meet the director, and the guy had told him to come on by. It was easy to find, he saw as he looked at the map. Turns out he'd gone by it on his way to the dump.

"Don Littlefield," the director said, getting up from behind his desk. Aside from another guy in his office, the building was empty. Don was beefy and balding but had a familiar smile.

"Any relation to Cal?" Pete asked.

"Cousin," Don said. "This is David Viens; he's on the transfer station committee. Been on it for years and knows everyone. I thought maybe he could help."

"Do you guys know Benji Reeves?"

"Tim Shaw does the hiring," said David. "But we get to know who's working there. Hard not to, the amount of time we spend there. We're trying to firm up the rules for hiring, partly because of Reeves. Maybe get money in the budget for background checks."

"Why's that?" Pete asked.

"Started hearing rumors after he'd been here for a while that he was behind some camp break-ins and whatnot."

"You didn't tell the police? They didn't know him?"

"It was rumors," Viens said. "No one wanted to go to them with just rumors."

"No," Pete said, not getting it at all.

"It's hard to get guys," Don broke in, defensive. "It's not the greatest job in the world, and with the recession, you know, lots of

125

people are drifting from one job to another. But they don't like sorting garbage in all kinds of weather for minimum wage."

A familiar theme, Pete thought.

"Whatever he was up to, we had Tim Shaw look into it, but it was just nothing we could get our hands on," David said.

"Nothing that was a big deal," Don broke in. "We don't support criminal activity at town facilities."

"Of course not," Pete said.

Don added, "Reeves had worked there on and off for a couple years. Couple days a week when needed, more in the summer, less in the winter. Tim gave him the boot a day or two before the whole JP Donovan thing happened."

"He didn't tell me that," Pete said, trying to remember if it had been in the newspaper story. He didn't think so. He made a mental note to ask the editor about it. "You said Shaw couldn't find anything when he'd investigated?"

"Personnel matter," Don added, nervous. "Hirings, firings. We don't talk about them publicly. He wasn't let go for doing anything illegal."

"Tim just had enough," David said. "Reeves did his own thing, came in late, left before his shift was over, that type of thing. Tim would read him the riot act, and Reeves'd just smile and shrug."

. . . . .

Later that night over drinks on Cal's deck, the police chief laughed about Pete's exchange with his cousin.

"That guy, monument to great management," Cal said. "The truth is, the committee, Shaw, Don, it's easier for them to do nothing and blame the town budget. Shaw has his fiefdom over there, and my cousin and the town fathers are too lazy to interfere."

"What about the rest of the committee?" Pete asked. "Viens seems on the level."

"It's all about politics. Viens is fed up, wants to quit, but my cousin keeps convincing him to stay. I heard he's quitting after this term, no matter what. Doc Chapman, the committee chairman, doesn't seem to want to get anything done. The rest of the folks on the committee just keep their heads down."

"Great," Pete said.

"Welcome to small-town politics," Cal said, lifting his glass.

"You guys, the police, never heard about Reeves?"

"It's possible we heard about him. Didn't put a face with a name. Hard to say. All we have is me and three other full-time officers, one who's a girl who does all our office work. A lot of names come across our desk, but we don't have time to track down rumors."

Cal was using the usual friendly-pal tone, but Pete could feel the defensiveness behind it. He wasn't going to argue. If they didn't know Reeves, they didn't know Reeves.

"You talk to Eli Perry?" Cal asked.

"Not yet."

"He's a rough customer. Doesn't like cops."

"I can handle myself."

"I know you can," Cal said. "But a lot of cops who can handle themselves find themselves looking down the barrel of a shotgun in the middle of nowhere Maine without a body in sight to help them."

It hadn't been that long ago that Pete had felt that maybe staring down the barrel of a gun wouldn't be the worst thing for him. He couldn't tell if he felt it now or not. He pushed it back.

"I made some calls about you," Cal said, like he was reading Pete's mind.

Pete, startled, waited for the blow.

"I hope you don't mind."

"Not a problem." Pete could feel Cal's eyes on him. The tone of the conversation had changed since he'd asked about the police knowing Reeves.

"You understand, right? City detective shows up in town asking questions, I need to check it out."

"I understand."

"I don't blame you for not telling me you're on mental health leave. You don't know me."

127

"Thanks."

"But you're sharing my home, my food. My drink. So why don't you level with me? Maybe I can help you more if I know why you're really here. Not the version you told me last night, the real version."

"What'd they tell you about me?" He couldn't look at Cal. Could feel his face burning and hoped it wasn't noticeable in the dusk. The ice in his glass clinked as his hand shook, so he put it down.

"You had a breakdown and your future with the department is uncertain."

"I was diagnosed with PTSD," Pete said, his throat closing around the words. He didn't say them very often. Never, actually.

"I was also told you're a good cop. Very good. That you're tough as nails. They're rooting for you."

"I'm sure they are."

Cal didn't say anything. Pete trusted his hand not to shake enough to pick up his glass and drain it. He might as well unload, here in the twilight, in this soft, quiet place, to this guy he didn't know, but who seemed to care, despite the tension of the last few minutes.

"I totally lost my shit," Pete said, surprised, given how he felt, that his voice sounded okay. "It'd been building up for years. That's what they tell me, anyway. I was at the scene of a drug murder, not anyone you'd feel bad about. He had a little girl; she was hiding in the closet. I picked her up and couldn't put her down." That was the simple version. The one that left out the panic, the nausea, the nightmares, and the absolute inexplicable terror.

"I get it," Cal said.

"Do you?" Pete asked. "I don't want to sound like an asshole, but I don't. Plenty of other guys have seen the same things I have. None of them lost their shit."

"Everyone's different."

"I could've been stronger, but I wasn't." His ice clinked again and he put his glass down. "I'm ashamed." That's a part he'd never told anyone. Not Karen or Sid, or even the therapist they were making him see.

"I did two tours in Vietnam," Cal said. "I was a different guy when I came back, but nobody was talking about PTSD forty years ago. There were a lot of things I didn't care about anymore. The first year I was home, on the Fourth of July, I ended up in the closet, crying like a baby. The fireworks. Cecile will tell you. I had a long row to hoe."

Pete didn't say anything.

"It gets better," Cal said.

"I'm not in Vietnam. Not in a war. No one's shooting at me, at least most of the time."

"There are worse things than being shot at. Giving a shit can be a burden."

"Lots of bodies in dumpsters," Pete said, trying it out, his voice even. Seeing if he could think about it without the panic taking over, things he didn't want to remember coming back. He didn't think he could.

"It'll get better."

Pete didn't want to tell him the biggest problem was that he had to go back. He wasn't home from a war, just on leave. He'd spent two days in a warm pretty little town on the edge of the earth and, whatever was going on behind the scenes, it felt so much better than where he'd come from, where he'd have to go back to. He didn't know how he was going to.

"That brings us to why you're here," Cal said.

"I have a lot of time on my hands."

"Why are you here?" Cal asked again, refilling Pete's glass.

"Something happened to JP Donovan. The family has been hinky from day one. The story doesn't fit. I feel like if I can just figure it all out..." He trailed off.

"Things will be better?"

"Maybe. I'll feel like I've done something, like I'm not a total failure."

"Okay, buddy boy. Let's figure it out."

129

. . . . .

Pete stopped by the newspaper office the next day, but the editor wasn't there. He was disappointed, even though he knew she probably couldn't tell him why Benji Reeves was fired from the transfer station. He thought of calling her cell, but it felt like an intrusion.

He walked to the trailer park, more comfortable now that he'd scrapped the suit for a polo shirt and khakis. The day was warm, sunny. The weather had been perfect since he'd arrived. He noticed there was a little more traffic, more people in town as Fourth of July approached, but it was still quiet, if you didn't count the birds, the breeze through the leaves, the gurgle of the river as it tripped along to wherever it was going. When he was a kid, his mother sent him and his brother to his uncle's farm in northern Wisconsin every summer to get them out of her hair. It was a relief, away from her sad anger, the drinking, the awful boyfriend, and later the worse stepfather. The farm was quiet, and he'd walk the country roads, like this one, nowhere special to go, pretending he was someone else. He was an adult now, though, and knew wherever he went, he wasn't anyone but himself. Today the thought depressed him a tiny fraction less than it had the day before.

"Help you?" Eli Perry asked when he opened the door. He was massive, the tattoos on his sleeveless arms meant to intimidate. Pete didn't give a shit. He introduced himself.

"What do you want?" Perry asked.

"I understand you were friends with Benji Reeves?"

"Nope."

"Any information would help our investigation."

"Tough luck."

"If he caused you some problems, we're on the same side."

"We'll never be on the same side," Perry said.

"I just want to find out who he is, what he was up to, why he left."

"You'll never know who he is, because he's a liar and a con man. I can tell you one thing, though. He wasn't a missing kid out of Philly. What he was up to? Who the hell knows? No good. Why he left? Ask Tim Shaw. Or better yet, his wife."

Perry slammed the door.

Pete walked back to Cal's, feeling the little bit of good feeling and hope drift off with the breeze. He'd learned little since he'd arrived in town. Brian from the transfer station had never called and was probably never going to. Pete wished he'd gotten a number, instead of just giving him his.

"Hi, Detective." David Viens, from the transfer station committee, was climbing down a ladder propped against a house. "Any luck?" He walked over, wiping sweat off his forehead with a bandanna, then put it back in his pocket to shake Pete's hand.

"Not much."

A woman came out the front door. "Come and meet my wife," David said, not giving Pete time to answer as he walked across the neatly trimmed lawn. Pete followed.

"Kris, this is the detective from Philadelphia."

"Call me Pete."

"David said you're interested in Benji," she said.

"I am."

Kris looked at David, an unspoken question. "Might as well tell him," David said. "Kris is a friend of Wendy's," he said to Pete.

"Were Benji and Wendy having an affair?" Pete asked, hoping to get the ball rolling.

Kris laughed. "Nothing like that. He was a kid, though not sixteen. Kid like twenty-one."

"That's what everyone keeps saying."

"Benji followed Wendy around like a puppy. She felt bad for him. They were just friends. Anyway, Tim would've killed her." Kris didn't say it like she was joking.

"Probably not killed her," David said.

"Maybe not," Kris said, not looking convinced. "Some of it on Benji's part was probably to get Tim's goat. They didn't get along, and Benji liked to push his buttons, and that made it worse. You know?"

131

"Sure," Pete said.

"Wendy said Benji was a lost boy who needed a mother figure more than a girlfriend, so she'd listen to him, give him attention. You didn't hear this from me, but Wendy told me the reason Benji left town was that Tim was going to turn him in."

"For what?"

"Tim said he suspected Benji was breaking into camps, stealing drugs and selling them. He was seeing what prescription bottles people put in the recycling at the transfer station, then breaking into their houses and stealing the drugs."

"People didn't catch on?"

"He focused mostly on summer camps, weekend ski condos, the elderly or other people who might not put two and two together. This is what Wendy heard from Tim, anyway. Benji was smart, knew how not to get caught. Benji in turn told Wendy it was Tim selling drugs. Tim may have his faults, but he's not going around breaking into camps and houses, so that was just one of Benji's lies."

"No one told the police?"

Kris shrugged. "It was all vague, and there are a lot of break-ins, lots of people with drug issues. Wendy even wondered if Tim was making it up because he didn't like Benji and just wanted him gone. He never quite believed there was nothing going on between them. Benji told Wendy he was afraid Tim was going to plant drugs on him and then tip off the cops."

"That's why he left town?"

"That's what he said to Wendy right before he left. Or tried to leave. Ray Morin kind of screwed things up."

David broke in. "You have to know Benji. He lied all the time. Told people what they wanted to hear and knew how to get what he wanted."

Kris nodded. "Wendy said whether what Tim said was true or not, Benji was involved with drugs anyway. Back when they first met, a couple years ago, he told her that he smuggled them—um, sorry—up his butt. In prescription bottles or baggies, so if he got

132

caught, no one would find them. He offered to show her, but she said no thanks. She told me he might have just been trying to impress her."

"Do you think you could get Wendy to talk to me?"

Kris shook her head. "No, it would piss Tim off. She told me he was complaining about you nosing around, and she almost had a heart attack when you talked to her in the store yesterday."

"News travels fast," Pete said.

"Small town," Kris said.

"You should try Eli Perry," David said. "He and Benji were tight for a while but had a falling out. Had to have something to do with drugs, because everyone knows Perry's been dealing forever."

"I tried," Pete said. "He wasn't interested. Why didn't you tell me any of this yesterday?"

"I didn't want to say anything in front of Don. Then everyone would know—"

"Right. Small town. Can you guys think of anything else?"

They looked at each other. "No, I guess that's it," David said.

"Thanks. That's the most I've found out since I came to town."

"Our pleasure," David said. "Even if no one wants to talk to you, there was no love lost for Benji Reeves in this town."

CHAPTER 13
2009
Redimere, Maine
Saturday, November 14

Dawna put her tray down next to Guy Gagne. "Are you covering this for the paper?"

"No, just eating," Guy said. Then he intoned, like a TV broadcaster, "Redimere's annual hunters' breakfast, a gala event that raises thousands for the soup kitchen and food pantry, was the usual social whirl as politicians and VIPs gathered at four-thirty a.m. over venison hash and eggs—"

"Enough," Dawna said, laughing. "It's too early."

"Anything new?" he whispered.

"Nothing." A week since he'd found the gut pile, and there was no DNA match or anything else to answer the question of who it was or what had happened. Then, in a normal voice, "Have I missed anything?"

"Nope. The usual. Plourde taking a beating."

"This is the year Brian's going to get the Monster Buck," one of the guys at the next table was saying. Everyone laughed.

"You guys know I can't hunt because of my felony conviction," Brian said, glancing at Dawna.

"She don't care," another guy said. "Tell us about the Monster Buck, Brian. Is it twenty points or twenty-four?"

"I'll keep a lookout for you, Brian," said a good-looking man sitting next to him. Dawna had never seen him before. His smile was friendly, not mocking like the rest of the guys.

"You do that, Professor," Tim Shaw said.

Guy broke in. "Dawna, do you know Bernie's brother Sal?"

"No," she said, leaning over to the table to shake hands. So this was him. "Dawna Mitchell."

"Sal O'Dea."

"Watch out, she's the law," someone said.

Dawna saw wariness cloud Sal's eyes as he turned back to Brian. "Since I'm new in town, maybe you can help me scout."

Brian's eyes shifted toward Dawna, then back. "Maybe."

When Pete had filled Dawna in on Sal, she'd said she had trouble seeing someone related to Bernie do something like what might have happened to Leslie Lark. Pete had reminded her that all sorts of people do bad things. Now, sitting across the table from Sal, she still didn't feel that vibe that the bad guys gave her, despite the fact he seemed wary of her. He seemed like a nice, normal guy.

"Tell Officer Mitchell about that other ghost you saw," Moses Mosher said, and the table fell quiet.

"*Sergeant* Mitchell," Guy said.

"That wasn't nothing," Brian said, turning red and glancing at Shaw, who was watching him with an intensity Dawna found unnerving.

"What was it?" Dawna asked.

"He saw Benji Reeves?" Moses, now uncertain, his giant round head topped by that disconcerting bright red crewcut swiveling between Brian and Tim.

Dawna felt Guy go on alert next to her. "When?" she asked, trying to remember how much of the gut pile investigation had been made public. Not much. Certainly no one knew it was possibly Benji Reeves's innards that Guy had stumbled across, except her and Pete, and Guy, who they'd floated the theory by to see if it jostled any details from that morning.

"He's in Philadelphia with his new family," Shaw said. "Last any of us knew."

"It wasn't probably him," Brian said. "You know how you

135

think you see someone, but it's just because they remind you of someone or something like that, but you're really not seeing them at all."

"Like your Monster Buck," someone said, spurring a burst of laughter.

"But Brian—" said Moses.

"Just like the Monster Buck," Shaw said. "Figment of your imagination."

The other hunters, all but Shaw and Moses, had gone back to their food and conversation.

"When did you see him?" Dawna asked Brian.

He looked at Shaw again, scared and apologetic. "Maybe a few weeks ago. If it was him, which it probably wasn't. Walking down the Ridge Road. Could've been anyone. I know it was before Halloween because I was going to the Pour House to watch the baseball playoffs on the big screen. The Yankees and the Angels? It was game six, so I think that was on a Sunday. My TV doesn't work very good, but I've always liked the Yankees even though everyone else hates them. They have such a great tradition. You know the Red Sox sold Babe Ruth to them—"

"Right," Dawna said.

"Tim's a Yankee fan," Moses said. "Right, Tim?"

"Can't beat Jeter," Shaw said, still glaring at Brian.

"You better talk to the state police detective investigating the gut pile," Dawna said. "I'll have him look you up."

"I don't even know if it was him," Brian said, his voice small. "I don't know what I saw."

"That would have been weeks ago," Shaw said.

"Yeah, right," Brian said, his voice trembling.

"You need to talk to him anyway," Dawna said. She picked up her empty plate. "Time for this hunter to get to the woods. Guy. Gentlemen." She nodded at the group and left, aware of how silent the table was behind her.

. . . . .

Guy Gagne hadn't been hunting since he'd found the gut pile the

136

week before. At first he wasn't sure if he wanted to go back, but then he realized how ridiculous that was.

He walked way back deep into the woods near the base of the mountains, back in where he knew it'd be quiet, back, actually, near where he'd found the guts. He wasn't going to let one horrific moment stop him from going where he'd been hunting all his life, starting with his father after the old man came back from World War II. He barely remembered the dad who left in 1942, when Guy was four. But he remembered enough to know the man who came back wasn't him. He looked like him. Smelled like him—pipe tobacco and Old Spice. Sounded like him most of the time. But it wasn't him. Not yet thirty, his father had aged decades in the few years away. The easygoing laughing guy who'd toss him above his shoulders was quiet and distant. He never hurt Guy or even yelled at him, but Guy still avoided him. Knew instinctively to. The only time he felt a kinship was when the two were in the woods, communicating silently, his father leading, Guy following. They had the same talent for listening. The same patient ability to follow and wait for the moment. The same love of the crisp sharp air and the smell of pine needles and the deep primordial earth.

When his father went downtown to the garage where he was a mechanic one day and never came home—felled at forty by a heart attack—Guy starting going into the woods alone. He went year-round, but this month was his time of year. The crunch of the frozen leaves under his boots, the way the breeze rustled the century-old trees. As darkness turned to dawn it was so, so quiet. Most of the birds were gone somewhere warmer. The squirrels weren't awake yet. He never told anyone, not even his wife, Eileen, but he believed his father was there with him in the breaking dawn, whispering so silently he could barely hear him, pointing to the deer scat or scrapings, the partial hoof print in the mud. Deer were so quiet, so incredibly quiet. But he knew where they were, he could feel them. He wasn't going to let a pile of guts stop him from being here.

There was a big buck he had his eye on, it'd been out there

137

opening day and they'd played hide and seek around a slope of dense pines. He hadn't seen it or any sign of it the day of the gut pile. Didn't see any sign today, either. There wasn't even a new sign—fresh scat, scrapings—that his buck had been around. Dawna believed deer knew when they were being hunted. Sometimes they played the game, and sometimes they tired of it and went away. Guy thought it was more random. His knowledge was based on science, not feelings. Deer wander around. They usually have a circular range of a few miles. Maybe that buck is somewhere else, looking for the best branches, the best spots to sleep or find a nice deer friend or spot in the sun or shade. Dawna said that was typical human thought—that something that lived in the woods, was of the woods, couldn't be nearly as smart as we are. Guy usually retorted that if deer were so smart, how come they didn't invent guns and shoot back? Deep down he knew she was probably right, but he liked the conversation too much to admit it.

Being out in the quiet also gave him time to think. Today he thought a lot about that day a week ago, reaching into his memory for those details Dawna and Pete had wanted so bad. He hadn't heard gunshots, he was sure of it. He'd come up the back way from his house, after six, long after the shots would have been fired. He heard other shots, later from other directions, as dawn broke, but not those ones.

Today, though, in the quiet, he finally remembered what he'd heard as he walked through the woods. It'd been bugging him all week, the feeling he'd heard something that struck him as funny at the time. Now he remembered. Truck engines, two of them, and how odd it was to hear them retreating from the woods toward the Ridge Road instead of coming closer into the woods when dawn hadn't broken yet.

. . . . .

Bernie slouched back on the couch at the back of the newsroom and closed her eyes. It was way too early on Saturday morning to be up. Thank goodness for the couch. She'd added the lounge area earlier this fall, figuring if she was going to spend this much time at

138

the office, she needed a comfortable spot. The front door opened and closed with its signature spring-less crash.

Bernie, eyes still closed, heard Carol say to Guy. "Hey, Vince said he saw you at the hunter's breakfast this morning. Why aren't you out in the woods?"

"I was. Now I'm here."

"I brought breakfast," Carol said to Bernie. "I know you had a bowl of Cheerios or something, but hard work calls for substantial food." She put a large brown bag on the table and Bernie opened her eyes. "French toast and bacon straight off the grill from Choppy's," Carol said. "Debbie even threw in utensils and maple syrup."

"Debbie is a goddess."

"How was your date last night?"

"It wasn't a date."

"You dressed for it, so it was a date. I'm sure Bobby thought it was a date."

"He did kiss me goodnight."

"Did you make out in the car?"

"I haven't made out in a car since I was, um..." Bernie couldn't remember the last time she made out in a car. "He kissed me next to my car. We both had our own cars, thank goodness." Seeing Carol was forming a question, she added, "Firm, not sloppy, no tongue."

"Did you kiss back?"

"More or less. He hugged me, too. Probably to cop a feel. I was showing cleavage."

"I'm impressed," Carol said.

"Enough of this," Bernie said. Guy had stopped typing. "I'm sure Guy is scandalized."

"Waiting for it to get good," he said and began typing again.

"What does that mean for Pete?" Carol asked.

"It means nothing. I'm not getting involved with Bobby. I'm not getting involved with Pete."

"You're already involved with Pete."

139

Bernie concentrated on eating and didn't answer.

"He does love you."

"So he says," Bernie said, wiping maple syrup off her chin.

"Don't tell me you don't believe it."

"I believe he does for the moment. But someday, maybe in a month or two, maybe in a year or two, he'll hear me bitching about something or be watching me eat French toast, and he'll say 'What the hell was I thinking?' But he won't say it to me, just slowly fall out of love, and I'll see the signs, but I'll try to ignore them and get more and more miserable, until the inevitable awful breakup long after we should have."

Guy had stopped typing again. "You're a true romantic."

"I'm a realist."

"I've told you a million times," Carol said. "You're overthinking it. That all may happen or it may not. It hasn't happened to me and Vince."

"Or me and Eileen. We've been married forty-eight years," Guy said.

"How about this?" Bernie said. "I don't have the time. There's too much going on and relationships are exhausting. Always worrying about what he's thinking, whether he's annoyed with me, what I did that I didn't even know about that pissed him off, worrying about his emotions, worrying about my emotions, tripping over his socks on the floor, having to negotiate every little thing from what to eat to what to watch on TV. I can't take it. I don't have time."

"You trip over socks?" Guy asked.

"You know what I mean."

"No, I don't."

"That's because you're a guy. You don't have to worry about the socks or the emotions or anything else, just drift along in obtuse bliss."

"I take exception to that," Guy said.

Carol threw up her hands. "You are hopeless."

"And finally, how about this? I'm the newspaper editor, and I

140

can't have a relationship with someone I cover."

"You're already in love with each other," Carol said. "You're already compromised. The relationship just makes it official. You're both smart, honest, professional people. You'd figure it out."

"I'm not so sure."

"There are so many positive things to being in a relationship with someone you love and who loves you," Carol said. "I notice you don't deny loving him. Aside from sex, there's having someone there to support you and help you with your burdens. That's what it's all about. A best friend to love you and care about you no matter what. Like the Springsteen song? 'A true companion for this part of the ride'? You like that song."

"Don't try to sway me by throwing Springsteen at me," Bernie said. "That's the ideal. The reality is exhausting."

"How about Bridget Jones? Remember how much you loved that Mark Darcy loved her just for who she was? Didn't Pete say something like that to you that night you went to his place?"

"That was chick lit comedy fiction, not really something to base a realistic romantic philosophy on."

"You're hopeless," Carol said. "Poor Pete."

"Frankly," Guy said, "if that's how you're going to look at things, the guy is better off without the headache."

"Let's change the subject," Bernie said. "We have to figure out how we're going to cover Leslie Lark. I have a conflict of interest. Carrie, if she works out as an intern, could possibly do some light coverage, but I need to either hire a reporter with real chops or use you guys. I'll have my hands full as the gut pile develops, because Guy can't help since he found it." She said the last pointedly. Guy typed on.

Carol shook her head. "I can't help. We're best friends. I'm not objective either. Anyway, I have a major freelance magazine thingee that's going to eat up the next several weeks and bring mega-money into the house, so I'm not available."

"We can't just ignore it if it turns into something," Bernie said. She tried to wipe syrup off her fingers, bits of napkin tearing off and sticking to them. She hoped they couldn't tell how scared shitless she was about it turning into something. "My credibility would go right down the toilet. He lives here now, works here." She went back to eating while she waited for one of them to say something. Her sticky napkinny fingers stuck to the plasticware and the food tasted like cardboard. The only sound in the office was plastic forks and the soft click of Guy's keyboard.

Carol finally said, "What about Fergus Kelley? The guy who called you a couple times?"

"Ugh. Yuck."

"Vince kind of knows Leslie Lark," Carol said.

"Really?" Bernie said. "Talk about burying the lead."

"Hardly knows her. She took his Sustainable Marijuana course at the college last year. She was looking to be a medical marijuana grower."

"Sal told me she was mixed up with some bad pot guys, but he's been light on the details. He eventually told the cops, but I don't know how seriously they took him since he's so vague and says he doesn't know much. Another angle someone else will have to cover."

"Maybe Carrie will be good," Guy said. "Isn't she why you're in here at the crack of nine a.m. on a Saturday?"

"She doesn't seem promising. Very monosyllabic when I talked to her on the phone. Cow-like."

"If a cow could talk on the phone," Carol said.

"Her whole aura was cow-like."

"Depression and lack of sleep is making you judgy," Carol said.

"Yep, that's me." Bernie poured more coffee. She'd already had a pot or more, but she needed something to cut the edge off the sluggish unhappiness. "I'm going to send her to the West Vineyard selectmen's meeting Monday night. See what she can do. Guess we'll take it from there."

"I hate to bring it up," Carol said. "But did Sal ever say Leslie was so annoying he'd like to shoot her and truss her up like a deer?"

"Holy shit, I hope not."

"Vince heard it at the transfer station committee meeting."

"Hopefully that's just a rumor. I can't see him saying something like that. Then again sometimes he thinks he's funny when he's not."

"Family trait," Guy said.

The door opened with its usual crash.

Carrie—it had to be—looked around the newsroom, eyes large behind round 1980s-style glasses. Her gaze fell on Guy, who didn't look up from his typing. She blinked as though trying to see after coming out of a movie theater.

"She's in the back," Guy said.

"Carrie, I'm back here," Bernie said, watching the scene from the couch, but lacking the energy to get up and properly greet her.

Carrie came to the back of the room.

"This is Carol, she writes a column and does some freelancing." Carol stood up and shook hands.

"Hi Carrie, great to meet a fellow Watcher."

Carrie shook her hand.

"That's Guy over there typing. He's worked here since the news was printed on palm leaves with dinosaur turds."

Guy guffawed. Carrie stared at Bernie wordlessly.

"Why don't you sit down? Coffee? Thanks for coming by so early on a Saturday."

Carrie shook her head and sat down. Bernie handed Carrie her payroll paperwork. "You can fill out the parts I haven't, then give it back to me. You told me you'd be available Mondays after four, all day Wednesday and possibly some other days during the week, right?"

"Yes."

"I thought we could get you started with the West Vineyard selectmen's meeting Monday. It's at seven. We'll see how it goes."

Carrie nodded.

"I think if you do Mapquest—"

"I can find it."

Four syllables, we're making progress. "If I need you more

than what we talked about, are you available? I'd pay you by the hour."

"Okay."

"Here's an AP Stylebook." She handed it to Carrie. She waited for her to nod before continuing. "That's your bible. You've covered selectmen's meetings?"

"I've worked summers the past two years for the paper in my town."

"That's right. Milo?"

"Yeah."

A little town in the middle of nowhere way east. It might as well have been on the moon. "This may be a little different."

"Bigger population than Redimere," Carrie said, coloring. "I covered meetings in some of the surrounding towns. Selectmen, school board." Then, to drive it home, "Zoning."

Carrie was right. Redimere, at two thousand and holding steady, wasn't a roaring metropolis. "You know the drill, then. After the meeting, write the story up that night or early Tuesday morning. I need it by nine a.m. Tuesday."

"Okay."

"Deadlines are very important. Even though this is a weekly."

"Okay."

"If your computer's dead, if your car dies, if your phone dies, you still get your story in."

"Okay." Carrie, after that brief flush of emotion, was back to staring at Bernie with owl eyes.

"Call me and dictate if all else fails. Nothing in your life is more important than getting your story in."

"Okay."

Bernie's heart sank. Carrie didn't seem to be catching her sense of urgency.

"I have some rules. I'll type them up for you. Editor preferences."

"Okay."

Bernie handed Carrie a reporter's notebook and a couple of

pencils. "Pencils are better than pens. They don't freeze in the winter, they don't run out of ink. If the tip breaks and you don't have a pencil sharpener—you can get one for ninety-nine cents at Redimere Drug—you can use your fingernail or car keys. Record as backup but always take notes. If you're taking notes, you're paying attention. You have a camera, right?"

Carrie nodded.

"Besides the one on your cellphone?"

Carrie nodded again.

"Good. Email me after the meeting with your story attached and tell me how it went."

"Okay." Carrie stood up. "Do you want a web update?" It was the first question she'd asked.

"What?"

"A web update. I can do a shorter version for the website that night."

Bernie felt her neck get hot. "We're in the process of updating the website. Let's just concentrate on getting it for the paper."

"Okay."

"Better tell her about the dog rule," Guy said.

"What's that?" Carrie asked, looking around, like maybe there was a dog in the office.

"Don't mock," Bernie said to Guy.

He kept typing as he talked. "If there's a dog in the story, get its name and breed. Bernie hates it when someone has a dog in a story and doesn't have the name and breed."

Carrie nodded and looked at Bernie for confirmation.

"Yes, by all means," Bernie said. "If there's a dog at the meeting. That *is* one of my rules by the way."

Carrie nodded and lumbered out of the office.

"Knock 'em dead kid," Guy said as she left. She waved in acknowledgement.

"I don't think I've heard you rant about that one," Carol said.

"If you mention a dog in a story, the first thing every dog lover who reads the paper is going to say is, 'I wonder what kind of dog?'

The second thing they are going to say is, 'I wonder what the dog's name is?'"

Carol said, "I always put that in my stories, anyway. The ones with dogs."

"Because you are a top reporter," Bernie said. "I wish I had more of you. If there is a dog at the meeting by some chance, I guess we'd want a web update." She laughed. "Actually, I have to get that website going."

CHAPTER 14
2009
Redimere, Maine
Saturday, November 14

When Bernie arrived at the transfer station that afternoon, Sal was pulling newspapers out of the bin behind the row of recycling windows.

"Putting that Ph.D. to work, I see," Bernie said as she dumped an armful in.

"There's actually a science to this," Sal said. "Only problem is, I'm tempted to stop loading and start reading." The bin under the window was filled with newspapers. *New York Times*, the *Franklin County Irregular*, the *Lewiston Sun-Journal*, *Morning Sentinel*. Lots of *Weekly Watchers*. "Who says people don't read newspapers anymore?" He lifted an armload and stacked them on a pallet.

"Makes me sad," Bernie said. "All that work, all the scrambling, phone calls and emails all hours of the day and night, and yet here it all is in a recycling bin."

"At least people are reading it."

Bernie watched as Wayne Daggett's battered pickup pulled up. "I'm surprised Wayne would actually be dropping anything off."

He looked up. "That guy? He does his shopping here. Tim chases him away, but he's tenacious. He's here almost every day."

"He's a hoarder," Bernie said. "They made him clean up his property a couple months ago. They were going to put him in jail."

"No way to treat a mental health problem," Sal said.

"Thank you." Bernie watched Moses Mosher sprint like a lumbering red-headed hippo toward Wayne.

"Now that you and Brian are BFFs, you spending a lot of time with Moses, too?"

"Hard not to. He's Brian's shadow. I think he's mentally challenged."

"He is. I call him and Brian Lennie and George," Bernie said.

"Lenny and Squiggy?"

"No, doofus. Lennie and George, you know *Of Mice and Men*? Steinbeck? You were forced to read it in high school?"

Sal grunted as he lifted an armload of newspapers. "Brian and Moses aren't really like them, though. Wasn't George a dark little evil guy? Brian is like an over-eager puppy. Moses, though, I guess he's kind of Lennie-like."

"Let's hope not."

"He strangled a woman, right?"

"Lennie did, yeah." Bernie watched as Moses and Wayne sorted through the plastics bin. "What are they doing?"

"Wayne likes bottles. He likes those big gallon water jugs if the tops are still on and they're not dented. And, like you, his fellow hoarder, he likes prescription bottles. Moses has been saving them for him, though I get the impression it's on the sly."

"They come in handy in so many ways," Bernie said.

As Wayne greedily reached for a bulging plastic garbage bag from Moses, they were interrupted by a shout.

"Moses, no!" Brian Plourde had come around the side of the building. He snatched the bag from Moses.

"Those are mine!" Wayne said.

"We fish the prescription bottles out of the recycling to go in the hopper. Tim's orders, you know that," Brian said. "He said not to give them to you."

"Now there's a regular Algonquin Round Table," Bernie said.

"Here you were all sympathetic to the developmentally disabled just a minute ago," Sal said, throwing another pile of newspapers on the pallet.

"I'm here to help."

"Don't get involved," Sal stage-whispered.

"It's prescription bottles, so, you know, I can't help myself."

She walked over to the trio. "Why don't you recycle those?" she asked Brian.

"HIPPA laws," Brian said. "No one is allowed to publicly release any medical information or talk about a person's medical information publicly, and that means these, too."

"That's not how it works," Bernie said. "The Health Information Privacy Protection Act is limited to health care providers releasing information." People were always citing HIPPA as an excuse to not give her information. They were almost always wrong.

"Tim says so," Brian said, certain. "It's for privacy, anyway. He says people shouldn't be seeing what everyone is getting at the drugstore. It's nobody's business. We're supposed to put them in the hopper."

"That makes sense," Bernie said. "Not great for the mountain of garbage we're turning the world into, though."

"Everything that goes into the hopper gets incinerated at the place out to Orrington," Brian said. "The truck comes every Wednesday. Twice a week in the summer. Removes the dumpster behind the hopper, ships it to Orrington and incinerates it. So the environment ends up fine."

Right, Bernie thought, but she knew there was no point in arguing.

Brian waved the bag at Moses. "Wayne, you ought to go before Tim sees you. Moses, you bring this to the hopper and make sure you throw it in."

"I'll take them," Wayne said.

"Tim wanted me to sort the glass," Moses said, staring at the ground.

"I'm busy. I can't do it," Brian said.

The hopper was probably two hundred yards away.

"I'll do it," Bernie said. "I've gotta toss mine in anyway."

"I don't know," Brian said.

"I promise I won't read any of the labels." She crossed her heart.

"I'm going to the swap shack," Wayne announced, turning back to his truck. Then to Bernie, "See? I told you."

Right, Bernie thought, trying to remember whether the conversation in the newspaper office had anything to do with any of this.

"Wayne, no. Tim says—Oh brother." Brian watched Wayne scurry back to his truck, then looked at the bag. "Okay, I guess." He gave it to Bernie. "Seriously, don't look, okay? It's about privacy. Tim will get mad."

"Girl Scout's honor," she said, holding up two fingers. She couldn't remember if that was the Girl Scout salute or not. Brian nodded and went after Wayne.

"Told you not to get involved," Sal said when she got back to her car.

"What's the big deal?"

He laughed. "Tim rules the roost. Brian is scared shitless of him. If Tim knew he'd given you that bag of bottles to bring to the hopper, he'd probably kick Brian's ass."

"You know how uptight that is, right?"

"Yeah," Sal said. "I just sit back and watch the show and try to be a friend to Brian."

Bernie threw the bag in the back of her Subaru and bumped around down the hill to the hopper. She enjoyed the hopper, watching its slow, crushing maw relentlessly push the garbage through the hole, bags popping and crushing as they jammed in. Some days, she could stand transfixed, watching bags of garbage slide down the slick metal walls to be pushed and crushed into the dumpster for long minutes. Not today; she had too much to do.

She grabbed her bag of garbage with one hand, the bag of prescription bottles with the other. The bag wasn't closed at the top and bottles spilled out, bouncing and scattering across the wayback. With a silent insincere apology to Brian, she gathered them up, glancing at the labels. Didn't recognize a lot of the patient names anyway, but the familiar Redimere Drug label stood out on most of them. Lots of them were customers—she preferred to think of it that way, rather than patients—of Dr. Chapman. *I got into the wrong racket.* She dumped the handfuls of bottles into the bag and tossed both bags in, watching with satisfaction as they slid down the shiny wet metal wall, falling off the edge into the rectangular hole, the steel wedge pushing them, along with dozens of other bags and loose garbage, into the dumpster.

She caught Wayne's pickup driving slowly by, Wayne watching her from the window, shaking his head sadly. She looked back down at the bag, being crushed with dozens of others fifteen feet below, a roiling mass of bags and garbage, slowly being jammed through the hole, and wished, irrational as it seemed, that she could have that bag of pill bottles back.

. . . . .

Bernie had a driving need to talk to Pete about Sal. Overwhelming. She warred back and forth in her head—bad idea! bad idea!—but it didn't work. She wanted to see what she could find out about the Leslie Lark case, but a lot of it too, she knew, was she just wanted to talk to Pete.

His rusting Volvo wasn't parked out back of his apartment. *Where the hell is he?* She climbed the back steps to his door, knocked anyway, wondering why his kitchen looked so strangely empty.

"Looking for Pete?"

Agnes Dostie was at the bottom of the stairs with a wheelbarrow full of dead plants.

"Yeah," Bernie said, going back down.

"He moved, dear."

"Moved?" Her stomach dropped.

"Didn't he tell you?" Duh, obviously not, Bernie wanted to say, but she gave leeway to eighty-year-old women who could kick her butt. "He bought one of those camps out on the peninsula. Couple months ago. He's fixing it up. We're selling the house. Can't keep it up anymore. We offered it to him, but I think the poor boy wants

151

some peace and quiet. Hard to be a landlord anyway. He was one of the good tenants, but most aren't."

Poor boy? Bernie felt anger surge up and choke her. *How does Pete buy a place and move and never say a word?* "He moved?" She knew she was repeating herself.

Agnes looked sympathetic. "I'm sure it wasn't to get away from you, dear. It probably just slipped his mind to mention it. Maybe he thought he told you when he didn't. Happens to me all the time. More to my husband, though. It's that last camp down on Loon Lane, off the Pond Road. The peninsula on Patton Pond. I'm sure he'd love to see you."

I'm sure, Bernie thought as she got back in her car. *I just bet.* She tried to tamp down her anger as she neared the lake, remind herself that she'd wanted to talk to him. He forgot to tell her he was moving? She'd just been at his apartment a week before—in his bed, for chrissake, him telling her he loved her—and he hadn't said a word. It was hard to tamp down.

She drove down the dirt road to the lake, her car bumping on potholes, roots, and boulders. She passed a few tiny houses set back in the trees, exposed now that the leaves had dropped. Loon Lane still had old traditional camps—small cabins, most seasonal, some year-round homes—but modest, not like the roads farther out, where people like Dr. Chapman had big modern homes on the water. Ostentatious, she always thought, but still keeping our tax base healthy. She was glad, at least, Pete wasn't show-offy in his choice of lakeside home. The majority of the houses on Loon Lane were at the end, on the water, like they were on most of the other camp roads on the lakes. The silver lake blinked up ahead in the filtered sunlight. In summer she'd be driving through a green tunnel, but now, with winter coming on, it was gray and lifeless. A breeze off the water whipped the last of the leaves, the balsams and white pines that stuck up between the granite boulders that lined the shore swayed. The road widened as the first shoreline camp came into view, then a handful of others. None of them were anything fancy: a mish-mash of architecture, small, clapboard-covered, one or two log cabins, most with screened porches and upside-down canoes and woodpiles in the dooryards. Dirt patches passed for driveways.

The road came to the water's edge and paralleled the shore, where the grass verge and pines gave way to a broad vista with flat rocks that jutted out into the lake, whipped by the wind into whitecaps. There were two houses, and beyond them, one last small house, forest green, at the end of the peninsula, nestled against a grove of pines, its front yard flat rock dipping down into the water, and beyond it the lake, framed by the western mountains. As she got closer, she saw Pete's car parked next to a pile of lumber.

She stepped up to the door and heard banging and soft swearing.

"Hello?"

"Come on in."

It was one room, with a kitchen against the far wall. Kind of like hers, but no hallway leading to bedrooms, just a partition with the foot of a bed visible beyond the opening. Boxes, probably his belongings, were stacked against a wall. Power tools, lumber, and plumbing fixtures were lined up neatly on the floor. A French door with two huge windows on either side overlooked the lake. From where she stood, it looked like the water came right up to the house, though she'd seen the rocky yard in between when she'd walked up. Half-built bookshelves lined the space under the windows, and a pellet stove hummed against the wall. As unfinished as it was, she was envious.

Pete's jeans-clad legs, work boots on the end, stuck out from under the kitchen sink. He pulled himself out and sat up. "You found me."

"You can run but you can't hide. Aren't you afraid of getting broken into way out here? Haven't you read it in the *Watcher*? It's an epidemic. Beautiful spot, though. What a view."

He flashed a perfunctory smile and went back under the sink. "I'll take my chances. What can I do for you?"

All business. Okay. "Anything new on the gut pile? Whose it

153

is? Who dunnit?"

"State police are the lead on the case, and all information is coming from them. Sorry."

He didn't sound sorry, but she didn't expect much more anyway.

"Can we talk about my brother?"

"If your brother has information about Leslie Lark's disappearance, he should go to the state police. Otherwise I'm not sure what we'd talk about." The banging continued.

Bernie didn't say anything. What she wanted, she realized, was for Pete to reassure her that Sal wasn't in trouble, but she wasn't sure how to go about it. Talking to his legs and boots made her feel disconnected. The fact that the reception was less than welcoming didn't help.

He swore. "Somebody actually glued these pipe joints together."

"It's nuts what people do," said Bernie, just to have something to say. He grunted acknowledgement. Or maybe just grunted with exertion. As he wrestled with the pipe, he'd stretched out enough that she could see him from the lower ribs down. Despite the cool day and the wind, the house was toasty, and he wore a faded T-shirt. A flannel shirt was folded over the back of the chair and she leaned back and smelled it. It smelled like Pete, soapy and reassuring. He swore again and kicked one leg as he wrestled with the pipe, arching his back. His T-shirt rode up, exposing his flat stomach, the bottom of his ribs still discolored from last summer, a curly brown trail of hair...he'd asked her something.

"What?" she asked, feeling the blush creep up between her shoulder blades to her neck to her face. She felt like she'd been caught.

He slid out from under the sink, pinning her with that laser gaze that lately only seemed to mean trouble, and the spell was broken.

"I asked you what exactly it was you wanted."

She let out a long breath. What did she want? Right now or in general? "I guess I was hoping for some kind of reassurance."

"Your brother may be involved in something serious. He needs to take care of it. I can't help you."

Her anger surged again. Did he think he was telling her something she didn't know? "I understand. But you've investigated a lot of homicides, so I thought you'd have some insight or positive advice." It sounded too stiff. Not what she'd really wanted at all. "Since we're friends," she added.

From his spot on the floor, partially inclined, one arm gripping the counter above him, poised to go back under the sink, he looked vulnerable, despite his growing anger. "I really don't know what you want from me," he said. When she didn't say anything, he went back under the sink.

She knew they were talking about more than Sal. "I'm sorry."

She wondered if she should leave. Part of her wanted to, part didn't. The clanking and banging were distracting, and she wished he'd stop so she could figure out what to say.

"Once I get the plumbing sorted out, most of what I have left to do is cosmetic. After I got my arm back, I was really able to get going on this. I want to get as much as possible done before it gets colder."

It took Bernie a minute to register he was changing the subject, signaling all was forgiven, and trying to have a conversation. She should've felt relieved, but the anger, which had been ebbing, rose again, hotter and sharper. She didn't care about his stupid plumbing. His stupid house that he hadn't even told her he'd bought. *Let's talk about Sal. Or at least about the gut pile. Let's talk about us. Let's talk about all the things that are bothering me.* "My brother is telling the truth."

"Bernie." His tone said conversation over.

"Why can't we talk about that?"

He slid out from under the sink again, sprang to his feet with a pull-up on the counter, and wiped his hands off with a rag before looking at her. "I hope he is. I hope you are, too."

"What's that supposed to mean?"

He took a piece of pipe wrapped in plastic off the counter, and

155

pulled the plastic off, inspected the pipe way more than he needed to, then disappeared back under the sink. "I'm beginning to see what you meant about how we can't be friends, given our positions."

Bernie was stung. "I never said we couldn't be friends."

Pete didn't say anything. She waited, seconds turning into minutes.

She left without saying goodbye.

. . . . .

Sal had made lasagna. Bernie could smell it cooking as she entered and was flung back into childhood, coming in from the cold and dark to warmth and supper cooking, music playing. The smell of sauce, the lingering zip of the meatballs and sausage under it, garlic. Nothing smelled more like love to her. It made her feel better. A little.

Dubya didn't run to greet her like he normally would but stood in the kitchen next to Sal, looking at her with his tail semaphoring, *Look what we're having, Mom!*

"I made lasagna," Sal said.

"So I smell. I forgot to ask earlier, you get a deer today?"

"Naw. Nice hike in the woods, though. Everyone at the dump is saying the gut pile is this guy Benji Reeves. That's the guy your boyfriend was asking about Monday."

She knew damn well who Benji Reeves was. Another story she could have done a better job on. "He's not my boyfriend. Why are they saying that?"

"Guess a couple guys saw him around town, but not since the guts were found. I don't think anyone told your cop that. Reeves wasn't a popular dude. Some of the guys said Benji had a thing with Tim's wife. Tim doesn't like your cop very much, either."

"That was the story, Reeves and Wendy Shaw," Bernie said. "He's not my cop."

"They said that's why Reeves blew town. Tim was going to kick his ass."

"I'm sure he would have," Bernie said, wondering how much

Pete knew, Pete who'd first come to town because of Reeves.

"Wonder where they'll find the rest of him?" Sal said. "That's wild. Being field-dressed like that. Someone said he was castrated and his ass cut out. Someone who really hated his guts must have done that. No pun intended."

"If it was him. Like you said, there's the rest of him to find."

"Wouldn't see me doing that. With a deer, I mean."

"If you ever actually got a deer."

"I've gotten many, as you well know. Few hunters can do that rectum thing without ruining the meat. Whoever did it was someone who knew what he was doing."

"He's not a deer," Bernie said, exasperated. "So it doesn't matter if the meat is ruined."

"There's that."

"Maybe we should talk about this after supper," she said. Then she remembered what Carol had said that morning. "Did you ever say something at the transfer station like you'd like to kill Leslie and truss her up like a deer?"

"God no. Where'd you hear that?"

"Carol said Vince heard it at the transfer committee meeting."

"People are making things up. The only time I've talked about Leslie was my first day, people wanted to know where I came from, and I went on a little about how I had to get off her farm because she was the old ball and chain or something stupid like that. I may have gone on a little, but nothing ugly."

"That's what happens. Rumors get out of hand."

"Brian was really freaked out about Reeves. Guess they hung out together."

"They haven't said it's him," Bernie said, trying to remember if she'd talked to Brian for the story two years before. She hadn't. Shaw wouldn't let any of the transfer station guys talk to her.

Sal shook his head. "Poor Brian. The guy can't catch a break. Tim was up and down his back all day today, screaming at him in the office at one point. What can be so important at a friggin' dump?"

157

CHAPTER 15
2009
Redimere, Maine
Monday, November 16

S al had come in late Sunday night. Or rather, early Monday morning. He'd been at Brian's playing chess. As Bernie got ready for work he snored away on the couch, the cats tucked around him. He didn't have to go to work until noon, so despite her annoyance at him coming in so late, disrupting her fragile sleep, she tiptoed around. Dubya tailed her, poking her calf with his wet snout. She felt guilty that she hadn't spent enough time with him. "You know what? Today is take your dog to work day. I've just decreed it."

He did his happy dance as she held the door for him to follow her out, and leaped in when she opened the car hatch. He picked something up in his mouth, turned around, and grinned. One of the prescription bottles that had fallen out of the bag at the dump.

"Silly, that's not for dogs." She pulled it from between his teeth and picked up two others that she'd missed the other day, putting them in her courier bag as Dubya nosed her hand.

When she got to the office, she called Pete, knowing he'd be at work as early as she was. She'd be cheerful and friendly, pretend Saturday's awkward conversation hadn't happened.

"Were you on painkillers when you were first hurt?"

"Why?"

Remember, cheerful and friendly. "Thinking about prescription bottles." She put her feet up on the desk, watched dead leaves blow across Main Street, rattle against the window. "I'm always afraid to bring mine to the transfer station. Kind of too much information."

"Take the labels off."

"Is that what you do?"

"Are you asking my advice? Making conversation? I have a busy day."

"I'm not sure. I just feel like I want to know more about prescription bottles. Something about them is bugging me and I want to figure out what it is." She saw Wayne Daggett in her head, saying *See? This is what I'm talking about.*

"I got a prescription for Vicodin filled but never took it. I don't like anything stronger than aspirin."

"Where?"

"The hospital," he said. "In Farmington."

"You never went to Chapman or anyone here in town for a refill?"

"Since I didn't use the pills I had, no," he said. "Anyway, I wouldn't go to Chapman. I'd go to the health center, a physician, for pain meds. Why would I go to a psychiatrist?"

After Pete hung up, Bernie rolled one of the prescription bottles from her car in her hand as Dubya watched longingly. It was for Oxycodone, one of the others was for Vicodin. She didn't recognize the name of the person it was prescribed to, but she did recognize the name of the prescribing doctor. Chapman. She'd have to let it fester in her brain more before she could figure it out. Anyway, she had actual stories to deal with. Like the gut pile, though more than a week later the only new thing seemed to be that rumors had reached a fever pitch.

She called Pete a little while later to run the speculation about the gut pile being Benji Reeves past him. He gave monosyllabic snippy answers that left her bereft and more exhausted than she already was.

She tried Dawna and didn't get much farther, though she did confirm in detail that was a little too graphic for Bernie the ins and

159

outs of field dressing a deer.

And Guy. Guy! Her co-worker, her compatriot. The police told him it was okay to tell her what he found. Up to a point. He gave her an exclusive, but he couldn't describe it in more detail than she already knew. In other words, no details about the castration and rectum rumors. He took pity on her and gave her some color, even told her how he threw up. Otherwise, he wouldn't say anything. When she asked a question he couldn't answer, he mimed a zipper across his lips and shook his head. Frustrating.

By eight-thirty she was out of ideas.

"Well, if it isn't fair Bernadette O'Dea." Bernie was startled into reality by the door crash and a booming all-too-familiar annoying voice.

"Fergus Kelley." She almost called him Feckless. "What are you doing here?"

"Answering your prayers." He sat down next to her desk. His gut was a little bigger, his hair thinner and grayer, the red veins on his clumpy nose stuck out a little more. She tried to remember how long it'd been since she'd seen him. Almost three years? He never looked great, but now he looked like he'd aged a decade. Same food stains on his shirt, though. It made her think of Wayne Daggett. Dubya peered at him from his sleeping spot under her desk, then yawned and went back to sleep.

"I thought I'd talked you out of wanting to work here," Bernie said.

He laughed. "Boy, you haven't changed."

"No, I haven't," she said. People gave her a physical reaction. Usually it was mildly pleasant. With Pete it was always sharp, painful, and somehow good even when it was bad. With Feckless Kelley it was always an unpleasant shiver that made her wish he'd go away, and it was always a huge relief when he did. It interested her that, despite the overwhelming unpleasantness of her life, that feeling still stood out.

"You said you'd think about it, and a little birdie told me you called some of the folks at the old shop the other day fishing around

160

for someone. Namely, a reporter to save your ass. So if you're still looking, I'm still available."

"You don't want to work here," Bernie said, but her resolve was crumbling.

"Why not? I need a change of scene. This seems nice," he said, looking around.

"I pay a fraction of what you were making. I thought we went through this last time we talked."

"Like I told you, not a problem. I got severance, so I can afford to work below my worth." He grinned and winked.

Yeah, right. "The stories are mundane. Not what you're used to."

"Well, I heard there's a girl missing in Kennebec County, and a guy in town was asked about it who has the same name as you." Wink wink.

Bernie felt her stomach drop and tried to remember who knew the police had visited Sal. Not that it was a secret, but how would that travel over state lines?

"There's a body in town, too, so that makes two big stories. You going to do all that by yourself? You and this dog?" He frowned at Dubya, who was sniffing his shoes.

"Not a body. Just a gut pile."

"Whatever," Feckless said, moving his feet away from the dog. Another minus. "Look, I can help you out, and you can help me out. I know you need a reporter. I hear you're desperate."

"I'm not desperate, and whatever happened to Leslie Lark, my brother has nothing to do with it, and that's going to become clear soon."

"Easy." He smiled again. So fake, so condescending. "You know you can use me, no matter how innocent your brother may be."

She tried to run through her head how things would play out if she hired him. Feckless was a good enough reporter when he wanted to be, but lazy and only interested in doing stories that would get him attention. If it was "too small," he'd do a half-assed

161

job. She suspected he spent a lot of time sitting in a bar rather than being where he'd said he was, and his coworkers had to pick up the slack. She'd caught him claiming to bosses he'd made a call or checked a source or fact when she knew he hadn't.

On the other hand, she *was* desperate. She knew he could do what she needed. Anyway, she'd be his boss, so she could keep him in line.

"I could get you a resume. References. Clips," he said. "But you don't really need that since you know me." Wink.

Bad idea! Bad idea! "Okay." She couldn't believe it. Knew she might regret it, but she was wiped out. So tired. She needed the help. "Get me that stuff, though, for my personnel files."

"Great! Just gotta go down and get my things and close up the apartment. I can start Wednesday."

"What are you doing here? You didn't drive four hours just to have this conversation."

"I came up to do some hunting since I'm on extended vacation. Kill two birds with one stone. Since I knew you were looking, and you said you'd let me know, I figured I'd come up and see if I liked the place." He grinned and shrugged.

"Get a deer?"

"Came close. Really close. Jumped a huge buck. Massive. But it got away."

Sure. Right. "Next time."

After he was gone, she felt that relief she always felt when he left the room. "Did I really just hire Feckless?" she asked Dubya. He opened his eyes and his tail flopped, then he closed them again. "Yeah, I know," she said.

She emailed a former coworker she knew would be straight with her, confessed she'd hired Feckless Kelley, and asked if there was anything she should know, just to be on the safe side. She could already hear him laughing all the way up Interstate 95.

.....

Dawna absently chewed a breakfast sandwich at Choppy's as she watched her sister Debbie clear the counter, wait on customers, call orders to the grill. She wished her job were as easy as owning a diner. Here it was, mid-morning Monday, and she was still no closer on the gut pile. Well, a little closer. Guy's memory that he'd heard two trucks driving away from the area could be interesting, could be nothing. DNA tests, even if there was a match somewhere, would take forever. No evidence at the scene but shell casings, the sweatshirt cord, that huge dried puddle of blood, and the guts.

"What's up with you today?" Debbie asked.

"Can't talk about it."

"The guts in the woods?"

"Can't talk about it."

"Okay," Debbie said, moving down the counter. "But everyone else is."

Dawna knew that. It's a good thing Guy was the one who found it. He could keep his mouth shut. Everyone seemed to know already about the castration, the rectum. She almost wondered if others had seen it before Guy but not told.

Everyone in the department except Pete hunted, but the guys acknowledged Dawna was the expert, though with a lot of Indian jokes and stereotypes. She knew she was better, not because of her Passamaquoddy heritage, but because she was more observant. Paid more attention to detail and nuance. Stopped and listened. Pete had made her Redimere point man on the gut pile investigation not only because of her expertise and, as he put it, that she's the best investigator in the department, but because he was sure the guts were Benji Reeves, so he'd have to take a step back. That bothered her, too. Not because she didn't trust Pete, but because the state police didn't. It was old news and she should be used to it, but it wasn't helping. Neither was Pete's uncharacteristic off-kilter mood.

She was grimly musing over all this, when Bernie sat on the stool next to her.

"So, what's going on with the guts?" Bernie asked, then to Debbie, "Scrambled eggs, bacon and coffee with no—"

"Yes, I know, no creamer, just some milk. You don't have to say it," Debbie said.

163

Dawna liked the way Bernie got right to the point. No fake small-talk or buttering up. She just wished she hadn't sat next to her.

"No more than last time," Dawna said. "Which I believe was about an hour ago."

"This is a weird question, and very general, but any drug connection?"

Dawna could feel Bernie's eyes on her. She knew that seemingly innocent gaze hid a sharp mind that missed nothing. Weird, general questions always had a basis. "You know I can't say anything, but even if I could there's not enough information to know what connection it has. Why are you asking?"

Bernie stirred milk into her coffee. She had a habit of staring while she was thinking, sometimes right at you, maybe not even seeing what she was looking at, but Dawna could hear the wheels turning, the bearings dropping into place as Bernie considered the details, the angles. She'd seen it before and she didn't like being on the receiving end.

"Has Wayne Daggett talked to you about anything?" Bernie said.

"With this? No. He's obsessed with pill bottles lately, but not this. Why? Please don't do this to me."

"What?" Bernie asked, all innocence, blowing on her coffee, wide eyes and cocked head.

"Please. The chief—"

"Leave my little sister alone," said Debbie, setting Bernie's food in front of her.

"Just doing my job," Bernie said.

"You're badgering a helpless creature," Debbie said, putting her hand up to stop Dawna's protest. "Do it again and next time you order grilled cheese I'm putting pickles on top. A whole jar. And half-n-half in your coffee, too."

"I know when I'm beat." Bernie took a bite of eggs.

"Why don't I believe you?" Debbie asked.

"Can't blame me for trying."

164

"Nope," Dawna said. Now she would have to try to figure out what the hell Bernie was talking about and see if there was anything to it.

Bernie's cellphone rang. "Pete," she said to Dawna as she answered. "What's up?"

"I'm calling to make sure Sal's at your house. I'm on my way there with Trooper Frazer as well as some police who are going to execute a search warrant."

"What?" Pete was quiet for so long, Bernie thought her phone had dropped the call. "Pete?"

"I don't have to tell you any of this, okay?"

"Any of what?"

"Just get home."

. . . . .

A Redimere cruiser and two from the state police, as well as an obvious unmarked police car, were in her driveway. She'd called Bobby Dolan and left a brief breathless message on his voicemail as she'd fetched Dubya from the office, run to her car, him racing her with happy abandon, and driven back up the hill. When she threw the door open, Dubya leaped on Sal, who was standing in his underwear with a blanket around his shoulders, surrounded by Pete, Trooper Frazer, and several guys in suits, obvious cops. They turned to look at her as Dubya danced from them to her barking, *look who's here, look who's here.*

"Sal, don't talk," she said.

"I was just asking if I could put some pants on," he said with annoyance.

"Your car was found," Frazer said to Sal.

"What? Where?" Sal asked.

"Sal, don't talk," Bernie said. "I've left a message with Bobby."

"Bobby who? My car—"

"Sal." Bernie stood between him and the cluster of police. "He's not talking."

"Mr. O'Dea, we'd like to ask you a few questions in Farmington," Frazer said.

165

"Where did you find my car?"

Pete touched Bernie's arm. "Move aside, okay?" he asked. The fact he asked so kindly just made her angrier.

"Don't touch me," she snarled. "Goddamit, Sal, don't talk."

"What I really want is to put my pants on. That open door is not helping." He took the blanket from around his shoulders and wrapped it around his waist. "What's happening?"

"We'd like you to come with us to answer some questions," Frazer said.

"If you're not charging him, he doesn't have to go anywhere or talk to you," Bernie said.

"It would be a lot easier if he came and talked to us," Frazer said.

"Don't fall for that trick, Sal," Bernie said. "You know better." She turned to Frazer. "He's not saying anything without a lawyer."

Frazer ignored her. Bernie tried to avoid Pete's eye, but she could feel the heat from his stare.

"We also have a warrant to search the premises," one of the plainclothes guys said.

"I'd like to see it," Bernie said.

He handed Bernie a folded piece of paper. She opened it, looked, her focus so off the charts it might as well have been in Greek.

Sal slumped to the couch, his pants forgotten, the blanket in a pool around his bare feet, his face white. Dubya jumped up and sat next to him.

"Sally, why don't you put some pants on?" Bernie said. He didn't seem to hear. She grabbed the pair of jeans resting on his duffle bag and tossed them to him. They landed on his lap.

The cold wind blew into the room and Bernie slammed the door shut. "Until you charge my brother, he doesn't have to talk to you. You can't make him." She knew she was repeating herself, but no one seemed to be listening.

"We want to find out how Ms. Lark's cellphone ended up in your car, which was found in the parking lot at Bigelow Park this morning," Frazer said to Sal. "We don't even have to tell you that much."

"Bigelow Park?" Sal said. "She had my car, so yeah, her phone would be in it. Where is that? Why's my car there? Wednesday—"

Bernie turned her back on the police and glared at her brother. "Don't fucking talk."

Sal seemed to suddenly process what Frazer was saying. "Wait, where's Leslie? What're you saying?" He slowly started to pull his jeans on, not standing up. "I wonder if it was that pot thing."

"Sal shut up."

Frazer moved closer to Sal. "Please get up."

"Are you charging him? Because that doesn't seem like a lot to hang a charge on to me." Bernie wanted to make them say it if they were going to take her little brother away.

"Bernie," Pete said, taking her arm and moving her aside as Frazer jerked Sal up from the couch.

Bernie shook off Pete's arm, "Are you arresting him?" she asked. No one answered. The other cops stood quietly. Dubya was quiet now, too, watching.

Sal opened his mouth. "Don't fucking TALK!" Bernie said again, panic making her voice way too high-pitched and cracky. She knew she sounded like she was going to start crying. Maybe she was.

There was a knock at the door and a whirlwind of plaid and paisley blew in. Kermit O'Neil. "My client won't be talking at this juncture."

"Your client?" Bernie asked.

"We're taking him to Farmington," Frazer said. He'd cuffed Sal's hands behind his back and was pulling him out the door. "Can you move your car, Ms. O'Dea?"

Bernie was confused, angry, paralyzed. She looked around for her keys, then realized she'd left them in the ignition.

"Move your car," Kermit said to her, way too matter-of-fact. "Sal, don't say anything until Bobby gets there." Kermit took Sal's coat off the hook by the door. "This yours?" Sal nodded, dazed. Kermit put it over his shoulders. "The guy is in a T-shirt, and it's

167

thirty degrees out," he said, directed more toward Pete than Frazer.

"Please move your car, Miss," Frazer said.

Bernie wanted to refuse, but they all were looking at her, waiting. She slammed out of the house, backed it out into the street, tires screeching.

Frazer was already hustling Sal to the cruiser as she got out.

"Sal," Bernie said.

He looked at her, eyes wide, as Frazer pushed his head down and eased him into the backseat. Deer in the headlights, Bernie thought, then kicked herself for the cliché.

Pete lagged behind. "Bernie."

"Just go," she said, fury and the threat of tears making it impossible to say more. "Go."

He looked for a second like he wasn't going to. Then he did.

She turned to Kermit. "Where's Bobby? Why are you here?"

"He called and asked me to make sure your brother was protected. Come back in where it's warm."

The other cops stood, waiting, in the living room.

"We are executing a search of the premises as well as Mrs. O'Dea's purse," one of them said to Kermit.

"Where's the warrant?"

Bernie handed the warrant to Kermit. "It's a courier bag," she said to the cop.

"This is all in order," Kermit said. He drew himself up to his full height, which was about even with Bernie's five-three. "I'll find out what's going on and get this straightened out. Or Bobby will."

Bernie collapsed on the couch as the cops started opening drawers.

"Your purse, Mrs. O'Dea?" One of the cops stood in front of her.

"Miss. Ms.," she said, handing it to him. "It's a courier bag." She watched him dump it on the chair, her notebooks, camera, protein bars, pencils, tampons, and a million other things she didn't remember she had, spilling out. Dubya picked up an empty prescription bottle as it rolled onto the floor and trotted to the kitchen, tail high and spinning like a helicopter blade. She heard a cop murmur to him and turned to see him prying it from Dubya's unwilling teeth.

"Can you put the dog outside, Mrs. O'Dea?"

Bernie turned to Kermit, who was watching the search. "Does Bobby know what's going on? Where's Leslie? What are they looking for?"

"I don't know anything right now."

"What do we do?"

"Bobby's going to see what he can find out. They have to charge Sal within forty-eight hours, though if they don't find anything I can't imagine they'd charge him on the flimsy evidence they think they have. If they do, it'll be a day or two before they transfer him to Wiscasset —"

"Wiscasset?" This was going too fast.

"Right," Kermit said patiently, as though they were having a conversation over coffee. "The Franklin County jail is now a holding facility. Longer-term prisoners go to Wiscasset."

How could she have forgotten? The fact Franklin County's prisoners were now sent more than two hours away because of state jail consolidation had been the topic of numerous stories over the past year. Suddenly those stories meant something. "That's too far away. I need to talk to Sal."

"Sit tight for now. He could be home tomorrow."

"Miss, whose phone is this?" the cop searching her bag held up a cellphone, gingerly, between glove-clad fingers.

Bernie was about to say, "Mine, of course," but hers was still clutched in her hand, where it had been since she'd grabbed it in her car. "I don't know." Sal's, of course. But she knew better than to give them anything.

He put it in a plastic evidence bag. He took another evidence bag and filled it with the prescription bottles that had been in her bag.

She wanted to run screaming from the house, run after her brother, or Pete, get Pete back here. But she was paralyzed, rooted

169

to the couch.

"Don't worry," Kermit said. "I have to go. Don't talk to anybody. Particularly the cops." He gave Bernie a meaningful look, ignoring the three cops bustling around him. "Particularly Pete."

CHAPTER 16
2009
Redimere, Maine
Monday, November 16

Don Littlefield's crew got started mid-morning Monday cleaning up the scarecrows along Main Street and a couple of side streets. Usually they got to them earlier, but they were short-handed, like everyone else. One of the ironies of the Great Recession: lots of folks out of work, but town budgets slashed so they couldn't fill positions, and no matter how unemployed someone was, nobody wanted to pick up garbage for a living.

Weeks ago, the scarecrows had been fun and festive—for about five minutes, Don thought—but now they were ragged and soggy. The contest was dumb, anyway, but what did he know? No one came back to pick up their mess after the prizes were handed out, and it was up to him and the crew to get them. That's what it was, a mess.

He was glad he was driving the truck, not picking up the dreck. Old clothes filled with straw and leaves, or god knows what. They stunk, they fell apart when the guys picked them up. Worse than collecting garbage.

The guys tossing them into the back of the garbage truck had been bitching all morning. What'd they know? He'd done a stint on a real garbage crew in Bangor when he was in college. This was picking flowers compared to that. The town didn't have garbage collection, and the truck was used mostly to pick up the trash at town hall, the public safety building, the elementary school, the parks. Once in a while something like this.

He watched Bernie O'Dea's Subaru turn the corner and fly up the hill toward her house. That gal has a pretty heavy foot on the gas, he thought. Won't ever see good old Pete give her a ticket though. He felt bad for the girl, hooking up with Pete. Not that he was a bad guy, but must be better guys in town for a single lady with a good job and with no kids to get in the way. Pete was a moody fella, and he didn't even hunt. Didn't seem to have a lot that would attract a single girl who could have her pick of Redimere's bachelors. Hell, Don thought, if he wasn't married he'd make a play for her himself.

Today's job was tedious, but he didn't mind. Drive half a block. Stop. Drive another half block. Beat being back in the office dealing with paperwork and budgets. Stop. Start. Fifty yards at a time. They were on School Street when he heard the guys behind the truck yipping louder than they'd been. He turned up the radio, letting it and the drone of the truck's hydraulic lift and the crunch of its steel maw drown them out. What a couple of pussies. He closed his eyes, hoping for a thirty-second catnap before he had to drive the half block to the next scarecrow.

Frantic banging on his window jumped him back to life. Don turned, ready to rip the guy a new asshole, when he saw the mess on the guy's work gloves, a stark contrast to his bone-white face. Dark red, black, gooey.

He rolled down the window, trying to ignore the pitch in his stomach, hoping that wasn't blood. Gooey, thick blood. "What's the problem?"

"You gotta come out here."

Don heaved himself out of the truck. "Used to be a little bit of mess didn't bother a guy," he grumbled, going for bravado, praying he wouldn't need it.

As he rounded the back, he saw the other guy, Moses Mosher, bent over vomiting. Kid always was a little soft.

Then he saw the scarecrow. Only it wasn't one. It was a body.

Jeans soaked black, a hoodie, hard to tell what the original color was, soaked dark red and black, riding up around his neck. The hood up, but from what he could see, only a partial head, the rest a blown-up glob of blood, tissue, bone, and hair. The white, white skin of the torso, what was left of it, exposed. It mostly gaped open. Kind of like someone had field-dressed him.

Moses was crying. It sounded like he was saying, "Oh no, Brian, oh no." But the body, or what was left of it, wasn't Brian, because he'd just seen him a couple hours ago at the transfer station, begging off garbage truck duty because he had a cold and didn't think he'd be able to keep up.

"Shut up, Moses," Don said, annoyance not nearly the shield against what was in front of him that he'd hoped. "Brian isn't here."

Don choked back the vomit he felt rising and pulled out his cellphone.

He got Pete's voicemail. "Pete? Come on down to School Street, will ya? I think we found the body the gut pile belongs to."

. . . . .

Pete had just pulled out of Bernie's driveway and started down the hill toward Main Street when he saw the public works truck. Don and the boys picking up the scarecrows. Well, at least one thing was going right.

Then again, maybe not.

Don was waving wildly at him. Was that Moses Mosher vomiting on someone's front lawn?

Pete pulled over, watching the tail lights of the state cruiser ahead of him disappear around the corner at the bottom of the hill.

"What is it?" he asked Don, who was sweaty, breathless and white-faced.

"Just left you a message, just now," Don said. "The body, missing its guts. And other stuff." He pointed.

Pete walked over to what he thought had been a scarecrow. It wasn't. It was an eviscerated body, and though the clothes were soaked black with dried blood, he saw enough brown to know it was the same hoodie he'd seen on Benji Reeves. The stench that

173

rose from it was unmistakable. That familiar smell of blood and decomposing body that could even overwhelm a hot Philadelphia dumpster in the summer.

He pulled out his cell. "Dawna, let Libby know we've got a body on School Street. Looks like it could be a match for the guts. Keep it off the scanner."

"Where on School Street?" He heard the strain in her voice.

"Just around the corner from Main. Nowhere near Bernie's."

"Got it."

Don and his crew were huddled together, none of them looking at what was left of Benji Reeves. "You guys didn't touch it, did you?"

One of the guys held up his gloved hands, caked with blood. "Sorry. I wasn't really looking and started to pull it. Then Moses screamed."

"Not really screamed," Moses said, his chin and the corners of his mouth wet with vomit and his cheeks with tears. "Brian's not here."

"It's all right, we're here instead," Pete said. "Let's stay away until the state cops get here."

The four of them stood next to the truck, looking across the street, at the bare trees, the slate-gray November sky, at the mountains rising into the clouds, the pavement. Not at each other. And definitely not at the limp, stinking pile of skin, bones, and blood-caked clothes in the gutter.

An occasional car drifted by, slowed to see what was going on, but so far no one seemed to catch on. After all, it was just a public works truck and crew, a cop, and a scarecrow.

. . . . .

Bernie wanted to call in sick after the state police questioned her, which mercifully happened in her living room. They threatened they'd have more questions later. Took her prints right there, ignoring her tears of humiliation.

But she couldn't call in sick. She was the boss.

Almost worse than the confusion and questioning about the

174

cellphone and pill bottles was the call from her sister Theresa.

She'd just come in from walking Dubya after the cops left, something she knew didn't make sense, but she wanted to avoid people, work, questions. She went up the hill, up out of town. She wasn't going to go downtown after that scene. Her cellphone, which the police hadn't taken, thank god, was ringing on the counter when she got back.

"I don't know where to start," Theresa said, without saying hello, so loud Bernie had to hold the phone away from her ear. "I guess with the biggest thing. How does our brother get taken into custody and the rest of us don't even know he's in Maine?"

Bernie knew she wouldn't have to say a word. Yet.

"I expect him to be this goddam irresponsible, but I expect more from you. Do you have any idea what it's going to take to get him out of this mess? He was living in Vassalboro? With Leslie fucking Lumpkin?"

"Yep, surprise to me, too," Bernie said.

"Not according to Bobby Dolan, who I just had the humiliating experience of hearing from not only that my brother is in custody on a possible murder charge, but that the cops had talked to him *last week* about his missing girlfriend. At your house."

"We were going to call—"

"When? Never mind. Tell me what's going on."

"Sal showed up a couple weeks ago. He'd been fired—" She could hear Theresa draw in a breath to start yelling again, so she hurried the rest out. "He was afraid to tell anyone, so he was living with Leslie. He showed up here, then she disappeared. I guess they found his car, and it has her cellphone in it. I don't know how they get murder from that."

"That's obviously the short version. They haven't charged him, at least. I'll call Mom and Dad. You sit tight and do whatever it is you do, but when I have time from trying to sort this out, I want to hear the long version."

Bernie realized, with relief and guilt, Theresa didn't seem to know that Sal's missing cellphone had been found in her courier bag a little while ago.

"Bernie," Theresa said, her voice quiet, firm. "They'll figure it out. If not the cops, then Bobby. And us."

Bernie wasn't so sure.

CHAPTER 17
2009
Redimere, Maine
Tuesday, November 17

Bernie spent Tuesday morning in a weird state of suspended animation as she confronted a new world in which her loved and loving baby brother had been taken into custody to possibly be charged with murder.

An early phone call from Bobby gave her hope but added to her confusion.

The prints on Sal's cellphone weren't Bernie's, which she could have told them in the first place. She'd wracked her brain trying to figure out how Sal's phone got in her bag, but couldn't. Bobby said it didn't matter for now. While Sal's car was a circus of fingerprints, his prints weren't on Leslie's phone or bag, both found in his car. In fact, they were wiped clean. There were at least three sets on his steering wheel, even though Sal said no one had ever driven his car but him and Leslie. "He just bought it last year," Bobby said.

They also found the note he'd left her on her kitchen table, with his prints, hers, and someone else's. Good old-fashioned fingerprint evidence to the rescue.

Still. "Nothing makes sense," Bernie said.

"It's good when nothing makes sense," Bobby said. "If it did make sense and pointed to your brother, then you worry."

The best news was Bobby had worked his magic and they were letting Sal go, for now. He wasn't cleared, though. Bobby's call was followed by one from Theresa, telling Bernie she'd been elected to pick Sal up in Farmington.

"Pat and I have court," Theresa said. "Makes much more sense for you to get him. You're right there."

Of course! So much sense! Bernie lived half an hour away. So, not right there. She was busy, too. In fact so busy she doubted she'd get this week's paper out. Tuesday was her busiest day. But yeah, no problem, whatever. She didn't have the energy to argue.

As she sat at her desk her ears still rang from Theresa's lecture about keeping Sal in line, how the charges were still hovering, how if Sal screwed up, all their careers would be over.

She opened her email, looking for Carrie's meeting story, which she'd almost forgotten about. She hoped it didn't suck. Her heart sank as she read, "There was a fire next door so they canceled the meeting."

There was a fire and Carrie didn't let her know? Bernie would have told her to cover it. She stopped mid-curse when she realized there were attachments. A story, a lengthy one, about the fire, with quotes from the chief and state fire marshal, from neighbors and the homeowner. The family dog had died. Carrie had its name and breed.

And photos. Good ones. Firefighters silhouetted against flames and smoke. A child forlornly holding a dog's leash as a woman hugged him. Holy shit.

"We've got a fire story," she told Guy. It was great, but she wanted to cry. She had so much to do. So much. So many stories that she couldn't even remember whether they were being written or not. Twenty-four hours to put out the paper. She had to go to Farmington to get Sal.

"We need to talk about where we're at with the gut pile story, now that there's a body to go with the guts," she said to Guy. "There's a state police press conference this afternoon. Then there's the Sal story."

"We'll figure it out."

Her phone rang. She wanted to throw it through the window.

178

She answered it instead. "What?"

A pause. Then, "It's Carrie. I wanted to make sure you got my story."

"I did," Bernie said. She felt bad she'd been rude when she answered, so she tried to sound happy. Which she was, just overwhelmed. "Nice job."

"I tried calling you last night but your voice mail was full."

Right. "Sorry about that."

"I heard they picked up that body yesterday, too, and there's a press conference?"

"You did?"

"I have a friend at Redimere College I crashed with, so I'm still in town. I get state police email alerts." The most words in a row Bernie had ever heard from her. There were a few more. "Do you want me to come in and help?"

.....

Bernie had an early afternoon appointment with Dr. Chapman, since her prescription had only been for a week. She had to go, but she didn't want to take the time out, time crashing after her, like that poem she had to memorize in seventh grade, *But at my back I ever hear, time's winged chariot hurry near...* Drowned out, as usual, by the Talking Heads, *Can't write a letter, can't send no postcard, I ain't got time for that now...* That song. Always in her head, zipping and dancing through all other thoughts. She sat down in the chair next to Chapman's desk, trying to not think about how much she had left to do. She pictured driving to Farmington, feeling herself in the car, waiting for Sal to emerge, driving back, like if she could picture it, go through every step, it'd be done and over and she could get back to work.

"How's that new dose working for you?" he asked.

"Good," she said, wanting to add, except for this minute, when I have a seventeenth-century poem and a 1978 song competing in my head while I'm typing on my computer and driving to Farmington, trees zipping past, even though I appear to be sitting here, mixed for some reason with the elfin figure of Wayne Daggett

179

saying "See? SEE?"

Ain't got time for that now... "It lasts longer. Took me a while to realize I needed to take it earlier in the morning or I'd be up all night. Not that I'm not up all night anyway."

"Still doing the midnight walkabouts?" he asked, reaching for a pack of gum on his desk and unwrapping a piece as he stared at his computer screen.

"More or less." She wondered if he saved the gum chewing just for her, knowing how crazy it made her, how his gum chomping and snapping tore through her head like a jackhammer.

He held out the pack and she shook her head. "How about I prescribe a sleep aid?"

"I'd rather not take any more drugs."

He jammed the stick of gum in his mouth and sighed heavily, then, for a change looked right at her. He looked as tired as she felt. "Medication helps a brain function the way nature intended it to. If you had a broken leg, you'd want crutches, right?"

"I take the pill so I can get through the day, but that's enough for me. I'm just as happy to be who I am."

"Even if you can't sleep?"

"Even if I can't sleep."

"How's your anxiety?"

She didn't want to keep having the same conversation. *Off the charts. Duh.*

"Let me guess. Your brother is arrested, you're trying to run a newspaper. You're having sex with someone you shouldn't be. Yada yada yada."

"Yada," she said. "Except for the sex part. That was a one-time thing."

"I suppose you don't want anxiety meds either?"

"Nope."

"Suit yourself." He tapped the keyboard, snapping the gum between his teeth. She tried not to cringe with each snap. "That's something about that body," he said.

"Yeah." She didn't want to talk about it.

"Grisly. You must get a lot of details over at the newspaper."

Not really. Hardly any. "Yeah."

"Exsanguinated," he said.

"Exsanguinated," she repeated, rolling the word around in her mouth. "Exsanguinated."

"It means drained of all blood," he said. Snap. Chomp.

"I know what it means. I just like saying it."

"Yup," he said his eyes on the screen, working the gum with gusto. "Gutted. Castrated. Drained. Like a deer in the wrong place at the wrong time."

"Except he wasn't a deer."

"Half his head blown away."

Bernie hadn't heard that. She nodded.

"People are wondering if your brother did it."

"Who's saying that?" Her neck burned, the heat traveling up to her ears, down her back.

He stopped typing. Looked at her again. "I'm just telling you what I heard."

"Because someone said at the transfer station committee meeting he said he'd do that to Leslie? Because first of all, he never said that, and second of all, it's two different things. Third of all, he didn't know Benji Reeves and would have no reason to kill him. Fourth, my brother wouldn't kill anyone anyway."

"Pee in the cup?"

"Yes." She looked to make sure her bag was on the chair by his desk where she'd left it when she went into the bathroom. "Still not a drug dealer."

"Ha ha," he said, staring at the computer. He snapped his gum. Loud. Like a gunshot.

But now the gum didn't bother her. What he'd said about Sal didn't either. Because she knew, with a startling blast of clarity through the poem, the song, the driving, the empty newspaper pages, the noise, the gum, the anxiety, and everything else, how Sal's cellphone got in her bag.

. . . . .

"Everyone's talking about the body," Walt said, when Pete stopped in the Country Grocer to pick up a sandwich. "They think it's Reeves."

Pete couldn't see anyone else in the store, though he knew Wendy was out back. He kept his voice low. "What're people saying?"

"Mostly he had it coming," Walt said. "Consensus seems to be divided between something to do with drugs that pissed someone off and the mysterious Sal O'Dea."

Pete was about to respond when Walt looked beyond Pete. "What can I do for you, sweetheart?"

Natalie Perry was behind him. Pete moved aside, and she put a pair of man's work gloves on the counter.

"Are these for your dad?" Walt asked, as he sorted out the tag to scan them in.

"Me," she said.

"These are a little big for you. We have some nice kids' mittens over there."

"My dad is taking me hunting and I need gloves," she said.

A customer came in the store, wearing obviously brand-new fleece and the condescending expression of an out-of-stater.

"Officer, sir," he nodded to Pete, then to Walt. "I'm looking for the Four Seasons Guide Service? The GPS in my SUV can't seem to find Old Mountain Road."

"I'll show you on a map," Walt said. "Soon as I'm done with my customer."

"Tell you what," Pete said to Natalie. "I'll help you find a pair that's a better fit." He nodded to Walt. "And you can help this gentleman."

Natalie looked like she wanted to say no, but Walt handed Pete the gloves and Pete gave her what he hoped was a reassuring smile.

"I bet we can find a pair that's just right," he said, walking down the aisle. She waited a beat, then followed, gripping the shoulder straps of a new bright pink backpack and looking straight ahead.

182

Pete put the men's gloves—size large—back. "Hold out your hands so I can see what size you need."

She held out chubby and dimpled tiny ten-year-old hands. He squinted, making a show of sizing them up. She rolled her eyes, but he could see the hint of a smile for the first time since he'd met her. All the gloves on the rack were men's and women's, way too big. A rack nearby held mittens, but Pete didn't see any kid-sized gloves.

"I don't want anything pink," she said, shrugging the new backpack. "Pink's for babies."

"I wouldn't dream of it," he said. His eyes fell on a box of bright hunter orange knits. He sifted through and found a pair of mittens, not too big, ones where the finger tops flipped open.

"These are pretty cool," Pete said. "Mittens to keep you warm, but when you need your fingers, ta da! Why don't you try them on?" he said, feeling way more pleased than he should.

She put them on, flipped back the tops and laughed. "Ta da!" she said, raising her arms in the air, her smile all dimples and sunshine.

Pete laughed too, until he saw, as her coat sleeve pulled down, a constellation of round, upraised red scars on the inside of her forearm. He wanted to grab her arms for a closer look, fought the urge, felt that tightness in the pit of his stomach.

"I'll buy these," she said, turning back to the counter, her Disney princess backpack bobbing ahead of him.

"Find anything?" Walt asked.

"Yep," Natalie said, putting the gloves on the counter.

Walt scanned them in. "That's $12.99."

Natalie took a change purse out of her coat pocket. "I only have ten dollars," she said, after counting. Her lip trembled. "I'll put them back."

"I happen to have three dollars," Pete said, taking out his wallet.

"I better put them back."

"Consider it a loan," Pete said. "When you have it, you can come over to the police station and pay me back."

183

She looked at the gloves, then the three dollars, then up at Pete, her eyes wet. "I don't want you to think I'll forget."

"I know you won't," he said.

She turned to Walt. "I guess I'll buy them after all."

Walt rang them up, wrapped them in tissue, and put them in a bag, winking at Pete as he did. "You'll have some good hunting."

"I don't want to shoot deer," Natalie said. "But once I can shoot a gun, then I can make sure no one can hurt anyone else."

"Wow," Walt said, after the door closed. "You may have to put that little vigilante behind bars."

"Does she come in here often?" Pete asked.

"Often as anyone else."

"With her dad?"

"Yeah, most of the time. Why?"

"How is he with her?"

"Same as he is with everyone," Walt said. "Gruff. A little scary. What's up?"

"Nothing. A strange dynamic, Eli Perry with a kid."

"Who knows? Maybe he's father of the year."

"I doubt it," Pete said as he turned to go. "Doubt it very much."

CHAPTER 18
2009
Redimere, Maine
Tuesday, November 17

Bernie was anxious on the ride to Farmington. Anxious to get her brother, anxious to get back to work, hoping she didn't miss the press conference, thinking about the paper, the stories, the pages, thinking about Wayne Daggett for whatever reason, Sal's cellphone. All the things she had to do.

She hadn't told anyone about her epiphany that someone had put the cellphone in her courier bag last Monday when she was at Chapman's office. Sal had lost it that morning, almost first thing, at the transfer station. She knew Chapman had been there. Her appointment was later that day. Leslie had texted Sal sometime Monday about his car. Someone had texted back, Bernie had deduced that from the questions the cops had asked her. Why would Chapman do it? No idea. She'd Googled him. Nothing. He'd been in Redimere since 1999, though, so nothing was going to show up on Google she didn't know about anyway. It seemed so unlikely even she had trouble with it. But as Sherlock Holmes said, once you eliminated the whatever, the blah blah blah was what was left. She couldn't remember the quote, her head was too loaded with stuff, but she remembered the idea of it. She had to tell the cops, but she had to figure it out first and make it plausible, or they'd dismiss it. She'd thought of running it by Pete, but she couldn't remember if they were mad at each other, where that stood. She didn't want to

185

take the chance he'd dismiss it simply out of annoyance with her.

When she'd left for Farmington, Guy and Carrie had been working away. They seemed to hit it off, and Carrie seemed to know her way around the computer, so that was good.

"Don't worry," Guy said when he shooed her out the door. "We've got it covered."

But Bernie did worry. She worried a lot. She was going to pick up her brother who'd just spent a night in jail for something so confusing that the only thing she could be sure of is that he didn't do it. Whatever it even was, since Leslie's body, unlike Benji Reeves', hadn't turned up eviscerated. Exsanguinated. Or at all, for that matter. Chapman. What a phony bastard. "Lying phony bastard," she said out loud. It made her feel a little better.

Staged. That's what it seemed. Both Reeves' sad end and whatever happened with Leslie, like someone was playing a game. She didn't trust the police to be smart enough to see it like that. She knew what happened once they set their minds on one person. They stopped looking. No matter how scant the evidence against Sal, they may still like him for it, as they say. And Chapman? No way, not a doctor. They'd never buy it. She turned up the CD player, Talking Heads. Kept hitting the repeat button. *We dress like students, we dress like housewives, or in a suit and a tie...* She sang along. *I changed my hairstyle so many times now, I don't know what I look like.*

She was surprised to see Bobby Dolan at the jail when she walked in. "I thought no one was going to be here," she said.

"I had a cancelation at the courthouse and wanted to talk to you and Sal."

Bernie looked at her watch. "I need to get back for a press conference, and I have a lot to do."

"It'll just take a minute."

Bobby reached for her arm, his face all soft and squishy like he was going to say something intimate, but they were interrupted by Sal coming through the door. The relief made her giddy. She wasn't sure if it was from seeing her brother walk out of jail, or because Bobby had let go of her arm and stepped away.

Bernie hugged Sal. "You look tired."

"Let's just get out of here," he said.

Outside, Bobby walked with them to Bernie's car. "It's not over. It almost is, but not yet."

Bernie wondered if she should tell him about her Sal's cellphone/Chapman theory, but her brain was too full, the thought of trying to explain it exhausting.

"Sal," Bobby said. "I know you didn't kill Leslie or Benji Reeves—"

"Kill Benji Reeves? I don't even know Benji Reeves. The gut pile guy?"

Bobby gave him a reassuring smile. "We'll talk tomorrow. I can't stress enough that you need to stay home and go to work and nothing else. Keep your head down."

The music in Bernie's head swelled. *You ought to know not to stand by the window, somebody see you up there...*

Sal shook his head, hard, like Dubya trying to shake off rain. "What the hell is happening?"

"Sal, look at me," Bobby said. "Do you understand?"

"Yes."

Bobby turned to Bernie. "Bernie?"

"What's Sal and Leslie got to do with Reeves?"

"Something came up today. Obviously, Reeves isn't a story you can cover either now, so be careful."

"Obviously," Bernie said, too dazed to be annoyed that Bobby was telling her how to do her job.

"I gotta run. I'll talk to you two later."

Bernie called Guy. "Can we send Carrie to the Reeves press conference?" There couldn't possibly be anything that tied Sal to Reeves. But she'd have to wait for the press conference to find out what the latest fiasco was. When she turned the ignition, the music came on full blast.

This ain't no party, this ain't no disco, this ain't no foolin' around...

"Jesus, Bernie," Sal yelled.

"Sorry." She turned it down.

187

"Just turn it off."

She drove out of the parking lot, heading north on Route 27. Sal leaned his head against the window, staring at the passing scenery.

"How was the hoosegow? Anyone make you his bitch?" Bernie asked, feeling slightly better now that he was out of jail, now that she thought she could explain the cellphone.

"Shut up," Sal said.

"Just trying to lighten the mood."

"I'm not in the mood for the mood to be lightened."

After a few miles he said, "So gut pile boy really was Reeves."

"The one and only."

"I don't even know that guy. How could they think I had anything to do with that?"

"No idea. Did Leslie know him?"

"No idea."

They rode in silence, Bernie with the pedal to the floor. Maybe she couldn't cover the press conference, but she was sure as hell going to it so she could find out what the hell was going on.

Sal sighed, a low "Oh my god," and closed his eyes.

"Don't worry," she said. "Everything's going to be okay. I can almost guarantee it." She wasn't sure if she was trying to convince him, or herself.

. . . . .

George Libby, the state police investigator, was waiting in the conference room when Pete got back to the office, Vicki told him. "He said he wants to see you pronto. ASAP. The second you walk in."

"Okay," Pete said, biting back his usual Vicki annoyance, coupled with the annoyance of being ordered around by Libby. "Can you dig up the number for our DHHS child services contact?"

"Everything okay?" she asked.

"It's fine. Leave the number on my desk."

When he walked into the conference room, Libby launched right in. "The blood in O'Dea's trunk belongs to Reeves, not Lark, though Lark's blood is in the backseat."

"If the gunshots Dawna heard are what killed Reeves, O'Dea was asleep on his sister's couch," Pete said. "That's on top of the fact no one can find a connection with O'Dea and Reeves. It doesn't make sense. I'm not feeling O'Dea as the killer of either of them."

Libby smiled, that condescension from the state investigator Pete would never get used to. "He may have a nice sister, but I still wouldn't necessarily trust her to alibi him. Anyway, domestic violence murders know no class or education level, you know that."

"I know that," Pete said. He'd investigated more murders in a year at his old job than this guy would in his career. "That still doesn't explain Reeves. With the pot angle, Lark may not be domestic violence, and we don't even know if she's dead. O'Dea didn't say the things someone who's guilty usually says. Didn't try to explain away things or divert us. He was genuinely confused. Though there are things he's not telling us."

"There always are," Libby said. "We're not getting anywhere with the pot angle, anyway. Lark apparently was looking into being a grower, but so far it seems all by the book. The pot guys O'Dea told us about seem to not exist. It'd help if he knew more than first names." Even Libby's air quotes around pot guys irritated Pete.

"I talked to a friend of yours today," Libby said. "Cheryl Donovan."

"About?"

"See what she could tell us about Reeves, though if his murder had to do with any of that Donovan case, you'd think it would have happened in Philly. Called him JP. Weird disconnect there."

"I know."

Libby continued, "Reeves got along great with the mom, Linda, and with Cheryl and her kids. Not so much with Brandon, who would have been his half-brother if he'd really been JP."

"Yup." This wasn't anything Pete didn't know.

"Cheryl said that JP—the real JP, though she said 'JP before he went away'—never got along with Brandon and had accused him of

189

molesting him shortly before he went missing."

The Donovans had never told Pete that. Reeves had once, but he didn't believe him, couldn't figure out how Reeves would know. Pete felt a bolt of shock, betrayal. It must have shown.

"Cheryl said they didn't tell you because JP lied all the time, and Brandon would never do anything like that. She didn't want to get Brandon in trouble for what she said was no good reason. She hoped you wouldn't be mad." He smiled.

All that time Pete had spent with the Donovans trying to get information and they held out the one piece that could have led him to the truth.

"I guess one night she and Reeves were having a few drinks and she brought it up, that little JP had accused Brandon of molesting him all those years ago," Libby said.

"And?"

"She said Reeves flipped out, told her they were all crazy, got his stuff and moved out of Mom Linda's house."

"Really."

"Really. That was," he flipped through his notebook. "March 2008."

CHAPTER 19
2008
Philadelphia
August 21

Pete had seen Benji Reeves, or JP Donovan, or whatever he wanted to call himself, a few times in his last year in Philadelphia. He tried to talk to him, draw him out, but Reeves was cagey. Everything he said felt like a lie, or weighted to get a reaction, or just trying to screw with him. It was the verbal equivalent of a carnival funhouse, and it wore Pete out.

The last time they talked, Reeves came to Pete.

"Going somewhere?" he asked, that same smirk, as he came around the side of the trailer parked in front of Pete's apartment. "Can't run away from your problems."

Pete lifted a box into the trailer. He was sick of Reeves, sick of the Donovans. Sick of Philadelphia.

Reeves laughed. "Don't be mad. I never asked you to bother with me."

"There's a kid who's been missing for four years," Pete said. "He's got a family who missed him. Something happened to him, and I was trying to find out what."

"The family doesn't seem to give a shit anymore, right?" Reeves' smirk grew bigger.

"Someday I'll find out who you are and what your game is."

"The way you found out what happened to JP?"

Pete turned back to the stack of boxes on the sidewalk.

"I have some information you might like," Reeves said.

"I'm done with your games," Pete said.

"First you're busted down to some loser desk job, now you're running away to that little shithole Maine town. You either really fucked up, or you're the world's biggest loser. Probably both."

Pete knew better than to take the bait. Reeves no longer had the power to piss him off.

"Too bad you're not interested in finding out what happened to JP anymore, because I can help you out." Reeves sounded serious for a change. Pete could feel him waiting for a reaction. Reluctantly, Pete looked up and met those brown—goddam brown and definitely not hazel—eyes. "How much do you know about Brandon?" Reeves asked.

"Why?" Pete wasn't going to tell him he didn't know anything, except the guy was a criminal and a grade-A asshole. Reeves, he was sure, already knew that.

"You and me are a lot alike," Reeves said. "We're both orphans. No home. No one to love us. Am I right?"

"What do you know about Brandon?" It was pointless to tell Reeves he wasn't technically an orphan, but Pete knew how conversations with Reeves went. Around and around and around, usually right down the drain.

"You know how I'm different from you?" Reeves said. "I take what I need, then move on. You keep hoping someone will actually give a shit."

"You know nothing about me," Pete said.

"I know you, fellow traveler. I can see it." Reeves voice was low, almost seductive. "That hurt little kid inside never grows up, does he? Never stops wondering why no one loves him."

Pete shifted some boxes to make more room. Damn trailers were never as big as you think they're going to be. It's not like he had that much stuff.

"I bet you'd love to kick the ass of someone who abuses kids, wouldn't you? That's why I'm asking about Brandon."

"If Brandon's abusing someone, you should report it."

192

"Right, like anyone would believe me. He skipped town, anyway. Moved up to Massachusetts." He made a show of pausing for effect. "With his young girlfriend and her cute little kids. It's not so much who he's abusing now, though, as who he used to abuse way back when. By abuse I mean going all Catholic priest."

Cheryl and Linda had never said anything to Pete about Brandon abusing JP or anyone else. There were no reports, nothing on file. Pete had looked into Brandon thoroughly. Reeves was screwing with him. Pete kept shifting the boxes, even though he didn't need to, wishing Reeves would shut up and go away.

Reeves sat down on the edge of the trailer. "It's pretty fucked up that you're moving to the place they treated you like shit. Kind of the pattern, though, isn't it?"

Pete didn't like the way he'd put those last boxes in. He pulled at one to move it, but it was wedged in tight.

"Remember Wendy Shaw?" Reeves continued. "Back a couple years ago, I was walking by one night and saw her through the window. She had the kid, Aidan, on her lap, reading to him. It struck something in me, you know?" He waited, though they both knew Pete wouldn't answer. "You and me never had that. We had the opposite, right? Right then and forever after, I wanted to be in that house. I know some pretty fucked up things go on in that house, but I couldn't get that picture out of my mind. Like the Maine slogan, you know? How life ought to be. It's not that I wanted to be in that particular fucked-up house, but I wanted what I saw through the window. It exists, but not for people like me. I know that now. And I got news, Detective. It doesn't exist for you either."

"Don't you ever shut up?"

Reeves' voice was soft again, almost a coo. "You want to be the tough-guy hero, but you also want to have a warm house and soft lap. Someone to make you feel like you're worth something, not the loser everyone always told you were, right? The loser you know you are."

Pete tried to ignore the gaping hole expanding in his chest.

193

"You were going to tell me something about Brandon."

"Don't be embarrassed. Everyone needs to feel loved, even cops who pretend they don't."

Pete realized if he moved a couple boxes more sideways, he could probably fit in the last two. It was just a matter of finding the right fit.

"You know what Brandon said to me when I came home to the loving arms of the Donovan family? He shook my hand and said, 'Good luck.' He knew I wasn't JP."

Pete tugged on the boxes, trying to shift them.

"You know that rag Dykstra jersey he always wears? I know you know it, because it's all the guy ever has on. It's even in his police mug shot. Look for it again someday. Keep your eyes open."

"If you know something, tell the police."

"Not you though, right? The whole reason I'm here is I thought you'd stick around and see this through. But you're running away. Now you'll be too busy keeping the moose out of the strawberry patches. Or maybe keeping the idiots out of the garbage hopper, right?"

Pete tugged at a box hard, way too hard, and it ripped, books spilling and scattering into the trailer and falling to the pavement.

"That's right. I still talk to people up there. They already made a monkey out of you last time. Nothing will be different now. Once a loser, always a loser."

Pete waited until he heard Reeves walk away before he looked up from picking up the books.

CHAPTER 20
2009
Redimere, Maine
Tuesday, November 17

The news conference was held in the cavernous bay at the public safety complex to accommodate the amount of press who had shown up, the firetrucks pulled out into the parking lot. It was already getting dark at 4:15, and under the fluorescent lights, everyone looked washed out and tired.

Carrie had her notebook and pen, as well as her iPhone. Bernie had brought a camera, figuring the conflict of interest didn't go so far that she couldn't take photos. Guy was back at the office finishing up the paper, but they'd left a big hole on the front page for the story. "I found his gut pile, I'm the last guy who ought to be at a press conference," Guy said. "Don't ask me to fill in any details in the story when you get back, either."

Bernie had never seen an iPhone. "It's like a little TV screen," she said.

"I'm going to record video and put it on our website," Carrie said.

"We can do that?" Bernie asked.

"Sure," Carrie said. "I'll write the story first, though."

The body found tied to the telephone pole was indeed Benji Reeves. He'd been put there that morning, but had been dead more than a week. The official cause and time of death had yet to be determined by the state medical examiner.

195

He'd been gutted—like a deer—and the condition of his body was consistent with the gut pile. There was little blood left, most of it had long ago soaked into the ground back at the clearing where he'd been cut open, Libby said, his flat delivery belying the gruesome facts.

Exsanguinated. Bernie wrote it down even though she didn't have to.

There were no new details about the injuries—police wouldn't comment on rumors he'd been castrated and his rectum had been cored out or that his head had been blown in half by a shot at close range—despite the repetitive, sometimes creative, and sometimes stupid way the reporters found to ask.

"His real name is William Reade. Born in Methuen, Massachusetts. Also known as William Deeves, Mikey Priest. Mickey Law. Mickey Cardinal. Bernard Cardinal. Bernard Priest."

"I'm sensing a pattern," Bernie said. She wrote down "sexual abuse?" in her notebook. She wondered if that could explain the mutilation.

Libby continued. "He has a lengthy record of petty charges: burglary, passing bad checks, fraud and theft, a variety of drug-related charges, mostly possession, sale, and trafficking. He was twenty-seven at the time of his death."

"So why didn't the Redimere police recognize him when they picked him up in 2007 and he said he was JP Donovan?" one of the reporters asked.

"None of the charges were in this area. He has charges in the Bangor and Portland areas, other southern Maine communities, numerous charges in Nashua and Manchester, New Hampshire, the Boston area, but nothing after late 2005 or early 2006, when he first appeared in Redimere, so they weren't familiar with him."

"He'd given up a life of crime?"

Pete leaned into the microphone. "We have no record of any charges in Redimere and no crime reports with his name on them. He was not known to the Redimere Police Department, according to department records. As many of you know, the department's personnel has changed since 2007, when he was last in town, so I can only speak on what the record shows."

Bernie asked Carrie to ask about evidence found on the body.

"No comment," Libby said as Pete stared at Bernie, she guessed trying to send her a telepathic message to stay out of it.

Libby cleared his throat and Bernie sensed the awful thing she knew was coming but hoped wasn't.

"The car that belongs to Salvatore O'Dea in the Leslie Lark disappearance has evidence tied to Reeves."

A flurry of hands went up, shouted questions. The room blurred, and Bernie realized she was clutching Carrie's arm. She could feel eyes turn toward her, at least one camera. She looked steadily straight ahead, concentrating on Pete. He looked back at her, and she tried to guess what she saw in his eyes. Pity? Anger? She couldn't see clearly enough to read them.

"We're not releasing any more information about it at this time," Libby said.

Pete was asked about his role in the JP Donovan case, the fact he knew Reeves. Bernie felt the attention drift from her, but it didn't keep her head from buzzing, or make the desire to run screaming from the building, go away.

"I'm confused." It was a Portland TV reporter. "You came up here to investigate after Reeves, who was pretending he was a missing boy, went to Philadelphia."

"I was a homicide detective looking into a potential homicide."

"Now you're police chief here."

"Is that a question?"

"Kind of. As I said, I'm confused." Nervous laughter rippled through the press corps.

"I made some connections here on that case in 2007 and when there was an opening, it seemed like a good fit."

"Then Reeves came back here recently?"

"Apparently."

"That's all a coincidence?"

"Yes."

197

Libby stepped in. "Chief Novotny is not a suspect in Benji Reeves' death. His prior involvement in the JP Donovan case has enhanced our investigation."

"Can we get some details of Chief Novotny's prior role?" another reporter asked.

"No," Pete and Libby both said at the same time. Press conference over.

.....

Pete felt a presence at his office door. He looked up and his eyes met Natalie Perry's.

"Vicki?" he called out.

"I waited until she was gone out of the room," Natalie said.

"Come in and sit down." He hadn't heard back from DHHS about the cigarette burns. He felt an urge to usher her into the room, lock the door behind her, and never let her go home.

She sat in front of his desk, awkward with the backpack on, her corduroy-clad legs and torn sneakers dangling a foot above the floor. "I don't have your three dollars."

"That's okay. What can I do for you?"

"Do you arrest people who take things?"

"If we can prove they took them. Did someone take something from you? Are those boys bothering you again?"

She looked scared but defiant. "I took something."

"Tell me what happened."

She stood up and took off her backpack, the bright-pink Disney princess one she'd worn at the store. "Nice backpack," he said, trying to put her at ease and get the cigarette burns out of his head, remembering too late she didn't like pink.

"My dad got it for me after those boys wrecked the other one. I don't like it." She didn't have to root around, she knew exactly where to find what she was looking for. She stood before his desk, reaching her fist out to him, her black eyes, on his, tragic. She turned her fist over and opened it, revealing an ornate cross on a gold chain. A Celtic cross. He'd seen it over and over again, on JP Donovan's missing kid posters, on JP's neck in the photos in the

198

Donovans' living room and Cheryl's wallet. In his dreams and nightmares.

"Where did you get that?"

"A friend of my dad's left it at our house."

"Who?" He braced to hear the name JP Donovan.

"Reeves? I don't know his last name."

"When did he leave it?" Pete asked, moving it onto a sheet of paper with his pen, her eyes following.

"November 6."

"Are you sure?"

"Yes," she said with an annoyance that reminded him of Bernie. "They had a fight. He started it, not my dad. My dad didn't do anything wrong."

"I know," Pete said, not at all sure.

"It fell off. I found it on the floor when I was vacuuming."

"Are you absolutely sure it was November 6?" Pete asked. The Friday Bernie had come over. The night Reeves had been in his apartment.

"Yes."

"Absolutely sure?"

Her eyes flashed. Bernie again. He almost smiled. "I was waiting for Dad to take me to the father-daughter dance at school. I got a new dress. We went, but Dad was mad because of the fight, and we didn't have fun."

Pete didn't know what to say.

"I heard you and Mr. Pecoe talking about Reeves in the store."

"That's his last name. His first is Benji."

"Like the dog in the movie?"

"Right." Pete tried to remember what he and Walt had said. How he'd thought the store was empty, then she was standing silently behind him. Just like now, her stare steady, black eyes on his, clear of tears, though her face was flushed. "Are you sure that was his name?" Pete asked.

"My dad called him Reeves. And some swear names. Are you going to arrest me?"

199

"No," Pete said. "You did the right thing and brought it to me. You didn't steal, it, did you? He left it and you picked it up."

"I wanted to give it back, but he never came back."

"Why didn't you give it to your dad?" He could guess.

"He gets mad. I didn't want him to get mad at me like he did with Reeves. Benji."

. . . . .

When Bernie and Carrie had returned to the office after the press conference, Feckless Fergus X. Kelley was there, typing rapidly on a computer with two pudgy fingers, old-style hunt-and-peck.

"Figured you'd need me ASAP," he said. "I've already met Guy, and he put me to work."

Bernie was grateful, an emotion she'd never associated with Feckless before. "We can do your paperwork after we get the paper out," she said.

Bernie introduced Fergus and Carrie and sorted out the duties. Guy smiled at Bernie. "We're beginning to look like a real newspaper.

Now, hours later, as she got ready for bed, wanting to collapse and sleep for days, she wasn't sure how grateful she should be. Earlier that night she'd overheard Feckless telling Carrie a story. Carrie had listened with fascination.

"It was a fire on New Year's Eve. A kid died. A neighbor ran in when he saw the fire and carried her to the fire station around the corner. The cops wouldn't let me talk to him, even though he was a hero, running into the burning house, trying to save the kid. I thought that was really strange they wouldn't let me talk to him, so I knew something was up." Feckless paused, Bernie couldn't see him, but pictured him with that smirk, waiting for Carrie's reaction. He must have gotten it, because he began again in that self-satisfied fake Irish way he had. "Turned out it was because the kid had been murdered by her baby-sitter, strangled. She didn't die in the fire. The baby-sitter, a guy, was a friend of the mom's, jealous she was on a date with a new guy. The kid, eight years old, still had the ligature around her neck when the neighbor ran with her down to

200

the fire station. Poor guy—the neighbor—was beside himself. Cops wouldn't let me talk to him because they were afraid he'd tell me about the ligature."

"Wow," Carrie said. "That's an amazing story."

"One thing I'll never forget," Feckless had continued. "The mom was all dressed up in her party clothes for New Years. She came home when she heard about the fire, house still burning. She kept trying to run up the driveway to the house in her high heels, but it was coated with ice and she kept falling down. Her date, first date, guy barely knew her, kept trying to help her up, but there was no help for her. She just kept trying to get up the ice-covered driveway, falling down. Screaming and crying her kid's name the whole time."

"Amazing," Carrie had repeated.

It *was* an amazing story. The really amazing thing, though, was it wasn't Feckless who had covered the story, it was Bernie. He probably didn't know she could hear him from her office, and she didn't say anything about it to either of them, but it reminded her what a feckless wonder he was.

She was just tired, too tired, but knew that once she was under the covers, she wouldn't be able to sleep at all.

The phone rang. Bobby Dolan.

"Can you talk?" he asked.

"Since I was eight months old," Bernie said.

"Ha ha. I mean, is Sal around?"

"He's in the living room watching TV," she said, shutting her door.

"I'm worried about him."

"Me too. What did they find in his car that would link it to Reeves?" Bernie had been hoping all night it was nothing, explainable.

"Blood in the trunk was from Reeves."

"Oh god. I thought he was exsanguinated at the scene."

"It wasn't much. Smears." He paused, his voice going gentle. "Bernie, whoever had the car, whoever wiped her purse and phone clean, did it. Not Sal."

"I know."

"He's very fragile," Bobby said. "Against my wishes, he let them question him today. Did he tell you?"

"No. He's barely said a word. You let him talk?"

"He insisted. He said he has nothing to hide."

"Why did you let him talk?" She wanted to scream it, but didn't want Sal to hear.

"I advise the client, but he does what he wants. You know that. He told them all about going to Vassalboro to get his car. Said he never texted her, lost his phone, doesn't know how it got in your bag, doesn't know Reeves. He's telling the truth, but I don't know if they believed him."

"I know."

"Now they may dig up his med school history."

"That was decades ago. He quit med school, remember?"

"Yes, but the fact that he went into sculpture and one of his tools is a knife, that his artist bio—which is still on some gallery website—says the only thing he learned in med school was how to use a scalpel and I quote 'while medicine wasn't his cup of tea, his colleagues all agreed he was an artist with a blade,' isn't going to help him."

"Everybody in Redimere uses a knife. Half the people walk around town with a Leatherman or hunting knives. What about Wendy, working at the deli? I bet she knows how to slice up meat nicely."

"Calm down," Bobby said. "I want you to make sure he doesn't get too down, and for chrissake, don't let him talk. To anyone, but especially to the police."

"Don't worry. I'm my father's daughter."

"The chief counts, too."

"Don't worry."

"So maybe we can talk more over dinner some night this week?"

"I'm just so busy." It wasn't a lie, but either way, she didn't want to. The kiss had been okay, but she didn't hunger for another one, not like with Pete, she admitted. She didn't have the energy to make small talk, act pleasant, worry whether there'd be another kiss.

"Guess I am, too." He sounded disappointed. "Maybe when this is all wrapped up."

"Yeah. Maybe."

After she hung up, she wandered into the living room. Sal was on the couch, watching TV, drinking a beer, Dubya's head in his lap. She sat down next to him.

"How ya doing?"

"Okay."

"Whatcha watching?"

"Some shit."

"Your time in prison turned you hard."

"Stop bugging me. I'm fine."

She got up and opened the fridge.

"I thought you were going to bed," he said.

"I'm not tired."

"Going for a walk?"

"I don't know." She took out lunch meat and mustard. "Maybe I'll just eat myself into oblivion."

"I have a friend coming over."

"Tonight?" It was ten.

"Yup."

"Who?"

"Brian Plourde. He wants to cheer me up. We're going to play chess."

"I don't have a chess board or pieces and stuff."

"No shit. Why would the world's worst chess player have a chess set? Brian is bringing his. He's got one of those chess clocks too, with the buttons on top."

"You know who else plays chess?" Sal didn't answer. "Pete."

"Whoopty-la-la-diddly-do."

"Very hard, prison has made you." She'd had a flash of Sal and Pete playing chess in front of a fire, her nearby, reading a book. She

203

knew it was as elusive as the scenes in those windows she saw glowing in the dark night. "That's nice of Brian. Nice of you, too. He's kind of a goof."

"He's all right. Anyway, right now he's my only friend."

Bernie kissed her brother on the top of his head, and as his curly hair brushed her cheek, she was gripped with deep, roaring sadness.

"Good night, Sis," he said, eyes on the TV.

"Good night, Baby Brother."

. . . . .

She was reading when Brian arrived, didn't go out to say hi, figured it was time to try to get some sleep. She turned out the light and listened to the rise and fall of her brother's friendly laugh, Brian's long, overeager stories.

"One thing I was thinking, since I learned you're fluent in German," she heard Brian say. "I was just reading somewhere that German paranormal erotica is very big."

"You don't say," Sal said. Bernie could hear the smile in his voice.

"So I'm thinking, I was a creative writing major in college. I could write them, in English, right? You could translate it to German, and we could put it up on the internet. We could make a fortune."

"Sure, let me know when you have something ready," Sal said.

Bernie was floating off to sleep, Sal and Brian's conversation drifting in and out, but it wouldn't take. Now they were talking about hunting.

"You can still go out with us," Sal said. "You just can't carry a gun. We don't have to stick with the guys. We split up anyway, right? We'll make sure they don't go near Monster Buck territory."

"I really want to go out with you Sal, I really do. But I just can't."

"Come on," Sal said. "I'll give you a share of my deer. Don't let the guys get you down. I need a friend with me." Sal was doing that wheedling thing Bernie was so familiar with. The one that got him

204

his way.

"It's just with my felony conviction, I don't know how much I want to be out there right now."

"If you don't have a gun, you won't get in trouble."

"Yeah, well, I just want to lay low and all that," said Brian. "Anyway, after they talked about it in front of that cop Dawna at the hunters breakfast, it's like I'm on her radar."

"Dawna seemed more interested in you seeing Benji Reeves than illegal hunting."

There was silence for a few minutes, just the occasional click of a chess piece, the soft tick of the chess clock

Sal again. "When did you see Reeves anyway? It might help figure out who killed him. They think it might be me, but I didn't even know him. I'd hardly been in town a couple hours when they think he was killed."

Bernie wished she could see what was going on, what Brian's reaction was.

"I don't really know, long time before he was killed, though." Brian said after a long pause. "I don't even know it was him. I didn't see him when he was killed, it was weeks before."

"Where was it?"

"Out by Patton Pond. It was dark out, really dark, and I don't know." Brian sounded anxious. Trying to convince.

"You know I didn't have anything to do with him getting killed, right?" Sal said.

"I know, I know." Brian sounded overeager again. "I know you didn't."

More silence, more chess pieces clinking, the clock ticking. A nervous laugh by Brian and a fake swear from Sal—Bernie knew it was fake, she knew Sal well enough—then Brian saying, "Check and mate."

"You got me," Sal said. "Best of five, okay?" More sound of chess pieces.

"Didn't you tell Dawna you saw him walking down Ridge Road?"

205

"I never said that. It was out by Patton Pond, the other side of town. One morning so early, it was still really dark. So it probably wasn't even him."

"So what were you doing out there, anyway, that early in the morning?"

"I was scouting. For hunting."

"I thought you liked to hunt out by Plourde's Mountain. Your family spot. That's what you said before, right? Off Ridge Road."

"Oh, I hunt all over. Lots of good places."

"I could swear you told Dawna it was Ridge Road you saw him."

Silence, the click of the pieces, the clock ticks seemed louder, the silence so long Bernie wondered if Sal was giving up the conversation.

"Now you don't even want to go hunting," Sal said. "Check."

More silence.

"I thought I did. Want to go hunting, I mean, but now I don't." Bernie could hear the tremor in his voice as she lay in the dark. "I just changed my mind is all."

Silence. Click. Tick. Brian again. "Oh man, this is a complicated position."

"Whoops, I don't think you wanted to take my rook like that." Sal.

No sound from Brian.

Sal again. "Checkmate."

CHAPTER 21
2009
Redimere, Maine
Thursday, November 19

O kay, guys," Bernie said as her news staff—she had an actual news staff!—settled down on the couches in the lounge area at the paper Thursday morning. "Eat up." She nodded at the Dunkin' Donuts dozen.

"This is the first-ever news meeting in the O'Dea era at the *Peaks Weekly Watcher*," she said, raising her coffee mug in a salute. Guy, Fergus, and Carrie, with varying degrees of enthusiasm, raised theirs. "I won't make you do that every time," she said. "I appreciate you pitching in to get everything done this week."

"It was fun," Carrie said.

"I've always said this needs to be fun. Why else are we here otherwise?"

Fergus snorted.

"The issue is, I can't cover our biggest story. Benji Reeves being separated from his innards and my brother's car found in town with Leslie Lark's blood in it and apparent evidence linking it to Reeves." She tried to sound matter of fact. "Guy can't cover it either, since he found the guts, so Fergus and Carrie, you're the primary reporters."

Fergus raised his hand. He had that condescending smirk that Bernie remembered so well. The one she'd seen on so many middle-aged men in her twenty-plus year career. The smirk that said, "I have absolutely no regard for you whatsoever, missy, or anything you have to say."

She gave him a big smile. "Fergus? I see you have your hand up."

"With all due respect," he said—*bullshit*—"I'm the experienced reporter and Carrie's a college kid. The story ought to be mine. She can help."

Bernie wished she could mash Carrie and Fergus together and come out with the reporter she needed. One with Carrie's instinctive smarts, work ethic, and lack of bullshit and Fergus's...Fergus's what? Bernie tried to remember what he brought. Experience. Ability to work a news story. He also brought self-absorption, laziness, and a certain level of dishonesty. Every time she looked at him she felt that negative twinge, like passing roadkill. Not so horrible it wrecked your day, but it wrecked the minute.

"You'll both work the story under my supervision and Guy's. I can't get involved, but I think I can still supervise in a general way. Anything you're uncomfortable talking to me about, run by Guy. I'm not going to let stories go in the paper that I haven't read. Guy will keep me honest."

Fergus shook his head so hard his thin strands of graying hair would have flown off if they weren't pasted down with Brylcreem or some other disgusting wetness. "You should really consider taking a leave of absence or vacation or something until this is finished."

Bernie felt the explosion build, trying to figure out which part to lead it with, when Guy jumped in.

"Bernie's right. This'll work best. You two are new, and she and I know the ropes."

"I know the ropes," Fergus said.

"We know the ropes in Redimere," Guy said, calm and reasoned as always. "Bernie can back off when she needs to."

Bernie knew Guy could get her to back off. Pretty sure if Fergus tried she'd rip his head off and feed it to him.

Fergus rolled his eyes. Carrie raised her hand.

"You guys don't have to raise your hands," Bernie said. "Carrie?"

"I'd also like to do web updates if it's okay. I notice we haven't been doing them, but it's pretty simple. Did you see all the comments we got on the press conference video?"

"Of course you can," Bernie said, wishing she'd thought of it.

Fergus raised his hand and immediately started talking. "Why would anyone buy the paper if we're going give it away for free?"

Bernie tried to conjure what little she'd learned about the balance between web and print and how they worked together. Granted, it was 2009, and the internet had been around for a long time, but the newspaper industry still hadn't figured it out. She knew there was a good answer, she just couldn't remember it.

Carrie sat forward, more animated than Bernie had ever seen her. "It gets our name out there and legitimizes us as a news source. We can still have things in the paper we don't have on the web. It's amazing, though, what we can do. Videos, photo galleries. Documents that go with a story that we'd never put in the paper." Her eyes danced behind her glasses. "It'll make more people buy the paper, not less. I'm excited about all the things we can do."

It's possible Carrie was full of shit, but Bernie was sold. It almost made her want to cry with happiness.

Guy nodded, intrigued.

Fergus sneered. "That's bull. It's the fastest way for this one-horse paper to go right down the toilet. Give it away, lose readers."

"You'll have to live with it," Bernie said. "I don't want to get beat by the *Morning Sentinel* or *Lewiston Sun* on this story, right in our backyard. I'll work with Carrie on how much we'll put on the website, but the most important thing is content. So let's get some."

"I'd like to do a map, too," Carrie said. "It can show where the gut pile was, where Reeves' body was found. Where the car—" she looked at Bernie. "Oh, sorry."

"That's okay," Bernie said. Might as well get used to it. "That's a good idea. Kind of like the crime trackers map the police department has on its website."

"Right," Carrie said.

"If you want any tips, you can talk to Dawna Mitchell at the PD, she's pretty good with that stuff."

Carrie wrote that down in the notebook she'd brought to the meeting. Bernie noticed Fergus was the only one who hadn't brought a notebook.

"Here's another issue," Fergus said. "Your relationship with the chief."

Bernie's face got hot. "We don't have a relationship." She did air quotes around relationship. "We're good friends."

"Several people in town have told me you two are hot and heavy," Fergus said. "But suit yourself."

"I will." She reminded herself he was here because she desperately needed someone. Anyone, apparently.

"Carrie, don't you have classes?" Bernie asked. "Shouldn't you be in Orono?" It had just occurred to her.

"I'm good," Carrie said, looking Bernie right in the eye. "I'm where I'm supposed to be."

Bernie was happy about it for the moment, but didn't want to ruin the kid's life. She'd deal with it later, though, when she needed her less. "We've talked about getting police reports, talking more to the guys who found Reeves' body, seeing if anyone at the transfer station who knew him before will talk now, so start with that. I can talk to Moses Mosher, since he found Reeves' body and doesn't have anything to do with the other stuff. I've got another project I'm working on that'll keep me busy, too."

"The domestic violence thing or the pills thing?" Fergus said.

"How did you know about those?"

"Saw some notes when I was helping out yesterday," Fergus said with no shame. "Looks interesting."

"Both are in the very early stages," Bernie said, wondering if he'd seen the notes on her desk. Where else would he have? Irritating. She wasn't going to mention that the "pills thing" might have something to do with Reeves.

He winked at her, and she felt that road-kill twinge.

Carrie went to find Dawna, and Guy left for lunch. Fergus sat down next to Bernie's desk.

"I don't mind working with that girl, but she's green as shit and doesn't strike me as very bright."

"She's more than bright. She also has good instincts and works hard. It'll be fine. Let's do your paperwork."

She searched in her desk for the file that had W-9s, the annoying Homeland Security "he's not a terrorist" form, and the other paperwork. She wished there was a "he's not a lazy fuck" form, but then again, she didn't need a form to tell her he was.

Fergus put his feet up on her wastepaper basket. He'd taken off his shoes, and the smell hit Bernie like a wet wool slap. "I'm happy to help out, but I'm going to need some good clips to stay relevant if I want to move on eventually and get a better job. I don't want that girl screwing things up for me."

Bernie sorted the forms. She felt like kicking the waste basket out from under his giant smelly feet. "Carrie isn't going to screw anything up for you. What we need is to cover this news the best we can."

"You're the boss," he said as he took the papers from her and got up. She didn't miss the eye roll. She knew he'd meant for her to see it.

Damn right I am, you feckless smelly-footed piece of shit. She bit it back. If they were going to get through this, she'd have to keep her feelings about Fergus shoved way down and hope he just did his job. She hoped keeping it to herself didn't kill her.

. . . . .

Bernie needed to get out of the office and away from Fergus and everything else, and there were a couple conversations she'd been meaning to have.

"Vince, do you have a minute?" The door to his office at Redimere College was open.

"For you, my sweet, of course."

"Don't let Carol ever hear you say that," Bernie said. Vince was

211

a nice antidote for Feckless. "Carol said you knew Leslie Lark?"

"She took Sustainable Marijuana last year."

"Small world. What were your impressions?"

"It's not a total coincidence. We're the only school in the state that offers classes on medical marijuana. Leslie is smart, focused, and hoping to turn part of her farm into a certified growing business."

"I'm trying to reconcile smart and focused with the Leslie Lumpkin Sal went out with in high school."

"Everyone grows up. I'm sure you're brother has, too."

"He has." Sal in high school was a skinny pony, more interested in Dungeons & Dragons and chess than sports and other high-profile activities. Everyone in their family had some dork in them, but Sal had been one of the dorkiest, just a little less dorky than Bernie.

"She called me up a few times since with questions. She seemed intent on it and was able to grasp what she needed to do."

"When did she take it?"

"Fall semester 2008, so a year ago."

"Did she seem the type who'd get involved with the wrong people?" Bernie felt guilty, checking her brother's story. She wasn't even doing it for the paper, but for herself.

"No way. She was by the book, really into getting all the information and how to get certified. It's highly regulated, as you know, and she was aware of what she had to do."

"Totally different topic," she said. "Carol said someone at the transfer station committee meeting said Sal said he'd kill Leslie and truss her up like a deer." Okay, not totally different topic after all.

"Chapman said he heard Sal say it at the transfer station his first day," Vince said.

"You sure?"

"I am, my dear. Since I'd met your brother a couple nights before, I said it didn't seem in character. Chapman just smiled like an asshole. I can see why David Viens quit the committee. I regret taking his spot."

212

"Great." Meaning of course, not great.

"I wouldn't worry about it. You know how people talk."

Bernie was still stewing as she walked to the college's running track. She'd seen Wendy there on Thursdays this time of day many times and figured she herself needed a nice track run. Sure enough, Wendy was there. As Bernie warmed up, she watched Wendy run effortlessly, her long muscular legs almost floating. Bernie did her plodding circuits, waiting for Wendy to slow down for a cool-off. After she'd lapped Bernie more times than Bernie could count, she finally did.

"Hey," Bernie said, jogging alongside her. Wendy's cooldown was close to Bernie's sprint.

"I have a feeling this is more than a friendly chat," Wendy said.

Bernie knew she didn't have much time before a heart attack ended the conversation. "Got me. Now that Reeves is dead, can you talk about him? I want to fill out the story, and you're the only one who didn't hate him."

Wendy looked down at Bernie, half a foot below. "You don't have a notebook."

She knew she'd forgotten something. She couldn't run and write at the same time anyway. "I can check back with you for specific quotes later. I'm looking for background."

They did a full lap before Wendy said. "What do you want to know?"

"How did you become friends?"

"When he started at the transfer station, Tim hired him to do odd jobs. He seemed okay at first," Wendy said.

"Everyone said he was a master manipulator and liar," Bernie said, trying not to sound like she needed to suck in giant lungfuls of air.

"You just go right to the point, don't you?" It was hard to tell, with the running, but Wendy seemed nervous. She'd sped up, too. She wasn't breathing hard at all.

"I'm going to drop dead after another lap, so I don't want to waste time."

Wendy didn't laugh like Bernie had hoped. Or slow down.

"He was. He was also a lost boy. He'd been sexually abused as a kid. I knew he was telling the truth about that."

Bernie tried to think of a question that would get Wendy to elaborate on the abuse, maybe even lead to the domestic abuse in the Shaw house. Quickly.

"I helped him," Wendy said.

"What?" Bernie's legs burned and she was gasping for breath.

"When he came back, I slipped him food, blankets."

"Did he say why he was here?"

"Redemption."

"What did he mean?"

Wendy shrugged, looking straight ahead, not at Bernie. "That's what he said, with that laugh he had. I don't know what he meant."

"Can we stop?" Bernie asked. To her surprise, Wendy did. They started walking. "When was the last time you saw him?"

"I can't remember if I said we're off the record," Wendy said.

We didn't. "Tell me what you want off the record and it is."

"I don't want anyone to know I saw him or talked to him or talked to you about him."

Great. Bernie breathed long, deep breaths, trying to slow her heart down. Her legs were jelly. "No problem. Deep background. When did you last see him?"

"Couple days before they say he was shot. Tim found out I was helping him. He wasn't happy. Hated Benji and never believed we weren't having an affair." Wendy started jogging again, so Bernie did too.

"Is that why Tim was mad that night? What was he asking you about? He wanted to know where something was."

Wendy's pace picked up. Bernie's lungs and legs hadn't recovered. Now they were on fire.

"The thing is," Wendy said after another lap. "I need to talk to somebody."

"About Benji?" Bernie gasped it out.

Wendy picked up the pace. Bernie felt ridiculous lumbering

214

along beside her, trying to keep up, trying to breathe. Wendy didn't seem to notice. "It could be, but more than that. It's something I have to think about first."

"Should you go to police?" Bernie asked. Wendy was white despite the pace. She'd been clutching and unclutching her hands. She seemed terrified.

"No. I can't," she said. "I can talk to you. Maybe. If you keep it quiet." They did another half lap. "I have to think about it first."

"What—"

"It's about that night with Tim. With the gun. And more."

"Give me a hint?"

Her question, gasped and barely audible, was lost to the wind, as Wendy sprinted away, across the track and the field to the parking lot and her car.

. . . . .

Dawna watched as Carrie got out of her car, pulling a bag and camera behind her, then laboriously arranging straps, pulling, buttoning, and tucking before walking to where Dawna was waiting at the entrance of the tote road.

"Are you sure you're up for this?" Dawna asked. "It's a rough hike once you get in."

"I'm fine," Carrie said. "I'm not in bad shape, and I've spent a lot of time in the woods."

"Okay," Dawna said. "If this were still a crime scene, I wouldn't be able to show you, but they're done with it. I'm surprised no other news organizations have come to see it."

"Maybe they came on their own."

"Not sure anyone would have been able to find it. The road's hard to see if you don't know where it is."

"Seems like everyone in town knows," Carrie said.

"Just seems that way," Dawna said. "The hunters know it, maybe some other folks."

They walked down the old road for another ten minutes, the leaves crunching beneath their feet. It was a cold, gray day, the kind where the light never changes after the sun comes up. Winter on its way. Dawna could smell the coming snow in the air. She was itching to get back out and get her deer, but it looked like the season was going to end before the cases did.

"Here's where they found the shell casings," she said, stopping in the overgrown clearing. "They figured the shooter stood here." She stood at a spot near the tumbledown shack. "Reeves was over there in the woods, where the trail continues." Dawna looked over and saw Carrie was holding her phone to her face. "What are you doing?"

"I'm recording you. Video for the website. Is that okay?"

"I guess so," Dawna said. She wasn't sure, but she'd cleared being out here with Carrie with the chief. "If I tell you anything is off the record, that goes for the video, too."

"Of course," Carrie said. She put the phone down. "It just helps, you know? People can see it, not like in the paper."

"Sure," Dawna said. "He got off two shots." She'd moved to the edge of the woods, and pointed to rust droplets of dried blood, little dots, where the trail, narrow and more overgrown than the tote road, let into denser woods. "This is where they think he was standing. We don't know if both shots hit him or just one. See that blood? The drops get smaller as we go along. Farther apart. Like a deer."

Carrie took some photos. "It's pretty dark in here," she said as she and Dawna walked, more slowly now, pushing branches out of the way. "How did Guy even find the blood?"

"It was sunny when he saw it. He's got a pretty good eye."

Dawna showed her where gut pile had been. "You can still see the stain. Lots of blood. They found another shell casing here. Fits with what I heard that morning. Two shots, then a third about ten minutes later." Carrie was filming again.

"Where are those cellar holes that people talk about?"

"They're farther in."

"Can we see them?"

"Sure, but it's not easy. State police came up and looked as part of the investigation, but didn't find anything."

They spent another fifteen minutes, climbing, going over scrabble, pulling themselves up by roots.

"It's hard to believe there'd be cellar holes way up here," Carrie said.

"It's changed. They used to log. All this tree growth is new. New as in only a few decades, less than a century old. When people didn't depend on cars as much, they lived farther into the woods."

They climbed some more and came out on another overgrown road. "Here we are. The first one is back here." Dawna pushed brush aside and they plunged through it, and then more brush until they came to a rock foundation, a square hole, scattered with crumbled rocks, shrubs, and trees. "Wonder if the state police even came this far? It doesn't look like anyone's been here," she said.

"What's that?" Carrie pointed to a patch of bright blue under tall shrubs.

They scrambled down a ridge of scrabble. It was tarp, brand new. Underneath it a knapsack and sleeping bag, blankets, cans, and a Coleman stove.

Carrie took out her iPhone.

Dawna took out her cellphone. No service out here, so she texted Pete: "Found Reeves camp. Cellar holes."

CHAPTER 22
2009
Redimere, Maine
Friday, November 20

Bernie pulled up in front of Wayne Daggett's house first thing Friday morning. There were no lights on in the windows, no cozy look on this cold, gray day. His yard had been cleaned up, all the junk gone, but the grass was uncut, the shrubs overgrown and ragged.

He smiled with delight and ushered her in. They were off to an unusually good start.

"I see you're filling up again," she said. The living room could politely be described as cluttered, and it reeked of must, old paper, and ancient grubbiness. There might have been furniture, but it was hard to see under bags and newspapers, dirty stuffed animals, books, and clothing.

"They took my stuff, but not all of it. I know where to get more, anyway. You're here for the story?"

"Yeah." She wasn't sure what story, but that nagging feeling wouldn't go away, Wayne's grinning goblin head, his hand waving that yellowed *New York Times* pulled from a bag that rattled suspiciously like prescription bottles, had been popping through her thoughts all week.

He walked through the room and she followed, into another equally messy room. He turned on the light to reveal mounds of garbage bags, piled on the floor, against walls. He opened one, held it open for her to look in, smiling at her with the same toothless delight he'd greeted her with at the door, reminding her of Dubya. "Ha!" he said.

She looked in at a jumble of clear brown plastic, white caps, labels. Thousands of prescription bottles. He snatched the bag away as her hand moved. She wanted to touch.

"Are all these bags prescription bottles?" she asked. There were dozens.

"Most. Other bottles, too. Hid 'em in the root cellar when they cleaned me out. Ninety thousand seven hundred and seventy three."

"Wow."

"That's how many are Chapman."

"What?"

"Some are other doctors. All these bags over here"—he pointed to the biggest pile of bags—"that's Chapman. Ninety thousand seven hundred and seventy three."

"Why?" She wasn't sure why what. Why the bottles? Why Chapman? She was too dazed to clarify it for herself, or for Wayne.

"The newspaper article." He walked out the room and she waited, wanting to open the bags and look, afraid if she did he wouldn't tell her the rest. He came back with the yellowed *New York Times*.

"Can I?"

He hesitated.

"I can't read it if you don't let me."

He gave it to her. "You read it right there." It was from 1997, open to a story about a California doctor who'd lost his license after he'd overprescribed to a patient, not only drugs for her mental health issues but also painkillers, and she'd died of an overdose. Her mother sued. They'd settled privately. There were also allegations of insurance and prescription fraud that were apparently dropped. She knew enough about the legal system to know it was probably because he had a good lawyer, not because he didn't do it. Chapman.

"Why do you have all these bottles?" she asked.

219

"I like them. I've been collecting Chapman since George Bush."

"2001?"

"The other one."

"1989?" It scared her that she was beginning to speak Wayne Daggett. "Why Chapman?"

"He has more than anyone else." Impatient that she seemed so slow to understand. "Tim Shaw doesn't know."

"I don't think Tim cares," Bernie said. "He just doesn't want you to take them from the dump." She didn't give a shit about Shaw, her mind was racing through the implications of the article, the bottles.

"Shaw doesn't want me to have them," Wayne said, stubborn. "He doesn't want me to have the Chapman bottles. He told me to shut up about the Chapman bottles."

"We should tell the police," Bernie said. Everyone was always telling Wayne to shut up, so that was nothing new. She was getting tired of the Tim Shaw tangent. "The police won't tell Tim."

"They'll take them away."

"They won't take the bottles, but they'd want to know. You wanted me to do a story, right?"

"About Chapman, not the bottles."

"I can't do one without the other."

"No story. No story. Leave now."

"Wayne—"

He snatched the newspaper from her. "I was going to show you the special bottle. No more. Leave now. No bottles. Goodbye."

"Special bottle?"

"No more."

"I promise I won't tell the police. Honest."

He studied her, his eyes gleaming with more than their usually rheumy goo. He wanted to, she could tell.

"I like bottles, too, Wayne. I have a bunch at home. I'll give them to you if you show me the special bottle."

She waited, watching him consider it, knowing he was going

through the scenario, just like she would. He walked out of the room and she followed, again.

He went to a cabinet, the one piece of furniture that rose above the mess in the cluttered, dim living room. Took a key from a drawer and unlocked another draw. Took out a prescription bottle and handed it to her. He watched as she looked it over.

It was a normal bottle, empty. Not from Redimere Drug but from the pharmacy at Franklin Memorial Hospital in Farmington. Vicodin in large letters. In smaller letters was the patient: Pete Novotny. "Where'd you get this?"

Wayne snatched it away. "You saw. Now go."

"But where?"

"The dumpster at the colored man's store."

"The Country Grocer?"

"No police. Go."

. . . . .

Bernie popped into the police station.

"Vicki, can you dig up any reports you have related to Tim Shaw? Police responses to their address,"—Bernie wrote the address down on a post-it from Vicki's desk—"or that kind of thing? Also, anything to do with drug arrests or reports?"

Vicki looked like she wanted to refuse, though she didn't say anything.

"It's public record," Bernie said. She'd file a right-to-know request if she had to, but she liked to play nice first.

"Is that the guy we called DHHS about?" Vicki asked Pete as he came into the room.

"Who?"

"Tim Shaw?" Vicki replied.

"Why are you asking about Tim Shaw?" Pete asked Bernie.

"Who did you ask DHHS about?"

"Did I do something wrong?" Vicki asked.

"Let's go talk in my office," Pete said.

Pete waited at his door for her and closed it as she came in.

"Are we mad at each other today?" Bernie asked. "I can't keep

221

track."

Pete smiled at her, thin, but still a smile. "Not that I know of. How's Sal?"

"Good as can be expected," she said, taking out her notebook and pencil. She didn't want to talk about Sal with Pete.

"Why are you asking about the Shaws? Still doing that domestic violence story?"

"I have to do something. Every other story in town seems to involve my brother being a murder suspect. Who did you call DHHS about?"

"It's a private matter," Pete said. "What do you want to know about the Shaws?"

"Wondering if you guys answer a lot of calls there," Bernie said. "Also if Tim has been tied to anything to do with drugs."

"You'd be better off checking with the court in Farmington."

"I am," Bernie said, annoyed. "But calls to the house that didn't result in an arrest are public record, too."

Pete shrugged. "I can't say many."

"I can't say I believe you."

"Off the record, okay?"

"All right." That was a great start. She tried to look disappointed.

"We've gone over a few times. I'm pretty sure he beats Wendy, but we can't prove it. There's no sign he's hurting the kids. Wendy won't press charges or tell us the truth. There's not much we can do. I wouldn't be surprised if he's on painkillers or something, acts like an addict, but it's nothing we have a criminal record of."

"The town doesn't do drug testing for its employees." Bernie knew that, just wanted to say it out loud, make sure there wasn't some secret testing she didn't know about.

"No way the budget could support it."

Bernie tried to fit the pieces together, decide how much to say to Pete about Chapman, about the bottle.

"You need to let it be," Pete said.

"What was the deal between Shaw and Reeves? Aside from

222

Wendy. Drugs?"

"We still off the record?"

Bernie nodded.

"Shortly after Reeves left in 2007, Brian Plourde got busted for breaking into camps, stealing prescription drugs. I found some files of Ray's, mostly notes; he was looking at whether Reeves was getting addresses from pill bottles at the transfer station, breaking into camps, too."

"I did the Plourde story. Late summer 2007."

"Ray's notes were from well after that. I think Ray felt bad he picked up Reeves and believed the JP Donovan story. He never talked about it. I just found his files on it this week, buried in those boxes we haven't sorted out from when we moved into this building. It looked like he started digging after Plourde went to prison. Ray thought Reeves was the leader, Plourde the follower. Reeves left town, Plourde got busted."

Bernie stopped writing. "You and Ray never talked about it?"

"No." Pete shifted in his chair, looked away for a second. "Ray also thought there was something bigger going on."

"What?"

"His notes aren't clear, but Shaw's name was there. I asked Dawna, and she said he never said a word about it to her, either. So Shaw may have had another bone to pick with Reeves besides the Wendy aspect."

"Can I run something really stupid by you? It kind of has to do with this. Maybe."

"Sure."

"I was trying to think how Sal's cellphone got in my bag. He lost it his first day at the transfer station, early. His lawyer said Leslie texted early afternoon about his car and someone texted back, from Sal's phone, to come get it, but she shouldn't come to my house because I'd be mad. It went back and forth and they settled on the transfer station for Tuesday night, because no one would be there."

"That's about right."

Bernie could tell he was annoyed. She'd gotten that

223

information from Bobby Dolan. It hadn't been released to the public. "That wasn't Sal texting," Bernie said.

"I know, but don't put any of that in the paper. It's part of an active investigation."

"You know?" So was Sal off the hook? She was afraid to ask. "I was told as his sister, not a reporter." She paused to let her irritation pass. "I was at Chapman's office that day the phone vanished. I left my bag in the exam room while I used the bathroom."

"Chapman." He didn't look convinced.

"He writes a lot of prescriptions. A lot. Not just for behavioral meds. Painkillers, big bad ones. Sleeping pills. Every time I go in he wants to load me up with something new. I saw Shaw filling a Vicodin prescription from Chapman's office. I wasn't spying, just saw it. Those pill bottles in my car from the bag at the dump? He wrote most of those, and they're for all sorts of stuff." She'd wait to see how Pete reacted before she brought up Wayne or mentioned the special bottle. It could all go south and she'd screw it up if she did it wrong.

"We'll look into it."

"He lost his license in California in 1997. I don't know how he got a license in Maine."

"We're not the state medical board."

"Vince Addison said Chapman told everyone at the transfer station committee meeting that Sal said he'd kill Leslie and truss her up like a deer. Sal never said that. So Chapman's credibility sucks." Pete's expression hadn't changed. Passive, unreadable. It pissed her off. "Because he's a doctor you don't believe me? Prescription fraud is big business. Huge."

"I said we'll look into it."

She crossed her arms and looked out the window. *I guess we're mad at each other after all. At least I am.*

"When are we going to do some more shooting practice?" She was still looking out the window, but it sounded like he was smiling. Too bad, she was mad.

"Never."

"Bernie—"

"Never." She felt irrational tears forming and wasn't sure why.

"I have something for you." She looked back from the window. He took a folded piece of notebook paper out of his wallet and leaned across his desk, smoothing it out in front of her. It was her name and cellphone number in her handwriting.

"What's this?" she asked, trying to surreptitiously wipe her eyes.

"Remember when we talked in 2007?"

"I yelled at you."

He laughed, all crinkles and dimples and warmth. Her anger eased a little, though she didn't want it to. "I promised when we found JP Donovan's body I'd give you the story."

"Someone's found JP Donovan's body?"

"No, but with Reeves dead, there's still a story. I can't tell you until this is wrapped up and it's all figured out."

"All right." She was still too mad to tell him about Wayne or the bottle.

"I just wanted you to know I remembered."

.....

When Bernie got home she almost tripped over Brian Plourde, kneeling near the door, hugging Dubya.

He got up, shifted nervously, bounced on the balls of his feet. He looked different now that she knew maybe he'd been involved with Reeves. She'd known why he went to prison, but it seemed dark now instead of stupid and desperate. She wanted him away from her dog and wasn't sure if her brother should be spending so much time with him either.

"I came over to see if Sal can come over to play chess," he said, as though she were Sal's mother. "Moses' mom is going on a date, and he's coming over. She doesn't like him staying home alone. He's like a big 300-pound kid, you know?"

Sal walked in from the hallway, buttoning his shirt.

"Ready to go?" Brian asked.

225

"Just let me get my things. I'm staying overnight, Mom."

"Behave." She didn't know what else to say, and the two were out the door before she could think of a way to stop them.

She enjoyed her solitary dinner of leftovers. She had a lot to choose from since Sal had moved in, her months-long junk food diet coming to a happy end. She tried not to think, but just enjoy the food. Too many things in her head as usual. It seemed like a new thing came up every hour. After trying to read, then listlessly clicking through the TV channels, she knew she couldn't avoid the inevitable walk.

Some nights her walks had no purpose; she'd go wherever her feet took her until she was somewhere and had no idea how she got there. Tonight she had a destination. She knocked on the bent tin door. A hulking figure blocked the light from inside, then the door opened.

"What can I do for you?" Eli Perry asked.

"Can I talk to you about something?"

"Come on in."

She could smell something garlicky, inviting. "I'm not interrupting supper, am I?" It was almost nine.

"Nope, just putting Nat to bed."

His daughter, a funny little kid, barrel-shaped like her dad, only dark with black pigtails and piercing black eyes, came into the living room.

"Hi, Natalie."

"Hi." She didn't answer Bernie's smile.

"Get into bed, and I'll read to you after I talk to Ms. O'Dea," Eli said.

"I can read to myself." She went back down the hall.

He sat down, so she did, too. "You have kids?" he asked.

"Not that I know of," she said with an exaggerated wink. He laughed, and she did, too, happy he got it. Lots of times that joke caused confusion or a lecture on how she *would know* if she had kids.

"Raising that little girl is way more work than anyone told me," he said. "I didn't see much of her before her mom died. I missed out on a lot. It's hard on her. She misses her mom. I'm a poor substitute."

"What did she die of?"

"Cancer," he said quietly. "I think that asshole she lived with would have eventually killed her anyway. He physically abused Nat, too. I think he messed with her other ways, though she hasn't said anything. She's going to a therapist. She's a tough little nut, like her old man." He laughed, sad though. "She has scars. Nightmares."

"Sorry. She seems like a good kid."

"She is. Now what can I do for you?"

"Benji Reeves." He began to shake his head. "Totally off the record," she added hastily. "They have evidence from him, I don't know what, in my brother's car. My brother didn't even know him."

"He was a piece of shit, and I'm glad he's dead."

"Be that as it may."

"Did your cop buddy tell you the state police had me in for questioning on it?"

Bernie felt her face burn. "No."

"Reeves came over here a couple weeks ago. I told him to get lost. I didn't want him around my kid. He was being a pest, so I grabbed him by his scrawny neck and threw him out."

"He say what he wanted?"

"He said he had a game to run that he wanted my muscle for. Like we used to in the old days. I was more focused on getting him out than I was on listening to his bullshit."

"Was the game to do with prescription drugs?"

"Where'd you hear that?"

"It's something I'm trying to figure out. Mostly a hunch."

"We're so off the record that we're in another dimension."

"Okay."

"Reeves used to have a game at the transfer station. Addresses from prescription labels."

"With Brian Plourde."

"Exactly."

"Brian got caught after Reeves left," Bernie said.

"Plourde has a lot of big ideas, but his execution leaves a lot to be desired. Reeves was the brains, and Plourde screwed up without him here to do the thinking."

"Why'd Reeves leave?"

"Shaw sells drugs at the transfer station. Bet you didn't know that. He's a bad businessman, though, because he's also an addict. Reeves figured out how Shaw was getting the stuff. He asked me back then to help him. I'm not sure if he was going to scam him or get in on the action, but I wouldn't. I'd already had enough of his shit and didn't want to go to jail. It didn't help that Shaw also hated Reeves because his wife liked him. Reeves left town before Shaw could kill him. Poor old Ray Morin picked him up and brought him back. Presto-chango, JP Donovan. Free ticket to Philly."

"Reeves was taking a chance. Ray might've known who he was."

"Didn't have a choice. He had to think of something when Ray picked him up. I'm guessing, but I know Reeves. Obviously, getting picked up wasn't part of his plan, but Reeves loved a game. Loved taking a risk. So he probably got a kick out of it."

"Do you know who the supplier was?"

Eli wagged his eyebrows at her. "My guess is you already know."

. . . . .

Bernie was tired of not being able to sleep. Tired of being tired. Tired of way too much stuff zipping through her head. She lay awake after she got home from Eli's, everything looping through her head, an endless news crawl of headlines. Now it was almost two. At least tomorrow was Saturday. Or today, actually. She put her coat on over her sweatshirt and pajama pants, pulled on her shoes, and went back out.

Destination or none, when she walked she always paid attention to the houses and trailers, the shadows behind the curtains. Out in the cold dark night, she wondered about the windows glowing in the darkness. They seemed so cozy, but she knew better, knew it well before that night nearly two weeks ago

228

when she saw Tim Shaw chase Wendy out of the house with a gun. Knowing that didn't stop her from looking, though. Sometimes she thought she'd started walking at night just so she could go home to her warm house and fire, her dog and cats and bed. The comfort she felt at the thought was almost as much of a fantasy as the windows, because she'd still toss and turn and have a million thoughts running through her head, the anxiety building until she got up in the morning.

The other reason she walked was that it helped her think. What Eli told her didn't explain what had happened to Reeves, and certainly not Leslie, if her disappearance had anything to do with Reeves, didn't explain Pete's Vicodin bottle in Wayne Daggett's grubby hand, but helped a little. She wished she could run it all by Pete. It had become clear earlier today she couldn't. He wouldn't even bite on Chapman. She'd be nuts to tell him she was getting information from Wayne Daggett and Eli Perry. He'd have her carted off to the state hospital. She liked to have things figured out before she presented conclusions to someone who was inclined to brush them off. She'd been on the receiving end of too much dismissiveness over the years, too many eye rolls about things that made perfect sense to her.

She walked aimlessly, breathing the crisp air, wood smoke and that elusive coming snow smell giving the air some bite. The night was cloudless after the gray day, and the Milky Way spread above her. It always seemed brighter, with more stars, when it was cold. She tried to pick out constellations, something she was never good at. She tripped over a pot hole and gave it up.

Thanksgiving less than a week away and she hadn't even thought about it. Too much to do. How was she going to get the paper out? She didn't want to have to decide which sister's house to go to. Maybe she'd just stay home with Dubya and the cats, under a blanket with a book. Her brain circled back to the prescriptions. Is it obvious it's Chapman? Why can't my head be organized so I can figure it out? It was the millionth time this month she'd asked herself that, and still no answer.

A car approached, its headlights blinding her. She stepped off the shoulder onto the grass as it passed. She heard it turn around, and a minute later it came back up behind her. All these nights of walking and finally some perv was going to ruin it? She looked straight ahead and picked up her pace. The car slowed next to her and she walked faster, wondering if she should break into a run, which would be impossible given how sore her legs were from yesterday's conversation with Wendy. A window went down and she fought the urge to look.

"Hey." It was Pete.

She let out her breath. "Hi."

"What are you doing?"

"Taking a walk."

"At two-thirty in the morning when it's thirty degrees out?"

"Yes."

"You're not even wearing orange."

"How would that make a difference this time of night?"

"Get in."

"I just got out here."

"It's late and freezing. Get in and let me take you home."

She'd walked a good two miles, and she was tired and didn't really want to walk all the way home. She got in.

He watched her buckle the seatbelt. "You have to break this habit. Some drunk could run into you."

"That could happen during the day."

"Or something worse."

"Ditto." She didn't have the energy to argue or explain.

"I know things have been rough for you," he said. He drove through downtown and turned up the hill toward her house. "I always wonder how you're doing." She could feel his eyes on her.

"You see me all the time. Every day. You know how I'm doing."

He pulled into her driveway.

"Did you check out Chapman?" she asked.

"I said we would." Terse.

"Thanks." She got out of the car.

"Is your brother here?"

"He's spending the night at Brian Plourde's. They're in some kind of marathon chess thing."

"I'm coming in."

"Oh really?"

"I'll help you get to sleep."

"Not tonight, cowboy." She couldn't believe he was serious.

"No, not that." He took his guitar out of the back. "Let's go."

"You're playing with the band again?" she asked.

"First gig since the cast came off."

Dubya popped his head up from where he was curled on Sal's blanket on the couch, his tail doing a helicopter spin.

"Want a beer?" she asked.

"Sure." He sat down in the chair and took the guitar out of its case. As she put the beer down next to him, he said, "Turn out the light and lie down on the couch."

"Is that an order?"

"Do you want to sleep or be a smartass?" he asked, plucking at the strings.

She shooed Dubya off and put her head on Sal's pillow. She looked expectantly at Pete, lit by the glow of the pellet stove. Dubya jumped back up and settled by her legs.

"Close your eyes." He strummed, humming, then singing, low and soothing. "Relax, Bernie, go to sleep. Pete's here so you don't have to count sheep."

She laughed and opened her eyes. "That's not going to make me sleep."

"Just relax."

He started strumming again and she closed her eyes. Dubya sighed and snuggled closer.

Pete finished one song and started another. It took her a minute to recognize it, the Talking Heads, only soothing, not hard-driving. *You make me shiver, I feel so tender. We make a pretty good team. Don't get exhausted, I'll do some driving. You ought to get you some sleep...*

231

She woke up to daylight, Dubya curled up in the chair Pete had been in. She could feel the cats around her, their purrs vibrating the couch. She was covered in a quilt that had been on her bed last she knew. She pulled it closer and closed her eyes, hearing Pete's guitar and low, soft voice, wishing she never had to get up and face the world.

CHAPTER 23
2007
Redimere, Maine
Friday, June 29

The heat was intense, the humidity thick, though the sun had gone. The night was dark, lit by occasional flashes of lightning, accompanied by a rumble of thunder.

Pete had finally heard from Brian Plourde. He'd asked Pete to meet at the transfer station, where no one would see them. "Top secret," Plourde had said. "You have to promise me you won't tell anyone you're talking to me. Anyone. Your wife, your mother, whoever."

Pete already could tell he was the kind of guy who was going to play it like Deep Throat. Pete would've rather been on Cal's deck, but he wasn't in Maine to enjoy quiet nights on the lake drinking beer.

The road out of town was dark and quiet. Every once in a while a firecracker went off, harmony for the lightning and thunder. Friday night before Fourth of July, Cal had told him. They'll be going off all hours of the day and night, despite the fact they're illegal. "We just don't have the manpower to go chasing them."

Better than gunshots. Pete turned down the dirt road to the transfer station, almost driving by in the dark, seeing the sign at the last minute, squealing the tires as he skidded onto the road. It was even darker than the main road, and he slowed down as he bumped along, trying to remember how far in the gate was. He couldn't believe Plourde would have access to the keys to the kingdom, so maybe he'd just be at the gate, but when Pete got to the gate, it was open. He drove in, wondering where he was supposed to go. He checked his cellphone. No call.

He drove past the recycling building, a low, black hulk against the dark woods and sky. Lightning flashed, and he thought he saw a pickup truck next to the office trailer, so he headed towards it. When he pulled up, though, there was no pickup, or any other kind of vehicle. He got out of his air-conditioned car, and the thick, wet heat wrapped around him, mosquitoes and something with a sharper, more painful bite attacking his exposed skin. Shorts, great choice, he thought, slapping at his sweat-soaked legs.

He tried the office door, but it was locked. There was no sign of Plourde anywhere. They were supposed to meet at nine, and it was ten after. He stood at the top of the concrete office steps, trying to make out shapes in the dark. The hopper loomed off to his right. The swap shack, and other buildings—he couldn't remember what any of them were—came into bright relief with a flash of lightning, then disappeared. Thunder boomed seconds later. Pete tried to remember the rule. As many miles away as seconds in between the lightning and thunder? The air felt like it had become thicker, heavier, as he stood there.

Nine-twenty and no sign of Plourde. Either the kid was playing games or had chickened out. He hated to leave if Plourde had something to offer, but he wasn't going to wait around in this dark, desolate place with a storm blowing in. He took out his phone. Plourde had said not to call him, part of his Deep Throat act. Screw that.

Pete's eyes were on his phone, so he only saw quick movement in his peripheral vision before a blow landed on the back of his head, knocking him to the ground. He scrabbled at the dirt, tried to shake off the pain and get up, but his legs were rubber. He braced for the next blow, trying to process through his spinning head and nausea what he saw, heard, smelled, anything that would tell him what was going on. He was looking at the undercarriage of his car, the action behind him. The only sound was movement, heavy breathing. Hands grabbed his and pulled them behind his back, zip-tied his wrists together, the plastic digging into his flesh.

"Hey," he said, the only word he could get out. The movement made his head pound. No one answered, but he could hear them breathe. He was being lifted from behind, still couldn't see who it was. Two of them, maybe, smelling like sweat, cigarettes.

They lifted him as lightning flashed, lighting up the hopper, which was now in front of him.

"Shit," one of the guys said, jerking Pete as the lightning made him flinch. The other one laughed, a sharp bark. The thunder crashed and then rumbled over them as Pete's feet left the ground.

"Lift," a voice said. The laugher, not the shit guy. Pete would want to identify them later. He tried to focus on what was happening, not on where he was being taken. "Hey," he tried again, more of a gurgle, his head pounding.

"Fucking storm," shit guy said.

"Shut up. No talking."

Pete was hefted over the edge of the hopper as the first raindrops hit, big fat ones that splatted on his bare skin and face, hissed as they hit the metal, still hot from the sun. It caught at the skin of arms and legs as he slid down on his back, head first. Through his sweat-filled eyes he could see two shadows at the top against the sky watching. He prayed for another lightning flash, so he could see who they were. It didn't come. Instead, the skies opened as he felt his head, then his shoulders go over the edge into the box in the bottom.

Over the sound of the rain as it hissed and splattered against the hot metal, he heard that laugh again, a loud nasal bark.

He landed on garbage bags, his legs above him. His head cleared more, and he turned over and slid forward, got to his knees on the garbage, which sank under his weight, plastic popping and sharp edges digging into his bare knees. The stench gagged him. *My whole fucking life is dumpsters.* The top of the sloped metal walls was a good fifteen feet away. With the rain in his eyes, the steady silver sheet of it between him and the black sky, he couldn't tell if his assailants were still up there. He wiggled his hands, trying to find slack to free them, but the zip-ties dug in deeper. He felt for sharp edges through the garbage bags to see if there was anything to cut the ties, but the rain, the plastic, his hands behind his back, made it pointless.

Above the rain another sound roared to life. An engine, loud enough to make the hopper vibrate. The garbage shifted under him. It wasn't the engine noise making it vibrate. The hopper had been turned on. He tried to stand up and lost his balance, landing on his back, as the garbage moved. The metal wedge that pushes the garbage hit his feet. He got to his knees, but the wedge knocked him back again. "Hey," he yelled, his voice working again. It was lost between the rain and the engine, even if anyone were out there.

He turned toward the opening to the dumpster. It was about three feet high. He had seconds to decide. If he didn't lie down, his upper body would hit the wall above the opening as he was pushed at it, probably breaking his back before he was cut in half. The other choice was to lie down and let the wedge push him in and hope there was enough give in the dumpster that he wouldn't be crushed when he was packed in.

He dropped and hit the garbage. Inside, feet away, he could see packed garbage bags, a lot of them split open, contents spilled. He tried to gauge how loose they were, how full the dumpster behind them was. Smells cut through the usual hot dumpster garbage odor. Kitty litter. Rotting meat. Strange how through the rain, through that overall smell, he could pick those out, he thought as he braced to enter.

He could almost laugh at the irony. Or cry. All those dreams about dumpsters, and he was going to die in one. He closed his eyes.

His lids were pierced by a blazing flash of lightning. An explosion of thunder on top of it crashed, echoing and booming so close it felt overhead. Pete's face was in the hole, the compressed garbage inches away, the smell suffocating, burning his eyes and filling his mouth. The light from the lightning turned everything white, erasing shape and color as the metal wedge pushed and folded his legs.

There was another crash, as loud as the thunder, but different. Everything went black, quiet, except the rain. No engine noise. The hopper had stopped.

For a long moment all he felt was gratitude as the rain pelted his back, his numb hands, the backs of his thighs. The metal wedge was cold and wet against his bent legs. The pressure would have folded his body up no matter how much slack there was inside. Panic overtook gratitude. He had to get out before the power came back and the engine started again. He tried to inch his head back out of the hole. He lifted it and banged the top of the opening, the same spot where he'd been hit, and the pain and nausea dropped him back down into the garbage. He took a deep breath and ignored everything except his need to get out. He inched backwards so he was sitting back on his legs. He pushed up with his legs, dizzy and sick, until he was standing on the garbage pile, higher now, that the wedge had pushed it all forward. He sat on the edge of the box, wondering what to do. If the engine started again, there'd be just enough room to put his legs up and brace them against the wall above the hole. Maybe. He tried it, leaning back and kicking his legs upwards. The movement caused him to slide on his back into the garbage, his head sinking down into it, his legs flailing. He pulled himself back up.

The rain had let up, the thunder and lightning had moved away. Clouds had parted past the tower of the hopper and stars blinked in the black sky.

"We're all in the gutter, but some of us are looking at the stars." The Oscar Wilde quote always appealed to him, even more when Chrissie Hynde growled it. It had been his battle cry since he was a teenager trying to fight his way out of his horrible life. He waited for it to inspire, but now that he was in it literally, it just depressed him.

Earlier he'd thought the night was quiet. No sirens or constant traffic, the night noises he was used to. Now he realized it wasn't.

Cicadas peeped a nonstop rhythm. The thunder rolled away in the distance. The call of a loon, then another one. He'd never heard one before the other night at Cal's.

He heard another noise. Tires on gravel. They stopped nearby and a door slammed, followed by another one.

"Hey," he yelled. "Help! Down here in the hopper."

"Fuck you doing down there?"

"Looking at the stars," he said.

"Don't go anywhere." A minute or two later, the voice was back. "You're that Philly cop."

"Yeah. Who are you?"

"Tim Shaw."

Then another voice. "Sgt. Ray Morin from the Redimere Police Department."

"Can you get me out?"

"We'll try."

Light played around Pete. A flashlight beam. "Your hands are tied? Jesus Christ," Morin said.

Pete heard a scraping noise, then Shaw. "I've got the pole we use to unclog this thing. It's got a hook on the end. Pretty sharp, so watch out. I'm going to try to hook your wrists and we'll drag you up. You're going to want to help any way you can."

Seconds later the cold metal of the hook poked against his arms. He lifted them so it caught under his wrists.

"I'm going to grab it around your arm," Shaw said. "Tense it up so it doesn't slide off, and use your legs to take some of the weight off. Brace them against the side and walk them up."

"Will this come on when the power comes back?" Pete asked as he felt the metal hook around his arm.

"Yup."

"Great." The hook pulled his arm up and back, wrenching his shoulder. Pete put his butt down on the angled wall, so he'd slide up, and got ready to plant his feet.

"Good thing the wall is so wet, that helps." Morin said. Pete had almost forgotten the cop was there. Pete heard a grunt, then someone said "Easy, easier," as his arms pulled up farther behind him, the wrenching in his shoulder almost unbearable. His feet hit the end of the wall and he pushed off with them, stepping backwards with first one, then the other, easing the pressure on his arm.

"That's good," Shaw said, breathing hard. "We're going to keep pulling."

Pete was just a couple feet from the top when the hopper engine roared to life, the metal under him vibrating. Shaw dropped the hook and Pete's feet went out from under him. "Shit," he said, feeling himself slip.

A hand grabbed the back of his shirt, then another his arm, then two more hands grabbed him, and he was pulled to safety.

. . . . .

It was still before midnight when Pete got back to Cal's, bruised, dehydrated, smelly, damp, and exhausted. It felt like it'd been days.

He let himself into the house, trying to be quiet. He wanted to take a shower, sleep. As he tried to wash the stink of the hopper off him, the friction burns on his forearms and the backs of his thighs stinging as the water hit them, he got angrier. Angry at the laughter as he was pushed in, at Shaw's amused patronizing after he pulled him out, at the cop's shrugs. Someone tried to kill me, he'd said. We'll talk about it in the morning, they'd replied.

In the morning, he took another shower. He could still smell the garbage. He hadn't slept, but it was just as well. He knew the dumpsters of his nightmares would've killed him.

"You got in late," Cal said as he handed Pete a mug of coffee. "You look like hell."

"Rough night."

Cal listened to Pete's story, with, Pete was glad to see, the outrage he'd expect.

"Let's get down to the station. I'll get Tim, Don, and Ray in there, and we can talk about it."

At the station, Don Littlefield seemed befuddled, Ray Morin annoyed. Shaw was contrite, but Pete felt the underlying disdain.

No one seemed upset, not even Cal anymore.

Pete had told them the night before about Brian Plourde's call.

"I talked to Plourde this morning," Shaw said now. "He said he decided not to go after all. He can't remember who else he told."

"He told me it was confidential," Pete said. "I can't believe he'd tell anyone."

"The guy's a goof," Shaw said. "He seemed like he was telling the truth."

"What are you going to do?" Pete asked.

Shaw looked surprised. "I told him he shouldn't be meeting anyone at the transfer station after hours. Took away his gate key. That was only for emergencies."

"That's it?"

"Someone having some fun, took it too far. Hard to say who," Shaw said. "I'm not excusing it, but you gotta know how those guys are with pranks. I'm betting someone was going to hit the emergency shutoff at the last second, but then the power went out. They knew I'd come over to check. So, no harm done."

"Someone tried to kill me," Pete said.

Shaw's face was blank. "Kill you? No. Someone just went too far. We don't even know who. Everyone in town knows you're here. So, probably a prank."

"I was asking about Reeves," Pete said. "I'm not sure why that would upset anyone enough to try to kill me, but it must have."

Shaw shook his head. "I understand it was an unpleasant experience. You're probably a little mixed up from it. No one was trying to kill you. Scare you maybe. Maybe you touched a nerve. How about Eli Perry? Anyone ask where he was last night?"

"Does he have access to the transfer station?" Pete asked. "Can he unlock the gate? Turn on the hopper?"

"Who knows? It's not rocket science. I wouldn't put it past him."

Cal had been listening, a judge waiting to render a verdict. "I know the boys at the dump like to mess around, but this goes beyond that. Pete's right. He could have been hurt or even killed.

240

It's more than just hijinks."

"Cal," Shaw said, his face flushing. "I can discipline guys, fire them if you want, but we don't even know who it was. It's all a misunderstanding."

"What wasn't understood?" Pete asked.

Shaw took a deep breath. Pete saw anger, mixed with that disdain again. No apology or remorse. No sincerity. "I'm sorry if my boys got out of hand. If it was even them. I'll be sure they hear about it."

Don, still befuddled, finally spoke up. "I'm not sure how we can discipline anyone if we don't know who it was. It wouldn't be fair to discipline everyone. I'm sorry, Pete, but it's strange you didn't see who did it."

"They hit me on the head from behind." Pete ached all over, the knot on the back of his head throbbed. The red marks on his wrists burned. So did the friction rash. He was exhausted. He knew his voice was strained, knew the anger was plain on his face. He knew there was probably a better, less emotional way to approach it. He used to be good at that.

"Did you see anyone when you got there?" Don asked Ray.

"Nope. Went to check when the power went out and got there same time Tim did. Didn't see anyone coming or going."

"Did Tim call and ask you to go over?" Pete asked.

Ray rolled his eyes. "No. We had a fire spark over there a year or two ago when a transmitter blew, so it's somewhere I check when the power goes out."

"Why do you care if I called him?" Shaw asked.

"Do you want to press charges?" Cal asked Pete. "You're within your rights. Against Plourde, I guess, though I can't see him doing something like this. Can't think of why he would."

The four waited. Cal sympathetic, Don befuddled. Ray bored, annoyed. Shaw with a self-satisfied smile, his cold eyes studying Pete.

Pete suddenly felt small. Small and stupid and beat and on the outside looking in. He wanted to press charges, but it was a fight he

241

knew would go nowhere. He hated himself for it, but he didn't have it in him. "I don't see the point."

Shaw smiled, clapped him on his sore back. "Sorry for the trouble, you know?"

Pete gave him a long, level look. He hoped Shaw got the message.

. . . . .

Pete's frustration almost choked him as he drove back to Cal's through steady traffic. Saturday before Fourth of July had clogged the town. The slow line of cars on the two-lane road, nowhere to pass, nowhere to detour, at least that he knew of, added to his frustration and anger. He'd seen the pity on Cal's face. Probably assessing Pete's mental health, figuring he was overreacting.

Is that what passed for fun here? Tying someone up and throwing him in a garbage hopper? They were right, though. He couldn't prove who it was. Before the meeting ended, Cal had asked Shaw if everyone had shown up to work. Shaw had kept his eyes steady on Pete as he'd reeled off half a dozen names, including Plourde's. Later, when he was alone, Pete had tried calling Plourde several times and didn't even get voice mail.

Plourde didn't seem to have a reason to set him up. Then again, Pete hadn't gotten enough information about Reeves to know who'd have a reason. It could have been Eli Perry. Could have been anyone.

Pete was beginning to wonder why he even cared. No one else gave a shit about JP Donovan, no one cared about Reeves now that he was gone. Everyone had moved on. What was he trying to prove? He'd been on a downhill slide for years, letting his marriage slip away, his life. He was useless as a cop. Didn't even know if they'd have him back after his shameful breakdown. And now he'd almost ended up dead—in a dumpster, the metaphor for his pathetic life.

Exhaustion overwhelmed him. He felt bereft but wasn't sure what for. He was glad he'd wanted to live last night, because sometimes over the past months he'd wondered if he did. He'd poked at it like a bruise, then backed away, too scared to answer. Now he knew, but where did that leave him? Nothing to go back to. No family. His job in shambles. His JP Donovan obsession now obvious to him as the farce it was, a way to keep the demons from devouring him.

A car up ahead swerved, a sudden movement to the shoulder and back. Pete hit the brakes, on alert. A second car, coming in the other direction, a hundred yards ahead or so, swerved onto the shoulder, then back onto the road. Brake lights on the cars ahead of him flashed. The cars directly ahead of him swerved, too, to the shoulder, back to the pavement, but he couldn't see why.

Then he did. A duck stalking back and forth in the other lane, squawking, charging the cars as they slowly rolled by. It took a second for him to notice the ducklings. Two were running in circles on the shoulder. More were squashed in the middle of the road, feathers and bright red smears. One clump had a little head sticking up. Another a tiny pair of webbed feet, pedaling desperately from a mash of feathers and guts.

His chest tightened. His shirt clung to his wet back and sweat blurred his eyes. He rolled down the window, desperate for air, even though the air-conditioner was blasting. The mother duck, frantically running back and forth, the pulpy red piles with feathers, still floating in the wake of the passing cars. The little dying legs, churning in the air.

Pete threaded through the carnage fighting the urge to stop like a couple other cars had. What would be the point? His theme for the morning.

It's just ducks, he told himself, just ducks.

The smell of the dumpster oozed from his pores with the sweat, and he saw those other ducks, from four years ago, in that other dumpster. He was shaking, soaked now with sweat, his hands slipping on the steering wheel. He pulled onto the bumpy shoulder, the car sliding toward the trees in the dirt and grass before it came to a stop.

He saw the store owner and the newspaper editor, helpful but confused, wondering what he wanted, why he was here. Cal, looking at him with pity, he could see now. Tim Shaw gloating. Eli Perry's disdain. The laughter as he went over the edge and slid down the wall of the hopper.

He put his head on his hands on the steering wheel and took deep breaths, trying to fight off the shaking, the sobs he knew were coming.

"Shit," he said. "Shit, shit, shit."

What was he doing here? The futility of it, the silliness of his mission grabbed him, but so did the terror. Now this. A panic attack over ducks in the road.

"I'm such an idiot," he said out loud, taking more deep breaths, trying to stop the sobs, the spinning. "A fucking idiot."

It was time to go home.

CHAPTER 24
2009
Redimere, Maine
Monday, November 23

Bernie's first stop Monday morning was the Country Grocer. She hoped to get Walt alone, but it was hard with the Thanksgiving week frenzy.

After loitering around the aisles dodging harried shoppers, she finally just came out and said it. "I need to talk to you really quick, in private."

"About Pete?" he asked hopefully as he closed his office door behind him. For a minute she thought he knew about the prescription bottle, but then she realized he was asking as one of Pete's best friends hoping for the love match.

"Kind of," Bernie said. "Why would a prescription bottle of his be in your dumpster?"

"I have no idea."

"Wayne Daggett found it."

"Wayne's been on high alert since I started inventory. I've been throwing out a lot and he's pretty much staked out the dumpster, but I can't imagine where it came from. Have you asked Pete?"

"No." She wasn't going to explain. "Can you think of anything?"

To his credit, Walt thought. "I've cleaned out a lot of trash the past couple weeks."

"Would you notice throwing out a prescription bottle?"

"Not necessarily. A lot of crap has collected over the years, especially out back." His eyes lit up. "Wendy, in fact, was frantic over some trash I threw out from the back room. But she wouldn't care about Pete's prescription bottle, obviously."

"Okay, thanks." Maybe she would, Bernie thought, though she had no clue why.

"What's this about?"

"I can't tell you now. Please don't tell anyone I asked."

"Even Pete or Wendy?"

"Especially Pete or Wendy."

.....

Vicki popped her head into Pete's office. "Eli Perry's here." She made her eyes huge and mouthed, "Help."

Too early on Monday morning for this, Pete said to himself.

Perry and Natalie stood in the outer office. "What can I do for you?" Pete asked.

Perry looked down at Natalie. "Don't you have something for the chief?"

Natalie held out her hand, clutching the orange gloves.

"What's this?" Pete asked.

"Nat?" Perry said.

Her lip trembled and she looked down, kicking one sneaker with the other. "I'm giving them back."

"I don't need you buying stuff for my kid," Perry said.

"I didn't buy those," Pete said. "I lent Natalie three dollars. There weren't any other gloves in the store that were right. She paid for most of them and they belong to her."

"Give them to him," Perry said, and Natalie thrust the gloves toward Pete. Pete hesitated but took them. "Want to come into my office a minute?" Pete asked Perry.

"No thanks. We're done."

"It'll just be a minute. Natalie can stay out here and talk to Vicki." It was an order.

Perry followed Pete into the office, then stood with his arms crossed, glaring.

"You don't have to like me, but don't take it out on Natalie," Pete said.

"Don't tell me how to raise my kid."

"There was no harm done with the gloves."

"Someone called DHHS, said I'd hurt my kid. I assumed it was Shaw. But then my kid tells me she's got a new friend, the police chief."

Perry stepped closer to Pete, was inches away. Pete didn't back up but felt his shoulders tighten, flexed his hands at his sides, ready. He was outweighed by more than a hundred pounds, he was still weak, his arm not recovered, his ribs still sore. Perry could crush him. He knew Perry wouldn't be stupid enough to do anything in the station, but Pete was pissed off enough to almost hope he would try.

"Does it matter who called?" He knew his calm didn't fool Perry.

"Yeah, it does, because I didn't hurt my kid. So whoever called wants to get me. Wants my kid taken away for no good reason."

"Maybe there is a reason."

"Who the fuck do you think you are?" Perry asked. He wasn't yelling. His tone was as even as Pete's, but the menace was clear.

"I called DHHS. I saw something and was obligated to report it." Pete felt himself spring a little on the balls of his feet. C'mon, he thought, try something. *Try something you big fat fuck.*

Perry stepped back and laughed, as though Pete had said it out loud. "You don't want to fight me, little man. You want to mind your own business and let me raise my kid as I see fit. If DHHS needs to look at anyone, it's someone who walks around town with a ten-year-old girl and gives her presents. That's the guy I'd worry about."

Pete caught him off guard, all the anger and disgust that had been building in him for days and weeks and months, maybe years, exploding. He hit Perry with his full body weight, his left arm pushing against Perry's massive neck. They slammed against the wall, Perry roaring in surprise and anger. Pete didn't say anything,

247

Maureen Milliken

didn't know what he was going to do next. In that moment he wanted to kill Perry, or maybe just let Perry kill him, he didn't care which. He pushed his left arm harder against Perry's neck, grabbing Perry's arm with his weak right arm, trying to twist it behind his back. He was up on his toes, their noses nearly touching, his eyes even with Perry's. Perry wasn't doing anything, not fighting back, and that pissed Pete off more.

"Pete!" He hadn't heard the door open but felt powerful arms around him in a bear hug, pinning his arms against his sides, pulling him back.

Perry sagged back against the wall, swearing.

Pete struggled in Dawna's arms. He could feel the cold buckle of her belt against his back where his shirt had ridden up. He suddenly realized how ridiculous he was. "Let me go."

"I need to know you're not going to kill him."

"I'm fine," Pete said, the anger gone, replaced with embarrassment.

"Go home, Eli," Dawna said.

"You need to get your boss under control," Perry said, rubbing his neck. "He's going to get himself hurt."

"Excuse me." They turned. Vicki was in the doorway, behind Natalie, who stared at her father and Pete, the same stoic look as always, but Pete could see the dismay. He turned away as he tucked his shirt in, trying to hide his shame.

"Come on, Nat," Perry said, ushering her out, her eyes still on Pete. Vicki left, too, closing the door behind her.

"What happened?" Dawna asked when they were alone.

"I don't know."

"He could have killed you," Dawna said. "He could press charges."

Pete sat back against the desk. "He won't."

"He's not a child abuser."

"I saw cigarette burns, and that was just her arm."

"Her mom's boyfriend did that," Dawna said.

"How do you know?"

248

"She was my cousin. When you get the DHHS report it'll say the same."

Pete took a deep breath.

"Natalie saw the whole thing," Dawna said.

"I'm sorry about that." Ashamed, he wanted to say.

"Maybe you should check in with a counselor."

"I'm fine."

"I know with PTSD—"

"This won't happen again."

"Eli's not a bad guy."

Pete's arm cramped, and he realized he was gripping the edge of the desk. He let go, flexed his hand. "I was playing with the band last night in Farmington, and someone there told me they'd seen Bernie leaving his place."

"Is that what this was about?"

"No. This was about Natalie and Eli and me not controlling my tempter."

"I'm sure there's an explanation for Bernie being at his house."

"I'm sure there is."

"You're wrong if you think Eli and Bernie—"

"I don't think that. I'm concerned about her judgment and her safety."

"She can take care of herself. I hope I'm not talking out of turn, Pete, but there are worse guys we should be focusing on."

She never called him Pete, it was always Chief. He couldn't look at her. "I know," he said.

She nodded, then left, shutting the door softly behind her.

. . . . .

Bernie doodled on her notepad, trying to figure out what to do about the prescription bottles, all the other stuff she had to do in the next two days, the stories she had to wrap up. It was the Monday before Thanksgiving. The paper was loaded with fliers and coupons for the upcoming weekend shopping craziness and she had to get it to press early, but she felt like right now she had forty-eight blank pages. She'd drawn big long columns on her pad, tried to line

up everything she knew with what was definite and what was
speculation. What was related to what with all the different things
going on, including the Shaws, Chapman, and Pete's bottle. It didn't
help. All she had were big long confusing columns with lots of
pieces of information. None of it had to do with getting this week's
paper to press.

Fergus and Carrie came in.

"What have you two been up to?"

"Pounding the pavement on behalf of Benji Reeves," Fergus
said. "No one wants to say shit about him. I was just at the transfer
station. Bunch of assholes."

"How about you, Carrie?"

"Police said they found some belongings in the knapsack in the
cellar hole, but not what."

Bernie's cellphone rang. Sal, calling from her landline.

"Hey, sleeping beauty."

"You need to come home right now." His voice shook.

"What's wrong?"

"Just come home, okay?"

Bernie got in the car, wondering what fresh hell her brother
was going to visit on her now. Though it was a good sign it was him
calling, not the police.

Sal was sitting in the living room with Brian Plourde, who was
even more pale than usual, his eyes rimmed red.

"What's wrong?" Bernie asked, flopping into the chair. She
shot Sal a look that said this better be good. Sal's look back was
wide-eyed shock. Okay, maybe it was good.

"What's going on?" she asked again.

"Oh my god," Brian said, his face in Dubya's fur.

"Tell her," Sal said. "Maybe it's nothing."

"No, it's something," he said. "When I went home today, there
was a state police cruiser parked in front."

"What did they want?"

"I don't know," he said. "I turned around and came here."

Bernie took her cellphone out of her bag.

"What are you doing?" Brian asked.

"Calling the police."

Brian leapt from the couch. "No, don't do that. Please!"

"Why don't you listen to what Brian has to say first?" Sal said. "You know how the police like to rush to judgment. Tell her what you told me, Brian."

"All right, but I'm not saying I'm not going to call," Bernie said. "At any moment."

Brian took a shaky breath and sat back down. Dubya jumped up onto the couch between Brian and Sal and put his head on Brian's lap. Bernie took no comfort that her dog seemed to trust Brian. He didn't have good judgment.

"I think it was because I was hunting, and I'm not supposed to because of my conviction," Brian said.

"The state police don't care about that," Bernie said.

"There's more to it," Brian said. "I shot this deer and it became a big deal." He looked from Bernie to Sal, then down at Dubya. "Shot a deer when I shouldn't have."

"Someone reported it?" Bernie asked.

"Here's the thing with that," he said. "It turned out it wasn't a deer."

Bernie knew without Brian having to say another word. "Benji Reeves?" Her cellphone was hot in her hand.

"It was a deer. He was, I mean," Brian said. "It was dark, but I know what I saw and it was a deer. Benji must have been right next to it or something. Anyway, he wasn't wearing orange."

"You must have noticed when you field-dressed him, when you slit him from stem to stern, pulled his guts out, cut out his rectum, cut off his dick, for chrissake, turned him over to let all his blood run out, that he wasn't a deer," Bernie said, her voice rising with each word. "Not to mention when you blew his head in half from two feet away. I'm calling Pete."

"Don't!" Brian yelled. "I didn't do all that stuff. Someone else did."

"Who?"

251

"I don't know."

"I'm calling."

"Do we have to?" Brian asked Sal.

"Yes we do," Bernie said. "Sal doesn't get a vote."

"I want to hear what Brian has to say," Sal said. "You wouldn't have done anything bad like that, right?"

Brian shook his head so hard Bernie thought she could hear it rattle. "No, I wouldn't. Not in a million years. It was a deer."

"Start from the beginning," Bernie said.

"There was a full moon that morning," Brian said.

"Maybe not that much."

"It matters," he said, annoyed. "It lit things up, and I needed to get out before dawn because I had to be at work at seven."

"Out to?"

"To hunt. I'd seen signs the Monster Buck had been out. No scat but broken branches, stuff like that. On the tote road out to the cellar holes. I just wanted it so bad. All the guys laugh at me, but if I got it, I could show them. I'd never have to hunt again after I got that buck."

Sal broke in. "You saw those signs and knew it was the buck?"

"Let him finish," Bernie said.

"I did," Brian said. "I knew it was."

"That's the same area you saw Benji, too, right?" Sal said, looking at Bernie, not Brian.

"I saw him out on Pond Road, remember?"

"That's what you said last time, but first time you said Ridge Road, and Moses said it was the cellar holes."

"I don't think I ever said that," Brian said. "You know Moses is retarded. He gets mixed up."

"I must be remembering wrong," Sal said, still looking at Bernie.

Brian continued. "I got to the clearing near where that old shack is and across, maybe seventy-five yards, I saw the buck at the tree line. Clear as day. I must have made a sound or something, because I saw a flash of white, its flag, I knew. I already had my gun up and ready, so I shot. It made a funny noise, high-pitched like, one I'd never heard before. I shot again and it took off into the woods, I could hear it crashing. So I followed it. It went right down the trail, too. I could see it moving up ahead but not real clear, because in the trees the moon wasn't lighting things up too good. I kept tripping over roots and things. The buck did, too, I think."

"The buck tripped?" Bernie asked.

"It was moving funny," Brian said. "Deer do funny things when they're shot. Then it turned and went through an opening. I saw it go and heard the branches crash, so I went in and it was in a clearing, just standing there. So I shot again." He took a deep breath. "It fell and I went over and it wasn't the buck."

"It was Reeves," Bernie said.

Brian nodded. "Yeah. I guess he was there, too. I shot him by accident. In the head. Instead of the buck. Like I said, he wasn't wearing orange. His sweatshirt was brown, like a deer."

"It was too dark for you to even know the difference between orange and brown," Bernie, said, punching her speed dial.

"I'm going to go," Brian said, getting up, dislodging Dubya.

"Stay," Sal said, his hand gripping Brian's skinny forearm.

"Pete," Bernie said. "We've got a situation at my house."

"I know," he said. "We're on your front steps."

Bernie opened the door to Pete and four state troopers. His car and two cruisers were parked haphazardly in her driveway and dooryard.

"Sal?" she asked. Pete shook his head, and her relief almost made her drop to the floor.

One of the troopers took handcuffs off his belt and went to Brian as Sal moved into the kitchen.

"Brian Plourde?"

"Who wants to know?" Brian asked.

The trooper cuffed him. "We need to talk to you about a murder."

"Benji Reeves," Bernie said.

"No," Pete said as Brian was led out the door. "Leslie Lark."

.....

Bernie returned to a reporter-less office.

"Where are Carrie and Fergus?" she asked Annette. "We have a big development."

"They went to lunch," Annette said. "Was it you who called the Drug Enforcement Agency? They're on the phone, kinda mad."

"What are you talking about?"

"I'll transfer."

The spokesman for the Maine DEA started talking, fast and loud, the minute she picked up, telling her in no uncertain terms not to publish a story about the impending bust of a Redimere doctor for prescription fraud. "You're going to blow our case."

"I don't know what you're talking about," Bernie said.

Someone had called, wanted quotes for a story. Fergus. She talked the DEA guy down, said they had no intention of publishing such a story, then booted up her computer. The front page of Thursday's paper came up on her screen, a headline filling the top of the page, "DEA Targets Local Doctor for Pill Pushing." Under it was a story, with a photo of Chapman, a poorly focused one of him walking into his office holding a takeout coffee. A byline, Fergus X. Kelley. Staff Writer.

She was still trying to digest the story, which seemed to be a compilation of her notes, including the speculation part, when Fergus come through the door, followed by Carrie.

"Who the hell gave you permission to put that story on the page?" Bernie said. She was trying not to yell. "Or even write it? It looks like my notes."

"Tough to get scooped with your own story, right?" Fergus said. "I saw your notes, but I knew he's your doctor and it's yet another story you're compromised on, so I helped you out."

"I don't even know where to begin," Bernie said. "Those were notes, a lot of it off the record, some of it just me speculating on where to go." There's no way it would have gone to print, because there's no way she wouldn't have seen it. He must have realized that and did it anyway, which pissed her off even more. Was he that

254

arrogant, or just that stupid?

"Was your information wrong?" Fergus asked. "The things about Shaw? Your boyfriend's pill bottle?"

She was so mad she wasn't going to bother to explain all the things he'd done wrong. Just kick his flabby white ass out the front door. As soon as this week's paper got out.

"Don't be so sensitive," he said. "There's enough news for everyone. I knew you'd react this way, but I was hoping cooler heads would prevail."

"I'm the only head that matters right now," Bernie said.

"I'm glad we didn't do that web update," Carrie said.

Bernie felt like her head swivel, *Exorcist* style. "What are you talking about?"

"It's moot," Fergus said, giving Carrie a warning glare.

Carrie ignored him. "Fergus wanted to put it up as a web update, but you'd said you'd work with me on web updates. He said that you said it was okay."

Forget swiveling. Bernie's head was exploding. "That's just—"

"You have to decide what you want," Fergus broke in. "Web updates? No web updates? It's hard to do any story here that you're not involved in. Like I said the other day, your affair with the police chief compromises you."

Bernie took a deep breath, tried to smother the explosion. They had to get the paper out, and it seemed impossible, with the developing news, the amount of work, the early Thanksgiving deadline. She needed Fergus to help. "You and me will have a meeting about this Friday."

"I'm going away for the holiday weekend."

"Monday, then. Eight a.m."

"If you fire me, I'll sue you for age discrimination," Fergus said.

"We'll talk about your status at the meeting," she said. "Let me just make it clear that my notes are private and anything that goes on the web goes through me." So much more she wanted to say. Actually, not say, just grab his self-satisfied neck and shake him until

255

his rheumy eyes popped out. But again, the paper, the paper, the paper.

"Suit yourself," Fergus said, going back to his desk.

"Sorry," Carrie said.

"It's not your fault," Bernie said.

"I went over to the police station, and even though Dawna couldn't tell me what they found in the knapsack, she told me that they found Brian Plourde's fingerprints on the steering wheel of your brother's car, and in some other places."

"Yeah, he was at my house when he was arrested. Let's get to work. We have a paper to put out."

. . . . .

Pete had felt Bernie's grip, tight on his arm as Brian Plourde was walked out of her house.

"We can talk later," he'd said, turning around.

"No." Her fingers dug through his jacket. "He said he shot Benji Reeves."

"Don't talk to anyone else," Pete said, as the doors to the cruisers slammed.

Now he was back in his office. He knew Bernie was probably waiting for a call from him, but she'd have to wait. The DEA had called, hopping mad, saying the newspaper was jumping the gun on the Chapman drug bust. He'd only found out about the Chapman drug bust himself when he'd called a friend at the DEA to run Bernie's Chapman theory past him. He swore he hadn't said a word to the newspaper. It wasn't his problem right now, anyway. But something still nibbled at the edges of his conscience any time someone said prescription. It wouldn't come to him. Didn't matter, he had more important things to think about.

For instance, the things in Benji Reeves' knapsack. They didn't seem like much, but Pete knew different. A worn Lenny Dysktra Phillies jersey with the sleeves cut off. A black skull earring.

Before he could deal with that, he had to deal with Brian Plourde. He'd denied knowing anything about Leslie Lark, despite the fact his prints were on Sal O'Dea's steering wheel and on a computer printout of directions to the transfer station found jammed in her wiped-clean purse. They were also on the note Sal had left Leslie, found stuffed in her purse, saying he was leaving, apologizing for being an ass, and promising to come back for the car later.

One thing Brian had been willing to talk about was the deer. Seemed to think, somehow, if he thought the guy was a deer, it would get him off the hook. He wasn't wearing orange, Plourde kept insisting. It'd happened plenty of times before in Maine, the shooter found not at fault.

But those victims hadn't been field-dressed, Pete had pointed out.

The state cops and Pete didn't always agree, but they were unanimous that Plourde had intentionally executed Reeves, probably as payback for going to prison for the pill break-ins after Reeves left town, then finished it off by gutting him like a prize deer.

"Obviously shows a lot of hostility," George Libby had said. Pete couldn't disagree.

Dawna knocked on his open door. "I can't figure out how any of it fits," she said, coming in and sitting down.

"What do you think of his story that he thought he was shooting a deer?" Pete asked.

"I have trouble believing anyone who says that, but it happens. Some pretty famous cases in the past thirty years. I just read an article about it that said the brain believes it sees what it wants to."

"It didn't hurt it was five a.m., and he and Benji had a history," Pete said.

"Maybe," Dawna said. "He could be telling the truth, though. That article said the brain only takes in fragments of images, then puts them together to form an image of what it believes it's seeing. That's why blaze orange works, and hunting fatalities went way down after it became required. The brain doesn't expect the blaze orange, and it short-circuits the forming image of the deer. Otherwise, if people want to see a deer really bad, they see a deer."

257

"I don't think if Reeves was wearing orange it would have made a difference."

"Here's an interesting thing," Dawna said. "Studies show that hunters who shot a person when they thought they saw a deer never say 'I thought it was a deer.' They say 'It was a deer.'"

"Brian didn't say 'thought.'"

"That's why I think he may be telling the truth. Here's another thing. After they do it and find out it's a person, when they replay it in their mind, it's so traumatic that their mind convinces them it was a deer. They replay it with a deer, not a person."

"I don't buy that."

"I can't imagine I would ever mistake a person for a deer," Dawna said. "But it's interesting."

"I still don't buy it. And anyway, he field-dressed him and all the rest of it, so obviously he got over the trauma pretty quick."

"I just think it's interesting," she said again, apologetic. "What we think we see because we expect to see it."

"I just thought of something."

"What?"

"I had a bottle of Vicodin in my medicine cabinet. When I moved, it wasn't there. I just realized that. I know it was there a couple weeks ago, because I saw it and thought about tossing it, but I didn't."

"Who's been in your place?"

Bernie, he thought. Knew that wasn't it. "Reeves. The night before he was shot."

CHAPTER 25
2009
Redimere, Maine
Tuesday, November 24

C arrie was waiting at the door when Bernie got to work at dawn Tuesday.

"Ready to rock and roll?" Bernie asked, wondering how she was going to get through the next twenty-four hours. She hadn't slept a minute the night before.

Carrie nodded. Good enough.

"Brian Plourde is being arraigned in Farmington at ten, do you want to go to that?" Bernie asked. "Get there early and get the affidavit from the clerk. That'll have all the details about what led to his arrest. I'll see if state police or Pete or Dawna or someone can fill us in."

"Okay."

Guy walked in with a Dunkin' Donuts dozen. "Figured we'd need these," he said, setting them down on the empty desk where all the food gathered.

"Those and about five more people," Bernie said. She started clicking through the paper's pages. Way too many were still empty.

"Anyone seen Fergus?" She almost said Feckless. She was beginning to not care about what she called him.

"If he doesn't show up, you, me, and Carrie can get this done," Guy said as he settled in at his desk.

Bernie's email pinged. Another release from the state police.

Brian Plourde's arraignment was postponed and the charge he murdered Leslie Lark was being dropped. Bernie's heart sank. Did this mean Sal was back on the hook? On the other hand, Plourde was being charged with Reeves' murder. She read more. Leslie was alive and in a coma in a hospital in New Hampshire.

Her cellphone rang. Pete.

"Have you heard all the news?" he asked.

"I don't know if I've heard all of it. Leslie wasn't murdered? She's alive? I don't know where to start."

"Can you come over to the station? I know you have a busy day. They're not going to have a press conference, because of Thanksgiving. People are off. They're going to issue a release, but Libby's here, and we can tell you what we know."

Bernie grabbed a doughnut. "You guys hold the fort," she said. "I'll be back. Fill the inside local pages with whatever copy we have. We're going to need the front and two inside jump pages for Plourde, Reeves, and Lark. If Fergus shows up, put him to work, but for chrissake don't let him write anything."

"Gotcha," Guy said.

"I'm on my way over to the PD to do some kind of interview. I don't know what it's about, the latest on Leslie, I think."

"Gotcha," Carrie said.

. . . . .

"You're going to need a bigger notebook," Pete said as Bernie sat down.

"Great," she said. "Can I record?" She dug through her bag for her micro-cassette recorder. She hoped the battery wasn't dead and it had a cassette. She rarely used it.

Libby launched right in. "I'm going to try to make this as simple as possible. Because it's not."

"So Leslie is alive in New Hampshire?"

"Just let him tell the story," Pete said.

"We're not clear on all the details because Plourde can't put together a normal sentence," Libby said. "But the Reeves murder and Lark whatever you want to call it—abduction maybe, we're still

260

figuring out the charges with the DA—are connected. Forget about Reeves for now, because we haven't untangled that.

"The Lark thing started when your brother lost his cellphone within hours on the job at the transfer station. She texted asking what she was supposed to do with the car, and Plourde says he texted her back and asked her to bring it. You know by now what the texts said."

"Why?" Bernie asked.

"We can't get a straight story out of Plourde. After that, the cellphone was put in your purse."

"Courier bag."

"Plourde says he did it, but doesn't remember when."

"Bill Chapman did it."

"Bernie," Pete said.

"This is where things get nutty," Libby said, ignoring Bernie. "After Leslie shows up at the dump Tuesday night, Plourde hits her over the head, plies her with alcohol and sleeping pills and drives her in your brother's car to Manchester, New Hampshire, where he left her on a park bench near a hospital."

"Why?"

"We haven't figured that out. No one said criminals are smart, and this one is not only not smart, but he has way too active an imagination. He said he was going to throw her in the hopper at the dump but changed his mind."

Pete's face turned red and he turned to the window. Bernie wanted to ask what he'd just thought of—it had to be important—but he didn't say anything. It took her a beat to tune back in to Libby.

"The guy makes things more complicated than they need to be. What we still don't know, besides the all-consuming why, is how Reeves' blood got in the trunk of your brother's car."

Pete turned back to face them. "Plourde's connection to Reeves is what ties it all together, we just haven't connected all the dots."

Forget all, Bernie didn't see *any* dots connected. "Why didn't

261

the car show up until days later?"

"Another thing Mr. Plourde can't explain," Libby said. "Unfortunately the more he talks, the less he makes sense. Others are obviously involved, but we don't know who or why. There was something at stake, something big enough to kill Reeves and maybe kill Leslie to cover it up."

They were done. Bernie tossed her notebook back in her bag. "Thanks, but I don't understand any of it."

. . . . .

Bernie and Sal knocked on the Moshers' door. Sal hadn't wanted to come, but she made him. She knew Moses might not talk to just her, but he would talk to the wonderful Sal. She also knew that, whatever Brian had done with Leslie, he hadn't done it alone.

Moses' mom opened the door, a woman about Bernie's age with a big smile and hair the same bright red as Moses', though with help from a bottle. When Bernie introduced them, she was delighted.

"Sal! You're the nice man who lent Brian your car. I'm glad you finally got it back. Sorry about that."

"No problem," said Sal, raising his eyebrows at Bernie as they were led into the living room.

"Moses!" she yelled over her shoulder, then turned to Sal and Bernie. "I'm Diana. He's so upset about Brian. He'll be glad to see you."

Bernie could hear heavy feet on the floor above. "I'm with the newspaper, actually, and we wondered if we could talk to Moses about Brian for our story?"

Diana's brow furrowed. "I don't know."

"You can stay, and if there's anything you're not comfortable with..." Bernie let the sentence trail off. She wasn't making any promises, just sounding like she was.

Moses shambled into the room, red-eyed and puffy-faced. "Hi Sal. Hi Mrs. O'Dea."

They all sat down. "Have the police talked to you?" Bernie asked him.

"No."

She was relieved. If they'd already gotten to him, it would mean he didn't have anything to say, given the scant information earlier. "We want to fill in some gaps about what happened with Leslie."

"She was supposed to be like Benji, but then Brian didn't want to do it because he liked Sal," Moses said.

"Like Benji?"

"You know." Moses drew a line down his torso from his sternum to his stomach.

"Why?" She looked straight ahead at Moses. She didn't want to catch Sal's eye or see the look on his face.

"So everyone would think there was a serial killer and it was Sal. Sorry, Sal."

"It's okay, buddy." Sal's voice shook.

"Brian liked Sal too much, so we took her to New Hampshire, where no one would know her. That was bad, though, and someone got mad just like Brian said they would."

Bernie was writing furiously. "Who got mad?" she asked carefully. She was waiting for Diana to jump in, but she was staring, mouth open, at her son.

Moses spoke slowly, like Bernie was an idiot. "Because they said to Brian to do Leslie just like Benji. I can't say who or they'll do me like that too. Then someone put the phone in your purse."

"We'll come back to that later," Bernie said. "Can you just tell me what happened with Benji and Leslie?"

"I just did."

"Why did Benji's body not show up for more than a week?"

"He was in the trunk. Brian didn't tell me he was going to put it with the scarecrows."

Diana found her voice. "Brian accidentally locked the car in my garage. He came by to drop Moses off, and they had, well, I thought, it was a nice young lady taking a nap in the back. I'd come out to tell them I had to go to my sister's in Scarborough, because she was sick, and I asked if Moses could stay with Brian. Brian parked the car in my garage when they got home later that night,

263

and he didn't realize he couldn't get back in without the remote opener, so it was locked in until I got home Sunday night."

Sal had turned whiter.

"Why was Benji in the trunk, Moses?" Bernie asked.

"I'm not supposed to tell."

"You better," Diana said.

"Okay, Mom." He closed his eyes and scrunched up his face. "We were supposed to put him in Eli Perry's garbage truck. The day Benji got shot, so it would look like Eli did it. But Eli's truck was at the shop. So Brian said he had to call it edible."

"Call an audible?" Sal asked.

"Yeah. So we needed to make it look like someone else did it. So he said we'd make it look like a serial killer. He left Benji in his truck, but when we had the lady's car we put Benji in the trunk. Then when he left the lady's car at the park, he put Benji back in his truck. He said I'd laugh when I saw what he was going to do with him, but I puked instead."

"He was in Brian's truck?" Sal asked.

"Since when?" Bernie asked.

"Under that tarp he keeps in the back. Just a couple days. Since when he was shot."

Sal blanched. Bernie knew what he was thinking. No wonder Brian's truck stunk.

"Brian said if we made it really complicated the police wouldn't be able to figure it out. He kept yelling at me to wipe up the fingerprints, but he was supposed to wipe up his when it was done. I guess he forgot. Brian is so smart. He's going to be a lawyer or invent computer games."

"Why did he field dress Benji?"

"Someone else did, but I can't say." He drew an invisible zipper across his lips.

"Maybe you won't say to these nice people, but you'll say to the police," Diana said. "Get your coat, we're going to the station."

.....

Somehow Bernie, Carrie, and Guy sorted the story out as much as they could and got the paper done, Bernie constantly interrupted by calls from the police.

Guy drew a flow chart on the office white board so they could keep it all straight, but it still didn't make sense.

"My head hurts from shaking it so much," Guy said Wednesday morning as they finished up.

Fergus had never shown up, but Bernie was just as glad. She'd be happy to never see him again.

"I think he's been sleeping in his car," Guy said. "I got in here one morning, and he was asleep on the couch. Turned out he'd hid upstairs until you locked up. I was going to tell you, but there was so much going on."

The thought of him in her office after hours sickened Bernie. She was about to say so, too, when her email dinged. It was the friend at her old paper, just now seeing the email asking about Fergus she'd sent the week before.

"He was fired, for making up things in stories, not laid off," she told Guy.

"Doesn't surprise me," Guy said.

"Great. Someone down there told him I was asking around about him. He called another guy at the paper, begging them not to tell me. That was yesterday."

"That explains a lot."

"Guess we'll never see Feckless again," she said, with huge relief. "Wonder where I'm supposed to mail his paycheck? His car?" She pushed the button on the computer that sent the papers off to the printer, ten hours earlier than usual, thanks to Thanksgiving. "I just want to sleep for a year."

When she got home in the breaking dawn, she was surprised to see Sal up and dressed.

"I can't get over Brian," he said. "I guess my feelings can't be hurt too much that he was going to frame me for murder, since he barely knew me. Typical Brian overthinking, though. That's what kills his chess game. I kept telling him that."

"Too bad you only had a week or two to school him in your

wisdom."

"Turns my stomach to know that body was in the back of his truck."

"Everything about this turns my stomach. Why are you up and fully dressed at six a.m.?"

"I'm going to visit Leslie."

"She's in a coma."

"Even so." He reddened. "I owe her that much. I wasn't truthful about that whole thing."

"No kidding." Bernie didn't want to hear Sal's story, finally, nearly three weeks after he first showed up. Just more information to load into her addled overloaded brain. But Sal wanted to talk, and talk he did.

When he first went to Leslie's in April, it was because he was ashamed of being fired, and couldn't think of anywhere else to go. He'd liked the farm, liked helping her out, and could see a life for himself. They had big plans for the marijuana-growing operation. But, Sal said, he was in a funk about plagiarizing and losing his job, and it affected his judgment.

"Leslie was being all anal about it, all by the book. I just wanted to do it. So I hooked up with some guys who ended up being bad news. They conned me out of a bunch of money and then wouldn't leave us alone. They knew I wouldn't tell, because I was trying to buy pot illegally, and I thought I could convince them to give me my money back."

"I can't believe you'd do something like that."

"I wasn't thinking straight for a while. I can't explain it," he said. "They came after me for more money, started hassling Leslie, and she got really, really pissed."

"She kicked you out?"

"Kind of. We had a big fight and that's when she dropped the bomb," Sal said.

"Bomb?" Bernie was trying hard to focus.

"She'd been seeing a guy last year. Bjorn Svensen. Can you believe that name?"

"I'll believe anything right now."

"He'd been deployed in Afghanistan with the 33rd Engineers and is coming back in a couple weeks. They'd decided, all by email apparently, to get married, and she wanted me out. I guess me messing up with those pot guys was the decider."

"So all that crap about her getting too serious was lies?"

"I'm not proud of it."

"Sal."

"I was so ashamed about the plagiarism and getting fired. It made me do crazy things. Really screwed up things."

"Positively Plourdian."

"New word. I like it."

"You left without your car because?"

"She kicked me out, said she didn't care where I went, so I went. Her truck was in the shop and she had my car, and I just wanted to leave. I left her a note saying I'd come back for it. I didn't want to argue anymore, since she hated me so much."

"The pot guys?"

Sal's face reddened under his beard. "She told them she'd call the cops if they didn't get lost and didn't care if I went to jail. So when she disappeared, I was afraid they were vengeful or something. Guess they weren't."

"Oh my god." She was so tired her eyes were cracking like eggshells.

"The blood on the floor? I tried to explain to the cops. All the animals and the stuff she did, there was always blood or shit or something on the floor. They tested it and it was not human. Guess they didn't feel the need to let me know that until I brought it up."

"How are you getting to New Hampshire?"

"Rental. I'm going to Angie's for Thanksgiving. That's where everyone is going this year. I was ordered by Theresa to tell you, since you've been too busy to answer your phone."

"I'm going to sleep for three days. I don't feel like talking to anyone or trying to explain."

Sal got up. "After Angie's, I'm flying to Florida to see Mom

267

and Dad."

"Good plan."

"I'll be back in a couple weeks. Is your couch still a short-term option until I decide if I'm staying?"

"You'd stay in Redimere?"

"Vince says there might be an opening at the college next semester. There's a vibrant arts community in town."

"There is?"

"Are you going to be okay here all by yourself?"

She looked up at her brother standing over her. "Listen to you being all concerned."

"Well?"

"I'll be fine."

. . . . .

Bernie took a nap on the couch, most of it in that limbo between sleep and wake, conversations and scenes running through her head, unsure of what was real and what wasn't.

Late afternoon she walked to the store to get groceries. A blizzard was coming Friday. Bernie's duties at the paper were done until the weekend. Even if there was more information available in the Plourde-Lark-Reeves tangled web, there was nothing she'd do about it until Monday. She was looking forward to hunkering down and riding out the storm.

The day had been gray and sunless, the wind sharp. Now it was getting dark. It matched her mood.

The Country Grocer was bustling, the day before Thanksgiving frenzy crashing into the oncoming storm hysteria. Bernie still wanted to talk to Wendy Shaw about Pete's prescription bottle, so when she saw her shopping, she made sure she walked out with her.

"I see you went with the fresh kill," Bernie said, nodding at Wendy's organic turkey.

Wendy flinched, then said "Better than frozen," with a shaky smile as she put it and a bag of groceries in her car. Despite her height, she looked young and vulnerable, a too-big Patriots sweatshirt hanging off her, her hair in a ponytail. Bernie wanted to figure out what was going on with the bottle, wanted a story eventually on domestic violence, but right now what she really wanted was to make Wendy feel like someone cared.

"Can we talk?" Bernie practically whispered, hoping Wendy wouldn't run away. She looked like she might.

Wendy's eyes darted to the store, then down the street. "You're good friends with the police chief, right?"

"Right."

"I found something of his Tim shouldn't have had. Now it's gone."

"Was it his Vicodin bottle?"

Wendy's face went white. "Oh god. How do you know?"

"Is that what Tim wanted that night?"

"Where is it?"

"In a safe place."

She looked stunned. "I hid it here, at the store, but Walt threw it away. Where did you find it? Wait, we can't talk about this here." Wendy looked like she was going to cry.

"When?" Bernie wanted to argue, *now dammit*.

"Tim has a poker game tonight. I can call you after he's gone."

"I'm home all night."

"He can't know." She got into her SUV, gripped the steering wheel, her knuckles white. She leaned to close the door. "I know what you think of me. But we've been together since we were fourteen. He's the father of my children." Her voice cracked. "This is very hard." She backed out into the street and then was gone.

. . . . .

Cheryl Donovan was on the phone, crying. Pete almost didn't answer when he saw her number, wondered how she got his. He hadn't spoken to her since months before he'd moved, had changed his cellphone number. He thought at the time he was done with the Donovans.

"He killed Brandon, killed Brandon," Cheryl sobbed.

"Calm down. Tell me what's going on."

She took a few shaky sobs. "JP killed Brandon."

269

"JP couldn't have killed Brandon since Brandon was still alive when JP disappeared six years ago," Pete said. Had it been six years? Good god.

"You know who I mean." Cheryl was calm now, except for sniffles punctuating the sentence.

Say he's not JP, Pete wanted to scream. But he'd been doing this dance with Cheryl for too long and was too tired to change it. "Tell me what happened."

"Brandon moved to Massachusetts after JP came home. Cassidy wanted to be closer to her parents."

"Yep." Now that she had his attention, he knew, she was going to string it out. He'd been painting the cabinets, but put the brush down. Sat down and put his feet up.

"Anyway, Cassidy's always accusing Brandon of things with the kids. You know."

"Actually, I don't."

"I'm sure I told you. She finally said something to her parents, that he'd done something with her son, and she and Brandon broke up. Her parents called Mom and it was this big fight."

"She reported him, right?"

"I guess so."

"So, the JP thing?" He knew if he said Reeves, it would set her off on a different track and he wanted to get to the point.

"Cassidy went back to get her stuff and found Brandon dead. The cops said it was an OD, but I know it was JP."

"You'll have to connect the dots."

"I'm trying to," she said, defensive. "I can tell you're being deprecating with me, but you can at least listen."

"Sorry, long day."

"What happened, which I thought you'd like to know, is that right before Cassidy broke up with Brandon, JP showed up. At their place. Springfield, Massachusetts," she said, brisk, businesslike, the crying long gone. "Brandon wasn't home. He told Cassidy that he knew Brandon had molested the, um, other JP."

Despite everything, Pete smiled as Cheryl tangled with the two

270

JPs. Serves her right. "He had, right?"

"Where did you hear that?"

"The Maine State Police investigator who interviewed you."

"I told him JP *accused* Brandon of molesting him. I never said he did."

"Did anyone report it?"

"You know, Pete, I thought we were friends. You're being mean to me and I don't like it."

"I'm trying to find out what happened."

She sighed, a big exaggerated one. He could feel her cigarette breath pinging off cell towers up the east coast until, five hundred and some miles later, it slammed into his ear. "JP lied all the time. He liked to cause trouble and he hated Brandon for some reason. So we didn't believe him. But Cassidy did this time, because of what she said he did with her kids. It's all bull."

"When was this?"

"Last month."

"Now Brandon is dead?"

Cheryl sniffled again. "Cassidy went back with her brother Monday to get her stuff. He was dead in the house, all decomposed. They said he'd been dead for weeks." Cheryl's sniffles came harder and faster. "The police said they think it was an overdose because none of his bones were broken or nothing. Cassidy said the last time she talked to him was the day she saw JP there and then her and Brandon broke up. After that, Brandon wouldn't answer his cell."

"It's a stretch to say he was killed and that Reeves did it." He already knew, though. The Dykstra jersey, the skull earring. He'd been planning to make some calls when he could get his head above water on all the other things. Brandon Donovan, dead or alive just didn't seem that important any more.

"He told Cassidy he was going to make sure Brandon never hurt any kids again. He told her Brandon killed JP!"

Talk about burying the lead, as Bernie would say. "Let me get this straight. Brandon killed your twelve-year-old brother JP—"

271

"I didn't say he did it, I said Cassidy said—"

"Reeves told Cassidy he knew Brandon killed JP, and was going to make sure Brandon didn't hurt any more kids." Pete had thought something like that all along, confirmed when Natalie had handed him JP's Celtic cross. Another trophy Reeves had taken from Brandon, who'd taken it from his little half-brother when he'd killed him. All these years and he finally knew it for sure and all he felt was empty exhaustion, not triumph.

Cheryl started sobbing. "Why would he say Brandon did that? Why would he kill Brandon? It's all lies. Brandon never hurt JP. JP just lied about it all the time before he ran away."

"All right."

"That's all you can say?"

"I appreciate you telling me."

"You know, there was a time, if you had tried, I would have gone to bed with you," Cheryl said. "Now I just think you're an asshole." She hung up.

No argument there. His phone vibrated. Cheryl calling back? It was Bernie. He was tired. Probably more questions that only she could see the importance of about things that weren't going to get solved tonight. He resolved to call her back tomorrow. No, Friday. Just because he was working Thanksgiving didn't mean the rest of the world was. She was going, he was sure, to a feast with her giant family. The tribe, she called them. She probably wouldn't even remember she'd called.

CHAPTER 26
2009
Redimere, Maine
Thanksgiving Day

Bernie had waited all night for Wendy to call, checking her phone to make sure the ringer was on, making sure her voicemail wasn't full. She'd even tried Pete, finally resolving to tell him about the bottle and Wendy Shaw, but he didn't answer. She didn't leave a message, feeling dumb for calling. She didn't want to call Wendy, her fear of Tim was contagious. She was probably just getting the kids to bed, all that nighttime stuff people with kids do. Bernie woke up to the sound of her phone as dawn broke through the windows.

It was Eli Perry.

"Sorry to call you so early on Thanksgiving, but I'm bringing Nat up to my folks in Colebrook and there's a problem you want to know about."

"What problem?" Bernie went from groggy to alert the minute she heard Eli's voice. They didn't have a call-and-chat kind of friendship.

"That reporter of yours is stirring up trouble. He called me yesterday asking all sorts of shit. I know you didn't say anything to him about our conversation, he seemed like he was fishing, but he was asking about Chapman, about Shaw. In fact, a lot about Shaw. Prescriptions, the whole shooting match."

"Shit."

"I told him to go fuck himself, but he said he'd get the

273

information from Shaw."

Bernie's hand clutching the phone shook. She shifted it to her other hand, but it didn't help.

"When I got up this morning, I started thinking if he throws that stuff at Shaw, there could be trouble."

"What was he asking?"

"It didn't make a lot of sense," Eli said. "I almost got the impression he knew little bits and, like I said, was fishing, what was going on with Chapman, Shaw, any connection to Reeves and why a bottle of Vicodin belonging to the police chief would be floating around."

"Wendy was going to call me last night, but didn't. I have to go over there."

"Don't go over. Call the cops. Call your boyfriend."

Bernie was too scared, too totally scared shitless, to point out Pete wasn't her boyfriend. "Shit."

"Call Novotny, okay?"

Calling Pete would be dumb. If everything was okay, he'd be annoyed. He was already mad, if she remembered right. She had to take her pill. It was hard to make good decisions otherwise. The lack of sleep, the constant circus of information dancing in her head, a dozen competing trains of thought she couldn't turn off, weren't helping. Wendy probably hadn't called because she was mad, thinking Bernie'd told Fergus her secrets. Now it was Thanksgiving, and she wouldn't even be thinking about Bernie.

Fergus had gotten hold of her notes. It was virtually impossible to read her handwriting, but apparently he'd made out enough. So instead of helping at the paper he'd been skulking around town screwing things up. She'd just go over to the Shaws' and smooth it over. Fucking Feckless Fergus Kelley better hope and pray he never crossed her path again. She guessed he was trying to scoop her on her own story and sell it freelance. First thing Monday she was going to fire him, whether he showed up for their meeting or not.

Right now she had to make sure everything was okay at the Shaw house.

.....

Pete knew he wouldn't get the information he wanted on Thanksgiving, but he needed something to keep him occupied as he sat in his cruiser on empty Main Street. He phoned the Springfield, Massachusetts, police department. The investigator he wanted to talk to wasn't there, of course, but they'd email the Brandon Donovan report tomorrow.

As he rang off, Bernie's Subaru careened down School Street and turned onto Main, about twenty miles over the speed limit. He toyed with the thought of pulling her over. He felt guilty about not answering the phone last night. He wanted to talk to her, but not about this. About anything but this. Too much noise, as she would say. She was probably late getting to one of her sibling's homes. The thought of her and her big happy family spending the day together, eating and drinking almost hurt. His family had never celebrated Thanksgiving. His mother indifferent, his stepfather uninterested. His father, who sporadically came around all false cheer and apology, always off doing something else.

He logged onto his dashboard computer, and Googled Brandon Donovan. Nothing much. A drunken driving arrest in Springfield in a local newspaper's police log from a year ago. A request to join his Linked-In network. Seriously?

He had no doubt Reeves had killed Brandon. Did Reeves' death here have anything to do with that? Seemed unlikely, but it made it hard to tie things up. Things had come together a little with Moses Mosher's story, at least the Leslie part. He was stubborn, despite his mother's prodding and pleading, about the Reeves killed and gutted part. The police had let him go home, figuring his mother would do more to get him to talk than a night in jail would. So many ends to tie up. JP Donovan, Reeves. Leslie Lark. Chapman.

The DEA told him they'd been looking into Chapman for months, were poised to bust him and Herb Varney at the pharmacy for prescription fraud, probably Monday.

Dr. Gum, as Moses called him, had been the one to text Leslie

Lark. Just like Bernie thought. But Dr. Gum had been very mad that Benji Reeves had been sliced up. Two trucks, just like Guy said he'd heard. Why did Chapman care? And who else was there? "He called it overkill," Moses said. "But they really only killed him the one time. Brian did, because he was a deer." That's all Moses would say about it.

Round and round and round everything went.

The DEA suspected Tim Shaw, too. There were too many prescriptions with his name on them, even for an addict. Pete was glad, the humiliation of being thrown into the hopper, the indifferent aftermath, still burned. When he first came to town as chief, Cal had told him to let it go. Move on. Pete never discussed it. He knew Dawna knew, and Don Littlefield. Some others. He'd never tell Bernie. He'd moved on, more or less. But every time Shaw looked at him he could see that gloat, that triumph. He couldn't wait to nail him. He suspected Shaw was selling the pills at the transfer station, and the DEA said they were happy to include it in Monday's raid.

His cellphone rang. Bernie. He could picture her, stopped by the side of the road, impossible for her to talk and drive—she always said—with some trivial question, some thought that couldn't wait. He'd talk to her after the weekend, after the Donovan thing was tied up, the drug raids, maybe they'd even be somewhere on Reeves. Then they could talk without all the noise and tension. He ignored the call and tried to ignore that same ping of regret he'd felt the night before.

. . . . .

Bernie got out of her car in the Shaws' driveway behind Tim's mean-looking Ford F-150. The morning was dark, no sunrise, things just gradually getting lighter gray. *The sound of gunfire, off in the distance. I'm getting used to that now*, Bernie sang to herself. Someone had a fire going in a fireplace and the sharp smoke mixed with the crisp air. The storm warnings felt right—the TV station's Storm Watch team, a whole team needed!, had assured viewers it was barreling up the coast and would be here by the next night—she

276

could smell it in the wind that nipped at her cheeks. The Shaw's house looked dark and cold.

As she walked up to the door, she could hear the baby crying. Wendy probably had her hands full with the kids, with trying to cook Thanksgiving dinner, that oversized turkey.

She tried to rehearse what she was going to say, anticipate the Shaw's anger, wondered if they'd believe Feckless was acting on his own. She pushed the doorbell, but didn't hear it ring inside. She knocked. No answer. Knocked harder. Nothing. The baby's cries were jagged, relentless. Wouldn't Wendy pick him up? Bernie had helped raise her siblings. She knew how impossible it was to leave a baby crying, especially when he sounded that desperate.

She tried the knob. The door was unlocked. "Hello?" She stuck her head in the living room. Kids' toys scattered on the floor, the TV showed the Macy's parade with the volume off. "Hello?" Louder this time. *Maybe they can't hear me over the baby.* A foul odor drifted in the air. Garbage, maybe spoiled meat.

"Wendy? Tim?" The baby's wails got louder, piercing. The kitchen was beyond the living room, through an archway. The light was on and the grocery bag from yesterday, along with the raw turkey, was on the counter. Wendy shouldn't leave that out, was Bernie's first thought, the reality not settling yet, that it had been a good fourteen hours since Bernie had seen Wendy with the turkey and the groceries. The baby's cries were from the right, where a hallway must lead to bedrooms.

"I'm going to check on the baby," she said loudly, ridiculously, to no one.

The cries came from behind a closed door. She was about to push it open when she saw a smear of blood on the door across the hall. Leave and call the police, a voice in her head said. The smell of the rotting turkey was rank and cloying. Overwhelming. The blood on the door looked dry, but not like it'd been there long. Her pounding heart almost drowned out the baby's wails. She pushed the door open.

Wendy was asleep on the floor. That's what it was, because it

277

couldn't be what Bernie thought. Something had spilled. Coffee, maybe. A whole pot. Not coffee. The color was wrong. A can of paint. The baby screeched, huge loud cries with desperate breaths in between.

"Wendy?" She was sleeping on the floor. In her clothes. The same Patriots sweatshirt and jeans she'd been in yesterday. Her eyes, or eye, the one that was still intact, stared up at the ceiling, her face white. She wasn't sleeping. It wasn't coffee. Wasn't paint. Blood, more than Bernie thought possible, pooled around her on the carpet, soaked the front of the sweatshirt, clotted in her sandy hair. One arm was bent at an impossible angle. The baseball bat that had been used to kill her was on the bed, blood smeared on a green and yellow quilt, pretty spring flowers coated with red and brown.

The baby's wails were earsplitting, one after another. Bernie wondered how he could breathe, where he found the strength. She'd get him, take care of him. First she had to call Pete. Or someone. 911. Pete was easier, on speed dial. She hit the number and waited, heard it ring. Heard his voicemail click on, his low soothing voice.

She'd just put the phone in her coat pocket, when her hand was jerked back. But it wasn't her arm being jerked, it was her head. Tim Shaw spun her around, banged her face-first against the doorjamb.

"Fuck you doing here?" he screamed.

"The baby," she said as he twisted her arm behind her back and pushed her into the living room, then to the ground. She heard a ripping noise, felt her hands being bound with duct tape behind her back, his fingers digging into her flesh and the tape pulling at her arm hair, burning her skin. "The baby," she said again. She couldn't think of anything else.

He flipped her over by her bound arms and wrapped the tape around her legs. At least he wasn't killing her. Would he tie her up if he was going to kill her? She wasn't sure she wanted to know the answer.

"Where's Aidan?" she asked.

278

"Shut up. Why the fuck are you here?"

"I heard the baby—"

"Not that you stupid bitch." He stood up, breathing hard. She could see his face clearly for the first time since he'd grabbed her. Under the five-o'clock shadow his skin was dead white, dark circles under his bloodshot eyes. He was covered in sweat, shaking. She thought he'd look furious, but he looked nervous and desperate and it scared her more than furious would have.

"What'd my idiot wife tell you?"

"What?" Her cheekbone throbbed where it had hit the doorjamb. It was making her head ache. That and the smell of the dead turkey in the kitchen. And the blood, which she wasn't sure if she smelled or imagined. The smells made it hard to think. The way she was lying on the floor, with her hands taped behind her and her legs taped awkwardly together made her back hurt. Her fear, the smells, Wendy dead in the other room. She couldn't even process this conversation. Tied up again by someone who wanted to kill her. This never happened to people, but she gets it twice in five months. What were the odds? She'd laugh someday. If she lived. Hot tears coated her cheeks. "I don't know." Her voice quavered.

"That reporter called up yesterday with lots of questions. He said he got it all from you, you told him to call. What do you know? Who've you told?"

"I don't know anything."

"He said you knew it all. About the pills, Chapman. He said he didn't know anything, he was calling because you told him to."

Fucking Feckless. "He's a liar. I don't know anything." She sounded hysterical, she knew it. Didn't know how else to sound, even if she could choose.

Shaw's face flushed and she braced for a blow, but instead he fell back onto the couch and ran both his hands through his hair. "Tell me," he said. "Are the cops coming for me?"

"I don't know what you're talking about," Bernie said.

"What did Wendy tell you?"

"She didn't tell me anything."

279

"She told you about that bottle. I should have taken care of things right when she found it."

"That Saturday?" Bernie asked. He seemed calmer, but she wasn't sure if that made him less dangerous. She could tell he was tired, even more than she was. Her phone vibrated in her coat pocket.

"I came home that morning with blood on my jacket, pants, boots. She knew it wasn't from a deer."

Benji Reeves. Bernie almost said it out loud.

"She pretended it was a deer. She wasn't so good at pretending when she found the pill bottle in my pocket after I left for work. Aidan told me. She was doing the laundry and screamed. Dumped the pills down the toilet and flushed. He said he thought there were spiders in it, because Mommy was acting like she does with spiders." He laughed, a ragged hoarse noise that made Bernie's heart sink. "She told me she threw the bottle away, but she didn't. She lied. I took the rubbish to the station that morning, and when I went through all of it at home, no bottle."

"Where's Aidan?"

"In the bedroom with his brother."

Bernie wanted to call out to him, make sure herself. The baby's cries had quieted to sobs of "mamamama" and hiccups.

"Did they see Wendy?" Bernie couldn't say "dead," was afraid to, afraid it would dump her off the tightrope she was on.

"No. Jesus. What do you think I am? I locked them in when I saw her car coming up the drive yesterday, right after I got off the phone with your friend, that reporter."

"He's not my friend." Maybe the kids didn't see Wendy die, but they must have heard it. She tried to not think about it and focus on what Shaw was saying.

"He knew all about me and Chapman anyway, from you. How did you know?"

"I didn't. I don't. I don't know what you're talking about." She really didn't. She was trying to figure out what Pete's Vicodin had to do with Reeves. What it had to do with Shaw and Chapman. *Believe me*, she wanted to say. *Please.* She knew she looked pathetic, bound on the floor, but knew that wouldn't help win him over. The smell of the rotting turkey, the discomfort, the baby burbling sadly in the other room made it hard to focus on how to play it. She was no good at chess.

"Wendy was bringing food to Reeves, treating him like her third kid or whatever. Aidan told me that, too. When Plourde called up crying because he shot the guy for a deer, it was the happiest moment of my life. I enjoyed field dressing that piece of shit."

"That was you?"

He was trembling. His work boot, inches from her face, did a dance on the carpet. She inched away. "Chapman was paranoid Reeves was going to blow his deal, just like last time. Reeves was smart enough to get out of town that time. Don't know why he came back."

"Chapman told you to field dress him?" It seemed like Shaw needed to talk. It was possible he was high on something, though she wasn't good at figuring that kind of thing out. Maybe he was detoxing. She couldn't tell.

"Shit no. He was bullshit when he found out, not that Reeves was dead, but about the field-dressing. Plourde was afraid he'd get busted, go back to prison, for shooting Reeves. He'd kept me out of it last time he was busted, but said didn't think he could do it again. I didn't have any choice. You get that right?"

Bernie nodded. *Sure. Right.*

"His idea was to make it look like something worse than an accident. Plourde and his big fucking ideas. Chapman said to make sure he didn't have anything on him that tied him to us. I searched Reeves, found that Vicodin in his pocket and took it for myself. Plourde said Reeves liked to smuggle stuff up his butt so we should do what we did. I knew it didn't matter if he had anything up there, but what the hell. Like I said, it was a pleasure after all his bullshit."

"I understand," Bernie said. As long as he was talking, he wasn't killing her. A little fake sympathy wouldn't hurt either.

"Plourde fucks everything up," Shaw said. "He was going to

281

pin it on Perry, but that got fucked up. Then the plan to pin it on O'Dea, that was nuts. I didn't know about it until it was too late. I kicked the shit out of him." He laughed again, a hoarse, grating noise. "Your brother never knew what he was walking into. Just like the time Plourde and that idiot Mosher dropped your boyfriend in the hopper. A couple of fucking idiots who don't know when enough's enough."

Shaw seemed to have wound down. She had more questions, but she had to stop thinking about things that didn't matter and start thinking about how to save her life.

The baby was murmuring now, his whines and hiccups barely audible. It was so quiet without the piercing cries, such a relief. The silence didn't last, shattered by the sound of cars on the road, tires squealing to a stop.

Shaw pulled back the drape a fraction. "You call the cops?" He spun on her, furious again.

"No," she said. *Did I?*

The phone on the table next to the couch rang.

"Fuck." He pulled her against the wall, the sharp metal of the baseboard heater dug into her hands, then gouged her forearm as he let her drop. From her new position, she could see what she hadn't before, a trio of handguns lying on the coffee table that hadn't been there when she'd first come in the house.

The phone still rang. Shaw paced, his hands on his head. The baby started crying again, building to a wail.

"Dad?" Aidan's voice from in the bedroom. "Dad? Colton's crying. Dad? I have to go to the bathroom. Dad? The door's locked. I have to pee."

The phone rang. Then a voice, amplified, from outside. "Tim, pick up the phone. This is the police. Pick up the phone."

Shaw paced, oblivious to the voice, to the phone, the crying baby, oblivious to Bernie on the floor, watching him. As he paced he picked up one of the guns, hefted it.

"Dad? Daaaaddee? I have to pee."

Shaw just paced.

CHAPTER 27
2009
Redimere, Maine
Thanksgiving Day

The wind blew the last dried leaves, the litter, the sand from last winter, against the lifeless downtown buildings. Everything looked drab and dead from Pete's seat in the cruiser. There'd been little traffic, just an occasional car passing through. But now things were getting interesting. He watched from where he was parked at the side of the Country Grocer, out of view, as a car with Massachusetts plates pulled up in front of the Watcher and Bernie's new reporter, Fergus Kelley, got out. Pete wasn't impressed by what little he had seen of the guy so far.

Pete watched as Kelley tried the Watcher door, but of course it was locked. Stood, with the wind blowing his gray strands of hair up, buffeting his windbreaker, looking like he was trying to figure out what to do. Pete hated himself for it a little, but he was enjoying watching someone who looked like more of a loser than he was. Kelley went around the back. Pete wasn't worried. There was nothing back there and the back door had a dead bolt. Kelley would be back around soon enough. Pete didn't know what he was watching, but he could tell from the guy's body language and the way he looked up and down the empty street that he was up to no good.

He came back around the front. Tried the door again. Nope, still locked. He looked around. Began fiddling with the door handle. Okay, that was it. Pete got out of the cruiser.

"Can I help you?" he asked as he crossed the street.

Kelley started, then smiled. Pete had seen it a million times. The smile of the guilty asshole who thinks he's smarter than the cop.

"I have to get into the office, have some work to do."

"On Thanksgiving?"

Pete could see him forming a story, all the little lies building on his smug face, when a pickup truck roared down the street. Slowed. Stopped. Eli Perry got out.

Great, Pete thought. This is all I need.

Natalie smiled at him from the passenger window. He smiled back and she waved. He waved, but braced for Perry.

"Did Bernie call you?" Perry asked.

Pete was taken off guard. Mostly by the question, but also by the fact Perry was wearing khakis and a sweater vest over a dress shirt. "About what?"

"Shaw?"

Kelley was inching toward his car, and Perry reached out his giant ham of a fist and grabbed him by the upper arm.

"What's going on?" Pete asked, full cop mode.

"This piece of shit has stirred up all sorts of trouble at Tim Shaw's and I think Bernie is over there trying to make it right."

"I didn't—" Kelley said, trying to pull away.

"What's this about?" Pete asked Kelley.

"Tell this guy to get his hands off me. He's the one you should be hassling. I was just doing my job, calling with some questions on a story Bernie was doing. Helping her out."

"Bullshit!" Perry roared, shaking Kelley.

"Shaw wasn't any help," Kelley said, cringing away from Perry as much as he could, given that his arm was still squeezed in Perry's fist. "He didn't know what I was talking about, so no big deal. Let go. Are you going to make him let go? I'm filing charges."

"What did you ask him about?" Pete asked, fighting the urge to run to his cruiser, get in, and do a hundred miles an hour to Ridge Road.

"Just pills. General stuff. Bernie had some notes about Shaw's wife, Reeves, bottles. Wendy and a prescription bottle with your name on it." Kelley leered at Pete, but Pete ignored it. He saw the same alarm in Perry's eyes that he felt.

"Bernie went to Shaw's?" he asked Perry.

"I told her not to. I told her to call you," Perry said.

Pete was in his cruiser in seconds, speeding up Main Street in the same direction Bernie had earlier.

.....

There was no clock in the room, something Bernie always hated. She liked to know what time it was. Time was hard to measure as she sat on Tim Shaw's living room floor, propped up against a wall, the baseboard heater digging into her lower back. The decaying turkey got smellier, the baby wailed, punctuated sometimes by Aidan's cries that he had to pee, he was hungry, he wanted Mommy. Meanwhile Mommy, like the turkey in the kitchen, lay decaying on her bedroom floor. Bernie's legs and hands had long ago gone numb. She had a headache and couldn't tell if it was from being banged against the doorjamb, the smell, watching Tim Shaw pace around the room, not eating, being too hot in her coat, being scared absolutely shitless, or a combination.

A small part of her brain laughed at the folly of being in this situation again. But last time she had Pete. She wondered if he was outside. The amplified voice wasn't him, it was a woman, who alternately begged and cajoled Shaw to pick up the phone, which rang on and off throughout the morning. Hers vibrated in her coat pocket occasionally. The fact that she could still feel it against her numb thigh made her feel a little better.

Shaw had gotten out his hunting rifle. Bernie couldn't figure out why the handguns on the table—all bigger and uglier than the one Pete had tried to teach her with—weren't enough.

Bernie had tried to talk to Shaw, pretend all was normal. He paced, ignoring it all—the ringing phone, the amplified police voice, the crying kids. The dead wife. He occasionally answered her, but mostly ignored her, too. She couldn't remember if she'd taken her

285

pill that morning, but it didn't feel like she had. She couldn't hold a thought, the turkey smell and the smell of blood—real or imagined? She still couldn't say—overwhelmed her.

"At least let the kids go," Bernie said.

"I'm not talking to the cops," he said.

She wanted to ask what his plan was, but she didn't want to know. He didn't seem to have one, anyway. "If the baby wasn't here, crying, you could think."

He pushed the drape aside, slightly, as he'd done over and over again. She wanted to ask what he saw, ask, stupidly, if Pete was out there. That would make her feel better, like there was hope.

"I know you love your kids" *despite the fact you brutalized and killed their mother.* "They'll be safe and then you can…" She trailed off. Can what? Kill me? She hoped maybe he'd just kill himself, as awful a thought as it was. A few times, he'd picked up the handgun, put down the hunting rifle, looked at it, weighed it, lifted it. Toward himself, not her. He had yet to threaten her life or point a gun at her, and for that she was grateful. She knew better, though, than to think she was safe.

Colton's wails, which had died down, picked up again, the same pattern all morning. For how long? Bernie had no idea.

"Someone out there could probably change his diaper, give the kids some food. Aidan's probably wet his pants. If it bothers me, it's gotta bother you. How long have the kids been locked in that room? Since yesterday? You don't want a child abuse charge on top of everything else."

That's when he taped her mouth shut.

.....

It'd been hours, but Shaw finally picked up the phone. They'd been in the cold wind—the state police negotiation team, the sheriff's department, the fire department, which had blocked off the road, a couple ambulances Pete prayed they wouldn't need, press and TV crews at the end of the road—everyone waiting, watching, blowing on their hands, stamping their feet, bites of snow hitting bare faces and hands. Few were sitting in cars staying warm. Everyone was waiting.

Shaw picked up the phone and Pete could feel the tension relax for the first time since he'd arrived, seen Bernie's car in the driveway, tried calling her. How many hours ago was that? It seemed like days. When there was no answer, he'd walked around the house until he could find a window to look in. The bloody horror of the Shaw's bedroom.

Beth Gardner, the state police negotiator, had been cajoling Shaw all morning, like he was a friend. She was patient, calm. Now she was talking to him. Not long enough though, Pete thought, as she took the phone from her ear.

"He's confirmed at least one live adult hostage." She looked at Pete. "Your friend, Bernadette O'Dea." Pete felt the breath he'd been holding all morning release. "I didn't tell him we knew about the wife. I've convinced him to let the kids go. He'll call back when he figures out how he wants to do it."

Her phone rang. "They're too young to come out alone. Let us send someone to get them," she said in answer to whatever Shaw had said. Everyone knew the plan was more than that—to get eyes on the inside of the house. They'd discussed it all morning. Everyone knew Shaw knew, too.

"Imagine them walking out that door alone to this wall of cops and firepower. They've been through enough. You can set the ground rules," she said.

"He's going to think about it," she told the waiting group.

They waited. The wind picked up and the trees along the road and behind the house swayed, their branches clacking. A last gaggle of geese flew through the frigid air, way too late on their trip south. A group of crows that had been roosting in the trees behind them all morning cawed, an accusing, unconvinced audience. Other than that there was silence.

A lifetime later, Gardner's phone rang.

"He wants Novotny."

The commander, his name was Caldwell, looked from Gardner to Pete, annoyed. "If that's what he wants," Caldwell said.

"He wants you on the lawn, your duty belt, coat, shirt all off."

Pete started toward the lawn. *Whatever it takes.* He was focused on what he would do when he got in the house. He wasn't leaving without Bernie.

"Listen," Caldwell said, taking his arm and waiting until Pete turned to look at him. "The object is to get the kids out safe. Check out the scene, see if you can get him to come out, release O'Dea. But don't do anything to endanger those kids. Get those kids out. That's the number one priority. If it ends up being the only option, it's the only option."

Pete nodded, his attention on the house.

Caldwell squeezed his arm, Pete's bad arm. The jolt of pain didn't bother him. All he could think about was the house. The kids. Bernie. "Don't be a hero. Get the kids out of there alive."

Pete was figuring it out, playing it through. Take down Shaw, get the kids, get Bernie, get out. His muscles were tense, ready. He wasn't going to leave that house without everyone.

He took a deep breath and nodded and Caldwell let go.

Pete left the circle of cruisers and cops and stepped onto the lawn, exposed, the wind felt colder there, sharper. The slivers of snow bit his face. He took his coat off and dropped it on the grass. The wind cut through his shirt. He dropped his duty belt, feeling more exposed than he had when he lost the coat. Next came his shirt. He faced the house, his arms held away from his body.

"Untuck your T-shirt, lift it up and turn around, three-sixty, slow." Pete did, the wind burning his bare skin. He didn't care. *Get the kids, get Bernie, get out.*

"Lift your pant legs to your knees and turn around again."

He did, feeling ridiculous, a clown doing tricks for an unfriendly king. *Kids, Bernie, get out.*

"Hands up."

He raised his arms above his head, then held them away from his body. There was no movement behind the curtains, no sign Shaw was watching, but Pete knew he was. He hoped Shaw could see the look in his eyes, know he was coming to get him. He was

288

glad Shaw had asked for this showdown. He'd been waiting for it for more than two years. He wanted to be sure Shaw knew.

The only sound behind Pete was the snap and static of police radios and the wind through the trees, the branches clacking. Even the crows had stopped. Pete stood steady, staring at the house, waiting to be told to go. The cold cut through his T-shirt, stung his bare skin, but it was separate from him. All that existed were the kids, Bernie, what he would find when he got into the house. What he would do.

"Go. He wants to see your hands all the way."

Pete walked, hands half raised.

The door opened. The older boy, Aidan, held the knob, staring at Pete with wide blue eyes that told Pete he'd seen way too much.

The house was dim and cold, stank of decaying meat. A TV, sound off, sent jumpy shadows around the room. A light was on in the kitchen. Pete didn't look at either, he was focused on what was in front of him. Aidan scurried back into the room. He and the baby were already in coats and hats. So much for distracting Shaw by having him gather the kids' stuff.

Shaw was beyond distracting anyway. He was standing in the back of the room, in the dim light, out of the line of fire. His arm was around Bernie's neck as he held her in front of him. The barrel of his gun was pressed to her temple. Her mouth was duct-taped shut.

The kids huddled next to their father. Aidan stared. Colton sat on the floor, red-faced and blubbering, his fingers in his mouth.

"Far enough," Shaw said when Pete stepped into the room, close enough to see that the side of Bernie's face was bruised. His anger kicked up a notch.

Bernie's hands were tied behind her back and her lower legs duct-taped together from ankles to knees. If Shaw hadn't been holding her up with his arm around her neck, she'd fall over. Pete's eyes met hers. "Are you okay?" he asked.

She nodded as Shaw pulled his arm tighter around her neck. "Don't talk. Get the kids and get out."

"Where's Wendy?" Pete asked. Calm. Conversational.

"Get the kids and get the fuck out."

"Mommy's sleeping on the bedroom floor," Aidan said, looking at his father.

Pete caught Bernie's eye. *I know.*

There were two handguns on the coffee table, a rifle propped against it. They were about a foot away from Shaw, maybe six from Pete. He calculated the odds, kept his eyes on Bernie and Shaw, trying not to give away he'd seen them. Shaw was sweaty. Wiped out and shaking. He was either on something or coming down. Either way, it made him more dangerous.

"Ma ma mommy," Colton said, grabbing his father's pantleg and pulling himself up. "Mommy!"

Shaw didn't look. He pressed the gun against Bernie's temple. "She's asleep, honey," he said. "This is Pete. He's going to take you outside. Mommy will come when she wakes up."

"No! Mommy!" Colton started to cry in earnest, burying his face in his father's leg.

Pete took a step.

"No!" Shaw yelled. "Not one more step." To make his point, he jammed the gun hard into Bernie. She winced and closed her eyes. "Colton, go with Pete."

Colton blubbered "No no."

"Aidan, get your brother," Shaw said. Aidan stared, white faced. "Now!"

Aidan reached his hand out to Colton. "Come on, we're going to have ice cream," he said.

"No! Mommy!"

"Colton, come on," Aidan said, his voice breaking, pulling Colton's free arm.

"Mommeeeeee," the toddler screamed, a heartbreaking wail, and clamped onto Shaw's leg again. Shaw remained expressionless, the gun jammed against Bernie's temple, but his eyes were wet. Pete felt a glimmer of hope.

"Let me get Colton," Pete said.

"Fuck off."

"We can all go outside and no one gets hurt." *No one else*, he almost said.

"Get the fuck out. It's too late for deals." He kicked the leg Colton was clamped onto. "Aidan, get your brother."

Aidan, crying now, grabbed his brother around the chest, pulling him from his father's leg. "Come on, Colton," he said, sobbing. The baby continued to wail, but let go. Aidan staggered backwards toward Pete, his shrieking brother in his arms.

Bernie's eyes were still closed, her lips moving slightly. If Pete didn't know her better, he'd think she was praying.

"Get out," Shaw said, the menace in his voice cutting through the baby's cries.

The boys were next to Pete now, the little one whimpering, the older one grasping his brother's hand, looking up at Pete, waiting.

Pete had known from the second he was told he was going into the house that he wasn't leaving without Bernie. Hadn't considered any other possibility.

"Now," Shaw said. "Or everyone dies. Everyone."

Bernie opened her eyes, locked them on Pete's. No tears, no blinking. The message was clear. *Leave.*

It was a shock, accepting he'd have to leave without her. One he wasn't prepared for. "Let her go. I'll stay."

Shaw laughed. "I'm not stupid."

Bernie's eyes narrowed and despite the duct tape he could see she was smiling. Telling him he could go, she'd be okay.

"Get the fuck out now," Shaw said, his voice shrill, rising.

There was nothing Pete could do. No heroics, no last-minute plan. Shaw was past compromise or negotiation. Nothing. He had to take the kids and leave.

Bernie was probably going to die.

He kept his eyes on hers. They still smiled, but he could see the fear.

He picked up Colton, held his hand out to Aidan. "Shaw—"

"Fuck times I have to tell you to get the fuck out?" Shaw

jerked Bernie's head back and jammed the gun against her throat. She gurgled, startled. Terrified.

Pete fought the urge to drop the kid, leap forward and beat the living shit out of Shaw, grab Bernie and pull her out the door.

Colton's head was on Pete's shoulder, his arms tight around his neck, holding on for life.

Aidan's tiny, moist hand grasped Pete's. "Ouch," he said. Pete eased his grip.

Shaw took the gun from Bernie's neck and pressed it against her temple. Pete could feel Shaw's eyes on him, but he kept his own on Bernie. *I'm sorry. I love you.* He willed her to read it in his eyes.

Hers were wide, staring back, the smile gone.

Pete didn't know how he turned around and walked out, but there he was, in the biting wind, walking back to the circle of cops, his legs moving under some other power. Someone applauded, lonely claps in the cold air. The absurdity made him want to punch something.

Colton was crying again. Someone took him from Pete's arms, pried loose Aidan from Pete's paralyzed fist. His shirt, coat and duty belt were in his hands. He'd forgotten how cold it was, forgotten that he was in a T-shirt until that moment.

"Let's get you in the ambulance, where it's warm," Caldwell said.

"Not in front of the kids," Pete said.

"Two ambulances."

"Might need more," he said, and Caldwell nodded. Pete felt disconnected, couldn't understand how calm he seemed. His brain was screaming.

"What's the scene?" Caldwell asked as they ducked into the back of the ambulance with Gardner. Warm as it was, Pete's hands shook as he put on his shirt. He tried to button it, but the buttons slipped through his shaking, numb fingers.

"Bernie's taped up. He's got at least four guns. Doesn't look like any window would give us a clear shot."

"We can gas it, storm him," Caldwell said.

Gardner didn't say anything, but Pete felt it. *Hurry up the inevitable.*

"He's done," Pete said. "He's willing to die and take Bernie with him." His voice still too calm. His brain still screaming. He gave up on the buttons and pulled his coat on, crossing his arms and leaning against his knees, trying to stop the shivering.

"I get that feeling, too," Gardner said.

"Hopefully the tear gas will disorient him and the hostage can break away," Caldwell said.

"Her legs are wrapped in duct tape," Pete said.

"I guess we'll take our chances."

. . . . .

Bernie knew hope was dead when Pete left. He wasn't going to save her, couldn't. It wasn't TV or a movie where the brave, brilliant cop has one last trick up his sleeve. Pete was brave and brilliant, but this was real life and he was an unarmed man hampered by two little boys, facing a guy who killed his wife with nothing to lose and a loaded gun. Several. She felt like laughing, now that it was almost all over. Forget being in a situation like this twice in her life—in five months, no less—but surviving it? She wasn't that lucky.

Luck has nothing to do with it. Go down fighting.

"Fuck," Shaw said as the door closed. "Fuck fuck fuck." He dropped Bernie and she fell awkwardly, landing on her side.

"So much for your big hero," he said, but as an afterthought, no longer interested. He began pacing again, careful to stay away from the window.

"Shit. I have to think. Shit shit shit."

With a long grunt, he pushed a hope chest across the door. He'd blocked the back door with the refrigerator hours ago. She'd heard him pushing it earlier. At the time she'd wished he'd throw the turkey away, the decaying smell sickening her. That was the least of her problems now. She felt for the jagged metal corner of the baseboard heater. She felt a surge of joy as it cut into her wrist again. She'd been working on it for some time, afraid he'd notice the duct tape was partially cut, the wet blood she could feel on her wrists and hands, when he dragged her to her feet earlier, but he'd been too focused on Pete.

He was banging around in the cellar. She moved her wrists up and down, the tape catching on the metal, awkward with her painfully numb arms. A couple times the baseboard clanged as it slipped loose from the tape, and she stopped, held her breath, afraid he'd hear.

He was breathing hard and swearing under his breath in the kitchen, and now was back in the room. He didn't look at her, glanced briefly out the drape. "Shit."

Bernie didn't care what was going on out there. She was more interested in what he had in his hands—each held a five-gallon gasoline can. Shit indeed.

He splashed gasoline around the room, end to end, letting it fly up the walls and furniture, it hissed as it hit the TV, which now showed a football game, the bright high-definition colors warping as the gasoline coated the screen. Some of it splashed on Bernie's legs, her arms and coat, though he didn't look at her or act as though she were there. The smell was nauseating, worse than the turkey. It filled her nose and made her skin itch. Her head spun, got lighter.

He moved to the hallway. She could hear the gas splash on the walls, then the bedroom door open, lots of splashing and movement.

She sawed her wrists against the edge of the heater, not caring how much noise it made or how much the jagged metal cut and pulled her skin. She didn't care about the blood seeping down her hands. All she could think about was getting them free.

When her hands sprang free, she was born again. *Should I try my legs?* The clanging in the hall told her no. She pulled herself up by the table, her legs buckling. What little feeling she had in them was pain. She leaned forward, wobbling. She grabbed the nearest gun. It was big, much bigger than the one she'd used at the range with Pete. It was too large in her hand. Too heavy. There was a loud clang. Like a gas can being thrown against the wall. It sounded like he was in the bedroom again, like he was pulling sheets off the bed. He was sobbing now, swearing.

Don't panic, think. Where was the safety? Then what? She went through the steps, the image of Pete shaking his head and laughing as she kept forgetting about the safety. What else?

She wished she could brace her legs. An image of Pete reaching to steady her as the recoil from her first shot knocked her back, his hand firm on her back. She could only stand by squatting slightly and leaning her thighs against the table. Her legs trembled. She was afraid to let go of the table with her left hand. She'd fall over, but she had to hold the gun with both hands. Even then, it was too heavy.

He was in the hall, his sobs loud. No more splashing or clanging.

She let go of the table, gripped the gun with both hands, her finger on the trigger. Heard Pete's voice telling her to point lower than intended. *Most people end up shooting a tree branch.*

Shaw was sobbing in the hall, out of sight, but close. Now his step on the carpet, shuffling, slow. Pete's voice. *Focus. You'll hit your target if you think of what you're doing and focus. Don't panic. Hold steady and focus.*

She pointed the gun at the hallway as Shaw appeared, a lighter in one hand, a gun in the other.

. . . . .

When Pete heard the shots, all planning went to the wind.

"Bernie!" he screamed. Someone grabbed his arm, said "wait." He pulled away and ran across the lawn. Heard steps behind him, felt them, but didn't care.

He tried to push the door open, but something blocked it. Oh god, a body? Her body? No, it was too heavy.

He leaned back and kicked as hard as he could as he felt hands on his jacket, one grab his arm. He shook them off, pushing harder. The door cracked open as an arm snaked around his chest. He felt, more than heard someone yell. He couldn't hear the words through the roar in his head. Didn't care. He surged forward into the narrow opening, his jacket coming off in someone's hand, the arm around

295

his chest slipping away. He smelled gasoline. There were hands behind him, bodies, some pulling at him.

"Bernie!" he yelled, "Bernie!" The door edged open farther and he fell inside.

She was face down on the floor, the back of her coat smeared with blood.

"Bernie. Oh my god." He put his hand on her arm, thank god warm and alive, and she rolled over and sat up, a gun clutched in her hand, eyes wide and wet. He took the gun from her and put it on the coffee table, as legs, boots, swarmed around them. People yelled, barking orders, grabbing him, reaching for her. She didn't seem injured, the blood from scrapes on her forearms and wrists. He pulled the duct tape off her mouth, then held her face between his hands, her tears soaking them.

"Are you okay?" He had to yell to be heard over the din, the roaring in his brain.

She shook her head, sobbing.

"Oh baby, I'm so sorry. So so sorry," he said, hugging her to him, holding her head against his chest. She squirmed away.

"I killed him."

Pete saw through the legs and chaos Tim Shaw struggling to get up, then pushed back down. "It's his shoulder," someone said.

"He's okay," Pete said. "Just winged him."

Bernie picked at the tape around her legs with blood-covered hands. "Get this off," she said, her voice rising. There was a crowd around them now, questions, hands gripping him again, pulling him up. He shook them off and pulled the tape off her legs, his fingers trembling. "I'm so sorry," he said again.

She didn't look at him, but picked at the tape, her fingers sliding, shaking worse than his.

"Let me do it," he said. He moved her hand away, gently, not wanting to let go of it. She looked at him, tears streaming down her face. "Let me do it," he said again.

"I shot him."

"I know. It's okay. He's fine." He wanted to hug her again, but she looked away, her fingers working at the tape.

"Get this fucking tape off me." She was sobbing, huge gulping ones. "It's not okay. It's not. It's never going to be okay again."

CHAPTER 28
2009
```
Redimere, Maine
Thanksgiving night
```

Bernie had showered until the hot water ran out, but she could still smell gasoline. Her head hurt, she was exhausted, but jumpy. She hurt everywhere. He legs ached. The cuts on her arms stung. Talking to the cops had been an exhausting blur, their questions repetitive, nonsensical. She was angry, though she wasn't sure at who. She tried eating, watching TV, but everything just seemed so stupid, so she turned it off. It turned out she hadn't take her pill that day, but it didn't matter now, it wouldn't do any good. Her phone rang a couple of times—siblings. She didn't answer. She wondered if they'd seen the news or were just calling to see how her Thanksgiving had gone.

Pete knocked on the door early evening, like she knew he would. She didn't want to answer, but couldn't figure out how not to.

Dubya, happy to have someone to play with who was more fun than Bernie, jumped on him. It gave her a chance to move out of reach before he could get in the hug she saw forming.

"You want something? A beer? I don't have any Thanksgiving food." The thought of turkey made her gag. She didn't think she'd ever eat turkey again.

"No thanks," Pete said, puzzled.

She leaned against the counter and tried to meet his gaze. He

298

ignored Dubya's dance around his legs and put his arms around her.

"How are you?" he asked, his hands firm against her back, pulling her tight against him. The stubble on his cheek rubbed against her. He smelled like sweat and gasoline, the familiar warm soap somewhere way underneath, too hard to find.

"Okay." She pulled away.

"Really?" Definitely puzzled. She knew her reaction wasn't what he expected, but she didn't have the mental or emotional energy to let him comfort her. She wanted to be alone with her anger and regret at letting things get so out of hand.

"I just need to be alone to process everything."

"We've been through this before," Pete said. "Not this, but like it. You were so brave. Again."

"I suck," Bernie said, knowing she sounded like a petulant teenager. "Wendy's dead. Nothing that happened today should have."

"It wasn't your fault. It was Tim's and his alone."

"Wendy wanted to talk. There's a lot I could have done differently." Bernie was embarrassed at the quaver in her voice.

"Oh, Bernie."

She started putting away the dishes, so she could keep moving, wouldn't have to look at him. "I just want to be alone."

"I'm not sure you should be." At least he hadn't followed her to the sink.

"It's not your call." She knew he was trying to help and that she sounded bitchier than she had a right to. She didn't care.

"I—"

"Can you please leave?" She sorted silverware frantically, the forks and spoons banging into the drawer. She was desperate for him to go before she broke down.

"I don't want to leave you alone."

She threw the last of the silverware in the drawer, not caring where it landed, some bouncing out on the floor, then faced him, feeling the explosion and not able to stop it. "I know you can leave, I already saw you do it once today."

299

The minute the words were out of her mouth, she wanted them back. Desperately. Pete's face went white. Stricken. Punched right in the gut. Well, now he knew the real her. She was almost relieved.

"Leaving that house today without you was the hardest thing I've ever done in my life," he said, quiet, soft, not with the anger Bernie deserved. He was making it worse.

"Go please."

His green laser stare was so intense it took a force of will for her to not look away. Dubya stood between them, his head turning from one to the other. He trotted to Bernie and lay down, his snout on her foot, as though he could sense the earth splitting in half, swallowing Bernie whole.

Pete went to the door, opened it, and walked out.

She'd been going back and forth about Pete for months, but now she'd made sure there was no debate, no back and forth left.

She sat on the couch and Dubya jumped up next to her. She buried her face in his fur and he nuzzled her arm. "I'm sorry Dub. Really, really sorry." She started to cry, wondering why she was apologizing to the dog, wondering if she'd ever stop smelling gasoline or rotting turkey, or seeing Wendy's battered body, but mostly wondering why she just couldn't be the person anyone else wanted her to be.

.....

Pete was surprised to find Dawna in the office when he got there the morning after Thanksgiving.

"Aren't you off?"

"Mountain of paperwork, just like you," she said. "Some Thanksgiving."

"I've had better."

"We're supposed to get a blizzard tonight."

"Yup."

Dawna followed him into his office. "How are you?"

"Okay."

"You don't look it."

"Tired." He smiled to show he was fine.

"Did you hear back from Springfield?" Pete had called her Wednesday night, after he'd called Libby, to fill her in on the possibility Brandon had killed JP, Reeves had killed Brandon.

"This morning. Brandon, the real JP's half-brother, thirteen years older, death undetermined, possible overdose. Lots of pill bottles around. They figured he'd been dead a few weeks. They don't know whether it could have been anything other than an overdose, he was too decomposed. They have no reason to investigate. He was cremated."

"You think Reeves killed him?"

"I'm certain of it."

"Why didn't Cheryl Donovan tell you about Brandon abusing JP? If you'd known, you could have figured it out."

"People see what they want." Pete was too tired to talk.

"How did Reeves know Brandon killed JP back in 2003?"

"He saw the necklace that Cheryl and Linda were always going on about, the Celtic cross, once when he was over at Brandon's place. Rifling through his things, typical Reeves. Then he nosed around talking to JP's old friends, other people. Finally went up to confront Brandon in Massachusetts. That's what he told Cassidy, Brandon's girlfriend. She told the police. They were interested, but again, looks like an overdose. With both Brandon and Reeves dead, no one cares to pursue it."

"The Donovans pretended Reeves was JP to cover for Brandon?"

"That's what I think."

"Maybe the sister would, but the mom?"

"The fact they didn't tell me JP had accused Brandon of molesting him, after I befriended them, all that digging I did—that they knew I was doing, that they encouraged me to do—says they were covering for him."

"Big leap from covering up sexual abuse to covering up murder," Dawna said. "Sexual abuse, people pretend it didn't happen, rationalize it. How can you deny murder? It was their son

301

and brother, but he killed a son and brother."

"People believe the easiest thing."

"Here's another theory," Dawna said. "They were afraid of what Brandon might have done and wanted to believe it wasn't true. They wanted JP back so bad they were willing to believe Reeves was him."

"I don't buy it. It was always strange how they accepted Reeves. Covering up for Brandon explains it. If JP's not dead, everyone can stop looking." Pete's head was pounding.

"You were the only one looking."

"Missing kid. Someone's always looking."

Dawna seemed like she wanted to say something. Hesitated.

"What?"

"Maybe it's like Brian's buck. The brain convinces you you're seeing what you want. It's especially true when someone's suffered a trauma. Easy to fool yourself."

"I don't buy it."

"I read in that article that trauma has a great effect, alters what people see. It's not because they're lying to themselves. People who have killed a person thinking it was a deer, most of them didn't want to kill someone, so it's traumatic. Their brain puts the deer there instead in their memory. They don't have any control over it."

"Some people, maybe."

"If Cheryl and Linda thought Brandon killed JP, it caused them tremendous pain." She got up to leave. "The human mind can only take so much pain before it has to protect itself. It sees what it wants."

. . . . .

Pete walked out of the Country Grocer feeling foolish that he'd picked up the New England habit of stocking up when a storm approached. Water, because everyone buys water when a storm's coming, beer, a bottle of whiskey, bread and sandwich meat. He hadn't eaten anything substantial in days, but wasn't in the mood to cook. He'd looked forward to getting his kitchen finished, now he didn't care. It was a lifetime ago.

302

He shifted the bag from his aching right arm to his left as he pushed the door open, nearly stepping on Natalie.

"You ought to scoot home before the storm," he said. It had already started, the cold gusts pushing leaves and debris in twisters, sharp, hard flakes of snow stinging his face and bare hands.

"I'm okay. Do you still have my gloves? My dad said I could make three dollars shoveling snow and can buy them back."

Pete was surprised. "Sure. Come by any time." He put the groceries in his car. She watched, making no move to go.

"Everything okay?" he asked.

She pulled up her sleeve, uncovering the cigarette burn scars, watching his face. "You have them too."

He wanted to deny, but couldn't. Not to her. "I do."

"I saw them." She touched her lower back, waited for him to nod to show he understood. "When you and my dad were fighting."

"It was just me fighting, sweetie. Your dad wasn't."

"They hurt. Not now, but they used to."

"I know."

"Do yours?"

"Not now. It was a long time ago. I was a little boy."

She nodded. "I won't tell anyone."

"Thanks," Pete said.

She put her hand out and he took it, soft and warm despite the biting air. *Duckling*. It tore through his mind, along with searing horror, then left. Natalie hadn't seen it behind his eyes or wherever that kind of horror lives. She was smiling, all lit up and dimples.

"See ya," she said, turning and hopping off the wooden walkway of the store. She walked a couple yards, then started skipping, her pink Disney princess backpack bouncing as the cold wind whipped the last leaves of the season against her legs.

Pete got in his car, trying to ignore the lump in his throat as he watched the backpack bob away.

CHAPTER 29
2009
Redimere, Maine
Friday, November 26

Pete put the groceries away. The storm had knocked out the cable; so much for watching basketball. He still had painting to do, unpacking. Instead he called Sid.

They talked about the standoff, Sid walking that line between concern and not pissing Pete off.

They talked about Bernie.

"She must hate me," Pete said. "I don't blame her."

"She doesn't hate you," Sid said. "She's tired, like you are. She'll come around." Sid couldn't resist. "How can she ignore the magnet pull of your legendary charm?"

Pete tried to laugh, but his lack of charm wasn't really a joke anymore now that there was Bernie. He changed the subject to JP Donovan/Benji Reeves.

"I think that's as good as it's gonna get," Sid said. "Makes sense."

"More or less." Pete had dismissed Dawna's theory, so maybe it was exhaustion or despair, or whatever the hell it was, that kept it nipping at him.

He ran it by Sid. "Do you think they could believe Reeves was JP just because they wanted to so badly?"

"The human mind is a magnificent and crazy beast."

Pete took a deep breath. Closed his eyes. Dove in. "I keep

thinking about that time we found the ducks in the dumpster. The ducklings. That same summer we found the kid we thought was JP Donovan. I have nightmares about it. I don't know why." Pete laughed, but he knew Sid could hear the desperation, the question.

Sid paused. A long one. The wind howled around the house, the roof rattled. The lump Pete had felt in his throat all afternoon had turned into a bigger one in his stomach. He wanted to know, but he really, really didn't.

Sid finally spoke. Gently. "Man, you know that wasn't ducks, right?"

Pete felt the tightness, the rise of bile and panic and terror. "It was ducks. In an old Rubbermaid container. They were bloody —"

"Pete."

"One little one was quacking —"

"Pete," Sid said, more forcefully. "Those weren't ducks."

Pete didn't answer. Couldn't.

Sid continued, gentle again, like he was talking to one of his kids. "It wasn't ducks."

"I remember ducks. Ducklings," Pete said, his eyes still closed, trying to fight off the tide.

"Pete."

He did remember. It wasn't ducks. Not ducks at all. A tiny girl. Still a kid. It turned out she was fourteen, but she looked ten. Her ebony skin caked with blood, her teeth knocked out and her face so swollen her parents could only identify her from her still-fresh caesarean scar. Her twins, two weeks old, their throats slit. They'd had yellow and white bows in their hair—tiny bows, painfully small—to match the onesies with dancing ducklings. Matching the dancing Daffy Duck on their mom's T-shirt. One was alive, barely, making a squawking noise through her slit throat, the bows in her hair, tinted with blood, jiggling as she struggled to breathe.

Pete had pulled the lid off the Rubbermaid container—always him who had to jump into the dumpster—and saw horror.

He must have made a noise—now, years later, he could still only hear the rushing in his ears. Then Sid. "What is it? Pete? What is it?"

Pete had collapsed into the soft garbage, wanted to bury himself in it.

"Ducks," he'd said.

"What?" Sid asked. Pete didn't answer. He heard Sid's hands on the dumpster, his feet scrabble up the side until he looked over the edge, half-smiling at his buddy sinking into the wet mounds of garbage. He wasn't taking in yet what else was there, next to Pete.

"Ducks," Pete had said again, staring up at Sid, willing him to agree.

Now as the storm howled outside, so different from that humid June day, Pete's horror was still as real.

Sid said again, more softly. "Those weren't ducks."

Pete took a deep breath, let it shake down into his chest. The wind rattled the window and he watched the snow, a blinding fist of white, batter the glass. That's when it had started. That moment more than six years before. The dreams. The panic. He took another breath, deep as he could, to see how it felt. He wasn't sure he could say more. He didn't want to break down. Not now, all these years later, just because he realized what he'd known all along.

"You all right, brother?" Sid's concern was more than he could bear.

"Yeah." The snow blurred, a white cloud. He tried to see ducks in it, but he saw three bodies, bloody and raw, the tiny one squeaking her last breaths. He saw the dead kid, a few months later with his floppy sneakers and basketball jersey, just another body in a dumpster. He saw all the bodies and blood before and since, in dumpsters, in rivers, hallways, on the street. His brother, in the open coffin his mother had insisted on, the funeral home makeup and ghastly wig barely disguising the damage the brick wall had done when he'd slammed into it with that stolen motorcycle.

Bernie, in that house, her huge eyes over the duct tape. Both of them knowing he was going to walk out and let her die.

"I'm going to hang up now." He didn't want Sid to have to prop him up again. It was too much.

306

"Let's talk."

"I'm talked out," Pete said.

"You shouldn't be alone."

"Well, I am, and I'm fine." Pete hung up, cutting off Sid's protest. He sat back and stared at the snow, swirling, dark and angry, battering his little house.

. . . . .

Bernie should have felt comfy with the fire going, the dog and cats curled up with her on the couch. She was in her favorite material—flannel. She'd made lasagna and meatballs from Sal's leftover sauce, the food equivalent of love, in an attempt to convince herself she wasn't a mean, hateful person who wasn't worthy. It tasted like wet cardboard, shame, and disgust. She tried reading a book, but after she'd read the same page three times, she gave up. Flipped on the TV, but couldn't settle on a channel. Then the cable went out, like it always did, so there was no point anyway. She stared at the fire, wondering if she should put her coat and boots on and try a walk despite the blizzard.

The phone rang.

"What fresh hell?" she asked the snoozing animals. She didn't want to pick up, or even check the caller ID. She didn't want to talk to her siblings or parents. You never know, though. Could be something big. Could be Pete, though she couldn't imagine he would call and even if he did, she had no idea what she'd say. *He's never calling again. Get used to it.*

It was a Philadelphia number. She considered not answering. Sid had called her once in a while over the past few months to check on Pete, try to do some match-making. She wondered if he was going to yell at her for how horrible she'd been, not that it would be like Pete to tell anyone. If Sid was going to yell at her, though, she deserved it. Penance. She picked up.

. . . . .

It took Bernie twenty minutes to make what should have been a less than ten minute drive to Loon Lane, the snow a blinding tumble of waves that buffeted her car, the road feet deep in some spots, nearly

307

bare in others, often invisible, as the wind whipped it around. She'd brought Dubya. She didn't know why, because she was pretty sure Pete would turn her right back around, despite the weather, but at least she'd have a dog with her if she got lost in the storm. *Just like Jack London.* Thanks, Sal. Just like.

Once she got to Loon Lane the only thing that kept her on the road was the trees on either side, guiding her down the peninsula. The car rocked as she reached the open part and the wind hit it. She slowed to a crawl, not sure she'd be able to see Pete's house, afraid she'd drive into the lake. During a lull, she saw a flicker of light, and steered toward it, then the house was in front of her, light spilling from the windows.

She gathered the pan of lasagna and the shopping bag with sauce and meatballs, bread and wine, the wind knocking her back against the car. Dubya, snow sticking to his thick Velcro fur, trotted to Pete's door like he'd been going there for years.

She took a deep breath and knocked.

Pete looked surprised, not mad. His eyes were red-rimmed, but he seemed sober.

"Is everything okay?" he asked, stepping back so she and Dubya could come in. "And Dubya." Dubya shook himself, a cascade of snow flying through the air, then danced around Pete's legs. Pete knelt down and tugged his ears, kissed his head.

"I thought you might want some lasagna," she said, walking to the stove. "I didn't know if your oven is hooked up. If not, it's still lukewarm."

"In this storm? What are you doing here?" He walked over, stood too close. She handed him her coat.

"Is the oven working?"

"Yeah," he said, hanging her coat up. "What are you doing here?"

"About twenty minutes at 350—"

"Did Sid call you?"

Bernie felt her ears burn. She couldn't lie. "He was worried."

"I'm fine."

"I'm sure you are. But I'm here, so we might as well eat."

She put the pan in the oven and the pot of meatballs and sauce on the stove, turning on the burner. He was inches from her. She wanted to apologize. To explain what couldn't be explained. She was afraid that his lack of anger and the fact he didn't seem to hate her was so fragile that she'd shatter it and bust everything wide open.

"How are you?" he asked.

"I'm fine too."

She poked at the meatballs with a serving spoon. Harder, she knew, than she needed too, tears stinging her eyes.

"I just find it peculiar that we're both fine," she said. "I can't imagine that's really true."

His arms were around her. She let go of the spoon and turned into them, pressing her face against his chest, the flannel, smelling of soap and wood smoke, warm on her cheek.

His lips, dry and soft, touched her forehead. Then his breath soft against her ear. "Why are you here?" he whispered, barely audible.

"I just am," she whispered back.

The house creaked with the wind. Over his shoulder she could see the snow swirling outside the window, the lake not visible through the furious waves of storm that battered the house. She knew she should say more. Apologize. Anything. Everything had been so awful. She had been awful. Every scene of the last three weeks was playing in her head. Every conversation. It all seemed wrong, skewed. She'd said such an awful thing to him earlier. Why *was* she here?

She felt his lips on her forehead again, not a kiss, but just there, barely brushing. "Stop thinking," he whispered.

She took a deep breath, the war in her head between her feelings and her words and everything else in between spun crazily. She breathed in flannel and soap and the strong warmth of Pete.

"Just be," he said against her forehead, his embrace tightening.

The house creaked in the wind, the window rattled, the snow a swirling riot, clattering against the wooden sides and the tin roof. But that was outside.

She took another deep breath and melted against Pete. She was inside, where the house glowed in the flame of the pellet stove, soft light caressing Dubya on the couch, snout on paws in sleepy contentment. She closed her eyes and smelled the sauce, meatballs, lasagna, the aromas from the deepest heart of her life that always told her love was in the room. Under it, the flannel, and heat of Pete's body. His heartbeat, strong and steady, against her chest. She matched her breathing to his, slow and deep.

His mouth was against her ear, his warm breath in her hair. "For now, let's just be."

She felt herself relax for the first time in maybe forever. Everything else swirled and spun away like the snow outside. She was inside, in the soft warm.

Yes. She didn't have to say it out loud. Didn't have to say anything or think anything. Let's just be.

-30-

Acknowledgements

Articles by Roberta Scruggs in the Lewiston Sun-Journal (2002) and Yankee magazine (2003) gave chilling insight into the psychology behind hunting accidents and were a huge asset to me while writing this book. My brother, Jim Milliken, set me straight on Pliny the elder and my Latin usage. I'm grateful to my sister, Nicki Beauregard, her husband, Todd, and father-in-law Arnie for use of their camp in Lempster, New Hampshire, where many of the original scenes that became this book were written. My readers Rebecca Milliken, Kathy McGrath Fitts, John Radosta and Scott Monroe were a great help, and extra thanks to Scott for the editing, the conversations and questions about hunting, the scouting trip, and the use of one of his photos. This book wouldn't exist if it weren't for Dixiane Hallaj and S&H Publishing for rolling the dice on me. Thanks to all.

About the Author

Maureen Milliken is the city editor of the Morning Sentinel in Waterville, Maine. She grew up in Augusta and worked for a variety of newspapers in New England before returning to Maine in 2011. Her Bernie O'Dea mystery series novels *Cold Hard News* and *No News is Bad News* reflect not only her love for all that is Maine, but also her lifelong affection for the newspaper industry and fascination, of course, with the darker side of life. She lives in a small central Maine town, where she watches where she steps in the woods.

For updates on Maureen's next book, go to maureenmilliken.com or follow her on Twitter @mmilliken47. Like her Facebook page facebook.com/maureenmillikenmysterywriter.

Made in the USA
Middletown, DE
04 September 2016